THE LIFE OF GOD

(as Told by Himself)

The University of Chicago Press

FRANCO FERRUCCI

Translated by **RAYMOND ROSENTHAL** *and* **FRANCO FERRUCCI**

THE LIFE OF GOD

(as Told by Himself)

Chicago and London

FRANCO FERRUCCI was born in Pisa, Italy, and is
the author of several novels and books of criticism.
He teaches at Rutgers University.

The University of Chicago Press, Chicago 60637
The University of Chicago Press, Ltd., London

© 1996 by The University of Chicago
All rights reserved. Published 1996
Printed in the United States of America

05 04 03 02 01 00 99 98 97 96   2 3 4 5

ISBN: 0-226-24495-4 (cloth)

Originally published as *Il mondo creato*,
© 1986 Arnoldo Mondadori Editore S.p.A., Milano.

Library of Congress Cataloging-in-Publication Data

Ferrucci, Franco, 1936–
    [Il mondo creato.   English]
    The life of God (as told by himself) / Franco Ferrucci ;
translated by Raymond Rosenthal and Franco Ferrucci.
        p.   cm.
    ISBN 0-226-24495-4 (cloth : alk. paper)
    I. Rosenthal, Raymond.   II. Title.
PQ4866.E77M6613   1996
853'.914—dc20   95-52043
                                                    CIP

TO THE GEMINI

THE LIFE OF GOD

(as Told by Himself)

1

For long stretches at a time I forget that I am God. But then, memory isn't my strong suit. It comes and goes with a will of its own.

The last time it came back to me I was sunk in one of those late-winter depressions. Then one night I switched on the television set, and a firestorm of events burst before my eyes. I saw a volcano spewing lava, a skiing race in the Alps, a film on Paris as it was forty years ago, hunting in Ecuador, an office in Ottawa, open-heart surgery telecast live, a documentary about submarine landscapes of the North Sea. Life caught me again in a hypnotic net. As the camera circled around a flower on a seabed, I suddenly remembered that I had created all this. From that moment, I began feeling as I always do when I remember that I am God. I felt like a child again, eager for springtime, ready for open skies.

I admit, right from the start, that it was foolish to create winter. I couldn't help it, though. It banged at my door and demanded to be let into the world. It was stirring inside me, insisting on being recognized. I've always been a bit of an oddball, full of contradictions, and for all my love of the light I still have my dark side.

Winter wasn't my only half-baked idea. I can't really warm to the heavy, damp days of in-between seasons either. How pigheaded the rain seems, coming down as though everything were about to turn into water, or as though gray clouds and wet asphalt were all there is to the world. I am not talking about thunderstorms, which nobody likes except me and a few other dramatically inclined souls, poets and lovers especially. I am inside the thunder as well as the lightning. I am inside all blasts of passion, for it is there that I rejuvenate myself.

The thought of childhood warms the cockles of my soul. When you are young, the sensation of life knows no limits, and the mere fact of existing is enough to feel happy. Even now that I am an aged divinity, I feel the same way in early mornings, in the infancy of my day. I lie in bed, my body stirs slowly and eagerly beneath the sheets. I blend laziness and energy. My feet point toward the northern hemisphere, beyond Canada, beyond the Pole. The right arm spans California and the islands of the Pacific. The left reaches out toward Europe and meets with the other in the Far East. Shoulders and head are stretched toward the bottom of Earth, toward the warmest of the warm seas. I am God just before breakfast, face buried in my pillow, as if resting on a cloud.

Judging from the firmament above, my early inclination for physical and mathematical games must have surpassed all others. I dream of my infant self roaming through space with measuring tapes, compasses, rulers, toys, all mixed together. The peculiar assemblage visible above still shows it. Take a walk outside and look at the disposition of the night sky: it is the room of a child at play. I left things all over, a clutter all around.

Some of my greatest heroes are the scientists of the sky. I admire them not just because of the order they impose on the heavens but because they are untroubled by the sidereal chill. I see them as a dynasty of polar explorers with furs and sleds, never afraid of catching the flu. Every time I think of them, I remember something I had forgotten. Galileo made me see myself as a child again, drawing on a sheet of paper as big as the sky, completely engrossed. Einstein took me back to the designing of the human mind, mapped out like a chart of the cosmos, and the complicated hither and thither in its corridors and rooms, with windows opening onto nothingness or onto the gardens of galaxies; and that feeling of always being late, with clocks keeping a different time in every room, and me growing older and younger with every passing instant.

In the beginning I was contained in something that could not properly be called space. I opened my eyes in a vacuum and could see it was bare: I was shut up inside it like air inside air. I became aware of myself when I realized I was wrapped up in nothingness. You cannot imagine anything more bleak. Emptiness all around! That was the origin of my universe: the impulse to go out and look for company.

In my impatience I was overcome by an urge to break out that strikes me now as comical, given the situation. I started crawling thoughtlessly in every direction, sensing that in a void one way was as good as another, answering to a need that pushed me beyond what I was able to understand, since in nothingness I could understand nothing.

In art I'm depicted as an old man with a white beard who gets it into his head at some point to create the world. In point of fact, I was merely an infant, heartbroken in my isolation, and with my first movements I was trying to find my way home. Of my very earliest years, I retain not a single memory. To judge by what I saw when I was old enough to look about me, they must have been pretty dull. The moment of creation has been described in a thousand different ways, in a string of fantastic hypotheses—absurd stories of incest, fathers devouring their children, gods fighting against Titans. The truth is that the world began when it dawned on me that I was all alone and I tried to do something about it.

Everything that came later was a consequence of that moment: of the great shudder that scattered the form within me throughout time and space, a closed fist that finally opens, a seed that explodes and shoots out leaves in every direction; until one of them manages to think and to create other thinking leaves, and among them one miraculous leaf succeeds in thinking of its seed, picturing it even, with all the effort that it takes up there at the top of the tree, so far away from the plant's origins, exposed to the winds and the trials of alternate heat and cold, and yet able to conceive the initial germ and its expansion. This thinking seed would be humankind, but at the time it was light-years away.

I cannot say how long I wandered aimlessly through the dark night of time. I was haunted by incandescent emotions that little by little cooled and became cold rocks in space. I walked for miles and miles, stumbling in the dark, trembling with loneliness; then I finally stood still in the vast blackness and let out a cry. I saw that cry rise like an arrow, reaching the center of the heavens and exploding into fragments that became stars. Where my cry had fallen stood a solitary, burning ball. I looked around, but there wasn't much to see. What the light revealed was, in fact, the vast monotony of my universe. I was so disappointed that I wanted to put out the light and go back to the dark.

It was then that I realized, for the first time, that I could not undo what I had done. Once I created something, I could not destroy it. The sun was up there forever, or until its own natural death. I could not play around with the created world, and make and unmake as I pleased. "I am not a candle or a castle of sand," the sun might have said; "next time think twice before you create something." I am only glad, however, that I could not unmake the sun, since it was to become my great friend. Even now, when it enters my room through the windows, I feel that I never made anything grander or nobler.

In that first light, I could see bodies flying off every which way. I was struck by their irremediable blindness. They couldn't see the radiance issuing from me and exploding at other points of the celestial city. Whenever I create something, it goes on reproducing, like a host of mirrors reflecting whatever I do, or a series of messengers rushing off to plant the seeds of my inventions. In fact, it is me all the time, with my inborn talent—which even I find mysterious—for multiplication. The fragments of myself, once launched, evolve on their own, taking themselves to the most unlikely places, like that cry that bounced off a thousand mirrors and created innumerable shards of light.

So the world is the shattering of an original point that, in my recollection, remains nebulous and indistinct. It is dispersed into a myriad of elements and partial units—molecules, cells, leaves of grass, animals that produce other animals through a part of themselves. It is a universe that appears fixed and yet continually breaking apart. At first sight, you might have called it an excessively nervous universe. But then, who was there to pass such a judgment, other than me? Sometimes I did have the feeling that my world had emerged from some big explosion that was still in progress, as if we had been spun off from another universe, run perhaps by another God whom I would never meet and who was wrestling with his own problems. I never indulged this possibility for long, since I couldn't abide the notion of a Being higher than myself.

Even then, however, I wanted to know what the point of origin was. I compared the fragments to one another, hoping to get back to a root that already seemed as distant as it is now. But how varied those fragments of reality were! Everything existed next to its opposite: light and dark, summer and winter, permanence and change, lightness and heaviness. And all those intermediate states, and those temperamental modalities of the weather! From the first moment of creation, I've never known what to wear.

My shards of light had created a gigantic spatial metropolis in which I began to look for a place to live. I established my foundations around the star that burned where I had first hurled my cry. It represented the only memory that I had of myself, and I wanted to continue from there, with my sun and with my planets in sight. It was my galaxy and, within it, my solar system—my neighborhood inside the exploding city.

For ages humankind thought the sun circled the earth, and not the other way around. To me, on the other hand, it was immediately clear; but then, I had a different vantage point, and the whole display, seen from below, could well lead one to the opposite conclusion. I thought of the sun as my home's furnace and generator, the point the tangled lines radiate out from—skeins of electric wires strung out like strings stretching through space—and multicolored coils, because I had come up with a spectrum of colors I really had no use for and stored in the room of the burning house I used as my laboratory. The sun went to work all on its own, as usually happens with my attempts at creation. All I have to do is light a fire, and it blazes up of its own accord; before I knew it, the sun was uninhabitable. Even I couldn't go near it, because of all the solar winds and explosions.

The sun was fine to admire from a distance, and my favorite observatory was the planet later known as Mercury. I made it my window on the sun. From there I watched the spectacles of the sky, with that ball of fire that took up half the horizon in a state of continual agitation. What I saw was a ballet of lights, with swift steps, acrobatic leaps, phantasmagoric costumes, swords flashing in the dancers' hands. Mercury was my scenic overlook, my box seat. To it I owe my perpetual tan, but also the eye ailment that obliges me to wear dark glasses in summer. But it's been years since I quit visiting Mercury, the balcony of my childhood dreams.

I took up residence on Venus. I wanted to cast off the state of solar lethargy into which I had lapsed, and dwell in regions more northern and temperate. Venus was hung with cloudy drapes, curtains that even today keep her hidden from prying telescopes, leading stargazers to imagine who knows what nudities within. In fact, there was no one there but me, opening rifts between the drapes in order to peer outside, like a boy peeping down the alleys of his own block.

I felt as though I were in some bizarre house where the rooms revolved around the central heating system. I discovered that on Venus the sun rose and set in opposite directions to those on Mercury. From this observation I concluded that while Mercury and Venus were both moving around the sun, Venus, unique among all her brothers and sisters, turned in the opposite direction. It figured. Shy Venus, wrapped in her clouds and thunderclaps, like a young girl in the secrecy of her bedroom.

Often the sun seemed to rise and set at a greater distance than before, and I would hear a confused noise that summoned me outside. I would look about, but I could see nothing. What was it and where did it come from? I was surrounded by a desert of silent stones. It was worse than Sunday on Wall Street.

I had to find a better place to live, and I began traveling through the neighborhood that had fallen to my lot, struggling with the rudiments of mathematics, calculating east and west and north and south. You can still see the vehicles I used to get around on: the comets carried me from place to place within the galaxy and then back again to the solar system. I moved through the stellar metropolis, from skyscrapers to shacks, from houses radiant with light to somber desolate mansions. Some stars seemed to have decided to give up the ghost. They curled up as if they had swallowed poison, and then they disappeared, leaving a black hole in the void. The more aggressive ones blew their brains out, exploding with a dazzle that lingered on the horizon.

The more I traveled, the more certain I became about where my real home was, and in the end I returned to settle down within its borders. The solar system was a veritable castle, with inner quarters enormously distant from one another, and endless corridors, and it took a comet rather than an asteroid to travel from one room to another. Each one was as large as a big piazza. First I visited two of the rooms farthest from the sun, Saturn and Uranus, but their iciness discouraged me. The rings that surround them are the sign of my quick passing so long ago: a hasty streak and nothing more. I didn't even bother to touch down once I realized how cold it was below.

Since then I've never been back; I've made do with the reports of astronomers. I'll never forget how I laughed when I read Galileo's remark "Saturn has ears," because he wasn't able to distinguish clearly the rings my trail had left round the freezing planet. To say nothing of when a couple of centuries ago an Englishman discovered Uranus completely by accident, and spent the rest of his life swearing he'd discovered it on purpose. He was less humble than I, who, being as far as I know a product of chance, am fully aware that everything I make or don't make is a matter of chance as well. The discoveries of Neptune and Pluto were a surprise. I'd never gotten that far; I didn't know that there were rooms in my castle so remote that not even a breath of warmth could reach them. I'm like a member of some decayed aristocracy: there are parts of my mansion I don't have a clue about.

My most ambitious project was transforming Jupiter into a huge airy living room. To get a better look, I contrived a system of flying rocks circling around it, and, very impressed with its colors, I glided down, only to encounter the biggest surprise of my life: I couldn't land. There I was, lost on a horizon traversed by electrical discharges, which created currents like those of an ocean in a storm. Tossed this way and that like a straw or a feather, I almost went crazy in the violence of that atmosphere, on the far side of which I could make out a rising plain, liquid and menacing. It was an overheated room full of drafts, and I decided to move out.

At that point I turned my attention to Mars; it looked calmer than Jupiter, though it certainly was a lot smaller. On board its two moons, I was trying to figure out in detail where I was going to be able to fit everything in, revealing incidentally one of my constant anxieties—the fear of not having enough space. It's the same fear that makes me uncomfortable in an elevator or a narrow corridor or a room without windows. Wouldn't agoraphobia have suited my divinity better than claustrophobia? This is an unanswered question in my theological system. In the end I left Mars behind too; I flew to the moon on a comet and took my first spin around Earth. The trip took almost a month, but when it was over I was happy, as if I'd finally found what I was looking for.

It was the finest room of them all: from above I could make out the shapes of its continents surrounded by some unknown element that gave off a shimmering glare as it reflected the sunlight. The whole enormous sphere rotated on its axis, majestic and captivating to my eyes, as if inviting me to come closer. I began my descent and glided gently, stepping lightly down the smooth steps whose names I still repeat nostalgically to myself: magnetosphere, exosphere, thermosphere, mesosphere, stratosphere, troposphere, and finally air, the air of my home.

Whenever I move someplace new, the first thing I do is look around and decide where I will put my plants. Once I was lucky enough to find a hothouse, but I was too distracted by events to take proper care of it. When I first set eyes on Earth, the place looked rather bare to me and in need of carpets to cover the soil and rocks.

Now that my vantage point had come down from the astral to the terrestrial level, what seemed a room in a castle became an entire house, as in a set of nested Chinese boxes. Earth proved to be already a labyrinth of seas, rivers, volcanoes, and deserts. There were windows facing the warm sun and others that were distant and locked in ice. I roamed about in the guise of cloud and wind, I descended in the form of rain. I immersed myself in whatever I did. I was and I was not my world. I was the impulse that lived in it; and the world, inhabited by my soul, went its own way. I wandered alone, my head full of unformulated thoughts, and since no one was there to whom I could talk, I infused into the vegetation with which I covered the earth the accounts of my peregrinations. Every leaf was a star, every flower was a sun. The force of gravity was visible in the branches, the trunk, the complexity of the roots. Every tree was a galaxy, each sunflower spoke for them all.

The plants blossomed as I looked on. I multiplied them in an effort to get them to communicate with one another. A tree that rises in majestic loneliness contains the secret of wisdom: to be sufficient unto oneself, with roots stretching inside the earth. This was my original persuasion, at any rate. But why were there so many plants? Why so many different blossoms growing on trees and in meadows, among escarpments and beside the water, like thoughts dropped from another cosmos or pearls scattered from a tiara? Was I equivocating? Willow wisdom, magnolia wisdom, pine wisdom, oak wisdom, ananas wisdom, laurel wisdom—how many wisdoms was I able to conceive of?

I spread the plants beneath the open sky and doused them often, my body diffusing into rain. I was everywhere: in the sky, in the rivers and over the seas, even upon the deserts with pathetic, scattered drops. My drizzles and torrents were endlessly energetic. Once sucked back up into the air, they made their way again to the rivers, moved out to the sea, rose up again to the clouds. The constant motion was exhilarating, but I dreaded crashing onto the sand and rocks. I was haunted, too, by the thought that I might become lost in the cycle of precipitation and evaporation. It seemed that I knew that a significant part of me was condemned to an obscure underground exile, never to return to the skies. And so my fears, like all my other feelings, took on reality and became animated. Dispersed raindrops changed into insects, the embodiments of my anxiety.

Those insects, upon my soul! Their very conception was infamous. They took advantage of my frame of mind, all those inhabitants of fissures, interstices, filamentous channels, dark niches beneath the stairs! Each of them was born out of one of my bad moods, and each of them reminds me of it. When I read some time ago that, besides being the most ancient living creatures in the world, insects are also its probable future lords, I was overcome. Is their power really that great? And yet they are pervasive, a neurosis that scourges the earth in every corner of its soil. Whenever I see a cockroach I cringe. Lice and bedbugs, where did they come from? Did I really have all of these insects in my mind?

I have come to the conclusion that inside me was an immense world that emerged without warning and spread freely. I was operating wholesale, with a great vastness of vision, as if outlining a book and passing it on to unknown ghostwriters and editors for refinement. At this stage the details did not interest me: I had no patience for manipulating the structures of cells or the spirals of DNA. Perhaps there were thousands of minuscule and diligent artisans weaving the intricacies of living bodies, my simplest thought enough to put them to work.

I had no experience of life before I created the tree, except for an obsessive memory of being alone among the stars. Perhaps this explains my need for roots. Each plant, separate though it is from the others, belongs to the earth: the palm and the elm, the fir and the birch, the betula and the sassafras, all plunge fingers into the soil more grasping than those of a drowning man. I clung to the earth through the plants, but at the same time I was the wind that battered them, leaving them stunned before so much ferocity. A tree at the mercy of the wind nicely illustrates my twofold nature: my need to feel at once secure and unconfined.

Creation was a superabundance of hypotheses. The world was my notebook, filled with jottings and corrections. Or call it, if you prefer, a theater of perpetual improvisation. I would have a notion of a tree—and bang, there it was, roots and branches and leaves and trunk and bark, rooted in the earth, with arms flung wide in the open air. And then what? "There must be something else," I would say to myself as I stood upright, myself temporarily a tree. I would wait awhile for someone or something to come along, and then I would make another tree to keep the first one company. My longing for family led me to group plants together, so that chestnuts and alders sprang up far from the monkey puzzle trees, and farther yet from the banana trees.

Since I was interrogating myself about my own nature, one

family was not enough. Am I thorny and wild, or meek and hospitable? Do I prefer the sea and burning sand, or a coat of snow over my foliage, up in the mountain woods? Am I tender or rugged, am I fruitful or sterile? With each question another plant was born. All this led to some disappointing results. For despite my multiplying of plants and plant families, each remained locked in an implacable solitude. After spreading out in the air and digging deep into the earth, each plant would pretty much stop there. The effort continued through entire seasons, and new hope would return with each returning spring. Only some flowerless plants considered springtime a disappointment and withdrew into an impenetrable lack of promise. When touched, they stung and closed in upon themselves. But the rest kept throwing themselves stubbornly into every blossoming, determined that *this* spring they would be alone no more.

The illusory hope born again each springtime would become positively grandiose during the summer. All those trees so perfect in themselves were now more eager than ever to become something else. The whole earth was ripe with expectation. Everything grew still, as if before an earthquake. But the meridian ardor passed almost as soon as it arrived. In autumn I would register my disappointment with an additional ring inside the trunk of every tree. I had done everything I could to live on vegetation alone, and had not succeeded.

I came to the conclusion that my solitude was not only bad but probably irreparable. I developed a surprising antagonism toward the trees, a feeling like an invasion of voracious termites or an ice storm. I would shake the plants from crown to root, inflicting—somehow—pain on myself. But eventually I began to imagine another remedy for my loneliness, in the only way I knew how at that time, by filling the universal notebook with additional drawings and giving them life.

The process that ensued was a maze of circumvolutions and sudden turns, and in the end I could barely remember what I wanted at first. It all began with a new inkling of my nomadic spirit. Comets and planets were traveling on high, the infinitesimal world below was crowded with cells and invisible beings halfway between the vegetals and something not yet imagined.

At the center of this restless circle stretched a terrain of rocks, self-propelled waters, trees enchained by their roots. After so much time spent inside rushing rivers, the ocean's currents, and the winds that swept the continents, I hit upon the wish for a solid entity that could finally move around on its own and accompany me on a good walk. Was this too much to ask for?

My initial idea was to set the plants in motion. Even today I can see the signs of this aborted experiment in the superfluous appendages I gave to so many of them. Take it from me: the plants will not be budged.

Nevertheless, that attempt contained the idea that led me to the creation of animals. It had already occurred to me that my constant shuttling from one condition to another, from season to season and realm to realm, was a manifestation of my complex nature. In certain climates I would know only summer and long days, in others I would bury myself deep within icebergs. In a single day I would go from morning to noon, from afternoon to twilight, repeating the succession of childhood, youth, maturity, and old age. Everything mirrored my mutable character. I wanted both to be awake and to go to sleep—this latter inclination explains the existence of winter, and night, and cold, and the death of plants and the drying-up of rivers.

Reflecting on this profusion of diversities, I realized that life could be maintained only by a merging of opposites. It took me a while to get to this point, and it was my first great philosophical thought. I expressed it through a monumental glaciation that left the earth chalky with snow, rigid and pensive for an entire geological era. The universe had learned that life and death were two sides of the same coin, and that the first was inconceivable without the other. During a nostalgic boreal sunset, I added an important clause to this truth, namely that death is also the reservoir of life. Almost by magic the glaciers began to thaw and a new era was born in a lavishment of flowers. A reasoning God definitely affects the climate.

At last my incongruences seemed justified. From that blazing insight was born the idea of a duplicate being that, in order to reproduce itself, had to enter another, which would in turn split into itself and its offspring: day and night and winter and summer would be repeated in the noon of love and the spring of fecundation.

Enthusiastic about this notion, I spread it everywhere: through the woods over which I flew, in the water into which I dove; and the world was thronged with cartilaginous plants, swimming and wriggling in pursuit of themselves so that they might multiply. A great libidinal agitation began to transform the very face of Earth.

MOMENTS of rage were not alien to me, and they still return, though with less violence and at greater intervals. In order to soothe my soul I would walk along the rivers, along the beaches, around the mountain lakes. Nothing much emerged from the surface, though I knew that underneath swarmed a manifold existence. Occasionally I would plunge in, just to look around, but I was unable to hold my breath long enough to study it properly. Aquatic life thus remained a mystery to me as I nourished my reveries on the seashore. I did not begin to explore it in earnest until the first time I tried to kill myself.

A serious crisis had overcome me that sad autumn, among the yellowed plants and the hopeless flowers. After another summer waiting for an interesting new life form to appear, I had become convinced again that nothing was going to change and that the coming and going of seasons was all that I would ever see. It was at that point that I wanted to die. I climbed to the summit of a rock that rose sheer above the sea and allowed myself to topple over the edge, certain that I would not survive.

What a tremendous fall! To this day I suffer from vertigo at the memory of it. A howl came out of me as I plummeted into that space of blue. I was already regretting my act and wanted to turn back, but it was impossible. I had wanted to die, and this was itself an act of creation: I was creating my own end. I crossed the liquid threshold and plunged into a vortex of forgetfulness.

I can't tell you much of those watery inceptions, since I remained oblivious for some time. Consciousness returned in steps now minimal, now gigantic. As if awakening after a fainting spell, I became aware of blurry motions that had no apparent direction, amid shadows that appeared and disappeared, through a light that was not light. At last my eyes could see—and there, present, overwhelming, and immediately swallowed by the dark, was a swordfish. Every so often I live again that reawakening at the bottom of the sea to which despair had driven me. Life undoubtedly had cared for me and prevented my death—a token of filial gratitude on its part—but that exile was hard punishment!

I SAID that I regained consciousness, but I did not know who I was or what I was doing down there. I had a confused recollection of how it all happened, a glimmer of illumination within me. I could see thousands of things milling around the bottom, and for a time I thought I was no more than a pair of eyes wandering about. Now I can explain what occurred to me, but at the time I only intuited it, in a subterranean and decisively aquatic manner. I was there so that I could be reborn. I was drifting in the sea, disembodied and clueless. The silence was deafening.

The world of fish was inhabited by angels of ozone. As I swam among them, I gradually learned how to breathe in a completely new way and to orient myself according to this space so different from the avenues of land and sky. But I felt held back, as if imprisoned in a dream or confined to an island by some tyrannical power. I became obsessed with an idea that would not leave me alone. The idea was this: I wanted to see how I was constructed. Perhaps because I had eyes in the front of a body that apparently stretched out behind me, it was impossible to take even a single glance backward. I was running after myself without ever catching up.

I remember still the soft warmth of the water I encountered toward the end of my migrations, the flavor of algae and the sensation of the eggs as they fell from me, the schools of fish as they moved among gorges of light and shadowy rocks, the inexhaustible variety of all the fish I pursued, looking for one that might resemble me. I must have been a solitary fish, because I never found myself in any of the groups that I admired from a distance. And so I continued my wanderings through the labyrinths of the ocean.

Ah, the deep, deep waters, the huge plants swaying in the mute wind of the currents! The flash of the lamprey and of the bass fleeing the shark's pursuit; the cod disappearing into the maw of the hammerhead, and the sudden shadow above me, like a heavy sky, during the regal passage of a blue or sperm whale; the spiny dogfish in the lethal net of the torpedo fish; the diminutive seahorses suspended like statuettes in midwater; the chimaera gaping astonished at the dolphin's bounds; and the incredible lobster that couldn't laugh at itself lest it choke, like a boy hiding inside a suit of armor in some museum. Everywhere was circus and theater, which was agreeable to someone as curious as myself. But inside this uninterrupted spectacle everybody seemed driven by the urge to eat another and by the fear of being eaten. Devouring, depositing egg after egg, migrating, getting gulped down by a lantern fish or a barracuda in the most romantic of coral reefs: that was what marine life finally amounted to.

I witnessed numerous attempts at escape. Underwater life, in both rivers and oceans, survived in the hope of emerging, because everyone preserved a confused memory of having fallen there, as had happened to me. Some part of every fish yearned to return and see what it had left behind. They had no inkling of the source of this impulse, because they were also very stupid. They exhausted themselves with wandering until a cold rigidity crippled them. The unlucky ones found themselves in ponds, with everything at a standstill. Nowadays, and this is even worse, they may end up in an aquarium, and who knows how they explain an aquarium to themselves.

I liked to swim close to the mobile roof full of arabesques and floods of light and watch the flying fish jump to the other side, then come back without ever revealing what they had seen. Common fish, unable to pierce the magic mantle, looked on them as wizards or as astronauts who had decided not to talk after a journey into space, never revealing whether they had seen God.

Finally I found a possible route of escape. There was a long strip of beach that the ocean waves covered during the day and left bare at night. At the time I didn't know anything about the power of the full moon, which from its distance controlled the tides of my oceans. This seemed to me a suitable passage for my reemergence. Right there I would be able to breach the wall of water.

But it wasn't so simple, since I had not developed the instruments for my undertaking. The first time I stuck my snout out of the water, I was dumbfounded by the violence of what greeted me there. An arid and burning air scorched my stomach and drove me back half-dead into the water.

I needed to proceed methodically. Each day I would take a small leap and remain panting on the sand, careful that only a small mouthful of air entered my throat before the wave returned and carried me back. The situation kept improving, and little by little, in the dark of my secret interior, right there above my stomach, I felt something taking shape, ever stronger and more assured, something that pulsated and enlarged when it came into contact with air—a lung!

I was also working on another indispensable tool. Now that I was no longer migrating from one ocean to another, I knew that moving in the old way wouldn't take me where I wanted to go. I would linger in shallow water and work on the fins I had on my sides, rubbing them against the pebbles on the shore. I spent my afternoons stretching them toward everything that passed near me, like an acrobat in training.

Moreover, I had found a confidant, the first friend I ever had. He would offer encouragement as I worked in my ceaseless, obstinate way. He was the strangest of all creatures, tormented in a later age by the mockery of boys, dragged ashore and pierced with sticks, the tender and taciturn jellyfish.

Trustful now of my beneficent lung, I waited for a moonlit night and jumped onto the beach, never to return. When I crossed the border, breathing immeasurable quantities of the air of freedom, I had already forgotten my wish to see what I looked like. There was no longer any need for it. I could postpone it until the invention of mirrors. The watery purgatory had come to an end.

Once out of my aquatic prison, I found myself scrambling about on shaky paws, my belly slithering in the muck, and I understood that my escape had succeeded only halfway. I had thought that once I freed myself, I would be restored as that fabulous being, hovering above the waters, about whom I had dreamed in my long exile. But matters were not that simple; it seemed I had first to pass through an amphibian stage.

Creation had begun to accelerate. My reaching landfall generated a great nervousness. My every thought was transmuted into a reptile, darting away into the grass. Some of these thoughts were innocuous, others were poisonous; one turned melancholically into a toad, another became a lazy turtle. These creatures seemed to cling stubbornly to the habits of old times, even in the way they decked themselves out: a monumental and vulgar elegance, with scales that recalled ancestors left behind under the water. I crept through their immense era, amid glaciations and heat waves that overlapped each other and flattened entire species and forests in their wake.

I managed finally to shake off my amphibian body and assume again the shifting shapes of a young, vigorous divinity. This was when I set about my first experiments in recording memory—efforts still rudimentary, but touching, if you think back on the spirit that animated them. I built entire scenes of natural memory by ingeniously depositing skeletons in sand and rocks. I scattered those traces in the hope of preserving something in the face of my certainty that everything was implacably passing and that the universe rotating around me would one day disappear before I could understand the first thing about it. The Alpine chain, among other mountains, helped me to this purpose. I set about turning it into a sort of library, crammed with manuscripts waiting for a geologist who would one day interpret the messages hidden in the folds of rock and earth.

I began decorating the stone manuscripts, and between one chapter and the next I slipped in my figures of reptiles and fish. Usually I deposited them at random, according to where the weather and my need to travel took me, but to one place I devoted particular care. It was a vast expanse of sea and coastline, in the middle of which was a bay where I spent an entire productive season. Here I settled to write the book on reptiles for the posterity of a species I was just beginning to imagine. I worked with exaltation and great commitment, there in my writing workshop upon the bay. My long working mornings and periodic sabbaticals took me all the way through Triassic and Jurassic times.

The reptiles were a curious mixture of superiority and inadequacy. At the bottom of their souls lay the concealed conviction that they were imperfect; at the same time a ruthless arrogance permeated their actions toward all other living creatures. Such was the result of their ancient stubborn dominance on the planet Earth, a dominance longer than that of the Chinese and Egyptian monarchies, more obstinate than a race of fakirs and rabbis. They had conquered everything. The fish-reptiles terrorized the seas and the amphibious reptiles controlled the borders between sea and land. On solid ground the warrior-reptiles roamed about with long necks and longer tails. Extremely conservative and not particularly bright, they were like old aristocrats in remote provincial towns, handing down to new generations both their idleness and a disquieting physical resemblance. It's impossible to imagine anything more enervating than the company of the ichthyosaurus and the mesosaurus. I found them limited and utterly humorless, and seemingly determined to live as long as possible. The Cretaceous period was the dark winter of my discontent.

The only way for me to find serenity was to go back to work. I carved magnificent mountains. I struggled to modify the light's nuances on the leaves of my beloved plants and on the sands along the fringes of the oceans. I achieved subtleties of contrast from one hour to the next of each sun-setting. I devised the markings of the caterpillars and created flowers by the thousands. I labored on the corollas and straightened tree trunks into living columns. I scattered water lilies over the ponds and chiseled elaborate butterfly wings. The snow that fell during winter days resembled the constellations, millions of years before the design of the snowdrop was penetrated by the gaze of the microscope. Every cell was the map of an imaginary country that I drew while dreaming of distant territories.

Later the flowers dried up, the snows melted, the butterflies died, but only to come back. In the springtime the entire universe seemed to breathe more deeply. It inhaled and said, "I am alive"; it exhaled and said, "There is beauty." Beauty was the expression of my thirst for understanding, just as a smile promises pleasure and the fragrance of a fruit anticipates the flavor. I wanted to understand my beginning and my purpose. But to whom could I say these things? I was still alone in the world. I was working for an animal that was unknown and yet to come; I pictured it as beautiful and intelligent, though curiously similar to a crocodile.

Solitude eventually got the better of me, and I began to fall into reptilian ways. When I realized what was happening, it was already too late, and I found myself imprisoned in their company. I was like some young avant-garde poet who returns from the capital after a period of untrammeled freedom. As he comes in contact again with the ancient world of his native town, there arises in him an urge for renovation. "I will create a new theater for these provincials," he tells himself; "I will organize concerts of serial and electronic music!" But soon he is attending Mass more and more frequently and has become an active member of the Parent-Teacher Association. In the meantime he grows balder and lazier, he doesn't want to leave the house anymore, and if he does go out with his wife and children he walks slowly, his head sunk between his shoulders. He has become a turtle. How many times, crossing villages on Sundays, have I seen myself during that reptilian time, when we breathed air in a group, stretched out on the rocks, looking at nothing.

I cursed my snake companions silently, withdrawing into my own shell. I turned mean, I became stingy. I fenced myself off, accumulated blades of grass in my cave, shut myself in for long naps. My mind became obfuscated.

ONE day I raised my eyes and saw the birds. I will never forget that moment, and I've kept it alive throughout the ages, in scattered paintings and writings, down to recent times. With the gaze of the reptiles, I stared at the birds as if they were lost poems. I could not believe that it was I who had made them, and I didn't understand why I had not noticed them until that moment. If the birds had looked down and seen those huge animals slithering and lumbering over the earth, they would have had the same thought I had: Who are they, and who created them? But entering a bird's head was not easy. Birds never stood still, and I knew that it would be a long time before I grasped their thoughts, if they had any.

In those long moments of astonishment, I anticipated all of humankind's attempts at flight, from Daedalus to the airplanes, from floating balloons to the missile ramps that look like falcons at rest. It is God's ancient aspiration to fly as an animal and not only as a wind. I have never been a bird, and in a way birds are still a mystery to me.

The reptiles, tormented by their own weariness, attempted to join the winged beings and produced enormous fowls that fell heavily back to earth. Filled with uneasy longing for their old, familiar scales, they dragged their huge paraphernalia behind them, like an evening gown much too long and heavy. They extended their bodies, lay on their backs, waved their legs, and thrashed their wings. Above them, elusive, the birds darted.

From the bosom of the old reptiles, which still kept their paws on the firm ground, finally arose a harsh condemnation of the restless and decadent sons who refused to be what they were and lost themselves in flighty dreams of transformation. The reaction took an authoritarian and violent form. To bring their prodigals back to earth, the truculent paladins of the old order rose up on their paws and began to terrorize the continents.

I had tolerated enough. I managed to slip out of my shell during one of those reptilian wars in which I was a constant deserter. For a while I rejoined the whole realm of nature. I remember my pleasure in inventing new amusements: to be an avalanche and roll down a mountain's slope like a growing white bowling ball; to shape the clouds into weightless tyrannosaurs and iguanas, and then dissolve them into rain.

I had to postpone a solution to the puzzle the birds were presenting to me. Was there another God at work, unknown to me, living in some other continent? That unpleasant thought resurfaces in me from time to time, but I always repress it.

Bored by the reptiles and mystified by the birds, I decided

that it was time for a fresh idea, and soon I hit upon a radical new concept. It was this: I wanted life to meditate upon itself so as to better comprehend itself. There followed from this that my next living beings should bear their children inside themselves, and that their eggs should open in the warmth of the womb instead of being hatched outside. Life would be born inside these new beings, and they would be its repository and transmitter. This became the sustaining idea of an emerging third state, after those barbarian fishes and ancien-régime reptiles. Here came the differentiated and industrious mammals, agile in trafficking and exchanging, tireless hunters, skillful builders of homes, and good savers of their possessions. Here came the bourgeois of the animal kingdom.

Parturition was a philosophical insight. I was obscurely and confusedly in search of the soul, as I would be for a long time to come. I had wanted the soul and had found the placenta.

I remember how those animals ran to and fro with their sharp teeth and useless tails, which were there to remind them of their reptilian and aquatic predecessors. Because of the odd absentmindedness that has distinguished me from the beginning of time, I failed to see to it that there was enough food for my creatures. As a result, they were caught up in an unceasing search for nourishment. With the fall of night, the animals became stupefied, swollen with sleep and snoring heavily. I took advantage of their slumber and went to work in the female bellies, respecting a division of labor that had been in effect for quite a while. They were sleeping, and I would make embryos.

Inside those wombs of mammal mamas I placed another almost finished thought about the world. I said to myself, "Just imagine yourself, God that you are, inside the cosmos. Aren't you perhaps like a small blob of flesh that stirs and presses? You too don't know how you came to this world. You too have no idea who put you here. Only your mother can tell you, and if you have a mother, she isn't around." I could see a part of my story in every fetus that came into being.

I had chosen the females to carry the burden because they were the more generous and patient gender. Restless troublemakers, the males let off steam in the hunt, showed their claws to the enemy, and scattered their seed into the wombs of their female companions, who would quietly receive it and eventually present their grooms with a flawless work: an entire litter!

The new arrivals acquired an impudent self-assurance. There were no longer only rodents; you could see larger animals in every part of the earth. My house was getting quite crowded. I moved from bears to monkeys to elephants. Content that life was proceeding in such leaps, I concentrated on details whose worth I intended to assess much later. Why should I have been so obsessed with perfecting the stomach? And yet I did, and I even placed two stomachs inside some ruminants, wishing them *bon appétit*. And what a great toy the brain became for me! It was patched together, poorly proportioned, and cluttered with gadgets, but I positively fell in love with it. Working on the brain made me feel as if I were creating a minuscule Earth all anew and from scratch. The world itself was enclosed in that fleshy, gelatinous sphere. I tinkered with it for millennia in every mammal I could get hold of. I played with its nerves and spine as if absorbed in an interminable puzzle. Some of those games reached a standstill, unfinished. When I could go no further, I'd turn to some other brain. The abandoned animals remained as they were at that point, with a flashing little planet behind their eyes, always sensing in the furthest recesses of their minds: God was here.

The creatures roamed all over, dazzling nature with their prowess. Yet I kept thinking that none of them could match the beauty of the birds. I often dreamed of flying and striking up a friendship with the eagle and the stork. Then I would wake up and see the bull and the zebra close at hand. I would shake my head and tell myself, "That's just how life is." I was being unjust. I was blind to the beauty of the antelope, but when an owl flew by, it took my breath away. Of course an owl, seen up close, is not really such a marvel; now that I am older, it brings to mind nothing so much as a discarded Halloween mask.

My patronizing attitude toward the newcomers tested their mettle and pushed them to assert themselves. They were trying to please me. Even though they didn't know who I was and never talked to me, they understood that I was not fully satisfied with them. They wanted to be loved by me, and I could not understand that. It happens in the best of families. The mammals felt deprived, while the reptiles couldn't have cared less about my disdain.

I thought I was quite a progressive fellow, and yet my prejudices persisted. Whenever I saw an earthbound quadruped, right off I would compare it with birds. It is strong as an eagle, it is white as a dove, and so on. I was even fascinated by the birds' language, for which I experienced a feeling close to envy. They sang or spoke an idiom whose rhythms, vocabulary, grammar, and syntax no one knew. The only thing that was certain was that the birds flew. It was easy to fall into the trap of thinking that they flew because they knew how to sing.

It was surprising that I should have such success giving language but not wings to the newly arrived inhabitants of Earth. I do not know how to explain it. But one thing I remember. When I tried to use the wings in order to bestow leadership on the world of mammals, the result was the bat—and I cannot remember a single kind word spent on behalf of this unfortunate offspring of mine. To this day its very name evokes vampires and nocturnal monsters, and even at that remotest time, the bat flew in darkness, as if it had been devised as a spy between two worlds. Other attempts of this kind soon aborted, with curious and somewhat circuslike results, such as lemurs and giraffes.

For a long period the bat industriously tried to deliver messages between the birds and the mammals. But it was useless, because the mammals obstinately refused to look up, and the spy had no one to talk to, much less report what the birds were saying to each other. When I finally listened to it, I could not get much out of its blabber, which sounded like some mountain dialect impenetrable to any visitors from the outside. From that time the fate of the bat was sealed. It drifted mournfully into seclusion and did not even go out anymore, except at night.

I did not know where to begin to master the song of birds. Until giving language to the mammals, I spoke through the winds, the currents of the seas and rivers. This natural orchestra intoned powerful but repetitive melodies. When I decided that mammals should rival the birds, I imagined an earthly orchestra that resembled the heavenly one. This gave rise to the idea of the horn, of the bassoon, and of the percussion instruments. The forest became a pit full of musicians. Voices were born that later would reign on the opera stage. Sopranos, contraltos, basses, baritones, and tenors invaded the bodies of the lords of the earth. When a herd crossed a plain I could hear from the distance single voices combine into a solemn chorus. It was all performed for me, and for me alone, and I was at once the audience and the composer. When humankind, their future masters, listened to them, they would remember me, and rightly so, since I had been the first to attend those ancient concerts.

The mammals ran, jumped, tumbled, and climbed, some even swam; but when it came to flying, nothing. Their voices merged into symphonies that unfurled effortlessly into the air, but they themselves never quite reached the clouds.

AT the moment I am writing aboard an airplane and am suffused with the sensation of that distant childhood. I sip my whiskey; the whiskey permeates me. I flutter inwardly with imaginary, somewhat torpid wings. Next to me a bearded young man is intently drawing something on a sheet of paper—it looks like a geological map. His handwriting is parsimonious and accurate. My calligraphy, on the other hand, is replete with flighty disorder. I scribble freely in the Edenic language, up and down my piece of paper.

I think I always knew that I would need people like the bearded young man in my world. I did everything cavalierly, and the engineers, agronomists, and all sorts of other technicians had to come to rectify my extravagant detours with prudent pencils, with numbers and arrows. With my second drink I drop off to sleep while the jet enters a fluffy blanket of clouds.

In my slightly alcoholic doze, all the species extinguished during the millennia of my early adolescence come to visit me. They arrive at random, like guests coming to a party given for people you wouldn't have time to see unless you grouped them all together. The strangest encounters take place and fade away. The multituberculates prick up their large ears, on bodies too swollen for their pointed greyhound snouts, and listen to someone complaining that his double nature as bear and monkey is not leading him anywhere, as will happen to a dancer who gets fat or an actor who begins to stammer. Actually, quite a few actors and artists are present, and they all despair of success and blame the world for it. On the other side of the room is a large cat spearing saltines and miniature franks with his saber tooth. He is chatting with a carnivorous snake, who skips the broccoli and cauliflower, aiming directly at the meat casseroles. They will vanish together in the nocturnal elevator that accompanies extinct species to subways without return.

Near the window several proto-ungulates gripe about their new shoes and regret the times when they walked barefoot on beaches and meadows. The mammoth is so tall that he can read the titles of the books on shelves just below the ceiling. One of these books tells stories about fantastic animals, winged horses, serpents with a second head instead of a tail, long-faced eagles, mules with a horn in the middle of their head. But those fantastic animals all existed!—so did a dwarfish parahuman who looked sillier than a crab.

There are new arrivals: a family of doomed equine visitors. The real horse does not show up, because he is at a party of successful folk, hanging out with lions, tigers, turtledoves, and other winners. The horse-dogs, the horse-toads, the horse-goats listen to the tale about the hippogriff that mounts into the sky with its great wings. Two dinosaurs, husband and wife, are out in the garden, partly because of their dimensions, partly because of that ancient feeling of superiority they can't seem to shake. They are conversing with a Neanderthal man and a Cro-Magnon, the latter more stuck up than the first.

I awake with a start while the plane is flying over the Nevada desert. The young man at my side is asleep now, in the belly of our metallic bird. "Back to reality," I say to myself. "Let's get back to the story of my youth."

A decisive turning point in my story occurred when I discovered the existence of pain. Maybe I had perceived it in the very beginning but did not comprehend it, like a child who even when he himself weeps does not know enough to say "I suffer."

Beauty and suffering were Siamese sisters, each turned in an opposite direction but inseparable. It is impossible for the magpie to appear beautiful in the eyes of the earthworm she devours, even if she has never looked as splendid as at that moment. If instead of being God at work on his memoirs I were teaching aesthetics in some university, I would try to clarify the notion of beauty as it is perceived by those who eat and by those who are eaten. For the latter, the magpie is forever a dark, misshapen, ugly bird, all beak and claws and disorder. And so the earthworm cannot embrace the serenity of classical art and becomes engulfed instead in the thorny forest of Expressionism, where colors are no longer colors but blotches of blood. The worm is one step from becoming a fiber in the body of that immense magpie; his view of life does not improve. Undoubtedly it is a better fate to spend a happy day with your loved ones at your side, dreaming that you are God or at least Leonardo da Vinci.

I digress, I digress. My entire world is a huge digression! For example, it was on one and the same day that I made the rhinoceros and the palm tree. I watched the monster run with lowered head, and upon his head the horn that I should have removed but didn't. I felt a need for reassurance, much like the urge to buy a bunch of flowers after a tough day at the office. And so I created the palm, the plant of youth. I took a swim in the most beautiful of my seas, and everywhere underwater I saw marine palm trees and scaly rhinoceri. Something similar happens when a small child building sand castles is suddenly startled to find a crab in his hand.

Then new troubles developed. I still clearly remember a festive day inundated by sunlight that gilded the leaves and the water of the rivers and grazed my cheeks and hair. From the peak of a wooded hill I looked down on what I had made, and swelled with pride. Today will be a holiday, I decided, the day of rest on which I celebrate my labors. Was that Saturday or Sunday? It's so long ago that I can't be sure, and I've never kept a real diary. In any event, that first holiday—let's call it Sunday—was followed by a bitter Monday, when everything seemed to turn upside down and into its opposite. A storm kicked up and a hurricane crashed down on the earth. I saw the plants ripped out of the soil and left to drift on muddy streams. I saw terrified animals trying to escape and meeting death and mutilation.

I couldn't recognize my own clouds. They had turned black and sinister, a menacing sight, and they hurled water onto the earth and filled me with consternation. Why so much violence? They seemed to be driven by an incomprehensible rancor, as did the other elements, each full of fury, all enemies.

I felt like a father watching a family quarrel that has spun out of control. I wanted to understand where I had gone wrong, but I could not, and so that fateful doubt came over me—the realization that I could err. When the storm finally weakened, I saw a placid crimson sunset, and my creation had the languorous beauty of a face after a fit of weeping. I sat pensively wondering what had happened. I spent a sleepless night during which I fell into a profound creative crisis. At about dawn I decided to take a first tour of inspection through my world.

I set out following the tracks of the sun. For a short while I felt almost comforted. After the excesses of the previous day, nature seemed to be doing its best to display a smiling face, but the illusion was short-lived. Late in the morning I sensed something in the air, an omen of misfortune. All of a sudden, I saw a falcon plunge like a flash of the blackest hatred upon a tiny bird hopping in front of me and then disappear with its prey, leaving a mist of feathers behind. An absolute calm settled down once more, and I was entrapped in it. I had the curious feeling that I was watching the world I had put together for the very first time.

The violence that the falcon had wreaked on the sparrow was not an isolated event: it was something that occurred continually, at every level of life. I saw the lions and other beasts that I had created exclusively for the sake of their beauty (I still remember the joy I felt when the lion and the tiger, the panther and the leopard, darted from my hands and scattered through the forest) pounce on other animals and tear them apart. I saw the spider catch the fly, and the fly pursue the microscopic insects I had strewn through the air in moments of somnolent idleness, along with nettles, dust, and other secondary inventions. Nothing seemed able to save itself.

I went farther on earth, walking across plains and mountains. I was so disheartened by the revelation of the faults in my creation that I decided to travel incognito. I disguised myself because I felt ashamed. In order to proceed more swiftly, I made use of the mesohippo, a most beautiful and proud creature who was very dear to me because he had been born in a moment of great happiness. I remember the sunny afternoon when the idea that produced him came to me: the idea of freedom, of tranquil absence of restraints. That powerful inspiration came out of me as a dancing figure with a floating mane. The mesohippo! The horse! Nothing else could compare with him. That same afternoon at the beginning of my tour, I went for the mesohippo and jumped on his back, and ever since he has been my favorite traveling companion and means of conveyance. I was especially relieved, at the time, by the fact that he ate grass and left the other animals in peace.

The mesohippo was partial compensation for the chagrin that possessed me that day. Hunger, fear, and anguish seemed to be everywhere, mixed with that same beauty I so often admired. Movement, even time itself, seemed to generate violence, decay, and death. They struck everything, dissolving it without destroying it, transforming it into something else. I had created some kind of monstrous mechanism, by now incapable of stopping, under the distant gaze of the sun and the stars.

For a while my distress paralyzed me, but I pulled myself together and decided to reason about what I was seeing. Before me was a world that devoured itself incessantly and managed its own transformations without asking me for comment or advice. The theater of hunt and war was everywhere. The fish pursued each other in the crashing torrents. The grottoes I had conceived as shelters were lethal traps for the pursued. The deer were savaged by the boars, animals that I had already regretted having put in the world, ugly, deformed, and ferocious as they were. From what bad moments of mine had all this come out? What state was I in when I conceived the hyena? What peculiar resentment had seized me when I shaped its mouth? I was not able to invent remedies; inherent in my act of creation was what these creatures would do and be. They were part of me! I was startled at the revelation.

I gave up on finding a way to help them and sat down in a corner of my enigmatic creation. I had the impression that the world was looking at me with a thousand eyes, as if it were trying to make some sense out of me. "Stop looking at me!" I yelled at a squirrel, which leaped up a tree and disappeared from my view. I waited for it, but it did not come back. Birds were swirling as usual, a herd of buffalo ran across the prairie. "God is sorry!" I exclaimed in a thundering voice. Nobody seemed to care.

The remedy that I found was to go to sleep. Sleeping resembles death so closely that the animals were already seeking refuge in it as if to anticipate their withdrawal from the chaos into which I had flung them. I myself took shelter in the cold of the poles, moving as far away as possible from the sun, whose warmth I took as a reproach. I shivered on the summit of the earth, without a sign of living beings around me except for the fishes in the grip of the ice and the seals that jumped into the water at the sight of a white bear. I watched that same bear tearing apart a penguin on a slab of ice, completely overcome by obtuse animal hunger; and I asked myself: Why all this hunger? Couldn't that bear busy himself once a year with something besides eating and sex—monotonous operations that merely keep him alive and give life to other bears intent on the same thing?

At that very moment there arose in me, as powerful as an instinct, the idea of an animal that could look at the world in a different way. I thought of a comely, thoughtful animal: a friend of creation, without violent and mechanical appetites. I was almost shocked by the force of this idea. It penetrated me and came out of me at the very same time. It was a vision!

I spent a white night in the whiteness of the aurora borealis, gripped by a new excitement, and finally I fell asleep. During my sleep I must have pushed the ice down with my feet, so that it covered the temperate continents and the tropical areas, and my whole creation went to sleep with me. It was the beginning of the longest glaciation in the history of the world. I fell into

it as if I wanted to slumber for a long time. I dreamed of kanga-
roos jumping all over the meadows, and of nightingales giving
recitals in my honor, and of beavers building a house on a lake
just for my sake. At one point in my dreams I knew that my
new animal was coming to meet me. I looked at the horizon
and down the valleys and over the rivers; and I thought that I
saw the shadow of a figure walking toward me. But the dream
ceased at that pinnacle of expectation, before I could gaze at
my creature's face.

When I woke up I flew toward warmer climates, having
ended my glaciation. I had premonitions about my newly expected animal. I already felt it stirring inside me and couldn't
wait to see it at work. But something became clear at the end
of that flight, after I reached some sunny and hospitable coast.
Maybe I had been sleeping too long in that bed of ice, maybe
it was the inevitable evolution of my organism. Or maybe it
was the price I had to pay for my grimly gained knowledge. In
any case, I discovered that my powers no longer existed as before. I could no longer create something totally new.

My first reaction was one of dismay. I wondered if I had
deceived myself until then, thinking that I was able to create
from nothingness, mistaking long processes for immediate and
final results, mixing up experiments in my own memory, trad-
ing causes with effects and vice versa. Was I myself—think of
the cynicism that suddenly transfixed me—was I myself a being who had been created? I was doubting, all of a sudden,
the very existence of God! I spent a season in consternation,
imitating the wolf and howling at the moon, but I finally rejected such absurd, venomous doubts. I knew who I was! Today, when I see adolescents grow old suddenly and quit writing
poetry, I remember those dark moments in which everything
seemed already accomplished and with no plausible purpose.

The end of youth forces a confrontation with reality. It's the
point when you have to accept a simple truth—that it is only
possible to modify what already exists. I decided to embrace
this fact, and I felt I knew what direction I should take. I had
to find an animal that I could transform into the most splendid
of beings, and I immediately started to look around. I became
like a visitor at an enormous zoo, or an archivist stunned by

the wealth of his archives. In every beast I discovered some merit, but I needed to concentrate on one alone. I must choose, among the many qualities, the one most useful to restore order to my possessions.

I rejected out of hand the earth's more ferocious inhabitants, the tiger, the alligator, the predators. Violent types wouldn't do for this assignment. Instead I turned to the birds, which had been the object of my prolonged admiration through the times. I went and lived with them for an extended period, overcoming all the practical difficulties that had frustrated me in the past. I concealed my identity and found a modest position among them as a kind of concierge and supervisor in a chestnut forest. I learned their dialects, which were incredibly various, and became acquainted with their goods and evils.

There came an unexpected revelation. I found in the birds something profoundly mediocre, something surprisingly commonplace. They were terrible gossips and took the most short-sighted view on any subject. After all that back and forth through the sky that had so nourished my imagination, they would return to their nests bursting with insipid stories about worms and bugs. They could think of nothing else; even while making love they chirped on about food in that clipped language I had worked so hard to master.

I tried to follow those that migrated. I thought that a well-traveled bird would hold more promise than, say, the rustic sparrow. I was wrong. An enlarged horizon was no help to the volatile race. They didn't look down, and they didn't look up. They resembled one of those instruments men nowadays launch into space, obtuse and semi-infallible (when there is a mistake, disaster is total): once put in motion they function almost independently, as if wound up by a spring. The migrators traveled stupidly, their heads empty of any ideas, uninhabited devices aimed at a goal that they attained without any joy. I had similar experiences with other birds and finally abandoned the project of trying to make something more out of the flying animals. Their level was not high enough, paradoxical as it sounds.

I quit my concierge and supervisor position and disappeared. The birds remembered me for a while as a strange fellow wrapped in a cape and never showing his wings. I don't think that they ever suspected my real nature. I could not bear the thought that I had once worshiped them so, my nose always pointing to the sky.

I had to discard one attempt after another. I was like a sculptor whose statue refuses to emerge from the formless stone. As I compared all the animals with my yet unborn one, I saw that each candidate had some defect or other that had not seemed irremediable until then. I was beginning to be certain that the survival of the world was at stake. I was determined to provide some relief for its discomforts.

Disappointment followed disappointment. The cat was too lazy, the marsupial was prone to getting lost, the beaver worked blindly and was undecided between the wet and the dry, the serpent was perfidious and unable to build anything at all. But something of each of these animals was destined to end up in the creature who came afterward, like a vestige of my experiments. We only have to look at our colleagues in the office or at people passing by: there is the dog, there is the owl, there is the mouse, the tapir, the anteater. Look at the lion, stretched back, eyes closed, immersed in sovereign and Olympian indifference. Look at the dog, how distracted he gets, scurrying left and right; and look at the fox, always late and never there when you need him. They all fit in the same room, along with rabbits and chipmunks, everybody looking into a different computer, exchanging jokes from one desk to the other, as if they were in a huge animal reservation. They all preserve in their faces and their gestures that remote interrogation of mine: Do you want to become someone else? Would you like to become humankind?

I took a new plunge into the seas and rummaged them thoroughly. I had forgotten how boundless my subaqueous territories were. There were fishes of all shapes, veritable water-birds with short wings on their backs and the same innate obtuseness as their aerial cousins. Not even the sharks were an exception, awesome and mechanical as they were, like mad submarines that think only of swallowing whatever they encounter. Clearly the fish would not serve my purpose. I eliminated the amphibians, too, because I didn't want any identity problems in my new hero.

In my despondency I retreated to an island in the warm seas. The place was thick with banana and pineapple trees. It suited me because the abundance of fruit kept the island's beasts unusually calm. One day I was sitting beneath a tree on the beach, munching a banana and wondering where in creation I would find the animal I needed.

Right then, from a branch above me, dropped the monkey.

I had forgotten that I had made such an animal. Of course you know by now that memory has always been one of my weak points. What struck me was that this monkey seemed to remember *me*. It looked at me with the stare of a schoolmate who recognizes you years after graduation. It wasn't a particularly distinguished monkey; I knew I must have made better ones. Of medium height, with a big nose, short legs, an elongated skull, lots of hair all over—this was not a handsome animal. But the eyes made an impression. Even in a zoo such eyes are to be found only in the monkey cages; eyes that look at me now as they looked at me then, and hold their gaze with the intensity of clutching fingers.

At that moment I also noticed the hand, which scrabbled on the ground collecting pebbles and twigs, without disturbing the attention fixed on me. And then I remembered completely. I even offered a smile to my old acquaintance, the equivalent of the "Ah, it's you!" that erupts in a train after fifteen minutes of mutual contemplation. "Ah, it's you!" The thought turned into words that reverberated in my mind. "I recognize you. *You're the clown.*"

The beast's reaction at this flash of recognition convinced me I was right. It rose erect on its feet like an acrobat or a gymnast preparing to perform. There was a suspenseful moment in that silent place. The monkey coiled up, its body like a spring under pressure. Then it released itself like an arrow into the air. An instant later it was back on the ground looking at me with a sly twinkle in its eyes. It had executed a somersault.

I felt that I understood a great deal in the space of that instant—God, the monkey, and the imminent humankind we would make together. Everything returned to me with the force of a thought that rises from the depths.

Yes, now I remembered.

At the beginning the monkey had a different purpose. In the vast world I had set in motion, its role was marginal. One day I had worked like a madman in the throes of an agitation that to say the least was manic. I had put the finishing touches on a lion, after several false starts on other animals. In the evening I rested, contemplating the lion as he came down the river, majestic; and then appeared the eagle, rising in wide perfect circles above the clearing and the water. As always happened with the birds, I did not know where the eagle had come from, but I felt good that it was part of my world. I was exhilarated, fulfilled, in the mood for play, for something light and unruly.

The idea of the monkey was born that evening. It too was the result of second and third thoughts and, indeed, of many subsequent rethinkings. It was finally realized with a decisive outburst in the last efflorescence of that magical day. After the king and the warrior, the court jester was created. It immediately performed perfect parodies of the lion and the eagle, drenching itself with water and crashing onto the ground, inspiring mirth among all onlookers. From the moment I created it, the monkey was capable of prodigious grins that displayed its enormous and dazzling teeth. Its descendants would learn how to laugh, but that original ancestor was already quite advanced in smiling.

To this day professional clowns paint huge cackling smiles around imaginary rows of teeth, but their eyes gleam, curiously sad, like those of orangutans. This contrast appears comical, at least so it seemed to me when I was racking my brains to write the world's *Ars Poetica*. Tearful eyes above bared teeth— it sounded like a good formula.

So it was that, at the beginning, I created the monkey as a living amusement in honor of the lion and the eagle. We all went to sleep, and when I woke up, I considered my latest production with greater calm. I realized that even as a clown, the monkey had several defects; and since I could not cancel what was already done, I made a number of adjustments. The eyes, for instance, were not sad enough. The comic effect was insufficient. How could I make them more melancholic, if not by making them more conscious of what they saw? The keener the awareness, the greater the tendency to melancholy. It was useless to frighten or hurt, because this would produce not greater sadness but only greater rancor. It was also useless for me to explain to the monkey how it must be, because it understood nothing of what I said. It was a spontaneous actor and had to be changed from within. Its eyes had to see more. The more you see, the less reason you find to rejoice.

I became practical about the whole issue. I had to enlarge that sort of warehouse that sat behind the pupils and in which all images were registered. I worked for months on the head of the monkey. The animal wriggled and twisted to escape my grip, and in the end I left the job half done, so great was my patient's resistance.

Finally I realized that a good clown must execute tricks with his hands, and my jester had proved pitifully inept at this. I lengthened its fingers, made them agile and mobile, all the while deaf to its screams and protests. The moment I let go, it leaped into the trees. An instant later I saw it hovering on high, balancing on a hanging vine, its immense mouth open below its extremely sad eyes, its tail twisted into a huge question mark.

"Zita!" I shouted. "I will call you Zita." The monkey disappeared in the foliage, and for some time I forgot about it.

But now, after that long glaciation, I found the proficient juggler once more in front of me. It not only ran and jumped like an acrobat but seized objects with hands never seen on any other animal before. What's more, a never-extinguished sadness was in its eyes. The monkey ran up and down the beach, scampering away from each wave with piercing shrieks of fear. I didn't know if this fear was real or feigned, but every time the edge of the water grazed its foot, the monkey would escape by jumping into a palm tree.

So that was it. Among all the creatures I had created, the

monkey was the only one that remembered me. The way in which Zita looked at me aroused my interest. I don't want to get sidetracked here into a philosophical discussion, but let me advance the hypothesis that perhaps it was Zita who created me, by recognizing my presence. When we fall in love, we don't bother to figure out who "really" did the choosing—well, it was something of this sort. I often ask myself at night, Where would I be without that first look? I would be flitting about the cosmos like a nameless shadow in search of someone able to recognize me.

At any rate, from that moment on, I devoted myself almost completely to the monkey's metamorphosis. Its role in the world was supposed to be that of a melancholy clown, a comic and decidedly minor character. I had now fathomed that these characteristics could prove essential in achieving a totally different role. The larger head and the hands conceived to perform the part of a tightrope dancer turned out to be just the tools for an unforeseen and inevitably dominating function. It was just another of my curiously roundabout operations, although it led to sensational results.

One surprise was the discovery of the tremendous effect produced by my old idea of play, which at first seemed just a casual thought, thrown out and lost in the recesses of memory, where, obviously, it continued to operate. Besides surviving and procreating like everyone else, the monkey had a purpose rooted in its being, albeit in a primary and summary manner, which was composed entirely of grimaces. Every comic knows that one sure way to evoke laughter is to imitate someone else, and the monkey had impersonated both the eagle and the lion in the forest's amphitheater. From then on, it kept busy imitating everyone and everything, even the mutable shapes of the trees and clouds. It almost seemed that the monkey did not have a personality of its own. Like a mirror, it reflected what surrounded it, and like a jester it commented on everything it saw.

That was the breach to be opened. In an instant of boundless vision, my guiding hope caught up with me again. The monkey must become conscious of what it did and said, and I thought I knew how.

I pushed my monkey insistently down the path of playfulness. I became its coach, devoted to its every performance, developing toward it the paternal feeling that coaches have for the youth in their care. In my determination to turn Zita into a superstar, I invented all sorts of exercises. In the morning we ran on the beach and into the woods, with no specific goal, as if we were clouds in the sky. Zita was seized by a kind of intoxication. My monkey now ran just for the sake of running, not to capture prey or escape danger. This was something unheard of in the animal world, and later only dogs and horses would catch on to the same spirit—art for art's sake, in a way. Zita and I ran all day, until the fatigue made us drunk. My pupil was always ready to commit itself totally, its pelt shiny with sweat, its eyes sparkling with physical pleasure, happy as it was to play in my company.

"Zita, jump!" There was no need for encouragement. And how my monkey did jump, how it climbed and grasped the branches with its incomparable fingers! And Zita would fly. Hanging from the branches of a tree or from a vine, holding on with one hand thirty feet above the ground. Its cries would scatter the fleeing birds, terrified by that gigantic creature pirouetting up there with no apparent purpose in mind. The monkey was now impishly disturbing the sleep of all other animals, who for the most part were terribly serious, totally unwilling to take part in any of my games.

There was only one thing that for the longest time I was unable to get my monkey to do. Zita would have nothing to do with water, neither river nor lake, well nor sea. This disconcerted me and I couldn't understand it. "Zita, jump in and learn how to swim!" I ordered in my most authoritarian tone. Not a chance. "What about the fishes, don't you want to imitate them?" But it was as if they did not exist. It took me ages to convince the monkey to play the dolphin and the frog, and it happened only much later, after several modifications of its nature. How different things are today! Just go to a swimming pool, or visit the beach in the summer. Everybody loves to play the fish, if only for a short while.

Zita and I went on to discover our greatest amusement: we would compare one thing with another and then with still another, and so on, ad infinitum. We were tracing a path for the conscious metamorphosis of my created world. We tumbled everywhere, elated by our game. It was a way to proclaim our happiness to all. Excellent pupil that it was, my monkey compared itself to every animal it saw, even to plants and rocks, bringing itself to an abrupt halt and imitating the perfect immobility of vegetation and mineral.

I took another close look at creation to see if Zita's antics had any precedent. Surely the plants and other animals had the knack of transforming themselves. I discovered a flower that in order to attract bees turned the color of flesh and gave off an odor of putrefaction. With the same aim, other flowers would cover themselves with magnificent spots. Serpents changed color so that an attacker could not distinguish them from the grass in which they hid. Certain male birds disguised themselves as females in order to be accepted, unsuspected, inside well-guarded harems. Caterpillars changed into butterflies, commencing a totally different life without any memories of the previous one, as might a human being granted the wish to become an angel.

There were lots of transformations everywhere, but Zita was up to something quite different. The disguises of the plants and other animals were efforts to survive or to find food or to propagate their species; none of them was really playing. My monkey, on the other hand, imitated for the sake of imitating, with a pure unmotivated joy, comparing itself to everything comparable.

What beautiful times we had. Hope was reborn in me after my long icy depression. The climate had become milder and made Zita's training easier. We both felt that an important event was approaching, a performance at which Zita's skill as a jester would announce the first day of the new era.

My fondest memory of our friendship remains our collaboration on a language that could surpass the infantile chatting that we heard all around us, from birds to mice. Along with the making of the sun, human language may well be my greatest accomplishment. But I want to be honest about it: Zita played an active role in the construction of its first prototype. We worked on it steadily, setting aside one hour every morning for language studies. A scholar of my acquaintance claims that words are already and forever inside people, who only need to take them out of their depths and show them to others, like old objects to be dusted and shined before being used. But I know that words first had to be created; only later were they stored in the soul.

Zita and I had to find every single term. In a meadow where the grass was short we disposed at random a number of stones of different colors and sizes. Each stone corresponded to an animal, or a tree, or a river. We identified each reference by running to it, and after a brief ritual dance that signified a sort of baptism, we ran back to our meadow and selected one stone among the many. In this way we slowly built up the first dictionary of our future communication system. From that moment on, that particular pebble was linked to the thing itself, and we passed the time combining words on the grass, drawing fantastic structures of grammar and syntax.

We got some help from my own creation. We laid three stones on the ground to signify the sun, and four stones and one small branch to picture the moon—it seemed natural to do so. As if rewarding us for that inspiration, the butterflies suddenly began to look like conjunctions, and the rivers like the infinitive form of the verb, and the blossoms like conditionals; reptiles became the past tense, and the birds the future. Animals ran like adverbs around us, their babies following like loyal adjectives. We reached a high point when we identified the falcon with an exclamation mark. We detected in the maze of a wild forest all the intricacies of the relative clause. For a long while my world rotated like a living dictionary, the revolving grammar of a foreign language that we were trying to learn. Above us immense clouds navigated like baroque paragraphs.

Chatting with stones became our favorite sport. My monkey would manifest its interest with grunts and yaps of different tonalities. It was looking for words—and how far it was from finding them! But we had made a start.

During this period of trial and preparation I had not lost sight of my aim: to succeed, if not in creating, at least in training an animal that could remedy the mistakes I had made in constructing the world. It was necessary for this animal to be able to think, and in order to be able to think it had to practice the game. The game was composed of imitations and analogies. It was a simple and ingenious model that I was setting in motion, and I was beginning to have some hope as to the result of my effort.

Meanwhile I noticed that in its feelings toward me, my monkey was passing through different stages. On certain days it rushed to meet me, emitting loud cries of joy, as though I were its best and most trusted friend. At other times it was irritable and inattentive, as if it were trying to avoid me. Those were the days on which it made terrible messes, exhibiting an unsurpassable clumsiness. On a few occasions it carried this attitude to the point of insubordination and a refusal to play, even trying to attack me, but these moods always ended soon in a heartfelt show of repentance in a clearing in the woods.

One of Zita's characteristics was a spontaneous and profound cowardice, the same that I would later find among the humans, who would call heroic any act that is less than cowardly. But then, who worships heroes if not those who are chickens at heart? Why should a truly brave man entertain myths of heroism? It took me a while to understand that cowardice was the firstborn of intelligence, but happily not an only child. Courage was its sibling, and always humankind would have to choose between them. Think how much God had to learn!

There were times when Zita would ignore me, pretending to be immersed in the search for food and for a mate, disdaining my every suggestion as the proof of futility. This was never very convincingly done, because immediately afterward I would surprise Zita at whistling, prancing, transforming love into a joyful and wild performance, turning meals into a kind of dance. I would have preferred greater stability in my monkey's temperament, but it had been conceived to live as a jester, and perhaps it never entirely forgave me for this. "Why couldn't you make me a lion?" it seemed to ask with its exaggerated moods and histrionic gestures.

Bless me, what an actor! I would chase it across the plain in a grotesquely menacing way, just to see it pretend to be afraid. What fun I had, running breathlessly after that primate, in the sweet season of the postglaciation, with all kinds of sparkling new buds and pleasant new brutes.

JUST then an entire section of the firmament suddenly collapsed, opening a vortex in the center of the sky. The sun darkened, a veil descended on the earth. The animals ran to hide, the birds cowered quietly among the plants, where I could hear the throbbing of their tiny hearts and could see the glitter of their feathers. In Zita's eyes appeared a grim shadow.

I didn't have the slightest idea what was going on. None of the animals knew much about the existence of stellar bodies, not even Zita, who rejected, along with water, the sight of the blue above the treetops. The attention of the entire terrestrial world, including the birds, had always gravitated downward. But I, the migrant and pioneer of life, had not forgotten my astral origins. I scrutinized the firmament, trying to track down the site of the cataclysm.

At last I thought I found it in the configuration that is now called Andromeda, a corner of the cosmos in which I had piled up a bit of everything, nebulae, old comets, unusable planets, broken satellites, but also some excellent stars that I did not know where else to put. I resolved to go back and look over those distant properties. I was motivated in part by remorse, the sense of responsibility of a landlord who has been absent too long.

I left Earth with a glance at Zita. *I'll see you soon.* I promised it without using words. *I'll be back right away.* Zita kept playing with some pebbles and did not look at me. Maybe the monkey was looking for the sign for hail and wasn't finding it; or maybe it had just fallen into one of its bad moods. I hurried away.

I had not foreseen that it would be so hard to orient myself up there, after having spent so much time on Earth. At first it was not difficult. I passed by planets still unnamed, coasted along the broad stellar gulf, and began to ascend one of the innumerable ladders that led to my solar attic. The sense of solitude that invaded me as soon as I left the atmosphere was still tolerable.

I had bundled up against the cold and had with me a sort

of sleeping bag in which to lie down because I remembered that nowhere in the entire universe was there a single soft spot except on Earth. I tried to keep my stops to a minimum. I proceeded by forced marches, tunneling through galaxies, circumnavigating constellations, recognizing the corners and corridors of my ancient castle, which was illuminated in the same sketchy fashion as before, leaving large areas of shadow and darkness, pits and caverns in the sky. The farther I advanced the more I felt that I could not love a place where one had to travel through an absolute lack of vegetation and be careful not to be burned by torches. I almost regretted having returned. "This is the last time," I told myself, lying down after reaching Orion, at a point of medium heat between the knees of what one day would be called the Hunter and was at that time a confused jumble of lights, like a chandelier shop.

After a spell of drowsiness disturbed by asteroids and meteorites, I got up to resume my journey, and soon found that I was lost in the sky. I had traveled only a brief distance past Orion, but when I turned around I could not see its familiar outline. I found myself surrounded by unknown, granitic planets at a junction that led off in several directions, none of which seemed right.

I was absolutely unable to place myself. I thought that perhaps my childhood haunts had changed in my memory; or perhaps they were unchanged and I could no longer recognize them. But no, the truth was much more unexpected and cruel. Never before had I been in the space through which I was moving now. These celestial bodies had formed after my departure for Earth and had filled a horizon that in my memory was vast and uncluttered, a sea of empty space.

I tried in vain to retrace my steps. I was unable to locate Orion, and nowhere could I spot Andromeda, lost who knows where. I was astray in a newly formed firmament that to me seemed chaotic and vaguely menacing, like the smoldering outskirts of industrial cities. That was the South Bronx of my solar system, and I didn't want to be there. I wandered aimlessly, surrounded by a crowd of stony-faced and potentially violent immigrants. New housing projects piled one on top of the other and threw into confusion the signals of recognition that had protected my childhood.

I kept on walking with my sleeping bag, not knowing where to go or where to stop. I was petrified by that world's tenacious will to survive and to expand, by its grim and infinitely silent demeanor. In my effort to overcome the anguish that was beginning to stifle me, I took a leap toward an observation point—a terrace atop an enormously high skyscraper—and from there I tried to scrutinize what was happening around me.

I will forever remember that period of bitter and studious solitude at the summit of a universe now alien to me, whose rules I was trying to grasp. I felt I was full of flaws and of limitations, but I was not about to collapse into resignation and indifference. A powerful will to comprehend kept me up there, braving the cold and a capricious and deceptive light. I took notes with my fingertips in the sky's sand, and in the end I shaped an alphabet to be learned by heart, with letters like figures, and I entrusted my discoveries to it.

For a time I was confused by the fact that none of the stars stayed still. Each revolved around other stars and, at the same time, rotated on its own axis, so I thought that the thing to do was to make a map of the firmament. It seemed arduous but possible. I had gotten over the wounded feeling inflicted on me by the realization that the cosmos was proceeding on its own and that my further contributions were not required. This was a vanity I needed to overcome.

I looked at the stars with a visitor's eye, like someone watching a party he has joined by chance, taking advantage of the fact that no one knows him in order to understand how the party works, noting the groups that form and dissolve again, casually, and the more stable groups that leave together even though their members had seemed to ignore each other all evening. That visitor would return home with the idea that the world is held together by invisible threads much like those that govern the rhythms of the stellar cosmos, a web of solitaries and multitudes that now and then declare war on each other and produce catastrophes that tear holes both in the earth and in the sky. I saw celestial recluses, unhappy to the point of self-destruction, flaring into the dark. I saw all those secondary figures in the family groups of the sky: the satellites as wives, the planets as lovers, in all their awkward arrangements. And among them all I saw the peculiar, omnipresent force of gravity trying to hold everything together and keep it in balance, like a marriage contract.

It was all more frightful than anything I had imagined. My ancient world was migrating into the void, like an irresistible flow of lava. I felt that sooner or later it would annihilate me. There must be a wall somewhere, an abyss, something to arrest that mobile mass, a point of extermination and a new beginning from nothingness.

The Earth I had left returned to mind. Amid all that rotation of boulders in the void, I saw the small, derisory grain in the cosmic forest as the shelter of my only possible hope. Earth! Earth, where death was not yet dominant, as it was in that mechanism without a hint of warmth. I wept in a corner of my cosmos now that, my divine adolescence behind me, I was compelled to face the seriousness of fate. Earth! By now it was certain: Earth was the flower of hope to which the cosmos had given birth.

It seemed that buried all along in the stony hearts of the monsters that surrounded me was the decisive, ineffable will to know. I understood then that what life was struggling for on my minuscule globe was the universe's great hope of understanding itself. I sobbed with compassion and pride, in my boundless solitude. Now I had a purpose, and playtime had ended. I must make haste and return.

But I truly was lost. For an interminable era I roamed through the interstellar void without the slightest notion of space and time, convinced that I would never find my way home. Thus in impotent anguish I consumed the most beautiful period of my youth, the moment when one would like to intervene positively in the matters of the world. Instead, I was forced to wander from place to place, among rocky masks in the hostile interstices of the stars. Today, when I go to the movies and follow stories of astronauts lost in space, I am assailed by the shivers of a troublesome memory, a long uneventful season spent searching for some trace of life. I know that the reason those films have a hold on people is that they obscurely remember something similar in my past, and they fear that it might happen again; they talk about it the way children talk about monsters in order to keep them away. I remember that one day (or night), having by then lost all hope, I regretted that I could not die myself, or become one of those round bodies destined to shatter against a black wall.

And then I saw a soft light with greenish-yellow reverberations, and it was framed inside a circle of petals like a flower, entirely unlike the rotating mechanical vortex in which I had been imprisoned. Around that light moved something as airy as a veil or a tuft of cotton, a ring of white clouds in which I suddenly breathed a different air, familiar to me from time immemorial. Earth was immersed in its air like a rose in its fragrance, azure and brown, white with snow at its two poles, and I descending, passing through the clouds, like a bumblebee filled with desire. In a moment I was following the coastlines and discovering the waters I had dreamed of during my wanderings in the sidereal desert, the water of the sea into which I now let myself fall. From it I emerged happily into the sun and ran among the trees and once more saw the birds and all the signs of the imperfect masterpiece of my genius, the living clock divided into seasons, into days, and nights, and hours, by minute gradations of light.

"We are together," I said to Earth; "our fate is joined." I breathed deeply. Oxygen had never tasted so good.

That is when I saw an animal still unknown to me, approaching on its two legs. But didn't it resemble Zita? That was Zita all right, judging from its eyes; but what a change! What had happened to its thick pelt? What were those odd sounds issuing from its lips? And why such dismay at seeing me?

2

I had reached an advanced point in my parabola, as I explained to Moses during one of our many long talks. We were sitting among the rocks of Mount Sinai, the desolate peak where we had agreed to meet. The people of Israel were camped in the desert below us. It had been a stormy day and the mountain's crest was surrounded by a mass of clouds. Forty days is a long time, but fortunately we had not lacked for topics of conversation.

Moses had climbed up there with a provision of bread, cheese, and water. He ate moderately and only in the evening, when the shadow of night rose in the sky. I watched him break small pieces of goat cheese from a large wheel, which every day became drier and more malodorous. To me it was simply inedible; my stint on Mount Sinai became an involuntary forty-day diet.

Moses and I had met at the Egyptian court, years before. I was among the few people gathered together for the ceremony of the adoration of Aton, the sun, which was slowly rising above Ikhnaton's temple. Aton was worshiped by the Pharaoh Amenhotep IV (who had changed his name to Ikhnaton) to the exclusion of all other gods; and Moses was one of the convinced followers of the new cult.

I had gone to that court in great haste, anxious to find an interpreter of myself. This was the first time that humans spoke about me in these terms. After so many false starts, somebody—the Pharaoh—finally seemed close to knowing me. He was a young and ardent man, already gnawed by an illness that was to consume him before his hopes could be realized. He wanted to convert his people to the cult of the Sun God, and this project pleased me because of my ancient liking for the great star. At the same time I realized that the propelling force of his ambition was in fact his illness. Ikhnaton felt his strength diminish day by day; pallor grew on the features the mirror showed him in the morning, a haggard face deeply furrowed, with dark circles under the eyes. He would go outside in search of the sun with the step of an invalid. He exposed himself to its rays all morning long, and a flock of dignitaries and friends went with him, sweating beneath the lash of the dog days. He turned to the sun for the life that was escaping from him.

I was alongside Moses when the emaciated monarch began to sing a hymn he had composed in honor of Aton, which at that point was reaching the summit of the sky, burning the air and filling the eyes of those present with black spots. Moses was sweating heavily under his ceremonial robe; it seemed to me that he was making a great effort to keep his composure. In the acrid odor of perspiration that pervaded the temple, Ikhnaton's voice could be heard chanting. It was a fragile chant that hovered tremulously in the air, like a small balloon attached to a very thin thread:

> All the beasts are happy with their nourishment;
> Trees and plants are blossoming.
> Birds rise in flight from their nests;
> They spread their wings in praise of Thee.

I made a sudden start, a reaction to the heat, I suppose, but also to the unrealistic idea that birds would be at all inclined to sing my praises. That was when Moses noticed me. He looked at me with that peculiar, attentive gaze that has struck me from time to time since the beginning of humankind. It was the gaze of someone who has recognized me.

The Pharaoh's voice continued:

> Ships travel south and north,
> Because all routes open up when Thou appearest;
> The fishes in the water dart in front of Thee.

Suddenly Ikhnaton's wife fell to the ground. Until then I had seen her with her back turned to me, wrapped in her silvery robe, her head adorned with a glistening crown. In its immobility her figure had escaped my attention, almost as though she herself were part of the temple. When she collapsed, felled by the sun's violence, a scene followed that was so absurd it seemed contrived. None of those present moved, since Ikhnaton continued to chant his hymn with fanatic indifference. Moses and I picked up the queen and carried her beneath the portico. I was struck both by her beauty and by the energy that I felt emanating from Moses' body. As she lay there, I seized that moment to look at his face and imprint his features on my memory, feeling certain that we would see each other again. He returned my gaze intently. The Pharaoh's voice continued to rise.

> Thou hast created the world according to Thy desire
> When Thou wast alone,
> The men, the herds, and the wild beasts.

A few months after that ceremony Ikhnaton died, and a revolt led by the priests of the polytheistic sect destroyed the solar temple and persecuted the followers of the defunct sovereign. Among the latter was Moses, who at that time had a different name, which I never learned. I assumed that he too must have been stabbed in some Cairo or Alexandria alleyway in the massacre that followed Ikhnaton's death. I forgot about him.

I went to stay in a village near the pyramids, where a tribe of Israelites lived. Their ancestors had been brought to Egypt by force, into a condition of absolute servitude. A short time before I moved to the village, the descendants of that ancient people had been released from slavery and allowed to decide their own destiny. Stay or leave, do as you please, was the message they received from the new Egyptian leaders.

It took them completely by surprise. They had been accustomed to obey, and the sudden gift of freedom left the Israelites uncertain and discouraged. They could not decide what to do. Close by stood the pyramids, erected by their own labor, and they had never been allowed to leave their shadow. Those solitary and enigmatic blocks of stone contained the only meaning left to them. The pyramids were visible signs of something they had made, and they were almost nostalgic for the time when the Egyptians' whips had driven them through the desert to haul the stone. Their attachment to those majestic buildings was made all the stronger by the innumerable Israelites who were buried inside the walls, people who had died at work, disappearing into the furnaces or among the chunks of stone. It seemed to them that the pyramids were also their funerary homes, not only those of the Pharaohs.

The Israelites no longer remembered with certainty where they had come from. They showed each other old maps that had become discolored by time and could no longer be read properly. At night, around the fire on which they cooked their meager family meals, they told each other various old legends that they had stubbornly kept alive, remembering them as best they could, although always in the form of questions. Was it true that their first progenitors were expelled from a beautiful Eden for no reason at all, or was it possible that they had committed some major crime? Nobody knew for sure. And what kind of crime could be committed in such a place, except possibly some minor infraction about eating fruit?

The game of questions and answers would continue. Yes, Joseph existed. But who was he—Jacob's brother or his son? And Isaac? And Abraham, what about Abraham? He was certainly important, but no one could say exactly why. In the house next to mine some people were speaking about Sarah and Lot and wondering to whom they were related. Then someone mentioned Abel, and there were clear signs of nervousness. The women tapped their temples as though remembering a frightful event, but in a confused way. Those evening conversations were made up of short, uncertain sentences that trailed off into silence.

In short, memory among them had become weak, and the tribe had remained stymied a few hundred yards away from the pyramids, incapable of choosing a direction. Some of the oldest maintained that they ought to go east, toward the side where the sun rose; others suggested that they go in the opposite direction. Nobody's argument was sufficiently convincing. Someone launched the idea of comparing their language, lost in the night of time, with the languages of known people, but the proposal sank amid general consternation. Vague legends floated in the air, like memories of dreams. I became profoundly attracted by the Israelites' loss of recollection and by their stubborn will to retrieve the past. In fact they would eventually succeed in remembering, to the point of possessing a memory that will last forever. But it wasn't so at the beginning.

Gradually it occurred to me that the Israelites, these exiled people, might be led to understand my nature better than humankind had yet managed to do, and that I could then entrust them to help set my creation right. I would need a partner in the effort, however, someone to appear among them and tutor them in my ways. It was then that, thanks to one of those providential interventions that seem to drive events, I chanced to meet Moses in a market in Alexandria. I had gone there to escape the somewhat oppressive atmosphere of the village in the desert, and I recognized Moses immediately even though he had disguised himself to avoid being captured as a follower of Ikhnaton. He was impoverished, barely getting by as a peddler of animal pelts, hawking his merchandise in a loud and raucous voice. For him, too, one glance in my direction was enough to renew our alliance. An instant later we were whispering in a corner of the market square, and our project took shape.

Moses had not rejected his faith. In fact, the debacle following Ikhnaton's death only made his faith stronger, and now he was seeking revenge against fate. The idea of an absolute God without rivals had grown gigantic in his mind, to the point of merging with the sky's horizon and with everything that might seem at once a limit and a threshold. If God was expected to come from such heights, Moses was certainly not going to wait for him to turn up in the streets of Alexandria. But when I did, he made the best of a bad situation and accepted it without complaint. So we met and went to lunch together. We tried to be equal to the event: God speaking to Moses, and all around milling servants, the acrid smell of wine, the hubbub of the populace, and no one aware that at a table, in that tavern, the future of the world was being discussed. Moses and I even drank to that, a cup of honey mixed with cool water.

Did Moses really believe that I was God? Even today I can't answer that question with absolute certainty. There was an impenetrable side to Moses. He would not be caught in the act of asking for something but seemed always to be waiting for a gift to be offered. He had gone into exile as he would go on an excursion, taking it for granted that he would return home. This is the stuff that leaders are made of.

Moses knew next to nothing about the Israelites and certainly never imagined he would have anything to do with them. I took him to the village and showed him around. We walked down the narrow streets and the alleys, we peered into the dark rooms crammed with people, we listened in on their conversations, mingling in the shadows with the anonymous crowd, until finally we became a familiar and accepted part of communal life. The Israelites overcame their first surprise at seeing us pry into their lives and soon convinced themselves that we had always been there.

Moses' interest was growing. He sensed in the Israelites a weapon to be forged and wielded. His eyes gleamed with a cold and violent light as he elaborated plans that seemed unreasonable to me. He actually thought of arming those wretches and leading them in an attack on the priests who had seized power, and he dreamed of succeeding to the throne of the dead Pharaoh and reinstating the cult of the Sun God. I had difficulty convincing him that this plan was absurd and certain to fail.

"This is what must be done, Moses," I would repeat in the low, firm voice that one uses with obstinate adolescents. "First of all we must find some territory to which they can be taken. In the meantime, we will help them to remember everything, not just in the past but in the future as well. This project is going to take a long time and we have to get started." When I explained to him that a true leader must be capable of the unexpected, I was finally able to persuade him: "It is better to conquer an unknown territory than to recapture a lost power." Moses' pride responded to this pronouncement. "I will have a new land!" he cried in a frenzy. I should have asked myself then whether I had chosen the right collaborator.

We concentrated on studying a somewhat confused map that I had found while rummaging in jars nobody had touched for many years. We had to turn it around several times before we saw which side was up and which was down, but in the end, after much discussion, we decided on a strip of land to the east of Egypt, beyond Mount Sinai, on the edge of the great

Mediterranean Sea. We pointed our fingers at the unnamed desert areas. This is Palestine, and this is Canaan, and this is Galilee. We amused ourselves by making up names: in the beginning there was the Word, at least this time.

Now that we knew where we were going, we had to get people moving. From that moment on I withdrew into the shadows, guiding Moses but leaving to him the glory that he seemed to need. He was obviously pleased by my discretion, and I did not mind, since I've never had the character of a leader or a demagogue. In fact, crowds make me feel uneasy. Even today I'd rather watch sports on television than mingle with thousands of agitated fans. I feel that I lose myself if I'm looked upon by too many people. Think of the problems this complex leads to in my case. It's no wonder there are so many unbelievers, and so many believers who don't know what they are talking about.

At first Moses kept to our agreement, and together we decided on how I should be described to the people of Israel. They had a tortuous memory of a divinity from the distant past, and as far as I could understand, he had not at all been a sympathetic God. Violent and aggressive, at night he wandered among volcanoes, exploding with rages that sent lava rushing down upon the tribe. They were all tremendously afraid of this God and feared that he might return to insult and punish them for some sin they had committed. The principal conviction of the Israelites was that of being very great sinners, though as far as I was concerned they did very little that was objectionable. They willingly repented, however, for sins it would rarely occur to them to perpetrate. The Israelites taught me that there is not much of a connection between guilt and wrongdoing. I have observed in recent years that a director of a concentration camp can feel perfectly at ease with himself while the inmates of that same camp can be obsessed by guilt. Humankind never ceases to surprise me.

I suggested to Moses that he should not bother with that particular God, whom I would not want to have even for a distant cousin, and that if the Israelites asked what God was called, he should answer that God was God and that was that. "Tell them that *I am who I am!*" I added. Why should they need to know more about me than that? I would reveal myself to them only later, once they had come close to the territory that I too had begun to think of as a promised land of happiness. I kept instructing him, but only after knowing him better did I discover that all the time he was listening to me, Moses was elaborating versions of my story that he thought the villagers could accept more easily.

Basing his narration on fragmentary clues and half-sentences, on scattered indications gathered, compared, and collated, Moses managed to compose a story that was credible enough. I listened spellbound to a new tale of creation: the six days of hard work and the seventh set aside for rest and contemplation of what had been accomplished; Abel and Cain, and Abraham and Isaac and Joseph and his brothers; the hallucinatory tale of the plagues in Egypt; and so on, up to that very day on which we found ourselves strolling around some oasis where we had gone to study and prepare. Every detail in this story took on a prodigious significance, and soon Moses too believed his creation. I did not expect at the time that I would eventually pay for the colorful net in which he was enfolding me; I did not suspect that I myself would become a prisoner in his mirage. I learned much later that all over the world other people were creating different versions of the same story, like professional writers adjusting the same idea for different audiences. Those were great narrative times, with countless people delighting in writing my epic. I felt like the David Copperfield of the created world, but Moses spoke of me as if I really were the God of the Old Testament.

Our lesson would begin in the cool of the oasis. We sat on the grass or strolled beneath the palm trees and along the edge of a tranquil pond. Moses was a diligent pupil, endowed with a stern memory, the very opposite of the Israelites, who tended to forget so easily.

"And what will you tell them?"

"I will tell them that I want to lead them out of the sorrows of Egypt to the land of Canaan, of the Hittites, the Amorites, and the Perizzites." And here would be a short pause, which he would then quickly dart past.

"Of the Hivites and the Jebusites."

"Who are they?"

"It doesn't matter who the Jebusites are. At this point I will drop the rod."

This was one of Moses' manias, and it came from his having learned to do some magic tricks from a charlatan he had met in the Alexandria market. The rod routine consisted in changing a twig into a snake, which writhed and spread panic among the spectators. It was a rather simple trick, but the first time it had startled even me. I was against this sort of thing.

"Must you really go for the business with the rod?"

Moses' expression would become so appealing that I would shrug and change the subject. I no longer considered it an important matter, and I was wrong, as I was to realize quite soon. But we still had to tackle the most irksome part of the tutoring.

"So, let's hear about Abraham's descendants."

Moses would take off:

"Abraham begat Zimran and Jokshan and Medan and Midian and Ishbak and Shuah; and the sons of Dedan were Asshurim and Letushim and Leummim."

"And then?" I would urge him on.

"The sons of Midian, Ephah and Epher and Enoch and Abida and Eldaah. Their grandmother was named Keturah."

"But finally . . . "

"But finally," Moses concluded triumphantly, "Abraham gave all his worldly goods to Isaac."

"And Rebecca, who is she?"

"Rebecca is the wife of Isaac."

"And Isaac's brother?"

"He was called Ishmael and his firstborn was Nebaioth and then came Kedar and Adbeel and Mibsam. Listen, I'm tired; enough of these names. I want to tell you what I've thought about Isaac's descendants."

The day before, I had told him confidentially that I had not succeeded in making any sense of the various legends that he had piled up with regard to Isaac's offspring and that I was about to give up the effort. He must have thought about that, because he rattled off a very beautiful story. When Isaac discovered that Rebecca was sterile, Moses told me, Isaac rushed to me and begged me to give him some children, and I granted his wish! Moses did not explain how Isaac had managed to find me. Redoubling my zeal, I impregnated Rebecca with twins, who collided with each other in her womb; and so she came to me to ask what this might be, and I told her that there were two nations in her womb, that two different people would issue from her and that one of those two people would subjugate the other. Rebecca gave birth to twins, one red and hairy, who was given the name Esau, the other white and smooth, who was given the name Jacob; and the first lost his primogeniture because of some business with the lentils that everyone knows by now. The story was invented by Moses that night before our chat. I listened to him with amusement, in part because I knew how much Moses loved lentils and cabbages, and I could see through this how a creative temperament works. He went on to tell me how Jacob managed to rob Esau of the paternal blessing, taking his place when he prepared the old blind father's meal. In order to make this event credible Moses had even imagined that Rachel, in cahoots with Jacob, had covered his neck with the skins of slaughtered kids, so that Isaac would mistake him for his hairy brother.

I couldn't quite grasp the gist of this story and I told him to forget it because the Israelites would never swallow it. I didn't understand that, on the contrary, they would have believed anything, so great was their need for someone to explain to them the mysterious events that cluttered their past. In this regard Moses saw things much more clearly than I. He managed to pass off Jacob, who later on would indulge in all sorts of tricks, as a decent man. And then Moses told how Jacob had gotten children, seeing that Rachel his wife was barren. Here too he was forced to fill incomprehensible gaps and smooth over the contradictions contained in the fragments that had come down to us. And he made up the business of Jacob going to bed with all the women in the house, getting a child from each one of them, with his wife's approval. I found it hard to understand why she did not ask me to help her as Rebecca did, but skillful raconteur that Moses was, he avoided repetitions that were not necessary for his purpose. When Moses reached the point where Rachel grants Leah to Jacob in exchange for a bunch of mandrakes, my patience came to an end and I decided to interrupt him.

"That's enough now, let's hear instead about Esau's descendants."

A bit disappointed, Moses began to reel off the litany. "Eliphaz, son of the wife Adah; and Reuel, son of the wife Basemath. And the sons of Eliphaz were Teman, Omar, Zepho, Gatam, and Kenaz. And Timna was the concubine of Eliphaz, and she gave birth to Amalek . . . "

FACE to face with Moses on top of Mount Sinai, I remembered all this. That had been a period of impassioned preparation. Moses was wholly taken up with the mission to convert the Israelites to believe in one God and lead them across the Red Sea to Palestine.

AFTER spending considerable time with Moses, I had formed a more definite idea of his character. He was animated by a strong need to believe in God, a single, august, potent God who would give him power over the crowd. He was ready to forget about the sun god worshiped at the Pharaoh's court and replace him with another divinity. This was a sign of his opportunism as a politician, but it was also the reason for his huge success with the populace. I watched him as he went about the village, amid the ecstatic admiration of all, telling the story of Joseph and Potiphar and Joseph being sentenced to jail and then his interpretations of the Pharaoh's dreams. Each time before leaving, he promised another story and actually offered a small preview of it—the same technique adopted later by the writers of serial novels. His listeners couldn't wait for him to return with the next episode. He never ran out of ideas. And so Joseph's brothers descended into Egypt and Joseph revealed himself to them, and then Jacob died and finally Joseph also died, leaving a message of hope to his people: "And God will certainly visit you and lead you out of here, and he will guide you to the land that he promised Abraham, Isaac, and Jacob!"

They all listened, enraptured. For here also began that part of their history that was closest to them and about which they held a memory that, if not clearer, was certainly stronger and more heartrending. It was the slavery in Egypt; it was the long-awaited explanation of an event incomprehensible through the centuries; it was above all, now, the advent of Moses, who told them about himself. I listened also, fascinated, as he told the story of a newborn babe entrusted to the river in a wicker basket, of the solitary childhood among the shepherds, of the apparition of the Lord's angel in the burning bush, and finally of God's visit and his promise of liberation. Here came the climactic scene. As everyone wept tears of joy, Moses stiffened and shouted, "That's enough! I want to hear from you the names of the sons of Reuben, the firstborn of Israel!" And his audience would begin to chant in chorus, "Enoch, Pallu, Hezron, and Carmi. And the sons of Simeon were Jemuel and Jamin and Ohad and Jachin and Zohar and Saul." Thus their memory was fortified and the pupil learned to surpass the master.

Moses had stirred up a great fervor among the Israelites. They were ready to follow him to the ends of the earth.

Now, at the top of Mount Sinai, Moses wiped his mouth after a swig from the water jug.

"Fortunately, they'll bring another provision of bread and cheese tomorrow," he said, talking to himself. "This stuff is disgusting."

Then he returned to the subject:

"I have already decided on the colors for the hangings in the pavilion of the sanctuary: violet, purple, and scarlet, and gold and copper buckles. Each cloth will measure twenty-eight cubits in length and four in width; and the tent will be covered with red ram skins, and on top of these will be placed badger skins."

Moses waxed fervid when imagining the decor of the sanctuary that he intended to build. I would let him run on, although I did not hide my lack of interest in this topic. He became agitated as he spoke, his eyes shining with expectation. He really was a peculiar fellow, Moses. Controlled and restrained as he was, he was seized by fits of cold fury that I had learned to fear. He did not drink wine, he ate very little, and it was my impression that he abstained from his conjugal duties. This thought had come to me the last time I had seen his wife Zipporah with that harsh and restless look of an unfulfilled woman.

Moses went on:

"And I want a curtain to hang from four columns of special wood, covered with gold and resting on silver pedestals. The altar will also be of wood, five cubits in length and three cubits in width. Look, I've made a drawing. Then it will have to be lined with copper, and the same goes for the shafts that will serve to transport it. But I still haven't told you about the court of the tabernacle and the twenty columns and the rug I want to place at the entrance. You know, violet and purple and scarlet cloth made of linen and embroidered all over. Look at these drawings."

I was irritated. This was Moses' least attractive aspect: an unexpected vanity that turned this ascetic athlete into something more like a housewife chattering about dresses and bedspreads for the new house.

And indeed:

"As for the priests' robes, they will be violet, and down the center you'll see a hemmed neckline; and I'd like them to be adorned with gold buckles and bells and pomegranates. And I want the tunic to be made of linen, and quilted; and the head cloth will also be made of linen, and the belt will be embroidered. The stockings must reach from the ankles to the thighs."

At this point I broke in impatiently, and Moses looked at me with surprise.

"But I haven't finished!"

"I want to talk to you about something else."

"But I haven't finished. I haven't said anything about the holy oil and the perfumes. The proportions are important. Myrrh must be blended with an equal mixture of cinnamon and canna, otherwise the holy oil won't come out properly. And the perfume must be ground in very tiny bits or it won't be holy. Therefore . . . "

I was forced to get up and walk away. I wandered along the ridge of the Sinai, which by now was wrapped in nocturnal shadows. I looked down into the plain through the thinning clouds. You could see the fires of the bivouacs gleam, and I thought I heard a distant murmur of voices and chants. They were right to celebrate a bit after the hardship of their journey.

It was on this journey that Moses had won his standing as leader of the people. I could still picture that most dramatic moment of the ordeal, in the middle of the Red Sea, all those hardened people crossing aboard two overloaded ships with the Egyptians in hot pursuit: the sudden storm that crashed down, like a wall of clouds, and water that dropped precipitously on one side, swallowing the pursuers' fleet. Moses had not revealed to the Israelites that the two ships had been stolen rather than bought with the money they had contributed for the purpose. His relief was huge when the storm intervened to save the fugitives. Standing on deck, his arms lifted to the heavens amid the whistling winds and the dazzling lightning bolts, he shouted with all his might, "God has parted the waters for us!" His pronouncement echoed down through the reaches of time and was already legend a few months later, when people began to say that the sea had opened to let God's chosen through and then had closed again, crashing down on their enemies.

Moses awakened the popular imagination and filled it with fanciful memories. Although it cost me considerable effort, I endured all of this, because I was counting on him to transmit my message.

I had told him everything: my encounter with humankind after returning from my voyage among the stars and my surprise at finding them so changed from what Zita had been, their mouths reduced to a slit, their hands different from their feet, bigger chatterboxes than all the birds and full of ingenuity. They had discovered fire, invented domesticity, and forged ahead on their own, remembering me across the generations by means of a series of incompatible legends (I belonged to an entire family of gods, I was a dragon, I wasn't there, I was dead). The profession of intermediary between myself and mankind was already born; there was the priest, the witch doctor, the shaman, and they worshiped me in the most varied guises and with elaborate rituals. Each one had the obstinate certainty that his way was the only right way.

There was a lot of work to be done and a lot to be corrected, but my first reaction on reacquainting myself with humanity had been one of unqualified enthusiasm, trusting as I am by nature and always ready to expect the best. That is the way I have always been: hypersensitive and moody, but also credulous enough to take the words of my flatterers as sincere. Every time I realize my mistake, however, my reaction is not one of revenge, but of detachment. I concede that God should not have such a profound need for affection that he immediately trusts whoever compliments him. But it is not his fault that he was born an orphan, that he spent his childhood alone and starved for affection. I'm being defensive, I suppose, so it comes naturally to fall into the third person.

Moses was very curious about my history; he wanted me to give him all the details, and he often asked me to repeat the same story several times, as when I told him about the way I taught humans to ask questions. There had been a time when the first humans, instead of simply asking me, for instance, "What do you want to eat?" would reel off a long list of foods much in the way a storekeeper hawks his merchandise. Challenged by this difficulty, I invented on the spot the gesture of the question mark: holding one elbow aloft like a jointed rod, joining my fingertips in the shape of a pinecone, and rotating my hand at my wrist. Accompanied by exclamations and grimaces, it was a gesture that survives even now among people living on that boot-shaped peninsula in the Mediterranean. I also recall that when writing was invented, that same gesture was transcribed in the form of a semicolon (as the Greeks did), then of a question mark. From that remote moment, we saved a lot of time in our talks. I told Moses about the first astonished questions that passed between me and those first speakers: "Are you really God?" "But where have you been?"; "What happened while I was away?" "And you, what is your trade?"

I went on with my story for days on end, paying little attention to chronology, jumping back and forth in time. Moses always listened with great concentration. Then it seemed he wanted to say something, but his voice failed him. He got to his feet, very disturbed, took a few steps on the sandy ground of the desert, and then fell to brooding. Finally he turned his gaze on me, and after a pause he came over and embraced me.

This was a moment full of hope. I had been recognized and accepted! I did not know that with that embrace he was in fact beginning to move away from me. I felt a stiffness in him after that first spontaneous effusion, and at the time I attributed it to a form of shyness. But actually, after his momentary emotion was over, he recovered his more authentic instinct and considered how he could make the best use of me. Moses' behavior was similar to that of many people I have known. He had been unable to sustain my gaze and so, like the rest, was destined to become either a beggar or a world conqueror. It always turns out this way with people who are not able to accept my real self once they have seen it.

We talked about the things we had to do. It wasn't only a matter of leading the Israelites to Palestine, but also of offering them moral and social laws. For as long as it took, we would isolate ourselves and each elaborate his own text. We divided the task as follows: I would devote myself to the general aspects, which—Moses dared not dispute this—belonged to me by right. He would concentrate on practical activities and on the organization of daily life. I thought I had taken the decisive role, and here again Moses showed greater foresight than I.

The weather atop Mount Sinai continued at its worst and we took shelter in a spacious cave whose ground we covered with fir branches. Thus began a memorable period of work, during which he and I carried on a kind of duel, each intent on giving it his best. We were separated by a wall of rock; before us extended the sky, thick with clouds. I sat down on a slab of stone and began to write on a scroll:

"I am your Lord, your God . . . "

I woke up in the middle of the night with my heart in my throat.

I had had the same dream again and was shaking with terror. It was a recurring dream of some distant memory, and while I wasn't sure that it always recurred in the same way, each time it seemed to me that I recognized everything. It was a memory from the earliest history of humankind, about which I had been telling Moses. In the dream I found myself standing in the clearing of a village before a witch doctor covered with the marks of priestly authority. Alone in the midst of a crowd, we looked at each other as though nothing else mattered but ourselves, and he stretched out his hands to offer me a gift. I saw myself advancing to accept the hideous carved figure. I understood that I had found a fearsome competitor in my own creation. Now man was molding me, kneeling before his sacred invention, which, in the dream, rose before my eyes. I tried to recognize my features in the sculpted wood, the hard, slanted eyes, the large swollen mouth, the imperious nose, the cheeks furrowed by lines, the tormented body. It was a piece of wood without limbs, covered with knots and contortions.

My reaction was amazement, and I continued to be amazed throughout the dream. I have a very uncertain idea of my appearance, and now I saw how others saw me. It was like being shown a photograph taken of yourself unawares. "Truly, is that me?" I cried out in my sleep. "An irate monster?" Why then did humans fall to their knees before me? Why did they say they loved me? I could not understand it.

After awaking, my anguish somewhat eased, I walked around a bit inside the cave and noticed that Moses was no longer there. The dream had reminded me of another important idea, which I immediately wrote down: "Do not believe in the images that men draw of me." That's how the sentence went, more or less. It was like saying, "Do not trust the likeness but come to me in person." Wasn't I entitled to as much? What honest painter would execute a portrait without having seen the person he is supposed to portray?

Having written this, I felt in such better spirits that I was ready to talk to my associate. But where had Moses disappeared to? I began to wander among the scattered rocks. Above me, huge stars shone like fruits in a tree whose leaves breathed secretly in the darkness. Some remote panic of solitude had been deposited in me like a seed and began to spread. I was alone, wandering over the skin of the earth, longing for company. From high on my mountain I saw the lights of the Hebrew encampment, and I set out for them.

As I came down the mountain I heard the murmur grow, until it became the roar of a mob. When I reached the first tents, I realized that a feast was being celebrated in the camps, and before I even saw a human face, I was confronted by a huge statue of an animal illuminated by hundreds of torches and a bonfire at its feet. I didn't immediately recognize the animal, but as I approached I could make out the muzzle of a cow or a calf. It was covered with golden stripes and gleamed atop a wooden pedestal, around which the mob writhed in a frenzy.

It was the most absurd portrait of me that anyone could have conceived, and I stood there looking up at it from below, humiliated and resentful. It was twice as large as a normal calf, and I thought that, as a statue, it was also ugly. I was disagreeably struck by its mouth, which was twisted into a malevolent smirk; or was that because I was looking at it from below? In order to get a clearer view, I took a few steps back and rose on tiptoe, twisting right and left, paying no attention to the turbulence all around me, until the mob crashed into me and flung me to the ground. I rolled into a corner, free from the crowd, and from there I watched the scene.

The village swayed back and forth like a tempestuous sea. Groups dispersed and came together again in the oscillating light of the torches. Those torches! I remember how Moses taught his people to cut the resinous branches and ignite them. I looked at the calf in anguish.

Then Aaron appeared. He was a character I had been unable to comprehend. He was Moses' brother and followed his every order, but always with reserve, as though they were things impossible to realize and even debatable from the standpoint of common sense. Now Aaron circled among the people excitedly, and when he saw me he approached without hiding his pleasure at the turmoil. He had never understood who I was, but he considered me to be the inspirer of his brother's projects.

"I hope you're satisfied now," I said when he was beside me.

Aaron sat down next to me and watched the spectacle as if from the balcony of a theater. "But isn't it wonderful how impassioned they are?" he said.

"A calf!" I retorted. "If you had to resort to an animal, couldn't you have found a more distinguished one?"

Aaron sighed patiently and started to explain.

"You shouldn't look down on the calf," he answered. "It is meek and tame, it supplies excellent meat for us to eat, and its hide protects us from the cold. But this is not what matters most. Just consider the joy of all these people. If you were God, wouldn't it make you glad? Wouldn't you take their well-being to heart? And do you know why they are so happy? Because here at last is something they can understand. These people have never followed any of my brother's lectures. They can't explain why their God shows himself only to Moses. Isn't a calf better than something nobody even knows how it looks? If at least God showed himself! If, for example, he decided right now to descend from up there and show himself here among us and explain a bit more clearly what he is about! But no, nothing. He seems to have no intention of paying us a visit. Perhaps we only want to convince him to do so. We made the calf out of gold so that it would shine from a distance. They gave me all the gold they owned, and it took me a whole night to melt it down and cool it."

I was by now close to revealing who I was, but I still had doubts and kept silent. Before us the orgy was in full swing. A young girl with curly hair had bared her breasts and was offering herself to the statue. An instant later she lay beneath the embrace of a young man, and they both rolled in the dust. I heard Aaron chuckle at my side, and I looked at him.

"He's her brother," he said to me, by way of comment.

I suddenly thought I recognized the man who was talking to me. As if in a dream, features that I have somehow always known took possession of Aaron's face. He was the witch doctor, brimming with compassion for the defects of his people and with secret antagonism toward me! He was the one who encouraged the crowd to create all sorts of images of me. It was he, the prophet's eternal brother, the compassionate organizer of festivals and sacrifices!

I heard the screams of the slaughtered animals. I got to my feet to see them, but before I could take a single step, something caused the crowd to swerve abruptly and issue a collective gasp. Moses had appeared alongside the golden calf.

Never was an apparition more spectacular. It was worthy of a great director and a great actor. Moses wore a black cape that reached down to his feet and made him look much taller than he was. I had never seen that garment on him and wondered where he had picked it up—perhaps he kept a wardrobe hidden in his tent. But even more sensational than his costume was his face. It is impossible to imagine anything more righteously irate. Two deep lines ran from Moses' eyes to his mouth. I wondered whether they had been drawn with charcoal or whether his very features had contorted to express the prophet's true feelings. The crowd fell silent, waiting for him to speak.

I threw a fleeting glance at Aaron, who had remained at my side. He had assumed the expression of a supernumerary at the arrival of the star, both admiring and resigned, with just a trace of resentment.

Moses burst out:

"So, this is what I find after my days upon the mountain— a people fallen into idolatry and licentiousness! God's anger blazes, people of Israel, and his vengeance shall be great."

In the silence that followed these words, the crowd was petrified with fear. I looked at the men and at the half-naked women, and their eyes, turned to Moses, were pleading for punishment. I wondered again what it was that gave a leader such mysterious power. They could have gotten rid of him in an instant and resumed their dance, but instead they were totally subjugated. You would have thought the power of some divinity had crushed them.

In a solemn, staccato voice Moses continued:

"This was to have been a great evening for all of us. The moment for true gratitude and festivity was at hand. I had descended from the mountain with the most precious of messages: I was carrying the Lord's tablets that were handed to me during my meditation on Mount Sinai. A great hope filled me as I came down, that of reading his new laws to you and offering thanks for the path marked out by him. Here, iniquitous, idolatrous, and blasphemous people, are the tablets entrusted to me."

I was gaping at Moses, incredulous at his words. We both knew very well that I had not written anything on a tablet. The crowd swayed in bewilderment. The Lord's tablets! And where were they, these tablets?

Then came the culminating moment of the performance. Moses let a minute pass in gloomy meditation. He surveyed the crowd with a distant and contemptuous glance. He bent down, picked up two slabs of stone that he had kept hidden behind him, and raised them up high so that the crowd could see them clearly. Then Moses flung the tablets against the statue's stone base. They shattered, and a great, convulsive cry rose from the multitude. I noticed Aaron beside me, his face wet with tears, tearing out his hair in despair at having lost my message. The crowd was overwhelmed by grief. The men comforted the women and mothers hugged their children, who wept as if they had lost their most beloved plaything.

For an instant I was relieved. It had occurred to me that Moses might have found the scroll on which I had been writing; instead he had destroyed a worthless pair of blank slabs.

Moses went berserk. He grabbed a torch and set fire to the calf's pedestal, which began to burn as though it had been waiting for nothing else. The crowd in its turn was consumed by a voluptuous and penitential frenzy. All of Israel gave itself up to suffering as one might to the embrace of love. I felt dismay and apprehension rise in me, and soon enough I understood how justified these feelings were. Moses must have sensed the crowd's yearning, because he decided to fulfill it. Surrounded by flame, he began to shout until he drowned out the roar of the fire and the clamoring mob: "The Lord demands proof of your repentance and of your obedience! Otherwise the lightning bolt will fall upon your tents, and not even a memory of you will survive. He commands that each of you take up his sword and murder his brother or son or mother, your closest and best-loved relative. This is the sacrifice that you will offer to the God who is your master. But that is not enough; when the flames of this fire are spent, I want you to gather its dust and mix it with water, and I want you, together with your remaining children, to drink that water, and this will be the sign of your newfound obedience. There will not be another chance for forgiveness."

Moses had pronounced his injunctions as though the second were more serious than the first; but both were accepted with relief by the crowd. And an indescribable scene began.

The first thing I saw was the brother striking, with a blow of his sword, the sister whom he had possessed in view of everyone, leaving her on the ground in her own blood. This was the beginning of the massacre, during which many accounts were settled in an instant. I saw each of the penitents make for a hated relative and kill him or her on the spot. Only those particularly anxious to make expiation flung themselves upon a person they loved, as Moses had commanded; others, uncertain, chose randomly, depending on who was within reach. The village was transformed into a slaughterhouse, and horror swept over me. I decided I had to intervene.

Even though I was certain I would fail, I ran toward the platform on which I had seen Moses, who, in the meantime, had disappeared to some strategic refuge. I was determined to address the crowd. I cannot say what would have happened if I had. As I was running toward the flames, which by now engulfed the statue, I tripped over a body squatting on the ground and tumbled in the dust. Next to me was a young woman with a child in her arms who in that infernal chaos seemed to be sleeping like an angel. She was holding him tight as though someone were trying to tear him from her, and her entire body expressed resistance. I looked more closely and saw that she clutched a knife against the child's body, and I met her eyes. It was clear to me that she could not do it. She would let herself be found like this by the village zealots, who were already checking that Moses' orders were carried out.

On an impulse I lifted her off the ground, and the three of us managed to cross the village without anyone stopping us. Here at least were two beings I might save. As I left the village with that human burden in my arms, I felt no desire ever to see Moses again. I directed my steps toward a small oasis I had discovered some time before, about ten miles from Mount Sinai. I walked all night and at the break of dawn, exhausted, I reached my goal, carrying the mother with the child held close to her breast, both peacefully asleep.

In the first light of dawn, beneath the vigorous and gentle palm trees, her face looked very beautiful to me, and I was glad that I had saved her, together with her son. But I was too fatigued to waste a lot of time congratulating myself. I stretched out on the grass next to them and gave way to intricate dreams.

When, with a refreshed mind, I recalled the events of the

previous night, it was as if they belonged to my recurring nightmare. Everyone had used me with the greatest nonchalance,
giving no thought to my objections. Moses had described me
to the Israelites as a jealous, vindictive deity, but he obviously
didn't believe this, since he had no worries about what I would
do in response to his misrepresentations. Whether humankind
cast me as a wooden totem, a calf, or a capricious landlord, in
each instance I was a kind of puppet. My pride was hurt, but
that was not the worst of it. I felt that my control over events
had slipped lower than ever.

We remained in the oasis for a long time, far from what was
happening in the world, protected by a natural shelter that
brought my childhood back to mind: the palm trees, the water
of the pond, the antelopes and the birds that swarmed in the
air, among the branches, and in the grass. I spent the days going back in time as much as I could, tracing the evolution of
my disappointment.

I had come to suspect that the human creature had reached a
dead end. I decided to leave the oasis for a quick survey of the
earth, and I saw that my fears were well founded. The same
pattern of events unfolded more or less everywhere, following
the mysterious process by which all corners of creation seem
to keep step with one another. I often imagine that on some
very distant star someone must be writing a book just like this
one. Wherever I went, among white, yellow, and dark popula-
tions, I could see the crisis that had seized the animal of my
hopes.

From the time humanity realized the inescapability of
death, I had encountered people who became obsessed by it,
clutching their heads in their hands, mesmerized as when you
stare at a hole in the wall and wait for something to pop out
of it. After futile contemplation they would pick themselves up
and return to their affairs with mechanical gestures and a
dreamlike expression. They seemed stuck in a parody of themselves, as if they had decided to repeat only the safe gestures
of the previous day.

I could see that some people had decided to let themselves

die, while others withdrew into cold and silent immobility. It was thus that two human families came into being: the suicidal and the derelict. The world is still crammed with both, and today the big cities are assembly points for these two related tribes. Collapsed on sidewalks, their faces cracked by the cold, their feet bare even in the depth of winter, they remember nothing but that far-off instant in the life of the world when humanity became aware of its mortality.

I had to do something to shake humankind from its torpor.

That is when the possibilities of mirage and illusion first occurred to me. It was an extremely hot summer. I was resting in a meadow, dazed by the sunshine. My creatures did not stir; even the horse drooped his head morosely. Only the insects— mosquitoes, horseflies, and bumblebees—flitted about, the crumbs and dregs of my creation.

The world seemed moribund to me, closed in its imperfection, like a prison with crumbling walls and tightly locked gates. Besieged by ugly thoughts, I arose and began to walk. Everywhere I encountered lassitude and oppressive heat. Male and female animals would not deign to look at each other. Whole species threatened to bore themselves into extinction. As I traveled through the outskirts of a village, I saw a man lying inertly beneath a tree and a woman a few feet from him, both looking exhausted and listless like dinosaurs in the hour of their defeat. I looked into the man's eyes, but his gaze passed through me.

Then I saw a vine laden with bunches of grapes, one of my decorative inventions, like the pineapple and the honeysuckle. I tasted them for the first time and found them good; then I began to squeeze the grapes. I worked under the inebriating sun, the hero of the grape harvest, the gatherer of the first vintage. It was twilight when I went over to the man under the tree and woke him up with the perfume that rose from my cupped hands filled with the aromatic and dense liquid. He drank and then the woman drank; soon after they were both laughing and flirting. By evening, the entire village resounded with the shouts and song of inebriated people.

Soon hemp joined the wine and the world was flooded with enthusiasm. But like wine, drugs eventually dazed and depressed those they inebriated. Jubilation was followed by the same gloomy immobility I had set out to cure. Stretched out on the ground, men and women gave themselves up to sleep. Sleep now became my chief enemy. I saw signs of its untiring and silent activity everywhere. If sleep won its battle against survival, it would become a messenger of death rather than a restorer of life. But sleep escaped me with diabolical skill. If I rushed to confront it, it eluded me, and even turned to hypnotize me. "I am the one who should dominate you," I would protest, "and not the other way around. You are the servant and I am the master!"

I tried to use cunning. I worked at my schemes late in the morning, the time when almost everyone was awake, so that I had at my disposal the crowd of humans who would fall asleep after me. My main effort was to penetrate the territories that sleep had occupied. I created dreams, divine messengers concealed in the folds of sleep, and they proved one of my more durable creations. They were like movable commedias del l'arte, each endowed with a basic plot and a series of variations to be chosen during the performance. People went around with reels of dreams inside themselves, never knowing which would be featured that night.

When I look out the window into the night of a city, I sense the immense crowd that sleeps, visited by dreams. One half of the world is submerged in dreaming's many-colored spaces, like the walls and windows of old cathedrals. Sleep is a fresco abode. I illustrated man's mind with the skill of a miniaturist. I granted each one dreams that sprang from something he had seen: a face, a place, a scene. I studied each person's life, clipping out important episodes and choosing others at random, and I set them within stories that contained the messages I wanted to transmit. I hoped to cast a spell on the sleepers, defenseless in their dreaming and ready to listen to my words. After the great seriousness of nocturnal contemplation (men sleep like philosophers), wakefulness would return filled with oblivion, tears, and laughter.

It was also necessary to do something to reinforce sexual desire, which had dwindled dangerously. I decided to invent clothes to cover the limbs of both men and women to see if they would become more desirable. The genitals figured prominently in my plan; they became invisible to the point of being dreamed about and even idolized. This proved an excellent ploy. The human body, which naked soon provokes only boredom mixed with irritation, once covered is clouded in an indistinct élan. Such is the power of illusion.

On the day I found her, Acsa—as her name proved to be—was wrapped in a mantle that left uncovered only her olive-hued face beneath hair as black as her robe. With the passing of time in the oasis, she cast off the burden that had been imposed on her. With each step toward happiness a part of her body was freed, her arms, ankles, shoulders. I caught myself shaking with a peculiar tremor when in our games our bodies would accidentally touch, and I found myself watching for hours as she slept alongside her son. I shuddered at the thought that, had it not been for me, death would already have taken her.

One evening, after a day of play, we ate on the grass. The child had fallen asleep and a quiet wind stirred the branches of the palm trees. We saw the pair of camels who lived in the oasis go by on their evening walk along the small lake, and songbirds flew about our heads. We were silent in the enchantment of the hour. Acsa looked at me, divested of all shyness. I had the unique and intoxicating sensation of being recognized. When this happens there is no mistaking it.

"You know who I am, don't you?" I asked her in a low voice.

Acsa nodded yes. She laughed with a happiness that spread all over her face.

"But how did you find out?" I asked. "Almost nobody ever succeeds."

Then Acsa told me her story as one would confide a secret. As a little girl, she had quite soon come to the conclusion that what people said about me in the village was false. She could not prove her suspicion because I never showed myself and she did not know where to search for me; she did not even know what I might be called, rejecting the name God as one falsehood among many. Unable to ask me for help and advice, she had found herself talking to me in the only way possible, writing letters as to an unknown correspondent. She certainly expected to meet me, like anyone who is happy for no apparent reason except the adventure of being in this world. When she felt she was growing up, her desire for life also grew. Her mind expanded, as did her body. Her breasts and pubis now offered opportunity for pleasure with herself and with others, but she ran into the wall of prohibitions that tormented the human world like a cloud on the horizon of joy. She wavered for a long time, confused by the possibilities that were offered to her; and, not wishing to harm anyone, she married a tailor of her tribe, and buried herself in the garments sewn by him, black, thick, and formless.

Acsa had changed into the shape of a closed flower, with imprisoned and astonished eyes. She adjusted to her life as if she were living it in place of another, and the hope of meeting me never abandoned her. It is a hope so strong that it never deserts believers until the last instant of their life. Some say that it follows them beyond death, though I wouldn't know: the dead disappear completely from my view.

Acsa would awake in the morning and look at the light as if I were inside it; and when her son was born, it was as if I had sent her a message that issued from her hospitable flesh, a living memory, a soul made of flesh indeed. Whenever she made love to the tailor, I occupied the air around her, entered her dreams and remained in them for long stretches, for whole journeys through the world. I had no idea that I had already spent so much time with her.

One day Acsa began to speak to me, and her hope of seeing me grew into a consuming desire. It was then that Moses and I arrived at the village, and shortly afterward the tribe abandoned the land of Egypt. Almost as in a dream, Acsa watched everything that happened up to the festival of the calf, which in a sudden fit of pride she had refused to join. When she saw everyone prostrate at Moses' feet, she was seized by terror about her son's fate. Only a few moments later I came to her side and carried her away.

In the oasis, she recognized me almost immediately, and her metamorphosis began. Now, with the sun disappearing behind the dunes, Acsa's prayer finally touched me. She reached out to me, as a flower turns to the sun or water caresses the shore;

and she threw off the burden of her clothes. She was becoming a butterfly, returning to me that which was mine: her neck, her shoulders, her hair, her breasts. Acsa's arms touched my body without shyness, because everything is permissible with God, and neither sin nor adultery exists. She quietly uncovered her belly, uncovered her thighs and her legs, and between her legs the flower of the garden that was her body, which opened up to me as though it had never wanted anything else; and so great was the ardor of her desire that mine too became as great as the oasis, and I entered into her and nothing mattered any longer until the seed sown with a cry reminded us both that all of this was done for the sake of life.

I felt now as if I were also Acsa, who in her turn was me. Suddenly, too, I felt at the mercy of a slow invasion coming from the leaves, the sand, the sky; farther off, I sensed it coming from the sea and from the lands beyond that sea, which extended to other seas. My universe was rushing toward me in happiness. It was like a reunion of old comrades or long-lost schoolmates, and it had all the jubilation and melancholy of such gatherings. The created world was celebrating me, and I was full of glory.

In the days that followed, Acsa walked about the oasis half-naked and happy. She called me her good and generous God and I saluted her as my most beautiful creature. Undoubtedly I was exaggerating, because the dahlia and the gazelle also have an extreme beauty of their own, perfect in itself, and so do other things that sprang from my hands during my most inspired moments. Splotched with sand, we would run and dive into the pond whose water remained cool even at midday, and then I would resume my account to her of the story of the world. Acsa never tired of listening to me, and for certain events she offered explanations of her own. For example, according to her, the torrents were the mountains' desire to reach the sea; and in fact a torrent is truly something of the mountain that sooner or later becomes sea. I was struck by how much she was able to see in me and my actions, and I felt that I, in turn, was learning from her. From the joyful gratitude that tied us together we decided to create love.

Love was certainly a game, but it wasn't only that. From that very beginning in the oasis, loving was more than the desire to make love; it meant adding to the flower its perfume and the memory of it. We decided that love consists in making the beloved at once familiar and divine. We made a list of all the things that seemed necessary to us. One absolute requirement is gaiety; without that you can neither begin nor continue the game. Laughing together means loving each other, and gaiety is the highest form of life, as those who possess it know. People try to make up for its absence with borrowed gaiety—the laughter that others induce in us with gestures and words—so that the tired organism recovers some hope-giving energy. But love means to give the other one's own gaiety, and in reality only a person who is already happy can truly love and win at the game. We wrote the rules in the sand, and it didn't matter that soon they would be erased by the wind—they were eternal rules.

The night when we arrived at the supreme rule, we closed the love game's inventory. This precept was contained in a brief formula, and Acsa was the first to pronounce it: "It should be beautiful to die," she said, looking at me. And I, who had cried over her with the joy and anguish of feeling myself separated from myself, understood what she said and helped her to understand it. We felt that love should never come to an end, but we saw at the same time that we no longer mattered much, because in the instant of love the entire universe attains a center and a purpose. At that moment death appears in a totally different light, like a fact that is not only necessary but, indeed, vital. And so we pronounced the golden rule: "Only those who do not fear death can love." Ecstatic with our discovery, we were surprised by a whirling wind. We did not run for shelter. I clasped the child tightly and wished I had a son of my own so I could protect him and teach him the reasons for life.

When I think about those rules of love Acsa and I invented, I don't know exactly what to say. Now that I am getting on in years, I realize that everyone who is in love creates some new rules. It is in the nature of that euphoric condition. Of course, I was not just love's co-creator but also the first to fall under the spell of our invention.

I wanted to stay in Acsa's company, now that we had created love and had experienced it to our great benefit. We could settle down in the oasis, bring up the boy, have a child of our own, live shielded from the greed and ambitions poisoning the world. I asked Acsa to marry me, quite clumsily, since she was already married; and she replied that she had already married me when she had thought of wanting to die. So in fact we were married, and we celebrated the event with a supper of fruit. That evening I fell asleep in a state of confused happiness, like an adolescent at the end of a day filled with premonitions.

LATE that night I awoke with a start. The oasis lay enveloped in the soft nocturnal sounds I had learned to recognize. But there was something more, an indecipherable presence that altered the intensity and direction of the animals' voices. Someone had entered the oasis.

I rose from my pallet, picked up a cudgel, and walked quietly among the trees. I moved about like the nocturnal beasts, guided by instinct. I came to the pond and on its shore could make out the dark outline of a horse. I approached cautiously, and when I was a short distance from the horse's muzzle, my foot touched a body lying limply on the ground. It was a bedouin. He did not react when I shook him. I turned him over, face up, and saw that he was dead.

Beneath his unkempt beard a saber wound ran from his throat to his thigh. He must have exhaled his last breath in the effort to get off his horse and crawl to the water. I stood looking at him with a kind of apathy until I heard a noise behind me, and, turning, saw Acsa contemplating the scene. With her help, I dug a hole at the edge of the oasis; we lowered the body into it and covered it with sand. In no time the serenity of the night had returned, and everything was as it had been before, except for the presence of the horse, which now lay down, its muzzle to the ground.

But I could not fall asleep again. The apparition had greatly dismayed me; the outside world had penetrated my isolated and happy paradise. I gazed at the stars above the branches of the palm trees, and the meaning of this event forced itself on me: the world is suffering and tells you so through that man lying speechless in the sand, his breast torn open by the ferocity of another man. I envisioned the world as prey to slaughter, and I stood up overcome with anguish. Had I forgotten that I was God? Had I abandoned the hope of converting my creation into something better and more harmonious? Perhaps the bedouin had appeared to persuade me to return to the fray. I could feel the boundless energy of destruction operating even in my oasis, the overwhelming struggle for survival in which every animal and blade of grass was caught up. Rouse yourself, God, I commanded. Rouse yourself to find Moses again and explain everything to him.

I went back to Acsa, curled up in sleep, her child in her arms. I caressed her hair before leaving. I led the bedouin's horse out of the oasis, got up in the saddle, and galloped all the way to Mount Sinai, taking my bearings by the stars. I reached the mountain's slopes, let the animal loose, and continued on up to the peak, toward the familiar cave.

FROM the cave's entrance I saw him sitting at his stone desk in a pensive attitude. He had stopped writing in order to reflect, stylus in hand, staring at a point in my direction without seeing me. Then he recited aloud the sentence he was looking for.

"When an ox has butted a man or a woman, he shall therefore die. He shall be stoned and his flesh eaten. But the ox's owner shall be absolved."

Moses bent his head to write the commandment he had just formulated. I entered the circle of light cast by the torch that was affixed to the wall; he raised his eyes. He stopped and looked at me, his face impenetrable. We remained like that for a few moments, then Moses spoke.

"Here you are at last. Where have you been all this time?"

I moved closer to his stone desk and sat down opposite him. During my ride I had prepared my arguments, but now I found myself speechless. Moses continued:

"I've been forced to manage by myself. You can't even begin to imagine how many problems have arisen. The people are discontented. The tribal chiefs are always quarreling among themselves. I've been forced to employ an iron fist to restore order. Without being able to ask you for advice or to let off steam. All by myself, on this mountaintop where everybody thinks I'm confabulating with you day and night, when in fact there isn't even a dog I can talk to. Every decision falls on my shoulders and I must think up every law. Listen to these, for instance."

Moses rummaged among the small tablets scored with signs until he found the one he was looking for: " 'Whenever someone seduces a virgin and lies with her, he shall give her a dowry and take her for a wife. However, you shall kill the woman seductress. And whoever couples with a beast shall be put to death.' You don't know how I had to fight to get these simple rules accepted; and I succeeded because I invoked your authority. And where were you instead of helping me?"

He fell silent, challenging me. Finally I replied.

"Moses, you haven't wanted my help. Perhaps you haven't even wanted me around, because that way you've been able to do everything you wished. Just to give you an example, the three laws you just read don't please me at all, and you have presented them as my ideas. You have forgotten the important things that I had to say and have lost yourself in an infinity of details, some of them totally alien to my teachings. I'm not at all happy with you, Moses."

He seemed to mull that over. A great quiet settled upon this decisive dialogue with my prophet. What did I look like? I remembered a moment in the oasis, while Acsa and the boy were playing and I was walking on the shores of the pond and finally saw myself mirrored in the water. I saw a young face framed by a gossamer beard. You're a man now, I said to myself.

Moses spoke again.

"I know you are dissatisfied. When it comes to that, so am I. I had expected a God better equipped to give orders and assume command. Instead, I'm the one who must do all this. Just ask yourself if it could have been easy to dictate this rule: 'Do not pronounce a sentence in a quarrel in order to favor the powerful; but do not respect the poor man in his quarrel.' How about it? Where were you when I wrote these lines? Who was there, fighting with both rich and poor?"

"There should be neither rich nor poor," I retorted sharply.

Moses looked at me flabbergasted.

"What's that supposed to mean? There should be neither rich nor poor indeed! You're forgetting the obvious. Some God you are, with your head in the clouds, remembering now and then to return to earth and criticize your prophet. You forget that the poor exist! It's not a matter of discussing whether they should or not, but trying to see what can be done to stop them from becoming beasts and starving to death. Therefore it is necessary to put them to death if they couple with animals, but they must be helped to survive hunger and cold. Since the poor will always be with us, everyone must offer a generous hand to the needy among them. Didn't you see them with the golden calf? Am I supposed to guide them or not? Am I inspired by you or not? What do you want me to do?"

As he uttered these last words, the tone of Moses' voice changed and his appearance was transformed. His eyes seemed frightened, his beard began to tremble, a pallor settled on his face; and his hands, having dropped the stylus, were joined in supplication. I think I must have assumed a frightful aspect, because with a single leap he rose from his stone stool, threw himself at my feet, and grasped the hem of my robe. I was quite startled, but I decided to take advantage of this change. I placed a hand on his shoulder and told him to stand up.

"Do not fear my anger, Moses. In some ways your work is admirable. But we never did discuss certain important things that for a long time I have been writing down. The moment has come for you to read them. Wait for me."

I quickly went behind the makeshift wall that had divided Moses' work area from mine. It was pitch black in there, and I groped around until I reached a torch that I had once fastened to the rocky wall. I remembered having stored my writings in a hole directly beneath the torch and covered with a stone slab. I removed this and found the bundle of scrolls tied together with a string. I carried them to Moses, who was sitting again at his desk, waiting for me. I threw the scrolls down in front of him and went to sit in a corner of the cave, alone.

In the dark I thought of my writings, and I saw everything again. The first part of the narration unfolded before my eyes as a succession of images much like those that centuries later would be part of both sacred and profane stories. There had

been a moment when, following its initial coming together under the leadership of a chief, humanity had arrived at a point
of great suffering. Not even my gift of illusion sufficed to console and sustain it. Men and women were no longer able to
recognize me, so strong was their desire to merge once more
with the past of beasts and plants.

Humans became skittish, vindictive animals lost in a contin-
uous enigma. They were imperfect and confused, flooded by
fear because of the darkness that they carried within and
poured out over the external world, beclouding it. I strove
mightily to correct the mistake, sending messages that were
immediately changed into nightmares. By propelling humankind along the path of knowledge, I obtained, in the end,
the opposite effect, as happens to nagging teachers; when their
pupils leave school, they quickly throw off their books in order
to gain a sense of freedom. Even my disciples turned their
backs on the search for truth and delegated a few to transmit
it, as if it had already been achieved. Eventually, humans asked
only for someone to obey.

This was the beginning of the disaster. Humans invented the
rich and the poor, the powerful and the wretched, an infinite
number of roles, each of which enchained them ever more se-
curely, distracting them from the true task of understanding.
With the ease of clowns, they impersonated the king and the
priest, the warrior and the disinherited, suffering and enjoying
each role like strolling players. The king tried to augment his
power, the witch doctor jealously protected his function, the
warrior killed without restraint, and the poor, more under-
standably than all of them, humiliated themselves at every turn
just in order to survive. They rewarded those who fed them
with a veneration broken by outbursts of resentment, and after
each bloodbath, they would return the powerful to power.

I tried in vain to heal my people's souls, for the most impregnable bulwark was erected against me. Oppression was the in-
fallible way to prevent humankind from becoming the animal
I had dreamed of. It was a collective choice; no sooner did the
poor man escape his fate than he immediately devoted himself
to accumulating wealth. By using the power of illusion with
which I had endowed them, they would build inviolable castles

in which they lost themselves and died without understanding what had happened to them. I searched the world until finally it came to me to choose an oppressed and suffering people who would again find the path that I had meant for humankind to follow.

In the second part of my writings I set forth my plans for this new life, and I was wondering whether Moses had begun to read it. When the first glimmer of dawn filtered into the cave, I went outside to look at the stars fading away. Then I went back to him. He had just finished reading. He looked at me and remained silent, as he had the night before, burning within. I did not want to be the first to speak and so I waited. Finally a torrent of words burst from his lips.

"You've come back, Lord, and I recognize your word. Your hands have formed me; give me intellect and I will learn your commandments. I know that your judgments are nothing but just; and may my heart be made whole by your will. How blind I have been until now! If it is true that you were not here with me, I ought to have sought you! And now your word comes back to me like a light over my path; comfort me and I will be saved. I raise my eyes to you as the servant to his master, and may those who do not follow you be like the grass that withers before it is gathered. You who have done what you please in heaven and on earth, you saw my body's shape when it was not yet formed, and everything was already written in your book even as you created it. You protect those who love you and you destroy the iniquitous, and my mouth will sing your praise."

I listened with increasing discomfort. To whom was Moses talking? I was none of the things that he said. I was not at all omniscient, and I had made an infinity of mistakes, which I had hoped he would correct. It was as though Moses were talking to himself or to some phantom product of his overexcited brain. This no longer surprises me now, because I know that everyone finds what he wants to find in the things he reads.

"It is not true that I want to destroy the iniquitous," I said. "I don't even know who the iniquitous are. And, by the way, there can be no agreement between us if anything like the massacre after the golden calf ever happens again."

Moses looked at me with a smile I could not quite read. Some force unknown to me had drawn him into a place of secrecy and solemnity.

"The man who loves being corrected loves knowledge; and you will condemn the malicious. The prudent man hides what he knows, but the heart of the fool spreads folly."

I was trying to decipher these words when something moved in the corner of the cave where Moses' bed stood. The light of dawn shone in the cave and my attention was drawn to a blanket that kept stirring.

"Who's that?" I asked, lowering my voice.

"It's Cusita," he said, rising from his stone seat.

"And who is Cusita?"

"My wife," he replied as he gathered my manuscript, which was strewn about the stone desk.

"And what about Zipporah?"

Moses shrugged, as though the topic were of no interest to either of us, and he went outside the cave to a place from which he could see the encampment. The landscape was arid and majestic, and for an instant we forgot all misery and disagreement.

"Will you help me, Moses?" I finally asked my prophet. "Will you speak to the people with me?"

I was facing him but he did not return my gaze. In an instant his profile had hardened like the rocks on the mountain where we had spent forty days fantasizing about the past and future.

"That's impossible," he said. "They would never understand. It would mean the destruction of all my efforts."

"In that case I'll have to do it myself," I concluded. I left him and went back inside the cave to pick up my writings; then I set out for the valley. When, halfway down, I turned around, he was standing stock-still where I had left him, in the throes of a thought that had nailed him there. Perhaps he hadn't noticed my departure.

In the village, there was a changed and nervous atmosphere. Moses' authority could be felt everywhere, even in conversations in the tents. There was talk about what had happened the day before to Nadab and to Abihu, Aaron's sons, who had lit a fire in a censer and had offered it to the tabernacle. For some reason that was not clear to me, the fire was not in keeping with the prescriptions dictated by Moses, and from the tabernacle had leaped a flame that set the sons on fire. In this strange accident, everyone saw a proof of the alliance between God and their leader. But Moses certainly had more than one accomplice in the village. I have no doubt that this was a question of revenge against Aaron over that business with the golden calf. I learned that Moses would come at noon to speak in public—the ballyhooed descent from Sinai had by then become a habit of his—and I decided to wait for that moment to address the people myself.

I spent the morning strolling among the tents and looking and listening. I heard childish voices chanting the commandments by rote. There was one containing the names of animals they could not eat, which they repeated continually. The children ecstatically recited the list: the camel, the hare, the pig, the eagle, the falcon, the kite, the ossifrage, the vulture, the owl, the cormorant, the little owl, the hoopoe, the bat, the weasel, the mouse, the mole, the chameleon, the gecko, and above all the four-legged winged creatures. What were they? Nobody knew.

Noon arrived and the populace gathered in the clearing where assemblies were held. There was the aura that surrounds ritual events, both intense and distracted, and I was already asking myself whether I would have the self-assurance to address these people, who had not yet even recognized me. I tried to bolster my courage by repeating to myself: "Do it for them, do it for their children, do it for . . . ," but I couldn't think of anyone. "Do it for Acsa!" That worked better, and since then I have resorted to this formula again and again, all through the centuries and in my most trying moments.

Moses appeared punctually. Once again I had to admire his panache. He had dressed all in white, as he did for all his daytime appearances. On his arrival, the crowd fell again into that mood of calm expectation that I knew well. In the alternation between speech and weighty silence that was his specialty, Moses began to read the new decrees and moral regulations that he had thought up during the night. Among them were the ones I had heard when I arrived at the cave. Then he announced further decrees subdivided into categories, and the mob dictated them to the scribes scattered here and there.

Moses offered a bit of everything—instructions on how to purify lepers, a prohibition against men making love with other men, an injunction ordering women to go into hiding during menstruation, another concerning a wife's repudiation by her husband, a law establishing the culpability of anyone who had witnessed a crime, a rule that anyone who had had his testicles cut off could not participate in the assembly, an order that women in childbed be purified for one week after the birth of a male child (but two weeks after the birth of a female), and so on with a crescendo of impositions, all of them received with jubilation. I stood off to one side, going over my speech to the crowd, pressing the scroll against my chest. At that moment, Moses' eye caught mine and to my astonishment he seemed to soften. Changing his tone, he pronounced his last exhortation of the day, urging the chosen people to help strangers, in memory of their enslavement in Egypt. I got ready to make my appearance.

By that time the assembly had reached its most eagerly awaited stage, and excitement rose to a peak. This was the moment for the sacrifices, and everybody wondered whether this time they would involve animals or men and women condemned by the rules Moses had dictated. In my travels I had seen enough of such scenes to be able to recognize them immediately. It seemed to me that the taste for sacrifice gave off a particular odor, as if the people were exuding a sweat peculiar to cowardly and passive violence. I still encounter that odor in movie houses during action films or at boxing matches, and I immediately have to go outside in order to breathe, because I know that each of the spectators is committing a murder for which he will not be reproached. I hate sacrifices! And I hate boxing matches.

I could put it off no longer. I made my way through the crowd and stood below Moses. They were all looking at me, and some of them remembered that they had seen me talking to the prophet. Moses seemed uncertain what to do. I took advantage of his wavering, went right up to him, and stood at his side. A terrified murmur rose from the crowd. No one, not even Aaron, had ever dared do anything like this. Checked by a sudden attack of veneration, Moses didn't try to stop me, and I began my harangue.

I said absolutely everything, things that for centuries since I have struggled to recall. From my lips poured a stream of eloquence; I didn't know I had such powers, and so I spoke as one inspired. Up until then, I had expressed myself as best I could, through the wind and sun and the lowing of the herds in the fields, through all the sounds that can still lead the soul back to God; but on that occasion I expressed myself in the language of my listeners. I retraversed the stages of history that had brought us to that point. I crawled, I walked, I flew, I penetrated my audience, leaving them enchanted and dazed. They were not accustomed to what I was telling them. I asked them not to prostrate themselves before me but to stand up in order to understand. I offered them again the torch of a glorious mission. I raised them to my height instead of crushing them with my power. I spoke to the women as I did to the men, to the children as to the adults. I felt certain that I was reaching them.

And then I made a fatal pause, during which the crowd hung as if it were suspended between myself and Moses, and the destinies of the people of Israel wavered like the plates of a scale as it approaches the balance point. In that instant the irremediable took place. In the assembly's silence the voice of Moses rang out:

"Bring forth the adulteress!"

I looked at him, taken by surprise, and he went on, pointing his forefinger at me:

"You come here among us indifferent to the hospitality we have shown you. You make seditious speeches and trample underfoot the laws that we have agreed upon together. There is not a rule here that wasn't approved by the people. You pretend that you are addressing the people, while all along you go counter to their will. Do you remember," and here he turned to the crowd, "do you remember what we have decided about unforgivable crimes? Do you remember the fate of the man who lies with his father's wife, what punishment he should expect?"

The crowd shuffled their feet uncertainly. The effect of my

speech was still vivid. I could feel Moses go rigid with ferocious tension. But we did not look at one another; our battlefield was there before us.

"What is the punishment?" he repeated.

The Israelites swayed like a beaten animal. Above them drifted a murmur like a word that has yet to take shape, until someone declared:

"They must both be put to death."

"And then?" the prophet urged him on.

"May their own blood fall upon them," another voice cried, rising anonymously from the group.

"And why?"

"Because he has exposed his father's shame," two or three voices cried out together.

"And what if a woman accosts a beast to be mounted by it?" Moses continued doggedly.

This time a small chorus answered:

"Kill both woman and beast, and may their blood fall upon them."

The crowd was getting excited, and I was preparing to intervene again when Moses delivered the final and masterful blow.

"And what if a man commits adultery with the wife of another?"

"May the adulterous man and woman both be put to death!" By now the chorus was large and convinced. Just then the crowd parted and Aaron, impassioned and completely forgetting what Moses had done to his sons, dragged a woman toward us. I started to tremble even before I saw her. Then the hair fell away from her face and she looked at me.

"Acsa!" I cried, and at that she recognized me from the distant spot where she had been flung. I tried to rush forward but was immediately seized. Moses looked at me defiantly. At his side had appeared the tailor, Acsa's husband. I struggled, while Moses tore the scroll from my hands and showed it to the people.

"Not only is he an adulterer in the bosom of the village that sheltered and fed him, he is also a false prophet, and we have condemned the false prophets to perish. Do not fall in with his whims, do not listen to him! Your eye must not forgive him. The false prophet must be put to death; he has spoken of rebellion against the Lord your God who has led you out of Egypt and freed you from slavery, and he urges you to follow gods whom you do not know. All of his sins are written here!"

With these words, and in a surge of righteous fury, Moses tore my writings to pieces. Stunned, I watched them fall in shreds and scatter. Would I still remember them? The crowd became intoxicated. The climax of the assembly promised to surpass all their expectations.

Acsa lay motionless on the ground. With a desperate effort I freed myself from the hands that gripped me and ran to her, crouching over her body. She looked at me in the same way as she had in our oasis. She was not afraid.

"Tell them again who you are," she whispered, her face lighting up. "They do not believe you."

I rose to do just that, and a stone struck Acsa, leaving her lifeless. I looked at her in disbelief before a stone struck me too and flung me to the ground beside her body. The prophet's words hovered above us, like thunder.

"Kill him! Let your hand be the first laid upon him and then the hands of all the people."

How can this possibly happen, I thought in a daze. *Get up! Help me, Acsa!*

A second stone crashed against my head, and I plunged into a whirlpool of darkness.

I woke up on an island in the Mediterranean, my memory obscured. The blow to my head had made me forgetful of myself again. Clearly I wasn't dead. I cannot die before my creation, for I am, as it were, the breath that sustains it. Breath of the cosmos or no, I was going through an episode of amnesia.

I did not remember what I had written in that scroll that had been ripped to shreds and whose fragments had wound up who knows where. My reawakening took place only once I became aware that I *had* known them—aware of the extent of my forgetfulness. Until that moment, I lost myself among fishermen, hunters, peasants, artisans, inventors of tools, as in the past I had been lost between the wind and the water of the sea. I wandered east and west, but I returned as if by instinct to my favorite abode, the great mild Mediterranean studded with green and rocky islands. It was on one of these islands that I began to remember what had happened to me. I collected myself and set out to explore the past, which in the meantime had been recounted by the prophets of the great religions in a curiously distorted way. And so I encouraged philosophers to come forward, and assigned them the task of understanding how my creation had unfolded.

I had chosen Greece as my habitual residence, close to the most beautiful water of the Mediterranean and not too far from the East, where I liked to spend my vacations. I would move from one island to the next on boats laden with fish, among merchants of spices and fabric. As I mingled with them, I wondered why, in the midst of a crossing, the sailors' eyes would turn to the horizon and smolder with melancholy; and why, during a celebration, the people would pause for long moments, slow tears streaming down the women's faces. Nobody could explain this.

Then some men, leaving family and belongings behind, began withdrawing to mountain peaks and small deserted islands. They were seized by the desire to be alone and often by a contempt for the world. After living in this fashion for a while, they would eventually set about thinking. When you begin to think, the fields, the sky, the clouds, the rivers—everything— becomes luminous and dazzling. These solitary men of mine, in love with nature, devoted themselves to thought.

They roamed the Grecian woods and shores, naming things and trying to find me somewhere. One dived into the water and shouted with happiness, thinking he had reached me. The next tried to mix all the elements together, thinking that I could be found in some great cosmic salad. Still another breathed deeply to fill his lungs, discerning my divine presence in the air. They were new, strange, extraordinary people. They were able to live alone without suffering. They wanted simply to *know*, and they let their exalted minds rush over the world, in pure joy. I was proud of them!

Some of these philosophers grew so convinced that they had found the truth that they returned among the people and founded schools. One of these was Xenophanes, with whom I became friends and whom I visited often on the eastern coast of Sicily. I remember many conversations with him, as young servants poured heavy Sicilian wine and a boy named Parmenides hung on his teacher's every word. His devotion would be rewarded later, because Parmenides had a great philosophical career ahead of him and became, in fact, more famous than Xenophanes. At the time, he nodded yes to all of Xenophanes' pronouncements and happily let his teacher touch him under his student's tunic, something that happened regularly after the first flask of wine.

Xenophanes was very acute. He said on one occasion, for instance, that if oxen or horses or lions had hands and knew how to draw, the horse would depict God as a horse, the ox as an ox, the lion as a lion. "Mortal mankind," he continued, despite the late hour and his visible fatigue, "imagines that the gods were born and have faces, clothes, and bodies just like themselves." It was a warm night and the air was saturated with the perfume of oranges and citrons, a scent that comes back to me every time I open a book of Greek philosophy.

" . . . The Ethiopians say that their gods are dark-skinned; the Thracians say that theirs are red-headed." His cadences invited derision, and Parmenides obliged with a snicker. The guests knew they were in the presence of a virtuoso and thrilled to each of his daring thoughts.

Not everyone, however, seemed entirely caught up in the performance. Next to me two Sicilians quarreled in low voices over some sordid financial matter, and I got up to move away from them. Xenophanes saw me and raised his cup of wine in my direction. He smiled and shook his head in fond reproach: "God must always remain motionless, in the same place, nor is it becoming of him to move now this way, now that."

With his usual astuteness, Parmenides understood that it would not be proper for him to comment on his teacher's quip. The others too remained silent, staring first at me, then at Xenophanes. I sat down, as surprised as everyone else. As far as Xenophanes and the others knew, I was only a vacationing fur merchant. But I quickly realized that it had been a joke; Xenophanes' laughter reassured the guests, and I heard Parmenides laugh more loudly than the others.

"Drink, my friend!" the philosopher shouted to me from his place at the head of the table. "And remember, when you mix water with wine you must first pour the water. Take a piece of meat and be happy."

The disciple stared at me with a certain disquietude. Parmenides was asking himself the reason for Xenophanes' display of friendliness toward me, and I understood that he was jealously trying to guess my age. He must have come to some sort of reassuring conclusion, because he stretched out like a young girl and went to sit beside his teacher, who looked at him tenderly and caressed the black ringlets that fell to his shoulders.

"Did you write anything today?" he asked him sweetly. Parmenides nodded.

"And you didn't beat your dog?"

Parmenides said no.

"That's a good boy. Continue to treat it well. You know that in the cry of a whipped dog Pythagoras recognized the voice of a friend. Perhaps in your little dog there is none other than Pythagoras, who has decided to live in a house of philosophers. Doesn't this make all of you happy?"

By now I was groggy with Sicilian wine. I belched discreetly and one of the guests raised his voice in the philosopher's direction.

"Xenophanes, go on to another subject and show us the path. Tell us, who is God?"

I pricked up my ears now that the topic of the discussion had reverted to me. Xenophanes noticed my attentiveness, and he was vain enough to feel flattered by it, even though he knew me only as a vacationer on the shores of Sicily. He assumed an inspired air and spoke more or less like this:

"Whenever something is, it is impossible for it to have been born. And God is. Therefore God cannot have been born, hence he is eternal. If he is eternal, it means that he is the most powerful of all beings. If a being is not the most powerful of all, it means that he is not God. There cannot be many gods, because one would dominate the others and God cannot be dominated. But that's not all. If God is one and perfect, not even his parts can dominate one another. Indeed, he cannot have parts that are different from one another. Therefore God has no attributes."

Xenophanes' voice had become distant and seemed to be floating high in the room. Everyone had stopped eating and drinking and watched the teacher intently. Parmenides' eyes smoldered and his mouth had fallen half open with lascivious worship.

I myself did not miss a word. I wondered, What is this fellow talking about and where does he get such arrogant opinions? Why doesn't he ask me how matters stand? It's not true that I'm eternal, for in that case my world would be eternal. It's not true that I'm omnipotent, for in that case my creation would be so too. How can he possibly think that I don't have attributes? Everything that I've created is an attribute of mine! In the creator, essence and attributes are indistinguishable. I literally am that which I have made. I am Xenophanes who reasons, albeit in his own way, and I am the fur merchant who listens to him, and I am Parmenides, who, being ambitious, wants to take his place when he dies, and I'm the chunk of ox meat that I've left on my plate. How could I possibly not have attributes? What are the leaves and roots if not a plant's attributes? And what is a plant without leaves and roots? I swallowed half a cup of wine to check the impulse to intervene.

Meanwhile Xenophanes, after a moment of calculated silence, raised his arms over his head and held them aloft, like a magician before his next trick. Expectation was at a high pitch.

"And if God is equal to himself in all of his parts, it means that he cannot be finite or infinite, immobile or in motion, nonexistent or manifold, blind or seeing, white or nonwhite. He is smooth and round like a huge stupendous sphere."

And here Xenophanes delivered his theatrical clincher. His arms, which during the entire monologue had remained raised, came down together and slowly mimed the circumference of a sphere. We all saw it come to birth, as immense as the earth—by now many had accepted the idea that the earth was round—as hospitable as a woman's womb, as serene as a cloud. I myself was breathless. It was me that Xenophanes was describing! Astonishment swallowed up any impulse to protest. The descending arc accomplished, Xenophanes' hands came together in his lap. His gaze moved to Parmenides, who was now sitting at Xenophanes' feet and was beginning to writhe with wantonness.

"I now want you to listen to this young philosopher, my descendant, my heir, my beloved Parmenides. Just look at him in the triumph of his youth. How enviable his state is to us old men! For sixty-seven years I have been dragging my sorrows throughout Greece and Magna Graecia, and it is a rare comfort to lie satiated on a soft bed, drink sweet wine, munch chickpeas, and be able to teach a beautiful boy all that you know. Little by little, of course, and with great effort, because the gods did not reveal everything to mortals all at once. But by searching, men gradually find what is best. So speak, Parmenides, let us hear what you wrote yesterday."

As Xenophanes said these words I saw the young man lying at his feet blush violently. Certainly he had expected his teacher's request, so his blush must have come from excitement. As soon as he began to speak, Parmenides seemed transformed, as if a strong and inebriating wine had flooded his veins. In an instant he was truly like a god. Lucid, tense, transfigured, the young philosopher burst into a long monologue in verse, of which I remember only a few dazzling fragments:

> And how could being exist in the future?
> And how could
> it have been in the past?
> Because if it was, it is not; and so it is not, if it must
>   be in the future.
> Thus birth is extinguished and death disappears . . .
> Identical, remaining in the identical place, being lies
>   within itself and so
> remains there immobile . . .
> It is perfect
> in its whole surface, like the mass of a rounded sphere,
> which from its
> center exerts pressure on all sides with equal force . . .
> from every side identical to itself, it collides in equal
>   measure
> within its confines.

I shared the silence that had settled around the table, around Parmenides' beauty. He had become nearly ethereal, and his words were vibrant. I almost felt an impulse of desire for him, for his warm and precise voice. We were all caught up in an enchantment from which Parmenides himself finally roused us when he curled up in the arms of his teacher, who immediately smothered him with kisses. The throng of guests broke into applause.

"Why aren't you applauding, merchant?" Xenophanes shouted at me across the table. "Were you not pleased by my best student? Can you do better? Or perhaps you don't like my divine boy. Did you ever see anything more beautiful?" Xenophanes grasped Parmenides' shoulders with his hands.

I did not want to be drawn into an argument with him because I knew that it would be pointless, and I needed to meditate on what I had heard. I was forced, however, to give some sort of reply, for they were all looking in my direction. I cleared my throat and stammered out a question: "But how is it, Xenophanes, that you and your disciples never speak about Zeus or Aphrodite or Persephone? Do you no longer believe in the gods of our fathers? Don't you remember the ode of supreme Homer and the exploits narrated by Hesiod? Why do you neglect the fables that embellished our childhood? Do you regard them as a pastime for children and poets?" Before I could finish I was drowned out by a spontaneous wave of laughter. Everyone looked good-naturedly at me as if I were a naive barbarian, charming in his foolhardiness. I understood that I would have no reply to my question. Then we heard a great thunderclap, and a rackety rush of wind blew in from the garden. Rain was in the air. Xenophanes looked toward the door that opened on the darkness, and began to declaim:

The sea is the source of water and the source of the
    winds,
for without the great sea there are no clouds,
nor winds that blow from within,
nor currents of rivers, nor rains from the sky.
The great sea is the progenitor of the clouds and the winds
    and the rivers.

He fell silent, exhausted and happy. Parmenides handed him the cup amid the hum of the guests. At that point I left, just in time to avoid the storm.

So this is how it was. The Greeks had put in my place a shiny and impenetrable sphere so that no one would be troubled any longer with what I really was. They had set me on high, unseizable and perfect, far from the world's cares. It was only for their amusement that they continued to regale each other with the vicissitudes of gods, fauns, nymphs, and satyrs. To worship the sphere and disdain the old fables was the sign that one was making philosophy, rising above the credulous populace. Plato would soon depict me as a gentleman creating the world by dint of geometric calculations and would resort to mythological anecdotes only to make his idea more accessible. I was being disfigured as badly by philosophy as by the myths.

I retreated to an island to meditate on what I had seen and heard. One thing was by now indisputable: Philosophy had been born; a group of men was intent on reasoning about the meaning of life. This would forever be philosophy's mission, and from the very beginning I was an integral and profound part of it. Indeed, without a certain idea about me, philosophy itself would have been impossible. It has been said that you must divine the painter to be able to understand the painting. Hence it was necessary to divine me.

I could sense at this point a threat gaining strength. Men who could not deny me did the next best thing, transforming me into the sort of immobile being who would never, for example, write his memoirs. In fact, all that I have created dreams of telling its own story and in one way or another manages to do so. The mountains write with their geological strata, the trees with rings in their trunks and lines in their leaves, the animals through the traces they carry of their ancestors before them. Even a blade of grass writes and rewrites its biography. The universe is a book of recollections, the earth is a journal.

It was then that I merged with a man for the first time. I did so because I wanted a philosopher to speak for me, and I could only use an already existing person. At a certain moment, in the town of Ephesus, I felt I had found him, a man still young, shy, with a short beard. I can still hear his cry after I entered him: "Man is like a child before God, just as the child is before the grown man."

I had been after him for a while, following him in his rounds and observing him with his companions, until I managed to convince him. We were in the temple of Artemis, and a number of children nearby were playing dice. Suddenly Heraclitus and myself became one and the same thing. He felt he'd been penetrated by God, and I knew that I would remain a part of him until his death and that we would not be able to separate. While he lived, our voices would speak with the same intonation and the same inflection. When recalling all of this, I feel, as I did then, pervaded by the unexpected and potent yeast that was diffused through his body. Heraclitus seemed to awaken from a very long sleep, and he never again slept in the manner common to mortal men. He was no longer enclosed in an individual dream, now that his eyes were open upon the world of men, now that he was an adult in respect to them, as distant from them as I was from those children who had stopped playing and stared at me in astonishment.

"Don't look at me like that," I said in Heraclitus' voice, "I too will play with you."

I squatted and cast the dice. I was like the great god Time, who moves the pieces of the game this way and that, similar in all ways to a child. I felt possessed by joy, and the reassured children made the serene air of the temple resound with shouts. That's where a group of citizens of Ephesus found me. They surrounded me and asked me why I had not attended the day's assembly with them, and I replied, "Why do you wonder? It certainly is better to play with children than to do politics with you."

The tone of my voice was filled with the choleric temperament that Heraclitus would accustom me to. I left the temple and resumed my solitary wanderings. By now I fully inhabited Heraclitus' body, and as I walked with him I could hear his monologue: "How great and vast is the soul that I sense within me. It is impossible to measure its limits. It is as though there were a demon inside me forging my character. Unlike those who seek gold and dig up so much earth for such a small booty, I will investigate my soul and extract from it the secret of the world and of life, now that I'm inhabited by God and by the passion for knowledge. Because only divine, not human, nature can have knowledge. Only the wise man fears and desires to be called God!"

These sentences, which I heard Heraclitus repeat to himself during our interminable pilgrimages, now reach me like vestiges of a distant and extraordinarily happy time when, having cast off the doubts and uncertainties of adolescence, I plunged into the world in the same way an athlete enters the arena. I was free to roam as I had been during the most intense days of my animal life.

It will be clear by now that I'm not an easy character to deal with, subject as I am to violently contradictory impulses. Heraclitus, ever since he got to know me, had been obsessed by the problem that things are so often at odds with one another. He convinced himself that everything seeks harmony and that when harmony is achieved, a great sense of well-being bears witness to the equilibrium between opposing forces.

"Even a mixture of wine and cheese coagulates unless it is stirred," the bearded man of Ephesus would exclaim, seated at his table. As usual, he was speaking about me, just as he spoke of me when he walked through military encampments and lectured dumbfounded generals on the need for war, mother of all things, which enslaves some and frees others, and which alone generates peace, just as white creates black, and the harmonious the discordant, and so on, ad infinitum. The generals would hear that the living and the dead are one and the same, as are the man who is awake and the man who sleeps, the young and the old. The generals, he told them, were at peace and did not know it, and the shepherd up there, placid in his rude tent, was at war and unaware of it. The astonishment of these military men can hardly be described, and one by one they kicked him out. Heraclitus would climb the hill up to the shepherd's tent, and the humble man would offer him some milk and meat. He always refused the meat and drank the milk, looking down at the soldiers who were at peace and did not know it, while the shepherd dozed off as if he were not in fact at war.

AROUND that time I was summoned to a distant part of the earth to hear the speeches of another solitary man, who might have been Heraclitus' brother had he not been so docile and rotund—a veritable orb of quietude.

Perhaps they were indeed brothers, for when I asked him point-blank about Heraclitus, the Buddha stared at me with the enigmatic gaze he is now famous for, with his big belly resting on his folded legs and the face of someone who knows much more than he is prepared to say. "Brother of Heraclitus? There are things that are better left unsaid." A smile creased the Buddha's lips.

During that valiant age, I commuted between Heraclitus and Buddha as if I knew that I had to choose between them and that my choice would have great consequences for the future of the world. After crossing deserts and oceans, I would reach Buddha's house and invariably find him in the garden, meditating on the insects that buzzed around him or on the clouds traversing the sky. Heraclitus, on the other hand, forced me to pursue him over the hills and across the islands facing Ephesus. He never stayed still. I ran, like the sun, from the one to the other, from the Orient to the Occident.

I suspected that they were brothers when I heard one of Buddha's speeches quoted by a man whom I met in a tavern in a small village north of Benares. It was a winter evening. Before a fire of huge logs burning on the hearth, as the wind rattled the windows and doors, the monk, gaunt and ethereal beyond belief, recounted one of the master's teachings. Throughout the entire speech, nothing at all was said about me, and this pleased me. For quite some time I had distrusted anyone who used my name, suspecting such a person of manipulation and the will to dominate. I had found that those who knew me spoke of me without mentioning my name, because they knew that I am a puzzle that has yet to be revealed even to itself.

That stormy night in the tavern, I listened to the discourse of dharma, the true doctrine, the doctrine of the origin of human suffering, as if hearing an ancient fable on which I myself had collaborated. Then came the words that awakened in me the memory of Heraclitus: "Everything that is born is at one and the same time a thing that dies." They struck like a thunderclap that wakes you in the middle of a dream. I could still hear my Ephesian friend shouting in the dazzling light of the Ionian coast, "The road that descends and the one that ascends are one and the same road!"

Undoubtedly the Greek light had much to do with the way Heraclitus chose to describe me. His words were drenched in a violent sunlight, which at noon clung to the earth like a crab. He spent his time in the open, walking bareheaded over the hills and along the coast. At noon he would begin to show signs of mental ebullition, like an awakening volcano. Two hours later, in a meridian fervor, Heraclitus would reach his creative zenith. By now intoxicated with light, he shouted his thoughts into the wind-driven air, like gulls whirling in the ether. I had never before seen anyone more solitary than he. He was content to have little; a trifle was sufficient to nourish him, grass and cheese. In his frugality too he resembled Buddha. Both of them drank only water and shunned narcotics, the scourge of their fellow citizens.

This made it possible for them always to remember what they had thought and to write it down or tell it to somebody. In the dazzle of noon, Heraclitus, with his eyes closed against the sun and his soul glowing with ardor, would cry, "God is day, night, winter, summer, war, peace, satiation, hunger. He changes as the fire does when it mingles with smoke."

Perhaps this idea of the fire came to him from the innumerable sunstrokes he had suffered. Our walks would exhaust me, but he would be up again at dawn welcoming the sight of the friendly star. "The sun is new every day!" he would pronounce. Heraclitus maintained that the fiery ball was each time reborn intact, since it engendered ever new thoughts. Sometimes he walked until his feet bled. He would then stop to bind his pained extremities, and with a wild laugh exclaim, "The sun has the width of a human foot!" So much did he feel pervaded by the creator and destroyer of the world.

In order to follow him, I assumed the guises of servant, admirer, and disciple, but he would always chase me away, intolerant as he was of human company. I would then enter him again and we would work out his ideas together. "Say it better," I would tell him, "notice how all things are transformed by fire and watch how fire itself changes. It is sea and land and fiery breath, so much so that the sea often becomes fire again, as it does at sunset, in the conflagration of sky and water. This is the very order of the world; truly it is not created by a god but is an eternal fire that flares up and is extinguished at the right moment." I believed entirely in what I was saying, so great was our mutual influence. I too would be pervaded by fire, until we both burned like torches in the Hellenic noon.

A river ran along the foot of those hills. Every so often Heraclitus was seized by a great desire to be refreshed, and he would run and throw himself into the pellucid water. I was even happier than he to abandon myself to the currents. That river was a balm. We would plunge into the water and there would follow a great swirling and clash of whirlpools, of shouting and foam. After the heat of the sun we felt as if we were evaporating in the water. That is how my friend would put it after our swim, lying on the pebbled bank: "Forever new waters touch those who go into the same river, and souls, too, evaporate." "Do you like bathing?" I once asked him. Heraclitus was stretched out in the sun, and I heard him answer as if he were talking to himself. He said that it was a good thing for the soul to become damp; but a man with a damp soul was like a drunk, tottering about like a beardless youth. He added that a dry soul functions better and is also wiser. I listened bewildered. What did he mean? And then I understood that the sun was beginning to do its work on him. By now he was mumbling through his delirium.

I often thought about his proud solitude. Those sentences contained the violence of things never said to anyone. His hatred for the town was total. Every society seemed to him the realm of evil: any congregation of men was a malicious anthill to be avoided. The crowd was worth nothing. Only a few were worthy, and among those few, he was the worthiest. His self-appreciation was boundless, and he despised anyone who did not think as he did. Neither Hesiod nor Protagoras nor Xenophanes was immune. He called Homer a crook and wished he were still alive so that he could whip him. I often wondered why a person like this should so arouse my interest, and my visits to Buddha finally provided the answer.

I BECAME Buddha's friend and disciple by telling him a story, part invention and part recollection. I introduced myself as a young man from a noble and rich family that owned three mansions, one for the winter, one for the summer, and one for the rainy season. During the four rainy months I would not set foot outside the mansion, and I would spend my time surrounded by young girls who played instruments and offered me every bodily pleasure. I told him that I read the poets and listened to the music with tenderness and detachment, as though they were a message received along with the wind and the rain beating against the palace walls and windowpanes. My youth had reached its culminating point, the moment when you feel that, like a fruit ready to be picked, life will never be riper and fuller than it is now. Soothed by the perfume of the wine and the caresses of the young girls, my body would float into sleep like a cloud as torches cast shadows across the mirrors and tapestries of my vast chamber. "This is how I hope to die, Buddha!" I cried, gripped by my own story as though I had really lived it; and, to tell the truth, I was sure I had. But where, when?

Once, I said to Buddha, I had fallen asleep this way in the middle of the night, under the dim light of a single lamp. The girls had also fallen asleep; the rain outside had ceased and the wind had fallen. Shut away in the mansion's silence, I felt as though all of us were traveling together through the void of the night. The lute player had dozed off on her stool, embracing her instrument; at her side, most sweetly, rested the girl who accompanied her with her voice. Two other girls, having laid down their instruments, had fallen back on the cushions, their hands on their breasts or in their hair. But one girl, close to the window, slept restlessly, writhing in her dreams and muttering sentences through her drooling mouth. At that sight I understood the evil of life, and my soul was filled with aversion.

How heavy and saddening all of this was! How dead my musicians seemed to me, and I to myself! Suddenly the senses appeared but a deception, and our bodiliness, our individuality, only a hideous illusion. I wanted to wake them up, to tell them of my discovery, but they would have reawakened in their error, and would not have understood my words. Their fate was to achieve truth in sleep, like children and drunks. And so I decided to face the oppressiveness of this new insight alone. I left the palace and found myself in the Benares tavern, where one of Buddha's followers told me about the great man.

Buddha and I were alone, seated on the veranda outside his house. Everyone had disappeared. From the mountains that towered above us beyond the garden, silence descended like a tranquil wave. I felt it penetrate between my words, and I drifted into it, as though a path had opened toward my listener. I became inebriated by my story. The Buddha looked like a cliff that my small boat was approaching, furrowing the sea of silence with a slender wake.

When my tale ended, he spoke:

"My friend, none of this is oppressive, none of this is painful! Why don't you calm down?"

He told me things of great interest. If the origin of pain lies in the error of believing we are individuals instead of parts of a whole from which the misfortune of birth has separated us, then the secret of happiness lies in ignoring our needs. The wise man shrinks from the body and from sensation and from the torments of the mind, until all passions are canceled. At that point he is free; he lives by not living, in the beatific certainty that he can never be reborn. His reward will be to die forever, instead of being reborn in bestial or deformed guises or in human shape. "Young nobleman," he said, creasing his lips with the laughless smile that every so often passed over his face, "in your previous existence you must have asked yourself questions, you must have taken steps toward the truth, without even knowing what the answers were. Now you are more fortunate, because there is an answer: meditation, Nirvana! Do not go back to your young girls. Forget the life of the senses. Never suffer again!"

I was struck by the poetry of Buddha's words, and yet I felt rejection arise within me. I could not say this to him openly, but in my innermost core I was greatly agitated.

Buddha confronted me with something that I had not foreseen: along with energy, I had brought into the world a desire for serene quietude. But it had never been my intent to reject life. Life was the only thing that I had; how could I teach the renunciation of it? Imperfect though it was, I could think of nothing better or, quite simply, of nothing different. Life was what I knew; it included the dreams of men as well as their ignorance, and also the astounding inventions of Buddha, who now was looking at me awaiting an answer, certain that I would devote myself to meditating with him, until mind and body began to breathe with the great celestial lung, and not-knowing became a virtue. For me, love of the senses had never been far from knowledge itself, and now I was being advised to reject both forever.

Buddha prompted in me a nostalgia for passion. I recalled the furious buckings of Heraclitus and the uninterrupted cascade of ideas that sprang from them. This recollection prompted me to join Buddha's retinue so that I might present him and his followers with a different view of things. I disguised myself, as I am forced to do whenever I am unable to convince those who are dear to me. I knew that I would perhaps fail in my intentions, since Buddha and Heraclitus reflected somehow a tension within my whole universe.

Buddha was an organizer of unusual skill. His prowess in gathering proselytes was incomparable. Entire villages would convert as he passed through, and theirs was a definitive change. It never happened that someone illuminated by dharma would go back to being the same as before. Whoever converted never turned back, for they had attained the truth, and the truth does not allow for second thoughts.

At the opposite pole was Heraclitus, solitary and aloof, the first image of a figure that would become dear to me: the free thinker, the irreducible poet, lost in the dream of an empire that will never be recognized as his. Back to mind came his contemptuous words when he looked at the crowd: "The many are worth nothing and only a few count for anything." If I tried to discuss it, he would cut me short. "For me, one is worth more than ten thousand if he is better than the others." It was natural that with such an attitude he should find himself alone, something that suited him perfectly, in that aggressive and spiteful way of his.

But now, at the foot of the Himalayas, I joined the pilgrimages of the monks and admired the astute humility of their leader. In his total lack of contempt—even for an animal or for the most derelict of men—was hidden one of the secrets of Buddha's immense fascination. His people loved those who, even though superior, behaved as if they were not. Anyone was supposed to be potentially as worthy as the prophet. Indeed, as Buddha taught, who is not capable of renouncing? There is just no limit to the possibilities for deprivation! And so his disciples followed Buddha, dazzled by the revelation that they could become the humblest of men.

I could not digest all this talk of renunciation. One time I fell asleep from fasting and fatigue, and entered a dream where a stupendous woman was waiting for me. I tried to reach her, but she eluded me with the magic step of a dancer. In my efforts to follow her I fell and rolled over in my sleep, and was jarred awake. Before me stood the Buddha, and he looked at me, pensive and melancholy. I must have cried out, and my forehead was covered with sweat. I tried to compose myself, but my hands trembled and sweat began to drip down my cheeks.

"Do you see?" the Buddha said softly. "If there had not been desire, now there would be no suffering. Because pleasure engenders uncertainty, lust and greed engender fear, and to be free of these you only have to suppress their roots. Smile, my friend. Give up everything. Act as though you did not exist! Don't you feel you are flying? Don't you already feel you are flying?"

My trembling had ceased and the sweat was drying. We were sitting on a hill near Gaya, below the great mountains of Vindhya. Before us, as far as the eye could see, extended a jungle. I was seized by an impulse that I felt often during this period of submission, and like a young boy addressing his teacher, I raised my head suddenly and blurted out this question: "And what about God then? Who made all this? Have you no thought for God? Don't you care about what he might want?"

On Buddha's face I saw only the slits of his eyes and the cheeks covered with scars. He had always refused to touch the subject; in reality he must not have had a very positive idea of God. He seemed to consider God a muddler, perhaps disreputable, who in creating life had concocted something imperfect, even monstrous, an illness to be overcome. Dissolving into nothingness was the prescribed treatment.

Getting no response to my audacious outburst, I bowed my head in obedience. Buddha fascinated me much more than I wished. Before him I was overtaken by shyness. I could feel his hidden contempt for God, and I was unable to speak up in my own defense. It pained me that he was so uninterested in the good things I had been able to put together.

Heraclitus, certainly exaggerating, said that for God everything is good and beautiful and just, and that only for men was one thing just and another unjust. He gave me too much credit, for I saw all the problems I had created. Buddha, however, didn't give me any, and everything in the world was evil for him. I could not ignore his attitude toward me, since nothing is more powerful than denial.

At that very moment, before our eyes, the jungle caught fire. In no time the conflagration grew into a sea of red and liquid light that moved with crashing breakers. The Buddha seemed overcome. I could see his eyes narrow beneath the fire's glare, until, with unusual deliberation, he rose and withdrew into his house. I stayed there to watch the flaming forest. I thought of Heraclitus and of his words about fire as the essence of all things. It was as if he had written me a letter.

I could not move. I saw a burning tree, closed in flame as the skeleton is locked in the body; and a leaf, turned to ash and driven by the wind, floated to my feet. By evening the fire was almost burned out. Instead of the green forest, I saw a gray and black horizon from which rose spirals of smoke.

The Buddha had gathered his thoughts to compose the speech that he gave that evening to the monks assembled around him. This is the last memory that I have of him. In the darkness of the grassy clearing where we sat, beneath the sky laden with ash, he spoke of the day's event and drew his conclusions. "Everything is fire, my brothers," his weary and unmoved voice pronounced. "The eye is prey to the fire. Even the eye's sensation belongs to the fire; and all the rest is fiery passion, hatred, illusion; and so are birth, old age, pain, and lamentation. The ear too is prey to fire, and hence hearing; and the same goes for the nose and the sense of smell. The tongue is on fire, and so are the mind and the objects it contemplates. And so my disciples, as they realize this, will become indifferent to the eyes, to visible objects, to the faculties of seeing and hearing, indifferent to the body and the mind, and to all that the mind contemplates; and they will free themselves of all passions and never again be condemned to be reborn into a world devoured by fire. The goal will be met when life itself is extinguished. Brothers, we all have a great task."

As for me, I was already on my way to Greece. When I reached the vicinity of Ephesus, I went in search of Heraclitus. Arresting news had reached me. Living so long like a vagabond, eating so little food, Heraclitus had finally been struck by dropsy. I found him lying on the ground, swollen with water like a drowned cat. My surprise was so great that I forgot my previous roles and stood before him in astonishment, undisguised. I kept silent, dejected by his appearance. At last he made an effort to speak.

"Are you Zeus?" he mumbled through swollen and cracked lips.

I shook my head emphatically. Heraclitus closed his eyes and continued.

"I knew it all along. In any case you wouldn't tell me. You like to conceal your nature. And besides, who knows whether God wants to be addressed as Zeus!"

I shook my head again, but Heraclitus was not fooled. He launched into an angry monologue.

"Look what happens to me—just as I am about to die I recognize you. But now that you have revealed yourself, the least you can do is answer me! Teach me how to see beauty in things that are unjust and cruel! Tell me that the illness from which I suffer is beautiful! Tell me that men are to be praised in all and everything. Help me understand how shortsighted I am, since I am unable to grasp the harmony of opposites. Help me! Like the men who search for gold, I too have dug much and found little!"

I kept silent. How could I reveal to Heraclitus, who was about to die, the reality of my nature, after he had spent an entire life in the hope that I was perfect? I saw all of fate chained to the eternal evil of my weakness.

Heraclitus, disappointed, asked again: "Am I asleep?"

I shook my head. He looked at me wearily.

"Just like the lord of Delphi, you neither speak nor deny, you merely hint." He rose on his elbows. "I want to recover, I want to be able to see what happens. Enough of this childish game of moving everything this way and that, so that there is never any certainty. Leave, I beg you, there is something I must do."

I set off by myself along our customary paths, meditating on my failure and racking my brain in search of remedies for the future world. I had plenty of ideas, but I still had a long way to go. I mingled with the boatmen and helped them find pitch for their hulls pierced by the rocks. At night we munched roasted chickpeas, drank wine, and talked. One of them, who came from far away, told us later that Heraclitus had died beneath a huge mound of manure, because he believed that the heat would dry up all the liquid that filled his body. And so he died for lack of fire.

Now that man had begun to remember the past and measure time, the centuries went by like seasons. The universe had entered a phase of activity that has not yet ended, even though today it seems to be toward the end of its tether. It was the epoch in which I would deal directly with the new masters of the world. I would appear to them and give them advice; and people spoke about me as if they had just seen me around the corner. They addressed me with different names, but it was always me they referred to.

Sometimes, as happened with Socrates, I came quite close to recognizing my own views in what I heard. When I went to Athens to see him, I found him in prison, just before he swallowed the poison, his disciples clustered around so as to catch his last words. But what I heard that day was different from what was handed down later on. Socrates was put to death because he had been able to decipher my thought, something intolerable to everyone except his followers, among whom Plato was undoubtedly the most intelligent and the most ambitious.

Plato was entrusted with the task of transcribing the texts of the teacher, who, contrary to what was later said, had written a great deal. Plato took the liberty of making unlimited variations. He truly loved Socrates and looked upon him as a father, even to the point of attributing to him all his own tastes. Finally he made him talk of an astral and perfect world where I lived, a world that I have never seen anywhere but in the minds of men. Plato's invention was very successful, and he was helped a lot by his immense gifts as a writer. He was so conscious of his skills that he made Socrates condemn all the writers in the world. One brilliant liar was enough, and no more chances should be taken in the future.

The Greeks scintillated with intelligence and gaiety. They stole and transformed everything, as if they could change into gold the raw material of other people's laborious thoughts. They were so skillful that they became enamored with anything they undertook, producing ever more perfect works, replete with enchantment.

I remember a tutor from Samos who one day in my presence created the tale of Narcissus. A thick beard adorned his young, gaunt face, and he told this story, which I inspired in him during a philosophy class, walking amid the scent of the orange trees and the verdure of myrtles.

"Once upon a time there was a river that encountered a nymph and imprisoned her in its waters. So Narcissus was born, having been conceived in the water. One day someone asked an old soothsayer: 'Will this young boy ever attain old age?' 'Yes, if he will avoid knowing himself,' the soothsayer replied. Nobody understood, but listen how well he knew what was at stake. Narcissus reaches the age of sixteen. He is not yet a young man and he is no longer a young boy, and everyone, male and female, lusts for him. He does not give himself to anyone. He is devoted only to the hunt and is contemptuous of all contacts.

"But one day Echo appears, a nymph of the woods. Her fate was a much harsher one. She has been condemned by Hera,

jealous of a love affair with Zeus, to repeat the last words uttered by others. When the nymph flings herself at him, Narcissus rejects her. 'I would rather die than make you a gift of myself!' he cries. To no avail she shows him her naked body. In
the end, bitterly disappointed, she asks the gods to punish him,
and all the young girls rejected by him join in her request. The
gods grant the wish. Narcissus will fall in love, but he will never
be able to possess what he loves."

We were now close to the seashore, and the tutor continued
in his youthful, rough tones:

"One day Narcissus comes to a shady spring in the heart of
a forest. No one is there. The youth mirrors himself in the water
of the spring and falls in love with his image. Unable to tear
himself away from it, he continues to admire himself and begins talking: 'Oh, dear self, where are you hiding? Must I separate myself from you so that I can join you? If only I could
detach myself from my body! But this is a desire unheard of
in a lover. I wish what I love far from me, so that I might attain
it.'"

The tutor reached the high point of the story, and his face
was flushed with emotion. He now saw in it a truth that had
been concealed from him. Concerned, until that moment, with
the outside world in which he was unwillingly immersed, Narcissus has now looked into himself and is imprisoned by what
he sees. He now resembles a plant that instead of expanding
becomes so obsessed with exploring its own roots and the soil
in which it is born that it no longer grows.

"With a delicate gesture the young man pierces his chest and
is stained with blood. He yearns and is consumed, until he dies,
and having reached the nether world, he is unable to wrench
free from himself and he still searches for himself in the rivers
that flow blindly down there."

The beauty of this fable still haunts me, and I thought about
it as my peregrinations continued, taking me, almost by
chance, toward Palestine.

CONFUSEDLY, tempestuously, memories began to surface. I
overheard stories about Moses, about the prophets, about my
words that were handed down from generation to generation.

This arid and dusty land of Palestine did not admire beauty as much as Greece did, but here everyone clung to the certainty of truth as to the one thing that mattered. And for them, truth was God. The God of the scribes and the Pharisees, who, after many centuries, still imitated Moses, never missing an opportunity to enrich themselves and augment their power. I had predicted this to Moses, but he had not listened to me. I entered the temple and saw the merchants making their business deals, and I was angry. Whom were these people talking about?

And then I remembered Acsa and was filled with tenderness. I roamed about Jerusalem for an entire night, calling out her name and speaking to the stars. Where had her soul fled? I sought her until dawn, when I thought I recognized her in a sleeping prostitute who held her head low, as Acsa used to do when dreaming with her child in her arms. I woke her and we made love at the edge of the city, in a grassy meadow, while she was still sleepy; she could not keep her eyes open, and when she cried out with pleasure, I realized that she was not Acsa and that I would search in vain for my old love.

Still, I kept an affectionate memory of that girl, and after some time decided to see her again. When I went back to find her, I heard that she had married an old carpenter and that they now lived in a village of Galilee called Nazareth. Several days later I happened to be in the vicinity, and a downpour caught me by surprise. A gust of wind blew open the windows of a modest house. I entered to seek shelter from the rain and was faced by a young pregnant woman who gazed at me in ecstasy. From the adjoining room came the sound of a plane against wood; the husband was building a crib for the child she was to bear. I stroked the wife's hair and vanished into the wind beyond the window, which closed behind me.

A few months later, while I was traveling on a comet and looking down at the earth as from an airplane window, I recognized my friend of a single night, stretched out on the straw in a stable. The carpenter was busying himself at her side like an inexperienced midwife. The event had caught them during a trip to the city of Bethlehem. They had been unable to find accommodations at the inns and had taken refuge in the stable of a peasant's house. I descended toward them, and when I reached Earth the child was already born and his soft whimpers filled the poor abode. I drew near to look at him, pushing aside a donkey and an ox that stood near the pallet, chewing its cud; the infant clung to the mother's breast and was now sucking quietly. The woman saw me hover between the beasts in the dim light of the stable, then turned her gaze to the child. Jesus was born, but I did not know this yet; and, besides, how could I be sure that he was indeed my son?

I WAS to see him again years later when his renown was already widespread. I too had gone to Palestine to see the Christ. Jesus had just returned to Jerusalem after the banquet in Bethany that had been attended by Lazarus, the man who had been resurrected.

His arrival in town was a triumph. I mingled with the crowd and saw him trot by, on the small donkey he had chosen as his mount. I was with a group of Athenian scholars who had heard about the events in Palestine and had decided to gather the facts for a collection of essays that ultimately was never published. You cannot put together a Cynic, a Stoic, and an Epicurean to discuss the same subject and hope that a book will come of it. I was a sort of secretary to the group and lent a bored and distracted ear to the discussions, which had already been quite violent on the boat that brought us to Middle Eastern coasts.

I had no desire to take part in the disputations. I knew that, at bottom, it was a matter of deciding who should be the leader of the Peripatetic School of Athens, a prestigious position laden with all sorts of privileges. I had gone simply to acquaint myself with Jesus, the adventurer who had declared that he was my son and my envoy to the world. During that period I was living in melancholic solitude. I was frustrated by the decadence of that Greek culture that was so dear to me, and I was frightened by the fact that no one seemed to be aware of its decline. As I listened to the arguments of the three philosophers, I could barely conceal my irritation, and I turned my attention to the fish flashing through the water.

I vividly remember what a tremendous impression the

Christ first made upon me. It would not have displeased me at all if he had been my son. I could only object to the length of his hair, which was certainly excessive and gave him a somewhat feminine aspect. Yet his overall appearance was first-rate, and I was struck especially by his intense yet exceedingly tender eyes. You could not afford to meet his gaze if you did not want to succumb to it. I immediately feared for his fate.

Our meeting was witnessed by the apostles. They deserve a story apart. Some of them were good people, like John and his friend Mary Magdalene. Others were opportunists, and a few were downright scoundrels.

Much later, at my first reading of the Gospels, I noticed that the event in which I had participated was recounted in an oblique fashion, by allusions scattered through several parts of the text; and now, to put it together, one must skip from one part to another. However, only I, the sole survivor among the actors in the drama, can do this. I was never referred to by my assumed name, because no one except Jesus knew who I was. And he could not say anything.

John, in his Gospel, mentions our encounters: "Now there were certain Greeks who were coming up to worship during the festivities. So then, having approached Philip who was from Bethesda, a town in Galilee, they begged him and said, 'Sir, we would like to see Jesus.' Philip went to tell Andrew, and then again Andrew and Philip told Jesus."

In fact this back and forth of Andrew and Philip between Jesus and us Greeks took up an entire afternoon. On hearing that we wanted to write a book, the two apostles had become extremely excited, and they tried to take part in the interview. Each had his own motives. Andrew was impelled by ambition, Philip by a desire to control events and not allow the Christ's words to be misinterpreted. It was a very hot day. The scholars sweated like Theban plebs and cursed their gods in Greek. I remained silent. I had noticed repeatedly that John never stopped staring at me. He was alone among all the apostles to sense that there was something unusual and decisive in that meeting, and indeed he was the only one to hand it down to posterity, though in a distorted form. Since the book by my traveling companions never appeared, in John's Gospel we became the "worshipers at the festivities" instead of a group of philosophers.

Along about twilight we were admitted into Jesus' presence. We entered a dark room and for a while couldn't see anything. There was a lot of stumbling over benches and tools; somebody stepped on a cat and for an instant there was tremendous confusion. I could hear the Stoic begin cursing again, and at that moment another voice rose from a corner of the room, resonant, with a slightly strident edge that made it resemble the ringing peal of a trumpet. You would have thought he was reciting psalms, such was the assurance of his words:

"The Light will be with you only a little while longer; walk while you have light, so that darkness will not engulf you; for he who walks in darkness does not know where he is going.

"While you have light, believe in light, so that you shall be the sons of light."

There followed a brief silence. We had managed to settle down, some on stools, some on the floor, still others leaning against the wall, and we were peering into the darkness, trying to see who had spoken. Finally we saw Jesus, sitting on a mat in the darkest recess of the room. His eyes glittered like semiprecious stones. He examined us intently, one by one. Then his gaze fell on me and he seemed surprised, as though by a distant memory; then his eyes moved on to the others.

I too had the curious impression of having seen him before. I recognized something familiar in his face and movements, but I couldn't say of whom he reminded me. My colleagues were making great efforts to take notes and, after the speech they had heard as they entered, they did not dare ask for more light. I sensed their anger and a kind of fascination that accompanied it, and I knew that such a mixture leads to resentment. For the moment, however, they were absorbed in scribbling, squinting from the effort to see.

At Jesus' side stood a jug, which he picked up several times to drink; and from every drink he came away refreshed and with a shriller voice that added to the vigor of his speech. Because he was clearly inspired, we understood that he was not going to agree to an exchange of questions and answers. Without warning he burst out:

"The time has come for the son of Man to be glorified.

"In truth I tell you that if the grain of wheat, fallen to the soil, does not die, it remains alone; but if it dies it produces much fruit.

"Whoever loves his life will lose it, and whoever loathes life in this world will preserve it in eternal life."

His words resounded sharply in the room. From a small window there came a purple light that heightened the intensity of the scene. The effect of these opening remarks still lives in me. I had never heard anything so beautiful and so convincing before. Hundreds of memories crowded into my mind; the years and the wheat and death, brought together by those words, took shape before me like a dance repeated forever. Where had the Christ learned these things? They seemed to spring spontaneously from him, like grass from damp sod. I remembered the time when I had created man and the task I had given him. Christ also remembered it! I was filled with emotion and gratitude.

The Greek academicians exchanged petulant glances. Someone brought in a torch, and in the wavering light we saw Christ bring the drink to his lips and resume with new élan:

"If any of you wishes to serve me, let him follow me; and wherever I shall be there shall be my servant; and if anyone serves me he will be honored by the Father."

Jesus paused in meditation and this created a great suspense among us. He looked all around and was about to continue when a voice arose:

"But who is the Father? What are his attributes? Where does he reside? And is his universe arranged by links like a chain or in filaments that run parallel? Are you part of the universal soul, or do you place yourself outside it? And where did you obtain your doctorate? I must ask you to answer because it is the public at large that puts these questions to me, the public whose servants and guardians we are."

All eyes had turned toward the questioner, the Stoic philosopher, the most disagreeable of them all. This fellow's arrogance was boundless. Even now as he was speaking he took scornful pleasure in his technique, like a monkey that makes grimaces at those who watch it, and he moved his hands like a flustered bird, folding and rubbing them. My hostility toward him instantly became gigantic. I already had a soft spot for Jesus, and there was no point in denying it. At that very instant I decided to speak.

The attack of the philosopher had created an atmosphere of embarrassment. His colleagues, united by professional solidarity, continued to exchange glances of mutual congratulation, while rearranging their wads of foolscap. I kept looking at the Christ, who seemed to have become quite somber. He stared into the void and winced, contracting his eyebrows and nostrils. Without looking he seized the jug and drank an angry gulp. When he put it down his gaze had become a blade thirsting for blood, and only then did he seem to take notice of the question that had been addressed to him. He looked straight at the Stoic philosopher, whose trembling hands groped for the amulets he wore about him, and I was reminded of his Greco-Sicilian ancestry, devoted to all kinds of incantations to ward off evil. On his wrist he wore a bracelet depicting Mercury in flight, carrying in his hand the inscription ALETHEA. The first A was a snake's head, the final one a coiled tail. I thought with regret of Socrates and my first philosophers, who roamed the countryside and waded across rivers.

The Christ finally turned his gaze away from the philosopher to gather his thoughts. After a moment's silence we heard his voice come from a further distance and with greater deliberation:

"Now my soul is distraught; and what shall I say? Father, spare me from this hour; but it is for this hour that I have come. Father, glorify your name."

Amid the general dismay, I answered Jesus almost in a state of inebriation. I don't know what took hold of me, perhaps the general tension or perhaps pity for that man, mixed with admiration; or perhaps the strange magic that emanated from the Christ like a light in the darkness of that house. The fact is that I spoke. Once again it was John who handed down the episode, though in a distorted form meant to render it acceptable.

This is how he described the scene, after Christ's invocation to his father:

"And then a voice came from Heaven and said, 'I have glorified him and I will glorify him again.' Of the multitude that was there present and had heard the voice, some said that it was thunder. Others said, 'An Angel has spoken to him.' And Jesus said, 'This voice has not manifested itself for me, but for you.'"

Well, that voice was mine, and I remember how surprised I was at hearing myself speak in that way, in a tone that I myself did not recognize, altered and forceful. I too thought that it was coming from a different place in the room, perhaps from above, and I saw many of them lift their eyes and begin to talk of a miracle. I myself looked up, ashamed of what I had just done, and it was undoubtedly easy to imagine an angel hovering over those waves of shadow cast by the smoky flame. Only John and Magdalene had clearly heard me, and they stared at me. The Christ, after the first moment of surprise, grasped the favorable moment. He straightened and thrust out his chest and flung an epiphanic series of dazzling verbal inventions at his audience. He rose to his feet, frightening everyone with his sudden and arresting height, and he seized the torch and began to shout in a paroxysm of exaltation, "So be the sons of light!" and flung the torch at those assembled, who screamed with horror and scrambled to pick it up. Meanwhile he had disappeared through the inner door, like a shadow passing through a wall.

Following that incident he really went into hiding, and finding him became a difficult undertaking. During the subsequent days the three philosophers wandered through Jerusalem's alleyways, arguing with the apostles and trying to corrupt them. They certainly managed to do so with Judas and Peter, who were the greediest and weakest, and accepted money to set up a meeting with Jesus. But I knew where to go, where I'd be sure to find him, and without having recourse to subterfuge.

I went to see John and found him together with his inseparable Magdalene, burning juniper in his garden, which gave off an aromatic smoke that filled my eyes with tears. I exchanged a few words with him and the meeting was arranged. John sensed that my presence was important, but he did not want to know anything more. I had time enough to admire Magdalene's beauty in the perfumed garden, and I thought I understood why Peter hated her for the love the Christ felt for her. Then John returned and gave me Jesus' message.

He did not want to see me at his house and begged me to receive him as a guest in a place where he could take his disciples for a supper that I was supposed to prepare. Afterward he would speak to me privately, as it is customary to do with one's host. He was giving me orders, but my desire to see him was so strong that I did not demur or hesitate. In search of a house I could rent, I rushed through the streets and markets of Jerusalem, among goats, dogs, and baskets of cheese and wine, among vendors of spices and magic herbs, among male and female prostitutes, mingling with the world that I had created as the stage for the Christ's story. At last I found a middleman, who procured an entire house for me in a good section of town and asked me whether I needed boys and girls for the evening and wanted opium. He was not surprised when I refused, thinking that I had taken care of all this on my own.

Now I had to prepare the supper. I returned to the market and stocked up on bread, cheese, and vegetables. I went down an alleyway where in a half-dark shop rather good wine was being sold at a modest price. While I was bargaining and giving instructions to bring the jugs to the house, I heard some voices muttering excitedly behind a pile of barrels, and in the gloom I recognized Peter and Judas in the company of a man wrapped in a barracan robe. After two thousand years I still haven't forgotten the impression made on me by that conversation. They were selling the Christ! I can hear the sound of the silver pieces on the barrel top; I can hear the heavy footsteps as the three left in their different directions; I can see myself standing in that shop, wondering whether I had not been part of a dream.

There was not much time left. I gave orders to tidy the house, cook the food, and prepare the room with a number of tables arranged in a U. I hired some servants and immediately sent one of them to carry out the instructions I had been given by Jesus.

"Go," I told him, "get a pail of water and make sure that

Jesus' disciples find you. Then bring them here." He was an alert young boy who was studying mathematics and astronomy in Alexandria and had returned home for the Passover feast. He pocketed the silver talents and went off into the street; then he returned with Christ and the apostles.

While the others rested, waiting for supper, I managed to talk to him. The encounter took place in a room of the house and continued through the streets of Jerusalem, in the taverns where Christ stopped to swig down one cup after another.

As soon as we were alone I had a revelation. While I was still asking myself whom he might resemble, there came to mind a sentence filled with contempt that I had heard Judas utter in the wine shop a little earlier, which at the moment had seemed to me malicious gossip. I looked at Jesus, remembered Judas' words, and everything fell into place like the pieces of a scrambled mosaic.

"Is it true what they say about you, that you are the son of a prostitute?" I asked.

Jesus' reaction was uncertain. He stood up and nervously paced the small room, clasping one hand in the other, trying to control himself. Then he stood still and looked at me sternly.

"My mother is a saint," he answered. "No man has ever even touched her. You can see for yourself that she is a virgin. Go to the room where she is resting, take along a midwife, lift her robe. My mother is an angel, I'm telling you."

With every word of his, another of my doubts fell away. His resemblance to the girl of so many years before was striking, and I had to push to the bottom of my soul the instinct that urged me to embrace my newfound son. But my insistence would not have led to anything. I concentrated on the important matter. I told him that I was God, and that I did not recognize myself in the Father of whom he talked; that I saw my son in him, but a son like all others and nothing more; and that the splendid things that he said mixed truth with lies. It certainly was true that I wanted men to love one another. That was why I had created them, to remedy the evil that flooded the world; but this evil had not been caused by mankind, as people stubbornly insisted on believing. Evil was due to the imperfection of the world, to my own lack of skill. I had known this for a long time. Man must decide not to blame himself but to improve creation. I spoke as only God could speak to Jesus just before the crucifixion, and I urged my point with logic, patience, and passion. If I minced words on this essential point, how could I expect Jesus to fulfill the hopes that I had now started to place in him?

The Christ listened and grew even more somber. He seemed caught in a dilemma that was ferocious and without solution. He seemed to want to reply; instead he shook his head and threw himself impetuously at my feet. I was deeply disturbed. I made him rise and whispered to him:

"I need you. Why won't you understand? I'm not a leader."

"I know that," he said, "but now what happens to everyone has happened to me. Men are not free, and I must always take this into account. Do you know this, Father? Do you know that they will do nothing unless they become convinced that they must worship someone or something? I will have to get them to crucify me so as to be remembered. I could very well avoid it, but I have no choice if I want to save at least a part of what I have preached. And I began to lie a long time ago. I know very well that neither hells nor paradises exist, but this evening at supper I will give a special speech about the final judgment, which will never take place, and they will believe me. What else can I do? That is why I drink, and now I hope I shall die. I want to die. I would like to disappear but for the fact that it's necessary for me to remain in their memory. I have no other way to make them better."

Jesus' voice was hoarse with wine and dejection. We spoke in low voices like two conspirators. Over Jerusalem passed clouds as vast as angels; I could hear the sound of distant trumpets, as if in a dream. I too had become intoxicated by the smell of the wine, and I realized that I wanted to believe in the Christ, I the atheistic God.

"There, I see that you understand," Jesus concluded, looking around nervously. "I want you to know that I speak like this also to some of my disciples; to John, Mary Magdalene, Matthew. But they aren't the ones who will count. It will be the hard ones, those who know men, Peter . . . "

"Peter has betrayed you," I burst out anxiously. Jesus gestured resignedly.

"I know. And all the guilt will be placed on Judas. But I need Peter; on that rock my fame will be built. Without Peter there would be nothing left of me. I need an army of Peters in the temple of the centuries, so that now and then a John or a Magdalene may emerge to keep the flame alive."

"You are wrong!" I cried. I knew that this was the last thing I would have the time to say to him. "You are mistaken! You must immediately renounce Peter, this very evening at supper. Immediately elect John, Matthew, and Magdalene. If they are the end, let them also be the beginning. Don't make the same mistakes I've made!"

As he moved away Christ looked at me, and I understood his answer then better than if he had uttered it. "I do not want to die completely," his eyes said, "and Peter will erect a cult that will last through the centuries." We entered the large patrician hall, downcast and pensive.

I wanted to leave right away. Besides, I had other things to do. I was planning to survey regions that I had almost forgotten I had created, the polar areas inhabited by animals of which I had lost knowledge. Thomas, one of the apostles, approached me and begged me to stay, saying that otherwise there would be no supper. They had realized that there were thirteen of them, and that would definitely bring bad luck. Reluctantly, I agreed to participate in the banquet, and I sat down at one end of the table, almost hidden and unremittingly silent. That is why no one mentions me when talking about that supper. No one says that God was present, that he did not miss a word.

During the supper Jesus made some of his most beautiful observations. I listened to him, deeply moved and proud.

"Now abide with me and I shall abide with you; just as the branch cannot bear fruit by itself if it does not abide with the vine, so you too will be sterile unless you abide with me." He lifted his glass in my direction, as if for a toast. "I am the vine, and my Father is the vinedresser!" he proclaimed in a loud, intense voice. And this was not his only reference to me. All evening long he did nothing but refer to the Father, to the point that the apostles, astonished, asked him, "But why do you say that you will soon join the Father?" And the Christ answered by drinking and then looking at me fixedly: "I will again leave the world and go to the Father," he said. It was obvious that he meant it. They looked at each other, dumbfounded that Jesus was now speaking so straightforwardly, without similes. And they had no way of knowing that this was because I was there. My presence does not permit the use of similes.

Then Jesus had one of his brainstorms. He broke the bread into the wine and pronounced a speech that created a stir along the entire table. He added that someone was going to betray him and looked straight into the eyes of Judas and Peter, neither of whom dared deny it. Once more the apostles swayed as a group. The torches fixed to the walls cast a stormy light all over the room. The entire scene was like a stupendously inventive painting.

At that very moment Jesus looked at me again and said, "But I am not alone, because the Father is with me." Then he got up, left the room, and went to the olive orchard that lay close by.

What happened next was a sordid business, and I will be brief. The apostles, by now almost completely drunk, fell into a leaden sleep. Peter and Judas rushed to get the guards who were supposed to arrest their master. Peter, like the true traitor that he was, lay down on the ground and pretended to be asleep like the others, allowing the infamous act to fall upon Judas' shoulders. I went into the garden just before the arrest and saw Christ weeping, in the throes of hysteria. He was pouring himself one drink after another. When he saw me he screamed, "Take this cup from my lips!" and flung the cup at me. Perhaps he was ashamed; his voice was so loud and frightening that it awakened some of the apostles, but they were stupefied and immediately fell back asleep. Jesus was afraid and I was not surprised. Crucifixion is a horrible torture.

But he did nothing to try to escape his fate. When the guards arrived, Peter, roused from his feigned sleep, played out the scene of the sword attack on the high priest's servant, even cutting one of his ears; and the Christ, having regained his calm and dignity, laid a hand on Peter's arm and said, "Peter, put your sword back in its sheath. How could I not drink from the cup that my Father has offered me?" And he gave me one last look.

Surrounded by guards and dignitaries, he disappeared, leaving behind his drowsy and disoriented disciples. I fled from their presence.

I spent two days unable to decide what I should do and full of harsh resentment toward the world. On few other occasions was I so aware of the vastness of my failure. I got drunk and wound up sprawled on the ground, dreaming about great birds transporting crosses. On the third day I was awakened by the philosophers, who told me of their intention to continue the trip all the way to Rome, where a certain Caius, senator and grammarian, was waiting for them. "Adventurers!" I said to myself, watching them leave. The possibility of a common profit had canceled all philosophical dissension.

I was left alone in that huge house I had rented. "My Father's house has many rooms," as the Christ had ironically observed. I whiled away the hours sunk in a feeling of impotence.

Evening came and I set out through the streets of Jerusalem all the way to the quarters of the poor, where news had arrived by means of the rabble just released from jail. Everyone knew what was happening to the Christ. There were rumors about tortures, humiliations, mockery, and a pale Christ weak and intent on dying. I knew what it was; for a drinker the first day of abstinence is dreadful. With some vague idea of solidarity I went to a tavern and commenced drinking on his behalf. I played dice, I won and then I lost and then I won again. My own being seemed pretty well summed up by a game of dice in a tavern. I ended up in bed with a girl, on whose breast I caught myself crying out the name of Mary Magdalene, before submerging again in sleep.

I woke up late and didn't recognize where I was. I found myself lost in that house as though inside a universe I had not created. I stared at the stains on the walls and the ceilings until a clamor outside made me leap out of bed. The girl told me that while asleep I had shouted completely senseless things: that the poor are blessed because they will own everything and the hungry because they will be abundantly fed, and that most blessed of all are those who weep, because in the end no one will laugh as loudly as they. It was only a dream, I repeated to her. Then she told me about the event, in which the entire town had participated: while I was asleep, they had crucified Christ. I rushed out of the house. I began to run, following a crowd. I lost my way several times and realized that the mob had no idea where it was going, like a herd of sheep without a dog or shepherd. I can't say how many times I went full circle through Jerusalem, always ending up again in front of the temple. Insane rumors bounced from one person to the next, such as one that described Christ as changed into a ram with horns and tail and nailed to the cross, or another that told how a woman had been found beneath the garment removed from Christ at the moment of his crucifixion.

Finally I thought of following a squad of Roman centurions, which led me out of the city, along a grassy plain, and then up the slope of a hillock crowded with frenzied people. I ran ahead and saw them, the three crosses under the sun. Oh, yes, I saw them! I arrived precisely at the instant when the Christ, limp, parched, and defeated, howled of his thirst; and I saw the centurion who had arrived with me, having come from a tavern where he had been drinking and eating, take a sponge, immerse it in a liquid that they later said was vinegar, and raise it to Christ's lips. I saw Christ suck avidly and his face turn more ashen with disgust; and then I saw him spit, his saliva falling to the foot of the cross, where women, soldiers, and disciples moved about in great confusion. Finally he saw me as I stood there straight and stock-still, with my arms limp at my sides, looking at his arms, which were stretched out above him, along the arms of the cross.

I saw him look at me for an intense minute, beneath a sky darkened by oncoming rain, and I saw him go toward his death without joy, because he knew that he had lost, just as Peter knew it, who beneath the cross wept real tears of sorrow. I understood that Peter would have been willing to die at once for his teacher, but that he would also not have hesitated a moment to do again what he had done.

Christ became animated one last time and cried out to me, "Father, why have you forsaken me?" before letting his head drop on his shoulder, in the same way it inclines in all the world's paintings. One of the centurions looked at me inquisitively. John had sought refuge in Magdalene's arms, and an old woman hid behind her shawl. She was Christ's bogus mother. I turned away and left.

I descended Golgotha, descended through the centuries.

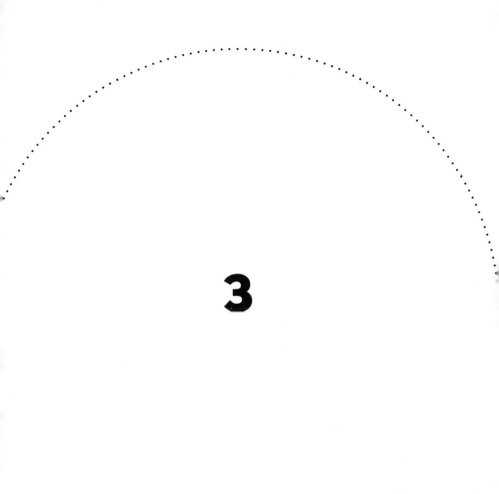

3

With the death of the Christ my youth was over. I realized that, for a long time, I had relied too much on the prophets to find answers about life and about the fate of mankind. I had needed certainties, and they obliged by putting in my mouth prescriptions and prohibitions I never even thought of. I was an adult God now and determined to free myself from prophets and emissaries. Without them, the universe suddenly seemed vast to me. I breathed the air as if I had forgotten its fragrance, and I immersed myself in the colors of creation and delighted in its shapes. I wandered like a perfect stranger, paying no heed to my appearance or my dress. I was the God who walks the roads, among uncaring animals; but men are not animals, and the naked sight of me is often frightful to them. There was talk of comets, spells, secret potions to explain the frenzy that would seize a village at my passing. I was almost unable to speak with anyone; it was as if I bore the plague. I had to find something to wear, a skin to inhabit.

After the death of Christ, humankind talked mainly about death, as though a violent sadness had shadowed the world. The melancholy type seemed to predominate. I saw examples that I will not easily forget: the priest who, convinced that he was dead, refused to leave his bed and was fed against his will while asleep; the merchant who refused to urinate for fear of inundating the world; the peasant who thought he was a wolf, with the pelt inside his skin, and roamed the fields slaughtering people; the soothsayer who never opened his mouth; the rich man who was convinced that his beard was growing within him and that it would finally suffocate him; the nun who cut her fingers off so as not to touch her body; and an endless phalanx of desperate visionaries. Their progeny survives still, a few inhabiting insane asylums, but most on the loose, raising families and holding down jobs until one day they jump in a river without a word or exterminate people they don't even know. Some think they are Jesus Christ but should tell nobody. Some think they are Napoleon and busy themselves with preparations for imminent war. Some think that they don't even exist, and that's the worst of all conditions.

I watched them with understanding and even sympathy, but I could not identify with any of them. Even in my darkest moments I try to remain hopeful, and a melancholy person, sooner or later, ends by irritating me. "Come now, bestir yourself," I feel like shouting, and in an instant I am already far away.

I did, however, encounter some melancholiacs of lofty intellectual attainment, like the philosopher Seneca. I had been following him for some time in his travels, his sojourns in the countryside, his solitary meditations, and finally I went to his house on the day of his announced suicide. He had received from the emperor Nero the injunction to die and had welcomed it almost with relief. He invited his acquaintances and the dignitaries of the court to a feast celebrating his departure from life, which by now seemed to him like a journey across a desert without oases. No water could extinguish the thirst at the bottom of Seneca's throat. Slaves, wealth, unchecked political power, lust satisfied on all occasions—nothing was enough to quench it. Seneca had everything! Hence his grim and unrelenting thirst.

I recognized his thin body and knife-sharp face, the slanted eyes that he could barely keep open—whether because of the wine or the tumult of his thoughts, I couldn't tell.

As I lay on the triclinium, I had time to reflect. Stretched out on my lounge, alongside a somnolent and bored patrician, I imagined myself the architect of a house that I had begun not a long time before and to which, each century, I would add a wall, outline a hallway, square off a room, amid a piling up of bricks and clouds. That house was history, crammed with famous people and obscure characters. In one of its rooms, on the mezzanine, I had met Seneca and witnessed an era at its end.

At first I had set out to convince him that solitude was the condition necessary to come into contact with me. Having such a notion accepted by a man like Seneca, with his tumultuous social life, was an ambitious project and required careful planning. I pursued him through the halls of imperial power. I would appear suddenly before him during the intricate conversations he had with his disciple Nero, who was already possessed by the idea of being a god. I followed him as he walked about, surrounded by a crowd of postulants and hangers-on, in a flutter of togas. He was forced to notice me, though at first he pretended indifference, a master at not seeing whatever he decided not to see, the original of a type I was to encounter again and again through the human adventure, diplomats, bureaucrats, ecclesiastical dignitaries, courtesans of every variety and ilk. I persisted with the obstinacy of a rejected lover, hoping for a sudden reversal, tolerating the discomforts of a life spent following in someone else's footsteps. I wanted to establish myself at his side in such a way that his gaze would no longer be able to slide past me.

Finally I realized that Seneca had recognized me even before looking at me. I had managed to get my hands on the letters that he wrote to Lucilius, a young patrician he had begun to tutor. I bribed the servant who carried the tablets from one to the other, and I read them before they were delivered, standing in a corner of the Forum, under the Roman sun, surrounded by senators who spoke about matters of little interest to me, such as the new system of rural taxation or the unrest on the Dacian borders. They were beautiful letters, discussing everything but above all describing the wise man's attitude toward life and the powerful who control it—inept riders of a capricious foal. Seneca had understood the farce of power, but he himself was unable to evade his ambition and pride; it was as though he were living two lives. I rushed through those letters in order to return them to the waiting servant, until I ran across the sentence in which Seneca finally acknowledged my presence. I reread it, tapping my knuckles with satisfaction against the wax tablet: "Live among men as if God could see you." He had finally managed it!

That day I went to give my thanks to Janus, the only pagan god I had created. Janus was claimed by the Romans, but I had thought him up myself, in a moment of condescension toward

religion and its rituals. Through Janus I wanted to say something very different from the role that was eventually assigned
to him as guard over the doors of houses, one face looking outside and the other turned inside, so as to protect both spaces.
My idea was more subtle, and the priests failed to grasp it. I
wanted to show to humans that their nature is twofold and that
one side of them is always turned toward the soul while the
other looks outside. This truth began to be understood when
Seneca, quoting Epicurus, would say: "When you are in the
crowd, and especially then, turn inward!"

It didn't seem much there and then, but this was a step comparable to the discovery that cosmic space has no limits. My
precocious monkey had, like me, reached adulthood and was
confronting my very own problems. Like a generous father, I
tried to help it by making it the gift of a space within, an inner
room where it could seek refuge from the pressures of the outside world. Naturally I was to some extent thinking of my own
needs. I imagined that solitude was what humans needed, and
I ended up making them all more pensive about life. Janus, as
it happened, proved to be one of my best self-portraits.

Nobody missed the feast for Seneca's death. Even his enemies had come and were received with cold politeness. Without them the show would not have been complete, for they
were counted on to tell Nero everything about the evening.

I immediately became aware of the spectacular character of
the event. The philosopher was offering his last performance,
and the hall was packed. The villa was stupendous, decorated
with all sorts of refined, elegant furniture and accoutrements:
Greek and Etruscan vases, murals painted by Oriental artisans,
pelts of African animals thrown over inlaid floors. Everywhere
you saw beds and lounges, and male and female slaves bustled
about. Not even in that most serious moment did the host forget his nature. The entire dwelling had been conceived of as a
multifarious, glittering space without recesses or dark corners.
Outside spread a garden of the kind favored by the Romans,
with geometric paths lined with bushes and a few plants. Everything was open on all sides, as though all the world's pros-
pects were endless and clear.

When I arrived the festivities were in full swing, and Seneca was conversing with a group of disciples, surrounded by the imperial emissaries, who did not miss a word of what was said. When he saw me appear, I was wearing the body and garments of a student of philosophy from Cordova, a follower of the Stoics. He was not deceived by my appearance, even though he pretended not to see me. For quite a while he had been thinking of me, and he knew that I never failed to be present at important moments. As I fixed my eyes on him, I saw him pale and almost falter; and the hundred lines in his face became a thousand, like a poisonous flower.

"What is happening to him?" somebody at my side whispered.

"He has just lain with a Numidian slave boy and before that with his daily virgin," another voice replied. "Don't you see that he is old!"

Ah yes, Seneca looked old as he pretended that he didn't see me. He declared to the assembled guests that he didn't mind dying because the wise man lives as though he has been given on loan to himself and is prepared to return himself without regret to the creditor who demands it.

"Do you want to know?" he asked all around, "do you want to know why men are so greedy of their future? Because they do not possess themselves." His eyes closed as he grappled with this thought. "You must search for something that will not decay with time and never be consumed."

I too, the student of philosophy, did not miss a syllable of his speech. Later on I would hear bankers and vendors of precious stones use the same words. For Seneca the wise man's virtue was like a bank account, a treasure in a safe.

I realized that my efforts to influence him had been at once a triumph and a failure. I had accustomed him to the idea of the soul, I had taught him the meaning of solitude to make it easier for him to recognize the new space I had created—and he had changed it for his convenience into a defensive fortress. For him the soul was like an impregnable citadel, protected by a thousand devices.

I spoke out, but almost as though to myself.

"Why do you condemn the future, my learned master? Surely the future is never still; it is the present after it has grown. You think, and here I agree, that life is a sickness; but you escape this malady by withdrawing into solitude as into a marble temple, shutting life outside. Seneca, you actually speak of an animal that dives into a hole—to escape what, if not life itself? Master, are you seeking death?"

I stopped abruptly when I remembered that I had come to witness a public suicide. Nero's dignitaries exchanged glances, already savoring the stories they would tell their lord about this challenge to the emperor's old tutor by an anonymous student, and the faux pas he had committed in speaking to Seneca about the will to die—after he had been ordered to do himself in!

I mumbled, no longer knowing what I was saying:

"I'm trying to make you the master of your soul, Seneca, before it masters you and leads you astray. You are the master, not your soul."

Fortunately I fell silent, because the atmosphere of the party had suddenly changed. Perhaps it was the wine, perhaps the drugs, perhaps all the lovemaking that filled the philosopher's house—the fact is that suddenly there spread through those present a sense of fathomless anguish. The dignitaries wrapped in their embroidered togas knelt on the ground, clutching their heads in a grief that was sincere and not just declaimed. The musicians struck up a funeral dirge, and the cupbearers began to beat their breasts, signaling the arrival of the fatal moment.

"It is time to die," Seneca proclaimed in a loud voice.

At that, the guests clustered in a circle around the philosopher, still holding their cups and, where possible, their women and slaves. I sat down in a corner, a spectator among others, unable to intervene.

It was dark now, and Seneca remained standing in the center of the room. The chant of the Greek singers, hired from a company in Rome to perform Sophocles' trilogy, faded away. A servant brought a torch in a vase, and the philosopher was illuminated from behind so that he appeared to us like a faceless phantom, a black shadow with a flame at his back. Silence fell upon the house.

"Do you remember Plato?" the old man exclaimed. A shudder of expectation ran through the guests. "Do you remember," Seneca continued, "the tale of the cave? I want to tell it to you again because I want you to know what I feel as I am about to leave you. I am the prisoner in that cave; behind me there is a fire and before me I see shadows against the wall of the cave. Man can only watch the shadows of reality; and these shadows are the things that surround me, the trees, the sky, the houses, the animals; and you too, friends and foes here gathered, are shadows among shadows. Behind me stands the truth of the eternal and incorruptible world, the house inhabited by God: the world of Ideas! I am about to go there, and there I shall no longer need a fortress in which to withdraw, because at every moment I will be free and protected. I leave this banquet, I loosen the chains that bind me; like a satiated guest who leaves the table after a supper with his friends, thus I abandon life. Hail and farewell!"

At that point there appeared a knife that Seneca had kept hidden under his toga. Everyone had been wondering what death he had chosen: to cut his veins, or drink poison, or slip his neck into a noose and let it be drawn tight by a muscular slave? The sight of his blade spread uncertainty. It was too long and thick to sever the veins. For an instant everyone thought that the knife was part of the performance, perhaps to symbolize the dying man cutting his bonds with life. But Seneca lowered the blade to his abdomen and immediately his robe was red with blood. The old man briefly struck a statuesque pose, then slipped to the floor amid the folds of his toga.

All around me erupted a clamor worthy of a sports arena.

"Did you see him stab himself? Nero certainly didn't expect him to do that."

"Why didn't he swallow that new poison from Macedonia that turns you the color of a snake?"

"I would have preferred the noose; I had already picked the slave."

I went out into the garden and stayed there, contemplating the stars, repeating to myself that the world of Ideas did not exist and that the learned master had died a pointless death. I heard the crowd leave, as when the match is over.

When I went back into the hall I saw that Seneca hadn't yet managed to die. In the hall, which had grown darker—the enormous torches had begun to flicker out—only close friends were still present. The small group of faithful watched the philosopher crawl about the house holding his guts in his hands, leaving tracks of blackish blood. The pallor of his face surpassed all whiteness. From his lips came a strident sob, and his eyes brimmed with tears. I understood that he was looking for me, and I went to stand at his side, silently.

"Why am I not dying?" Seneca whispered. "You who know, tell me why I can't die."

"Perhaps you are afraid," I said, not certain that I was right. Seneca looked at me aghast, and at that moment his shoulder was struck by the first of the knife thrusts that his friends were to inflict on him to help him die. He did not seem to notice and continued to stare at me.

"Perhaps it is true," he finally replied, "perhaps it is true that I am afraid. But why? All my life I have prepared myself for this moment and now I am unable to cross the threshold. I cannot rise from the table! So I am not as satiated as I thought. There is something that I have forgotten to accomplish, and I can't bear the thought of dying. Do you know what it is—do you know what it is that I forgot?"

The scene was extraordinary. Seneca sat on the floor and friends and slaves struck him again and again with knives that opened holes in his flesh, from which oozed a kind of bloody foam. I stood and bowed before the master, in my Iberian student's disguise; only Seneca had recognized me. His last words were uttered in the dialect of Cordova, where he had been born.

"Papa, Mama," he spluttered, his eyes rolling back, sinking into himself as into a den. Then he fell down onto his entrails and his soul escaped from a hundred wounds, fluttering through the room like a bird before slipping through the window and disappearing into the garden, beyond the trees. I have not seen it since.

Still the young student from Cordova, I left Rome and took refuge in my native land to meditate on what I had seen. But remembrance soon became burdensome. I occupied myself cultivating vineyards, forgetting Seneca and my philosophical youth, forgetting everything until my own divinity collapsed into oblivion. I awakened and fell asleep again in different and far-distant countries.

After a time I realized again that I was God. I found that I had become everyone's obsession, and the most harebrained plans were being attributed to me. I heard the evangelists and the men of the Church announce my arrival and the establishment of the Kingdom in apocalyptic tones, with a great sideshow of bizarre animals, dragons and serpents, bloodthirsty angels, rivers erupting from the sky, and chasms gaping wide in the earth to swallow the reprobates. "Just listen to this nonsense," I grumbled, traveling from one place to another.

I went this way and that. I took possession of the soul of a Roman bureaucrat, forlorn in a village in Gaul, and just as easily kept company with a follower of a Zoroastrian sect in Babylon. I exploded from the mouth of a freed slave in the truck gardens of Syracuse and flashed through the ecstasies of Christian martyrs. I was an early summer storm in humankind's history.

Wild rumors kept spreading about me. I was astonished to learn how many people swore they had known me personally or through those connected with me. A certain Simon Magus, a contemporary of the apostles and born in Samaria, claimed to have been sent directly by me to punish humankind if they did not believe his version of my story. He professed that I was some kind of lone wolf, a very contemplative fellow, and from all my self-absorbed activities finally sprang a thought that took the form of a woman named Epinoia, who initiated a series of creations, beginning with the angels and going all the way down to the earth and humans, but from the start everything has been deteriorating, and so it will until the moment when the world returns to me, who all this time have remained silent in the skies and never made a move. In short, the best course of action in his view was apparently to relinquish life. It was quite an ingenious story, as were others of the time, but it was totally false and not even of his own making.

Simon Magus knew a thousand tricks that he claimed he had learned from me. At Tyre and Phoenicia he happened to meet a woman he fell in love with. He carried her everywhere, introducing her as the reincarnation of that famous Epinoia.

He continued with his tricks, until on one occasion, at the imperial court of Rome, being anxious to obtain a large reward, he improvised an attempt at flight that came to a sad conclusion. He crashed to pieces on the ground without ever having spoken to me in his entire life, notwithstanding his noisy claims.

He was one of many, despite the fact that his name has survived and others have dropped into oblivion. Some of them built imaginary universes in which I passed through confused metamorphoses. For instance, the idea that the world had actually been created by a bad counterpart of myself received a lot of credence at the time. Some went so far as to maintain that I was two beings, one of which lived above, while the other set out to fabricate the world, seeking neither advice nor consent from me. Others said that all this mess was caused by certain angels swept up in a creative frenzy. The memory of the Christ played a large part in all these fabrications, but legends varied in his case too.

At night I would dream about angels and about an inferior and corrupt god, busy concocting malevolent schemes, while the poor Father, confined to his armchair in some bedroom, watches them through the window. In reality there were neither angels nor pairs of gods. There was only myself, capable of so many mistakes, something that I found hard to get across to humankind. Among all animals, humans were indispensable to me. Without them it would be an impossible effort to understand who I was and what I wanted. My only genius consisted in having created someone who might understand and describe me. Humans seemed to have convinced themselves that I had endowed them with faculties that I in turn possessed to a supreme degree—but I was waiting for them to become clever enough to explain to me who I was and why I was carrying on in such an unseemly manner. I did not receive the help I needed, and so I floundered, forced to incarnate myself in order to become visible to myself and others. Through the human mind I formulated extravagant hypotheses about myself, like a horse that dreams of flying and sees itself changed into Pegasus.

I was thinking about all this in an inn where I happened to

be sitting, surrounded by a clatter of dishes and a storm of curses. For the moment I was a mail courier, whom I had visited while he changed horses in a remote village in Scotland. I was dismayed by those curses and felt them as a personal and direct insult, as if everyone there knew that God himself had come into that smoke-filled room; and in fact I was there, sitting among them and listening to all that Babel-like confusion. Why were they cursing God with such animosity? I couldn't answer that, and tears filled my eyes. But the horses were ready now, and I rode off into the sleet, barely able to protect my bundle of letters. Twenty miles later the courier had dropped his anguished reflections and thought of nothing more than reaching his destination before nightfall. I let him go and set off again on my own.

I STILL carried with me from my youth a sustaining trust in my creation. It is impossible, I repeated to myself, that all of this turmoil has amounted to nothing. There must be a reason for the world to have come into being. Nourished by this hope, I endured all the sorrows that my vast, imperfect creation flung at me: hunger, sickness, the violence that raged beneath the frozen gaze of the stars. "Carry on," I exhorted myself. "Carry on while your energy lasts."

If I knew that I could not count on a vigorous adulthood forever, neither could I depend on remembering my divinity from one moment to the next. I tended still to become oblivious to myself, unwittingly assuming one incarnation after another. I would recall myself at unexpected moments and in unexpected guises, as when I found myself in a city called Murcia, on the Spanish coast of the Mediterranean, at a lecture by a leader of the Manichean sect.

I happened to be passing the lecture by chance. I was a ten-year-old girl working as a servant in a Carthaginian brothel. I had been sent to buy some flowers, and I stood there motionless, hugging a great bouquet, spellbound by the scintillating eloquence of the speaker. I did not understand much of what he said, but I was captivated by the images he employed to describe the primordial forces active in the world. There appeared before my eyes a spot of resplendent brightness, and in front of this spot a vortex of darkness opened: these were Good and Evil, which, I heard, have forever existed, each in its own territory, the Kingdom of Light and the Kingdom of Darkness. Then the Kingdom of Darkness decided to invade the luminous territory, and the conflict between Good and Evil began. The creation of the world was the battle of Darkness against Light immobile in its splendor; and the speaker described the phases of the immemorial struggle, with its warriors and other protagonists. Of all the names, I memorized only that of the Black Prince who commanded the armies of evil: Ahriman! The name of Good has disappeared from my memory.

I returned home, my head full of turmoil. After placing the flowers in the entrance hall, I climbed up to my room. On one of the beds lay the oldest prostitute, who mothered me and taught me the rudiments of the profession that I was soon to enter. We both came from the same village in the desert, and the life we had known as children was very similar. In my village a woman would be violated several times before being assigned to a husband as his housekeeper. The moment of the wedding was like the beginning of death.

Every so often a liberating angel descended into the village, and in my case it was this woman, who had returned for her father's funeral and had stayed not more than a few hours. She saw me in the street as I looked into a puddle of water, and I must have awakened some memory in her because, without hesitating, she approached me, took me by the hand, and led me away into the world of Carthaginian prostitutes all the little girls in the desert dreamed about.

Bursting as I was with revelations, I watched her sleep until—I don't know whether I too was sleeping or still awake—I had the impression that I could see everything. My short, poor life appeared before me like a spectacle worthy of being played out on a majestic plaza. I left my room and wandered around the house. Through the half-open door of one of the rooms, I saw two bodies on a bed engaged in the slow writhings that took place every day between the women who lived there and the men who came to visit them; and the man lying on top of the woman seemed to me as ferocious as the Prince of Darkness, while the woman seemed to me overcome and defenseless

like the territory of wounded light. Below in the entrance room
I glanced at the flowers I had bought, already arranged in vases
by expert hands. Back to mind came something the orator had
said concerning the world of plants, innocent creatures out-
raged by rapacious animals and above all by man, who, not
satisfied with trampling the grass underfoot, would tear off the
flowers with his hands, guided by Ahriman, the universal executioner.

As the sun rose, I went into the street and found myself at
the fish market where the morning's catch was being cut up,
and the stench made me sick right there, in a corner of the
market. As I tottered down a blind alley, trying to find the way
home, a dog came up to me as though it wanted to speak. Its
eyes were shining and full of affection, almost as if it knew me
and wanted to guide me, but when I stretched out my hand,
its maw opened with a snarl, its teeth reaching to grip my fingers; and as if in a nightmare I saw its body tremble and shake
beneath its white and black pelt. In the dog's very body I recognized the battle between the princes of good and evil, and with
a cry I cursed the darkness that invades light.

I got back to the house, ran to my room, and flung myself
into the arms of my sleeping protector. Against me I felt the
breast that was my bulwark against life. I wished that we could
both fly beyond the arena of light and darkness before the battle started in earnest, before I met up with the horseman of my
destiny. In that instant I thought I saw him coming for me, and
with a scream I fell to the ground, unconscious. For many days
they treated the fever that had stricken me, and little by little
I regained my senses, ready to become a whore and forget everything, just to survive, as darkness does, only wanting to endure, while light yearns to return to its fixed and eternal abode.

I forgot what I had learned and avoided the squares where
orators addressed the crowd. I shut myself away in the house
surrounded by the flowers and the attentions of my adoptive
mother. I forgot having remembered myself. The soul of the
young girl went its way without me, and I was cast outside
again, into the streets of Murcia.

In the darkest and most defenseless part of me—the part
that became frightened at night in dark places—in that part

remained a fear that the Manicheans might be right. It was a
fear that verged on certainty. Back to mind came the ancient
fables I had dismissed with a shrug, fables that told of an adversary of God who thinks only of damaging him and doing harm
to mankind by adopting a thousand disguises and every sort
of deceit: spirits, malign dwarfs, elves, kobolds, sneering satyrs,
and then Satan, Satan in person who seeks out Job and is
driven away by God with an irate gesture.

These are all fables, I repeated to myself. I've given humanity
too much imagination. But the idea that creation itself—and
not only the defects of individual creatures—might be the work
of forces of evil, this idea devastated me, for it seemed a frightful hypothesis about myself and the world. I could not brush
it aside with much assurance. I had to face the possibility
squarely—and so I spent whole centuries rushing from one
philosophy course to another, from one explanation of what
had happened to the next. People would see me go past, panting, out of breath, in pursuit of myself, like an eagle chasing
its own shadow.

During one of these excursions I landed in Egypt as a Roman
dignitary on a diplomatic mission; and, not knowing how to
spend a melancholy and solitary evening, I went to look up a
young man named Epiphanius, a Christian at the start of his
ecclesiastical career. The town was new to me, and I hoped that
he would take me to see something interesting. I also wanted to
talk to him about my problems and let off some steam. I
wanted to confide in somebody that my sudden memory of divinity was conflicting with my high social position and that I
was meditating on how to solve this unforeseen predicament.
As it happened, I did not have a chance to discuss this, because
things took an unexpected turn.

Epiphanius seemed nervous and didn't pay much attention
to me. We ate a frugal vegetarian meal that made me regret
having suggested our outing. My regret was compounded by
the stifling humidity, and I asked myself how Epiphanius could
wear so much clothing. I would come to realize that both food
and clothes were part of a façade for the benefit of his relatives
and servants. After dinner he asked me to go with him to attend
an unusual event, and it was thus that I participated in a gath-

ering of the Ebionites, a sect whose fame had not yet reached Rome. I went gladly, in the hope of improving an evening that had become tedious.

We reached a house just outside the city, isolated and surrounded by tall trees. Epiphanius knocked and the door was opened by a middle-aged man who let us in, looking at us in silence. We stood there for a good minute as if we were waiting for someone. A woman came and approached Epiphanius, offering him her hands, which he held in his for some time, staring into her eyes. They must have exchanged some sort of signal because suddenly a smile appeared on her face and on the face of the man who had opened the door to us. The three of them embraced and Epiphanius was taken to another door that led to the inner part of the house. They seemed to have forgotten all about me, and I followed them.

I slid along in their wake and entered a large hall full of people and tables set for a meal. We were immediately served meats, vegetables, and wine in an abundance that amply compensated for the frugality of our earlier meal. I was not sitting with Epiphanius, but I could hear his voice rise in ever more intoxicated, disconnected philosophical pronouncements. I decided to concentrate on the people sitting near me, three men and as many women, and I learned that they were married couples. On meeting I had held out my hand to each of them, and the women clasped it tightly for some time, staring at me and tickling my palm. The conversation was anything but interesting; the men talked about horses and the women about problems with servants, subjects on which I had nothing to say.

I made an effort to listen to other groups. At the table nearby there was an animated conversation about the political situation in Byzantium and the eastern Mediterranean. From the tone of his voice I recognized some visiting diplomat who seemed to be Syrian. His wife kept her eyes fastened on Epiphanius' table, where students and some young professors, with their wives and fiancées, had gathered. An uninterrupted chatter came from that side, and the jugs of wine passed around with greater speed than at any other table. The diplomat's wife seemed especially attentive to the movement of the bodies beneath their robes. Epiphanius, for his part, had taken off almost all his clothes and sat there in his undergarments. I kept trying to catch what they were saying.

I picked up bits of argument about the nature of sin, mixed with debates on beef stew and the metaphysical significance of menstruation. The diplomat's wife had apparently been listening in as well, because at that point she stood up among shouts of approval, lifted her skirt, and produced a rag soaked in blood. With glittering eyes she pirouetted, displaying it to the entire room. This was the signal everyone had been waiting for. A gust of madness ran through the hall as if a northwest wind had crashed through the windows and thrown tables and chairs to the floor.

In an instant all the furniture was pushed aside, and the guests were seized by convulsive excitement. The couples split up in search of new partners. Soon the floor swarmed with bodies. I saw Epiphanius bend over the diplomat's wife with an expression that was, to say the least, famished; but before he made love to her he plunged his hands between her legs, pulled them out bloody, and held them aloft, as priests do when they elevate the chalice. I had seen almost everything, but this was a spectacle that shocked even me. I stood frozen in a corner, filled with nausea by the gamy odor that had filled the room. I had eaten and drunk too much, unaware that the food was a prelude to this perverse Mass; and when a woman came toward me I disappeared, leaving her stupefied and gawking at the empty corner where I had stood.

But the meeting was not over, and further surprises were in store for me. After fornicating, the lovers gathered semen in their hands and raised their palms high, crying: "This is the body of Christ!" Others whose hands were dripping with menstrual blood shouted: "This is the blood of Christ!" I realized with a shudder that they were speaking to God and doing something they thought I would appreciate. I kept to myself, sulking above the mob of bodies, and it seemed to me that I was contemplating a pit full of snakes. I believe it was then that the idea flashed through my head that hell must resemble such a scene, and I immediately tried to suppress the thought. Too late! It had already spread through the air and taken hold.

Then came the climactic scene. A girl was led to the center of the hall and the guests clustered in a circle around her. Two men advanced; one seized her by the arms and held her still, the other spread her legs. From the crowd came an old woman with adept hands, and in less time than it takes to tell, she had groped in the girl's womb and extracted a blob of bleeding viscid flesh: a fetus. While the girl was being consoled and embraced by her torturers, the woman delivered the fetus to other hands, which placed it into a mortar and pounded and mixed it with herbs and oils; everyone, including my young friend Epiphanius, partook of it. Then they all knelt to pray. Not feeling too well, I left my observation post and escaped to the garden.

I sat down beneath a palm tree and spent some time there, planning visits to more reasonable lands. Then I saw Epiphanius come out, dressed as he had been at his arrival, and with the furtive air of a conspirator. I attached myself to him and we set off for home. He felt me close at his side but, seemingly ashamed, did not look at me. He walked quickly, his head bowed, and answered my questions unwillingly. In dribs and drabs I got him to explain to me that in those feasts the Ebionites represented sin in order to combat it better, and that the best way to defeat it was to refuse life as the last ultimate abode of sin. And so they ate the fetuses of the faithful to facilitate the soul's return to the common Father, who was supposed to be me.

I listened, almost beside myself, to this new invention. It gave me a sour pleasure to realize that Epiphanius, despite the air of self-assurance he had displayed throughout the night, had come from the feast devastated. When he got home he went to look at his mother and I saw tears on his face. He retired to his room and tore his clothes and hair, rolled on the floor, implored my forgiveness, swore to do penance, and denounced the guests at that perfidious Mass; as if all this would make any difference. I left him foaming at the mouth about his sins.

The next day I resumed my duties as if not much had happened. A Roman ambassador cannot be distracted for long by such a spectacle, and not even by God's presence in his soul.

I NEEDED a brilliant mind. Everywhere it was said that Augustine was such a mind, and that was enough to fascinate me, even though I did not quite believe it. People were too often mistaken. All my doubts disappeared, however, when through a window I entered Augustine's study and found him sitting stylus in hand, gazing past me. He did not see me pass, but somehow he had become aware of my presence, because he immediately began to write. I saw the astrolabe near the window and the open books scattered on the floor and on the dais that supported the desk. I saw a statue at the end of the room, at Augustine's back, and a platform covered with green cloth where I in turn sat down to peer at the pages he was writing.

My first idea had been to appear to Augustine in his dreams, though not in the bearded-old-man guise that a number of painters had saddled me with. I had learned that his greatest affection was lavished on his mother, Monica. So I decided to reach him by creating a dream in her. In her dream Monica stood upright on a small board, consumed by sadness, as I came to meet her. I asked her the reason for so much melancholy, and she replied that she feared for Augustine's soul. I told her to take heart and to notice that we were both standing together on the same slim board, that God was beside her. Here Monica's dream ended, and she rushed to tell it to her son, giving rise to inexhaustible rumination from that master of dialecticians. "What does this mean?" he inquired, "that where he is you are too, or that where you are he is too?" The mother fell silent, disoriented, and dropped the subject.

I tried other methods. When a dear friend of his died, I hastened to Augustine's side to console him. He spoke to me uninterruptedly, but without recognizing me. As we walked along, he told me that he was searching for me within himself and that some day he would find me in his innermost soul, through which he wandered like a visitor in a deserted castle. Without me this abode seemed to him empty and sad, and he roamed through its rooms racked with pain. He wrote books about aesthetics in which he maintained that the principle of beauty is the rule of unity, and this too was part of his effort to find and recognize me. Little did he realize that I am too easily distracted to qualify as unitary. Indeed, during this period I was busy with a great many projects, but I never forgot to come back to my chosen pupil.

I followed Augustine everywhere. He had left Carthage and gone to Rome, moving ever closer to orthodox Christian faith. Being the heretic that I am, I wanted more and more to entangle him in metaphysical doubts. I wanted to fix his attention on the universe I had created, which appeared to me so full of pain, despite all its beauty. I tormented him with the question "Where does Evil come from?" and I urged him to look dispassionately at the world.

One afternoon we were on the beach at Ostia. Augustine had met with Monica and together they were walking on the sand. I kept buzzing around him invisibly and whispered into his ear: "Just look, Augustine, look at the sea, look at the land: they are splendid but also troubled. Look at your mother, Augustine. You know that she drinks and that her drunkenness is a scandal; don't close your eyes to what is happening." I knew that Augustine's beloved mother, whom he considered perfect, drank on the sly among the servants, who pretended not to see but gossiped about it with relish. Augustine cut me short, declaring that his mother had gotten drunk only once, inadvertently. He was determined to see no evil in her.

I carried him to stormy seas, to forests filled with wild beasts, among men who administered justice and led armies on the battlefields. I made him listen to the cries of the wounded, I showed him the blood and carnage. I forced him to watch the death of famished children, who, if they had survived, would only have been sent to work in fields and mines, becoming crippled old men by the age of twenty. I wanted him to explain to me where all this came from and who might be responsible for it. I wanted him to look me in the face and acknowledge the limitations of my foresight and all my mistaken calculations. People who suppose that I never participated in the creation, who attribute it to a minor and ambitious god, are wrong. "I am all this, Augustine! If you don't understand, who ever will?"

Once I saw him shaken, his features gnarled by fear. He flung himself to his knees and prayed tearfully until, on his feet again, he screamed into my face, "Leave me, Satan!" Imagine saying such a thing to me! But I persisted. One Sunday in Milan I dressed up as a drunken beggar and displayed my anguish on the street, walking in front of him as he passed by with learned friends of the entourage of Bishop Ambrose, his confidant and protector. I wanted to make him understand how I often felt and that creation was badly in need of compassion and sobriety. He looked at me and discussed with his friends my state of misery and the poverty of the human condition without divine sustenance, and then passed me by. I tried again. I saw him doubtful and afflicted, and I urged him to open the New Testament so that he could draw inspiration from the first sentence that fell under his eyes, and give a new direction to his thoughts. I imitated to perfection the voice of a child in a house nearby and repeated several times in a chant: "Take this and read, take this and read!"

He went to the holy book and opened it. I stood beside him and tried to direct him to the page I wanted. I was thinking of a passage in St. Paul that describes suffering nature invoking assistance, but despite all my efforts I was unable to guide him to those lines. He seemed to resist, almost as though he were deflected by an impulse, and instead he chose another of Paul's sentences, where he advises men to shun debauchery and gluttony. At this, Augustine became very excited and ran to tell a friend of his discovery, leaving me to leaf vainly through the pages of the book.

I made one last attempt by sinking into nature and assumed the guise of a humble and repugnant spider weaving its web in a corner of the study. I had captured a fly and was moving toward it, and at that instant Augustine saw me. He stopped to observe the scene with great attention. Then he turned abruptly and dashed to his desk to jot down his thoughts. Later on I read what he had written by climbing up to the pages of the book, still open at that sentence. From those lines his voice reached me as though I were listening to him talk to me: "And what shall we say of the interest and attention that I experience when I sit in my house, and a tarantula hunts flies and a spider wraps in its web those that blunder into it? Then I rise to praise you, admirable creator and ordainer of all things; and life is replete with such casualties; the only hope is the immensity of your compassion . . . "

I slithered down from his desk and returned to my web, and the meal of a butterfly that I had caught only partially consoled me.

I must meet Augustine within the walls of his inner abode, I told myself. We made an appointment in the halls of his memory, and I arrived ahead of time in order to examine them at my ease. Since remembering has always been a weak point with me, I entered Augustine's memory with due respect and reverence. It was a spacious dwelling, and everything could be found in there. I was impressed by the number of books I saw—not only Christian books but also a great number of pagan volumes by the Latin poets and the philosophers whom Augustine so loved. They were set next to each other, prefiguring what was to happen centuries later in the courts of the Renaissance. Like a scholar in a library, I moved among the stacks of Augustine's memory, leafing through a book here and there, scrupulously putting it back in place, because I did not want to open any gaps in that prodigious habitation. I ventured into the recesses of the brain, where the sensations that helped humankind recognize external experiences were stored: the memory of light and of colors, the shapes of bodies, the variations of sounds, smells, and flavors, the distinctions between hard and soft, hot and cold, smooth and rough, heavy and light, inside and out. I roamed in ecstasy through the human mind.

I found Augustine standing by the window of his inner house, contemplating a boundless landscape composed of landscapes he had seen in the past. Here inside himself Augustine finally recognized me and embraced me. He took me by the hand and led me through the halls of his memory.

"Go ahead, look," he exclaimed, leading me into even the most secluded corners, "look at everything contained here, not only the sky and the earth and all I have already seen, but also my hopes for the future. In that niche are the images of events that I imagine could happen to me. Every time that I return here I feel the need to meet you. In that edifice there are my most complicated memories: dialectics, rhetoric, mathematics. How great is your divinity in having created such things!"

"I am happy that it pleases you, Augustine," I replied, trying to keep up with him through one room after another, "but I must talk to you."

"Wait," Augustine interrupted me as he fluttered to and fro, "answer me first. From where and by which paths did these ideas enter my memory? Perhaps they were here before I knew them, as Plato argued. But if so, how could I recognize them if they were not already present? Just look here in the cellar; there are even memories of when I remembered! And here are memories of when I forgot! Memory is like the belly of the mind, and memories are its food. This is what you have done, my creator, in the house of my memory!"

"Augustine," I kept saying, almost out of breath at that point, "Augustine, there is something I have to tell you."

"Just listen," he kept saying, pulling me in another direction, "I can say *rock* without seeing the rock and I can say *sun* without seeing the sun, because the image is in here." As he said this, he showed me his image of the sun, which I could look at directly because it was like the sun in a painting, whereas the rock lay motionless on the ground exactly like a rock. "And now that I am well I think back on when I was ill and I remember exactly how it was. Isn't this extraordinary! Just as when I am ill I remember health! But tell me, how can I keep the memory of forgetfulness if, by definition, forgetfulness cancels memory? Help me understand this!"

Had I had any breath left I would have explained to him that he was constructing a sophism and that to remember having forgotten is not the same thing as to forget. But I was exhausted, and Augustine continued to race through the innumerable dens of his memory. Images of Monica pouring milk from a pitcher, of his friend Alipio praying before an altar, of a garden studded with pear trees, of an ocean bathed in the light of the rising sun—all appeared before my eyes like fragments of a dream. "Stop, Augustine," I stuttered. "It's impossible for me to talk to you."

Augustine, in fact, stopped abruptly in one of the rooms of his memory. He had reached a half-dark space, with huge windows and beyond them a motionless landscape painted on the walls. I was beside him, panting, and waited to regain my breath before talking to him. But he, strangely composed and unaffected, only stared at the painted windows. Then he spoke to me again.

"This," he said, "this is the room where I collect the results of all this rushing about inside me. You and I should have decided to meet here. This is where I come to ask myself where the desire for you and the memory of the happiness that you can give originates. And do you know what conclusion I draw from this? That this memory could not exist if the happiness had not been there before. Therefore, I already knew you! There was a time when we were happy together, otherwise the possibility of it would not be preserved here in my favorite room. I come here every day to search for you; and I am happy that today you are with me."

Augustine had fallen into an ecstasy that did not really concern me. He looked at the painted wall and had the same expression he had had when contemplating the sea, clutching Monica's hand. I felt excluded. I knew he would not hear me, but I began to speak all the same, surprised at the timidity in my voice.

"I'm not here, Augustine. I'm everywhere, but not immobile as you see me. I was within your rushing and anxiety that led you from room to room, from corridor to corridor. When you think that you have caught up with me, you can no longer see me. You confuse reality with desire. It would be best not to do this, Augustine, and to accept desire for what it is, because desire is sacred and I too am filled with it; I myself have bestowed it on you. But do not take it for something that must exist at all costs, otherwise you will lose me. For example: that landscape is painted and you don't realize it. Let me show you."

I reached to take Augustine by the hand and lead him to the windows, but he had knelt to pray. His voice rose to the ceiling decorated with beams. I withdrew silently to a corner of the room and his voice echoed toward me.

"You were within me and I was outside. In my deformity I threw myself upon the beautiful things that you created. You were with me but I was not with you, kept away by your very own creatures. You have bedazzled my sight with your splendor and you have vanquished my blindness. You have exhaled your perfume and now I yearn for you. I have tasted you and now I am hungry and thirsty. You have touched my hand with your hand and now I burn with desire. Do not leave me: I cannot lose you again!"

But I was already on my way. I left the room and set off through corridors of the house, and it proved to be quite difficult to find an exit. I went past the books, the cupboards crammed with sheets of paper, and the chests overflowing with clothing and objects. I crossed the gardens of memory and found myself under Augustine's sky, brightened by a sun that I did not know. Finally I emerged from his memory and his soul and was again in the familiar world full of imperfect desires. Farewell, Augustine, I thought with regret.

I saw him for the last time when he was consecrated bishop at Hippo. I could not resist the temptation to attend, because I loved him in spite of everything and was proud of his excellence and his success in the world. It was a splendid day. The embellished church presented a majestic spectacle, the square before the building was packed with devoted people, and the sound of bells filled the air, as on a day blessed by God. The lips of the spectators moved in prayer, and sweet tears ran down the cheeks of women. And then I saw that they were searching for me and that I was present even though I did nothing to show myself. When Augustine appeared I felt held in the embrace of all those who without seeing me called out to me.

I too looked at him. He was dressed in a glittering robe, sitting bolt upright in a cart drawn by purebred horses, surrounded by courtiers and dignitaries decked out in all the insignia of power. Among the many thoughts that had escaped me was one of great importance: I had not considered the effect of such a vision upon a great and ambitious soul. It did not surprise me that Augustine wanted me to be fixed and immobile, the perfect insignia of power, since he himself admired power so much.

That's the explanation, I thought. They want me omnipotent

because they would like to be that way themselves. I made my way out of the crowd, tacitly wishing him good luck.

I thought it wise to hide from my believers for a while. I cultivated an ideal of utter simplicity, taking refuge inside a shepherd, a peasant, a humble artisan, a fisherman of the calmest seas. Sometimes I returned to the animals, but I discovered I could no longer be happy there. My soul had progressed too far, and from within a deer or a falcon I missed humankind; being a hurricane or a summer sunset satisfied me only so long.

Sooner or later I had to return to my most precocious creation. As I listened to their talk, I finally noticed that their imagination was haunted less by me than by a figure I knew nothing about. They called him the devil, and he had become an awesome and disquieting reality to them. Among all the eerie figments that mankind had created without my help, this appeared to be one of the most provocative. The Virgin Mother, the saints and the blessed ones who swarmed in the imagination, the angels who patrolled the skies, ready to execute my orders; none of these could be compared to the invention of the devil. I ignored him for a while but in the end I decided to confront him. I set out in search of Satan.

I began the hunt with determination. It was not easy for me to find him, because I considered him an impostor; the incredulous don't easily find what they are looking for. I went to places the devil was reputed to inhabit. I scorched myself on the rims of volcanoes. I almost contracted pneumonia waiting for an entire night surrounded by the lightning and wind and torrential rain of a storm that was, to say the least, infernal. But Satan was nowhere to be seen. I plunged into the midst of an earthquake he was supposed to have set loose, hoping to see him jump from the crevices of the wounded earth. Nothing.

I began to frequent forlorn and abandoned places, the ridges of mountains, dark forests, caves, chasms, and moors. I waited so long and with such anxiety that once I thought I saw him after two weeks in the Sahara, beneath the perpendicular sun of high noon. A vague form loomed on the horizon, like a moving cloud, and it approached with dizzying speed. During its brief and intense trajectory the cloud took on contrasting shapes; it became a bull, a snake, a bird with a lion's body, a flame-spewing dragon, a fish with horns. These metamorphoses concluded two feet from me, where a small desert toad squirmed and then vanished underground.

"You're not a very convincing devil," I grumbled. "There are no toads in the sand." I was so taken up with my aggravation that I skirted an oasis without noticing it and soon was dying of thirst.

I went into gold mines he was said to frequent in order to rekindle his accursed hunger, and I found that prospectors are very dull people, obsessed with only one idea. Since it was commonly believed that the devil was a great craftsman and engineer, I stationed myself in the vicinity of certain bridges and aqueducts that were supposedly built by him: again to no avail. In a desecrated church I was sure I saw him go by in the shadows in the nave. I rushed at him, grabbed him, we rolled about on the floor, and I suddenly realized that I was clutching in my arms a poor homeless fellow who was seeking shelter for the night. I let him go, and I myself went to an inn to sleep.

Everything led me to believe that the devil was the fruit of an overactive human imagination. But I also knew that when there's talk about something, it means that something does exist, and it becomes a matter of looking for it in the right place. Finally I gave in to the most obvious but distasteful strategy before me: I became an exorcist.

I set myself up as a carpenter in Westphalia, near Munster, and soon forgot I had been anything else. I spent much of my time caring for my twin sister, who was close to death from an illness incomprehensible to the doctors. Our apothecary had just left in a whirl of black capes after fiddling with a lot of useless instruments and potions. He had subjected her to a bloodletting but had stopped abruptly at the sight of the reddish water that seeped from her veins. We were old and had spent our lives together, like two faces of one and the same leaf. What was I going to do without her? I watched her breathe heavily. Her eyes were closed, and she was wrapped in her shawl. Then I shook myself and went to plane the table I had finished the day before. As the shavings flew, I realized that my face was wet with tears.

The son of the possessed man came to look for me, so I slipped into my coat and followed him as though in a trance. Exorcism had been my sideline for years, and this kind of call had become a routine, no different from undressing before bed or getting drunk on a Saturday evening. Meanwhile the man was explaining to me that he had already tried the priest but it had not helped. He said it was a sly and vicious devil who had taken over his father, a devil well versed in his trade as a prevaricator.

From the body of the possessed man emanated an odor that had almost made the poor priest faint. Still not satisfied, the nasty devil had begun to reel off his adversary's sins, and quite a varied list followed: thefts of the faithful's alms, drunken binges on consecrated wine, love affairs with the parishioners, one of whom, an eighty-year-old woman, had died in the sacristy some time before, and nobody had been able to figure out what had happened. The priest had fled, waving his sacred paraphernalia and followed by the howls that poured out of the possessed man's mouth. At that point they had decided to turn to me since I had a reputation of succeeding where the priests failed.

I was barely listening, caught up in my own thoughts. I had heard such stories a thousand times. I had never believed in the devil, and I was certain that every possessed person spoke for himself and said precisely what he thought, taking advantage of the fact that no one dared challenge the supposedly abominable presence in him. I had found that I possessed strange powers, and I used them with ease and almost indifference, in the way that a singer uses his voice or an acrobat his body. I performed my work with the nonchalance of an artist who exploits a natural talent. This is the secret of work well done. Of course there are tormented artists who are never satisfied with their talent and would like to achieve more than it permits. I asked myself whether God too belonged to the latter category, and I was surprised at the very thought.

"Enough now," I said aloud. My companion looked at me but said nothing.

Since my sister had fallen ill, unusual thoughts milled through my mind. I boasted of being a sensible person without caprices of any kind; and yet, for some time now, I had been visited by weird apparitions. At night I was plunged into long and painful dreams, intent on traveling along endless roads that at a certain point would come to a fork, and there my anguish was such that I would wake up moaning. A few times I thought I had seen a woman squatting on the stoop in front of the house, but an instant later she was gone. I had started to lose things, and this irritated me so much that in a kind of revenge I had caught myself fasting without being aware of it, while I watched my sister lying in her bed. The idea came to me that God was roaming about the streets of the quarter and was trying to reach me. Nothing quite so extravagant had ever occurred to me before.

We entered the house of the possessed man and were immediately surrounded by signs of opulence and high social rank. In the entrance hall maids and manservants jostled to get a glimpse of the exorcist. I passed through their midst and went up the stairs to the mezzanine, following the young master. I began to hear the howls that were familiar to me after so many years in the trade.

The room of the possessed man was packed with relatives and physicians. He rested on a broad seat, immobilized by a rope tied to a ring in the corner of the room. When I entered, he fell silent and watched me without a word. I heard his heavy breathing, which at this point was the only sound in the room, because everyone present had become quiet. I began to prepare the ritual: the incense, the book of magic formulas, the candles. I felt like one of those quack doctors I had seen come to my sister's house. I was the center of attention, and it seemed to me that even the personages portrayed in the paintings on the walls were staring at me.

I struggled against a mounting discomfort, and then another thought came to me. I began to think of God as the portrait of a man whose gaze follows anyone who looks at it, so that, if a hundred people look at it from different angles, the portrait keeps its eyes on each one of them. I was dumbstruck by what was happening. I was God now, but the realization came to me

at the most awkward moment, while I was holding the crosses
and images meant to strike fear in the devil, who was now staring at me through the sick man's eyes. All was clear: I had come
this far to meet my ancient adversary, and now we scrutinized
each other, both enclosed in the skin of someone else.

As soon as he became aware of who I was, the devil un-
leashed a savage dance. The possessed man began to writhe
and foam at the mouth, and I had the unpleasant sensation
that the devil was using that poor fellow to teach me some sort
of lesson. I tried to remain calm. "First I will get rid of him,"
I thought, "and then I'll deal with this other problem of being
God." The room was dense with an aromatic haze, and my
voice recited the formula to lift the spell.

"Come on, get out of there," I ranted in German and Latin,
"get out of there and stop all this, you ugly little monster; you
know that I don't believe in your existence. How can you take
advantage of a poor sick man who is close to death! Come out
of there, you scoundrel, or I'll give you a good thrashing."

The possessed man gave such a strong jerk that the rope
almost broke from the ring. The devil was annoyed by my disre-
spect and replied with a string of insults that sent a murmur
of fear through the room. The air was tense with excitement,
and I realized that the greater part of those present were looking forward to a spectacle like the one they had enjoyed when
the priest had been routed. "Clown," I mumbled; and I moved
forward to the sick man's side, holding the cross in one hand,
clutched like a dagger.

A surprise was in store for me. The possessed man regained
his composure and looked at me with a tranquil expression,
not without a trace of irony. As I reflected on this metamorphosis, he smiled and began to speak to me in ancient Greek, and
I answered him point by point in the same language, astonishing all those present who knew me as an ignorant carpenter.
In the purest Attic version of the immortal tongue, with the
voice of the old man whose body he inhabited, the devil asked
me to leave him in peace because he had at last found a comfortable dwelling in an elegant house where the cooking was
good, and which moreover was furnished with an excellent library—and I should know how fond he was of reading. In ex-

change he promised to be well behaved, not to curse the Madonna and not to sow heresies in the family. At this point I interrupted him.

"And why in the world should I make this pact with you? You are in no position to bargain about anything. For what reason would I go easy on you?"

"You know why," he replied. The possessed man's cheeks were taking on a greenish pallor, his lips quivering, as though rage were gripping him once again after a moment of forced calm. My interlocutor's Greek became dense with dialectal expressions, as though his cultural level were deteriorating. "You know why. I've always been your partner, even if you pretend you don't see me and, in fact, deny my existence. Do you know that if I weren't persecuted and tormented in this way, this same treatment would be reserved for you? Try to compensate me at least a little. Otherwise I'll tell everyone who you are, and then you'll be sorry."

"Go right ahead," I said, taking a step closer to him, as he fell again into the throes of a seizure.

"Damned worm!" he croaked in Greek slum jargon, and without warning he dropped his pants and spattered the sofa and rug with excrement. A sinister fetid stench flooded the room. Somewhere behind me I heard a kind of thud. One of the attendants had fainted. Seeing that there was no way out for him at this point, the devil flung a series of horrific accusations at me. He loaded the miseries of creation and the suffering of all humankind on my shoulders. The old man screamed diabolical insults at his exorcist, wallowing in his feces and urinating from his mouth. But even as the devil blamed me for everything, he fortunately forgot to mention my divinity. Without this important detail, his ramblings were incomprehensible to the possessed man's relatives.

I decided to put an end to it and flung myself at the old man, breaking through the pestilential stench. At that, defeated, the old man vomited up the devil. I saw it move in the vile slush, a lithe black snake that I couldn't grab hold of. Darting along the ground, it reached the window and vanished outside. The old man lay in a slime of refuse, half in a faint. His relatives hurried to his aid, and I pocketed my compensation. As I left the house, I could hear the old man's querulous voice behind me like that of a just-awakened child.

In the street I told myself that all of this had been a bad dream and promised myself to forget it. For a short while this was easy, since I immediately began to worry about my sister. I rushed home, burst into her room, and found her at a small desk near the window, busy writing a letter. I was stunned. My sister seemed to have become young again, and on seeing me she smiled, with a radiant look that I had never seen before. I was overwhelmed by joy and hope. I called out her name, went to her, held her in my arms, and this time I wept with a sense of liberation.

We spent the entire day as we had in our childhood, talking endlessly, holding hands. I found in her that part of me that had not yet been realized but had always accompanied me, like a faithful and discreet shadow, or like a mirror that reflected the shape of a woman. I prepared dinner for her, along with an infusion of aromatic herbs. As we sat by the fire in the common room, I ventured to confide in the woman of my life and tell her about that day's dramatic discovery.

I told her that I was God and that I did not know what to do about this new identity of mine. To tell the truth, I admitted, I could not get rid of the burden soon enough. I told her about my encounter with the devil and what he had said to me. I knew that he was right because I had long since become aware of the world's imperfection. I told her that I remembered the time when I had created the cactus so that it would be able to defend itself against birds, and the hedgehog so that it could roll up at the fox's approach, and that on that day it had seemed to me I was the fox and the hedgehog at the same time, each of them understanding the other without resentment. Considering the ambiguities of evil, being a carpenter had its advantages over being God.

My sister listened to me with her head bowed, bent over her embroidery, and she didn't miss a word. Slowly cheered by the wine and the warmth of the fire, I plunged into universal memory. I told her about the joyous labor of the shoots of a plant, and about the gaiety of growing together from one and the same root, as had happened to the two of us, who were a single soul that searched for itself in two bodies. I did not even know where these ideas had come from; I could not remember ever having had them before. But at the moment of divine reminiscence it is as though several gates open up and suddenly the most distant past emerges from them. "I don't believe this," I said to myself, "I am really God."

I had tired my sister, and so I stopped talking and picked her up in my arms to put her to bed. And then I realized that the gesture was exactly akin to carrying a bride to the nuptial bed. I was carrying my sister and at the same time I was carrying my bride. I had never gotten married, and this was new to me. The soft warmth of a female body that abandons itself, arms that close around you, as though there were no other way to shelter oneself from the world, the lips of the beloved parted on the verge of sleep—all of this plummeted down on me with the violence of a rainstorm on a thirsty forest. Was this what it meant to be God? I wanted to go on being happy, even if only for the space of a single night.

I put her down on the bed, slipped in beside her, and felt, so long after my birth, the warmth of a woman's breasts. I lay with her as if there were no other place in which I could find refuge. If this took place, the stars were not to be reproached. We were alone, in a blind spot of the world. We were brother and sister in love.

I dozed off and slept as if all the world's questions had been answered. At last two souls had met and knew why they had been born together. In the middle of the night I awoke and wondered what it was that had pulled me from such a blissful sleep. The night was splendid and the moon shone with its most silvery radiance. Being God would not be bad after all, I told myself, if only I could be a bit more self-confident! I did not have the time to develop my thought.

A loud cry jolted me back to where my sister lay sleeping in the glow of her miraculous recovery, and by the wavering light of a candle I saw before me again the approach of death in the ashen face and the rolled-back eyes. Her body, half naked in the spasms of agony, was once again the body of the previous day, as though the luminous evening had never occurred. I then saw our brief and now unrepeatable love lost in another star, where the world begins all over again. I was delirious by now, and as I clutched her in my arms and smothered her with kisses, my heart stopped. I was holding the devil in my arms.

Rigid with terror, I slowly tried to detach myself from his cold embrace. He had cast off the mask, and his voice reached me, strident and mocking.

"You thought you had put one over on me. Didn't you know that the devil can't be ordered around? Look at you, without strength and without faith. It was quite a feat to reduce you to this state! You have no idea how long I have been after you. I concentrated on becoming a woman to better deceive you, and I managed at last! You did not want to believe in me because you did not want to recognize who you are, but in the end you had to surrender, you've lost the battle. If you are not God to your very depths, victory falls to me. Now leave me in peace, for I must turn my attention to death."

My sister let out a hoarse moan and stopped speaking in that unnatural and distorted voice. She looked at me for an instant, then she shuddered and expired. I still held her body in my arms. Was it life that had left her, or was it the devil? I looked around and saw nothing suspect. A potted basil shivered in a breath of wind that entered through the door. Through the window floated a pale luminescence, almost a shudder traversing the shadows and announcing the coming of the day.

"No, no dawn!" I heard myself shouting.

I ran out of the house, my head lowered so that I could not see the sky. I fled from the town all the way to a hill, while brightness invaded the world as water pours into the breached hull of a ship. A rooster crowed from a farmhouse, other roosters answered, and by the time the sun rose above the trees, I had hanged my carpenter's body from an oak tree. "Just look, he thought he was God," I heard voices crying out inside me. I was convinced that I was killing myself to avoid the sun.

I AWOKE elsewhere, filled with shame. I was angry at having let myself be played with in that way and eager for a rematch.

I jousted with cunning. I began to set traps for the devil, behaving as he did, entering the bodies of unknowing souls in the hope of meeting my opponent there. We both learned from each other. For a long time I imitated him and became his monkey in the world's labyrinth.

I retired to an Irish hut where I found Isidore, a hermit who lived in extreme solitude. People would come and bring him food once a week, and he took advantage of this to ask for news about the world. In this way he learned of all the evil deeds that were committed there before returning to his prayers and meditation. Isidore had created an image of God for himself, and throughout his life had tried to enter into communication with him. He lived in God, conversed with him, and heard God tell him to keep the faith because the forces of evil would not prevail. Isidore wished to breathe with God, to become a fiber of his being and a thread of his mantle.

Whenever I have decided to come into contact with a soul of this sort I have experienced a slight feeling of remorse; I would be disturbing a saintliness that for me was incomprehensible but certainly admirable. An instant later I was reasoning with his mind and speaking with his voice. I did nothing at all to make Isidore change the idea he had of me. Now that he had become a God-hermit, he prayed with greater fervor, not to ask for favors and forgiveness, but rather for a message of peace to descend upon mankind. He wrote speeches and sermons about the future of humanity and was overwhelmed by visions of huge crowds listening to his words. He would awaken drenched in sweat and set out on long walks across the desert heights. He began to neglect food, and his body became aerial and vibrant. "Truly, my God, are we by now a single thing?" he asked himself, astonished and trembling. I didn't reply, but neither did I do anything to discourage this idea. I had decided to stand fast and wait for the devil to appear.

One morning, after a troubled and sleepless night, I kept up with Isidore's hurrying feet until we stopped on the edge of an abyss. In the distance we could see a strip of sea. It was cold up there and a harsh wind cut through the mountains. I was in a bad mood and was beginning to think that the devil was too astute to allow himself to be deceived and that I would never confront him directly again.

Engrossed in these thoughts, I heard a clang of bells and

barking of dogs. A flock of sheep benumbed with the cold climbed all the way to where we stood, and a shepherd left the flock and came to sit beside us. The moment I looked at him I was sure that he was the devil. If I had not been so anxious to find him I would not have recognized him behind his beard and his measured gestures. He was too beautiful and he did not seem to feel the cold. Isidore had not noticed anything and looked at the shepherd in silence. He took the tepid milk the man offered him, swallowing an entire cup in one breath. Watch out for that milk, I thought.

And indeed he must have put something into it, because Isidore began to rave. He told the shepherd what he was seeing at that very moment: hell, no less, gaping wide open beneath us, with devils flitting among the souls of the damned, wielding forks and whips; and fire and ice mixed together, and monsters standing watch at the gates of the various enclosures; and Lucifer, the king of demons, locked inside a rock. I stayed clear of the disquisition, but the shepherd listened attentively. When the hermit stopped to catch his breath, the devil said, "And what about purgatory? Don't you ever see that?"

"Purgatory," Isidore replied, "has never been accepted by our mother the Church. We still don't know where it is or whether it truly exists. It is a sin of pride to entertain a vision of it, before the dogma is pronounced."

"Come on, what are you talking about," the shepherd objected, in a conciliatory manner. "Of course purgatory exists. I've been told so by somebody who was there. It is a mountain divided into as many circles as there are sins, and at the top there is the earthly paradise from which you then fly to God's heaven. Ah, you have no idea how beautiful the earthly paradise is: a place of endless delights."

"Tell me all about it," Isidore exclaimed, as I lay quiet as a mouse, hidden in a corner inside him so that the devil couldn't see me. To Isidore's request the devil shook his head, almost as though he had realized that he was entering a territory that did not belong to him.

"No, I can't," he said, getting up and taking his leave. "You are a saint and I am a sinner. You are already close to God while I am nothing but earth and dust." He moved off toward his animals and disappeared down into the valley. I could not help but admire his performance, worthy of a perfect actor and impostor. Isidore was about to bless him from afar, but I was able to divert his attention just in time, bringing to his notice the sun that was piercing through the clouds. He lost himself in contemplation of the sky. "When will I fly to meet you, O Lord?" I heard him mumble as he sobbed quietly.

In fact Isidore's most arduous tests were to come. As I expected, the devil was on his trail. He announced himself with certain sly deceptions that were typical of his character. Isidore became absent-minded to the point of forgetting where he had put the lettuce leaf that was his dinner. He searched for it everywhere, in his cell and then outside the door of his hermitage, among the rocks of the courtyard, until he foamed at the mouth because of his longing for food, and then punished himself with a two-day fast. I didn't think this was such a great idea, considering that his body was by now skeletal and covered with sores. This new torture made an invalid of him.

As he lay on his bed he heard his window shutters creak, as if someone were shaking them in order to get in. He got up to fasten them from the outside, but a gust of wind slammed the shutters closed so that he was unable to go back inside and remained in the freezing-cold night, struggling in vain to pray through his chattering teeth. He was saved the next day by the person who brought him his weekly ration of food. He took refuge in his bed, wrapped in a fever and exhausted by his ordeal. At that point the devil made his regal entrance.

The scene had a strange beauty. One wall of the cell had opened up, and the performance began. Before the eyes of the two spectators—one of them stretched out on the pallet, the other hidden now in the molding of the cell's ceiling, above a crucifix that dominated the room from on high—the Prince of Evil displayed himself in his most professional garb.

To begin with, he was a consummate director with a wealth of scenic inventions. A landscape opened up before us. We saw lakes and mountains from which rivers descended, running through opulent fields and villages crowned with towers and steeples. From this landscape strode a well-groomed friar wearing a dark brown mantle. He advanced and then knelt before Isidore's bed and with his arms made a gesture of investiture and bestowal. "Take it, it is all yours," his lips whispered. Isidore stared at him with an inebriated expression and didn't say a word. "Come, do something," I whispered from above, "chase that cur away." Perhaps the hermit heard my voice, for he propped himself up on his elbows, let out a howl, and found himself sprawled in a thicket. An instant later the landscape had disappeared, almost as if a curtain had descended.

I detached myself from the crucifix and came down to Isidore's side, concerned about the state of his health. He was gasping, squirming on his pallet, his eyes popping, in a desolate protest against what was happening to him. "Be patient," I murmured into his ear. "As soon as I manage to catch the devil, I'll take care of him." He didn't seem to hear me and continued his lament, so I kept to myself in the cramped space of the cell. I listened intently to the wind outside.

The next day I was still on the alert, while the hermit seemed to have returned to his normal state. Night fell and we prepared to go to sleep. Isidore recited his prayers, to which I listened with a certain impatience, since I knew them by heart. I had become accustomed to the rules of cohabitation: I was careful not to fall asleep before he did, not to take up too much room in the bed, and not to invade his dreams with mine. We were waiting for sleep to come when suddenly the wall facing the bed once more disappeared, the sign that a new performance was about to begin. This time, instead of the landscape, there appeared a long hall furnished with tall shelves bulging with books.

In one corner there was a desk at which an elderly man sat, perhaps the librarian. Isidore watched the scene with an enchanted air, as if he were remembering something. And, indeed, as soon as the librarian stopped writing and rose to meet him, they both seemed to have known each other for a long time, and a smile flitted over the hermit's haggard face. The librarian looked at him with affection mixed with complicity, then began to speak as if continuing a conversation that had only just been interrupted. In brief, he proposed to make Isidore into the most knowledgeable man in the world. We were both spellbound and listened to every detail—which books to read entirely, which in abstracts; which useless notions we ought to forget, which other wise men should be contacted, and so on. It was a true and proper academic lecture, and it was all we could do to refrain from taking notes.

I completely forgot my plan of attack and actually felt like asking the librarian some erudite questions, but I caught hold of myself just in time. I don't know how this story would have ended if the devil hadn't made the mistake that exposed his dilettante and parvenu nature. It happened when he confused a quotation from Aristotle with a passage from Plotinus, and he was betrayed as well by the self-satisfaction induced by his success up to that point. I jumped to my feet and shoved him toward the open wall, against the shelves, which collapsed in a great cloud of dust. "But who are you," he asked me, consternated, before vanishing under the desk and taking with him the entire library. I was left alone with Isidore, who was staring at me as if I were a celestial apparition.

I decided to be one, if only this once, and flapping angel's wings I vanished from his side. I heard him burst into tears and swear that his guardian angel had saved him from a diabolic temptation. The walls of Isidore's cell were solid again at the close of this second act of devilish buffoonery.

Another day went by, with Isidore absorbed in prayer and penance, and I taking restless strolls in the vicinity. I trudged on the snow along a steep cliff above the sea, wearing a hood that barely shielded me from the violent gusts of the northwest wind. I saw a village, and in it a small church with a tiny bell tower. I rushed over and entered the hospitable warmth of the house of God, and there I lingered in the most protected corner, the confessional. I huddled in it, wiping the salty rain off my face. The small space was draped with a dark red cloth, and I rested my eyes on it. Outside, the wind beat against the rocks. I heard it rage and was happy to be sheltered. The cushion was so comfortable that I dozed off. Finally I was awakened by a young voice, and I saw a face move on the other side of the grille.

"I would like to make my confession," the voice said.

I was about to explain that there was a mistake, but I realized that the story would appear incredible. I tried to make the best of this new situation. I made the sign of the cross and instructed the penitent to do the same, feeling quite clumsy performing these unaccustomed acts.

"Go ahead, I'm listening," I encouraged him.

"It is an ugly sin," the voice added. "Truly I don't know whether I can be absolved."

"That's up to me to decide," I cut him off, displaying a sudden sacerdotal authority. Then I softened my voice. "My son, what happened to you?" I could hardly believe my own transformation.

There was a silence on the other side of the grate. Then the voice resumed, clear and firm.

"My sin is that I am the devil."

I stopped a moment to consider the matter. Then I ventured:

"When did it happen that you sinned so gravely? And why did you do it, my son?"

"The first time was a very long time ago. I need an exceedingly long penance, father."

"And yet you seem so young."

"I can be whatever I want to be," the penitent rejoined, and I noticed a decisive toss of his head. "Young, old, it makes no difference. As far as that goes, even man or woman. Right now, for example, I'm a schoolteacher in this small village, and everyone likes me. But in the evening I lock myself up in the house and practice black magic. Do you know what that means? Desecrated Masses, curses, the calling up of witches. In fact, I'm juggling so many nefarious projects at once that they're always behind schedule. Last night I was up until dawn working on an apparition that I'm supposed to present to a monk nearby; this is already the third one, and the first two went off pretty badly. Perhaps not all roles suit me equally well."

"But how did it all start?" I insisted. "Is it true that you were, as they tell us, one of the angels who rebelled against God?" (I uttered my name with considerable nonchalance.) "Is it true that you were thrown headfirst out of heaven and from that moment on you've played nasty tricks on everybody to get your revenge?"

"Nonsense," he replied. "I was created by humankind and

not by God. They are the ones who need me and call on me continually, and most of the time they aren't even aware of it. That's exactly what the monk did last night. What do you think of that? He thinks that he's calling God but in fact who he wants is me. Isn't that just my luck? And so everything that happens is my fault."

"Why then do you go to the monk at all?" I asked.

The devil sighed on the other side of the grate.

"That precisely is my sin, father. I'm unable to resist. I can't bring myself to say no. I'm vain and curious and a bit of a meddler. You see, I'm weak! I could have refused, but I'm always rushing around making deals, keeping busy. And there's another reason."

"What's that?" I asked, a little too eagerly. I was beginning to sympathize with him.

"It's that humankind is fond of me. Despite all the curses and maledictions they fling at me, I know that I occupy a large place in their souls. If they did not care for me, why would they seek me out? I too need affection. I'm not made of wood."

These words left me speechless for a few moments. Then cautiously I asked him:

"What do you think about God? How do you imagine him?"

"I haven't the slightest idea. And in any case it doesn't interest me. I have too much to do. Actually, I've got to go now; give me penance and absolution, please. I know that it doesn't count, because I'm not resolved to change my life. But give it to me anyway. Other sinners also continue to sin."

"I'll give it to you on one condition," I said.

"And what is that?"

"Tell me what you have in mind this evening for that poor little hermit."

"Why do you want to know?"

"Never mind. Tell me and I'll absolve you."

"I can't," he said, and his well-bred voice had again become distant. "What do you take me for? I'm a serious operator. I'll do without absolution. I've managed to let off some steam, anyway."

The head had disappeared from behind the grille—to my relief, because I had no idea how to go about giving absolution.

I peeked through the folds of the confessional's curtain. A slim figure was moving toward the church's exit, and treading lightly I began to follow it. How that devil ran on his way back home! He took the road through the fields and looked exactly like a young professor as he ran swiftly along the pebbly path. "There," I said to myself, "there goes the devil. Take a good look at him so that it will be easier for you to defeat him." I kept him in sight and followed him along almost impassable paths, and suddenly I no longer recognized him. Was it the same person as before or did he not resemble a farmer pushing his plow? A farmer! "Bravo, devil," I said to myself, "let's see what you come up with next."

I arrived at Isidore's hut and sat down to one side. Because of his endless penances, the hermit now looked like a scarecrow. I couldn't leave that cell soon enough, but not before realizing my plan. I prepared for the event by dozing beside his pallet until, after a rapid winter sunset, evening came. Soon it was dark but for a glimmer of moonlight through the shutters.

Several hours after nightfall, in the silence of the cell, the wall began to pulsate like a leaf in a breeze. A subtle and insidious music stirred in the air. Isidore sat upright, his body tight as a string and his eyes pointed at the wall. Suddenly, like a cloud, the wall dissolved and a woman appeared, stark naked. Her breasts and hips were opulent and robust. I stared at the black tuft of hair below her belly. She moved toward Isidore with a dancing step, and he barely breathed. "So this is what you are up to now," I thought. "Scoundrel! You know our weakness."

Isidore was little more than a heap of rags spread out on the bed. The woman stood before him, splendid in her nakedness. It was hardly a fair match. There was no chance that Isidore could make love to her, but the devil nevertheless wanted a victory. She wanted his humiliation and his surrender. She sat on the edge of the bed and looked at him with a smile of dazzling candor.

"Go on, take me," she told him, more with her breath than with words. "Take me, or at least look at me. Touch me! It isn't true that sin is not beautiful. Look at me and tell me that I'm not beautiful. Good is not the only thing in the world; nothing equals the sweetness of my lips. Do you see my breasts? I beg you! Sin is so sweet. It will be the beginning of a story without end. You can sin with me forever, until the most distant point in time. You will come to live with me, in the land of fire. I have in store torments for your delight—whips, pincers, flaming lakes. You do not know what I am capable of, if I set my mind to it. Look!"

I too was caught off guard. Suddenly her legs were spread wide open and the bush was a pink and humid abyss. Isidore seemed to succumb. Incapable of moving or rising, I watched him stretch out his hand toward her and I saw his lips move. I had to bend over to catch his words, but I managed to decipher them: "Come, Satan," he said, "come and give me sin. I have resisted too long. Come and condemn me. I'm tired of sacrificing to God."

This was too much. I felt offended by these words. Why did Isidore speak of me in this way? The woman was caressing her skin, and I trembled in the shadows, torn by conflicting impulses. Isidore looked defeated, a wreck without hope.

"Go on," the woman resumed. Her voice had become hoarse and vaguely menacing. "Come to me and abandon yourself, come close to me, and we shall renounce God. Just think if he were here watching this scene; how much sorrow he would draw from it! Think of his suffering. I have an idea: we could make it more outrageous with curses. Do you know how to curse? It is a delicate art, it requires thoughtful preparation. Repeat with me, but first listen carefully."

The disguised devil began to spout a litany of foul words against me, and Isidore, after some hesitation, did his best to repeat what he heard. The two of them cursed in unison—the woman in her obscene pose and the hermit wrapped in his everyday garments, bent over on the pallet. I decided I had had enough. I appeared before them without any commotion or sign of power. They both looked at me from the depths of their decadence, suddenly as mute as fish.

I spoke, addressing Isidore.

"Stop cursing. I cannot bear to hear you disfigure my name in this way. You spent your life invoking me and you haven't the slightest notion of me. How dare you insult me? And whoever told you that you must not make love? Whoever ordered you to come up here, far from everyone, to chew over your senseless prayers? Get up, if you can manage it, get yourself a real woman, look at her and touch her, and may it do you good. Do you really think that I attach any importance to your chastity? Show me what you are capable of. If you need some kindling, I'll go and get you a cup of wine. As for you," I said, turning to the woman lying on the floor, "we'll settle our accounts later."

I had spoken quite clearly, but it wasn't of much use. Isidore fell back on the pallet. I waited for a little while, then I prodded him with my foot. Finally he turned toward me and spoke amid sobs.

"Go away," he said. "Did you come to tempt me? Leave and take this monster with you. I will punish myself, don't you worry. Oh, I will certainly punish myself! Just look." And as he said this, moaning and writhing, he stuck a nail in his hand. I watched him with disgust, and at that moment the devil's voice reached me. It was the voice I had heard inside the confessional. I turned and saw him, the little well-mannered professor, sitting on the cell's only chair, with a bored and contemptuous air.

"There's no point in your insisting," he said. "You really don't understand anything. Without sin, love doesn't interest him. You don't understand the first thing about humankind. Is it really possible that you created all this?"

"What is there to understand?" I heard myself foolishly say.

"You have to ask me? I understood them immediately, although I arrived among them a long time after you. Men don't want you, and when you appear they disavow you. Especially hermits, you understand? And faithful wives, and those who do not drink, and consecrated virgins. They are my favorite partners. You know, we do a lot of things together, unless you show up and ruin everything. You've caused me to fail three times with this fellow. Now I'm fed up. You can have him."

"Wait," I cried. "Now that I've found you I'd like to ask you a few questions."

"Absolutely not," he replied curtly. "I am the devil. I don't owe God any explanations."

"I don't want explanations. I'm asking you to tell me what else you have understood."

"And I will tell you nothing at all."

"Then this will come to a bad end."

He looked at me with a mocking air. "And what would that be?"

I flung myself at him, but I had not foreseen his agility. I barely managed to touch him and he was already far away from me, outside the cell. I ran after him, determined not to lose sight of him. In the darkness his figure had disappeared, and I saw a tree with outstretched branches. Had the devil turned into a plant? But not only a plant, for suddenly rocks poured down onto the path and small snakes issued from beneath the stones. The pine tree against which I was leaning released a stream of odorous resin; a fox darted past me and a sparrow attempted to fly from a branch in the wintry frost. "Just wait till I catch up with you," I shouted into the wind.

I fell heavily to my knees and admitted defeat. I remained there stock-still, brooding over my situation. Finally I got up and walked until dawn, when I found myself again near the church of the day before. I went inside and was overcome by a great desire to confide in someone. I saw a priest enter the confessional, and I went to kneel before the grille.

"What is it you want, son?" I heard him ask.

"I want to catch the devil and I'm not succeeding," I blurted out, with more exasperation than I intended.

"And why do you want him?"

"I must make him pay."

"What did he do to you?"

That was a good question. What had the devil done to me? I had to admit that I wasn't sure. I was reflecting on the matter when the priest spoke again.

"Go home, son, and don't worry about it anymore. If you listen to me, you'll never meet the devil again. The devil exists only for those who believe in him. He can be made to disappear immediately—it's enough for you to want it—like a bubble, a breath, a stain of water. Go home and don't give the devil another thought."

I listened to him, perplexed.

"If that's the case, answer this question too. Why doesn't humankind love God? God as he is, I mean, and not the idea that they have of him. Somebody told me that they do not love him, and I'm beginning to believe it. Why should this be so? Can you answer this?"

I had the impression that the priest was smiling inside the red shell of the confessional.

"It is because of their feelings of guilt. Men are children. God has inscribed in them what they must become and their mission in the world, but they are not able to fulfill it, except with the greatest effort, and always very imperfectly. Don't you think this is vexing enough? They refuse to grow up! They find all sorts of pretexts not to recognize you and not to do what they must. They even invent a devil! But pay them no mind and go home."

I stood up.

"What sort of a strange priest are you," I exclaimed. "What sort of reasoning is this? Let me see you."

I raised my arm to lift the curtain, and at that moment I woke up in the open countryside, in full daylight. I was so worn out by the cold that I was unable to move. So it was a dream; and yet what the priest said must be true. If the devil does not exist, I told myself, then I will no longer run after him. I felt a great desire to leave this place and return to my Mediterranean haunts. But what about Isidore? What had become of Isidore?

I set out for his cell, and on my way I thought of telling him everything, absolutely everything, that the devil doesn't exist and that God does not expect men to fast and abstain from carnal love but wants them to help life to improve. I told myself to hurry, that if only I could say all this to that poor man, all would be well. I was filled with joy, as in ancient times.

I found Isidore in a state of ecstasy, far from myself and from the devil, longing for oblivion. He was undoubtedly absorbed in a conversation with his own God, and there was no way to make myself heard. Beside his pallet I vowed never to mislead again, not even for a joke or for a good purpose. I straightened his bed, placed the rosary in his hand, and adjusted a garment that had exposed his poor legs.

"Farewell, Isidore," I said. "I haven't explained myself to you after all. I'm always late."

I had now reached full adulthood, and I was soon brimming again with enthusiasm. I had a burning desire to busy myself among humanity, but too often I came up against hostility or indifference. I was stymied by entrenched convictions as by a fortress. Circling around this fortress, I occasionally managed to slip inside, penetrating wherever I could. I left traces, signals, messages. I felt like God's secret agent rather than God in person.

I felt neglected. It wasn't that people didn't talk about me, but it was as though they constantly referred to someone else. I had fallen into the hands of the theologians. If anyone dared to define me in a slightly unorthodox way, he was imprisoned, excommunicated, burned alive. The authority of the theologians was all the more formidable because the faithful wanted it; supremacy, it seems, is always desired most by those who are subject to it. Humanity remained young and immature, and so imagined for itself a choleric father. They did not want a God who was a brother and a friend. They did not want him as an equal.

I flew again over the wide expanses, over the fields, in search of sympathetic human beings. I went into peasants' houses as a hungry wayfarer, holding out my hand in the name of mercy. I entered their kitchens and saw for myself that their food was little better than that which was given to the most precious guest in the house, the pig in its pen, worshiped like a noisy and famished divinity. Perhaps they imagined God as similar to this pig, lost in an indecipherable language and the throes of a gigantic appetite. And finally, when the god is slaughtered, what is won is the reward of a great banquet in the heavens, portions of which are given as hors d'oeuvres to the communion of the faithful. Ever since I saw it this way, the ceremony of the Mass has filled me with feelings of horror.

I witnessed an army of plague-ridden people pass through one town where I had stopped to rest, and disappear over the horizon with its baggage of crutches and bundles. A real army

captured a village amid rapes and killings, until those tortured
no longer remembered their existence without outrage. I went
to contemplate the labor of those who worked in the stunted
fields and the poisonous cities. I forced myself to see people
dying of starvation, young mothers, with their children in their
arms, expiring before my impotent eyes. I observed the vi-
ciousness that springs from pain, knives glinting in assassi-
nations and nocturnal thefts, the rapacity of those who had
escaped death. I saw the silent incest between father and
daughter in rooms crowded with sleeping people. I saw boys
killing animals for fun, priests raising a drunken din during
Mass, soldiers disemboweling women prisoners, mothers beating their infants beneath the crucifix to obtain my forgiveness
for their sins, men burning their neighbors' houses on full-
moon nights. I saw governors and priests in their ceremonial
robes go past crowds of sufferers in the throes of veneration.
I saw gaudy likenesses of Christ dragged about on carts by ca-
parisoned horses. I watched processions of flagellants travel
through the regions tormenting themselves with whips and
goads. In a small castle where I went to ask for alms, through
a slightly ajar door I glimpsed a table where two men sat absorbed in a game of chess, oblivious to all else as though intent
on deciphering the mystery of the universe. Down below them,
in the animal pen, a woman with the eyes of a furious goddess
let herself be mounted by a ram. In the kitchen they handed
me a chunk of bread that was black and hard, and a handful
of rice. I sat down on the floor in front of a fire that blazed up
like the beginning of a conflagration.

Seen through my vagabond's eyes, the world appeared too
chaotic for comprehension; and that is when I finally went
mad.

I no longer remember well how it happened, whether it was
a sudden flare-up one sun-drenched noon in the middle of a
summery countryside, or a gradual transmutation of my being.
I was probably seized by a need to return closer to my divinity,
of which, it seemed to me, I preserved only a small trace. I felt
as though a flood of light had sucked me in like a tiny moth
that dissolves in the flame of a candle. I abandoned my bundle
of rags because it no longer mattered what I wore and where

I slept. I no longer cared whether I was naked or clothed, nor was I sure whether I was awake or caught in a dream. Around me were some who went mad with cruelty and committed acts that were worse than the causes of their madness. Others were crazed with terror, unable to move and almost unable to breathe. For my part, madness bestowed a tranquil and constant hilarity. Flowers caressed my beard and birds perched on my arms.

That is how my divine nature became manifest. In the villages the people came to meet me and took me by the hand to lead me to shelter. Even if they did not recognize me as God, they sensed that I brought God closer to them. When offering me food and drink, and showering me with gifts, they did not show the vexed gestures of irritated charity that I remembered. It seemed that I was bringing them a long-awaited happiness. I would refuse their gifts, which increased my mysterious prestige. They did not call me mad; they had another name for me, which I have written down somewhere.

I had entered my inner abode and remained locked inside it, lost in ecstatic contemplation of a beneficent universe. I wandered through the world as if in paradise; I smiled at the animals as though we were inhabiting the Garden of Eden, among placid rivers and hospitable grasses. I looked at the sun as though it would never set again and at the moon almost as at a sister. I glided over sorrow as water glides over the skin of a fruit.

I spent quite some time in this state, keeping no account of the years. Nobody thought of curing me because I didn't seem ill; they had never met anyone as happy. And indeed, without being aware of it, I inspired a great many people to change their lives. Madness became an integral part of the world, in the form of a desire for death that cannot be separated from life, as when, in dreaming, we seem to awaken while continuing to sleep. They laughed on seeing me, and when there is laughter, hope returns in the world. I was the addled God, wandering barefoot with a bunch of flowers in my hand.

This is how Francesco, the son of Bernardone, saw me as I walked through the Umbrian countryside, and he burst into laughter, as though the immense and manifold fabric of life had become clear to him in an instant. He cast off his sandals to run after me, turning somersaults like a jester behind his king. I knew all about jesters, having met them in the castles where I sought shelter as a beggar. I had watched them declaim and perform contortions before their lords after much guzzling and swilling. I had eaten together with them in the kitchen, beside the hearth, surrounded by the to-and-fro of servants and cooks. I had observed their faces decrepit with immemorial old age, as if they had never been reborn since the time when Zita was leaping among the trees. Those clowns were sad, as are all those who must evoke laughter, just as cooks are seldom hungry. But Francesco's laughter was joyous, and he never stopped following me, so that I too had my jester like the lords who gave me hospitality. Later in our association I often put on a friar's cowl in order to accompany him, and it was I who gave him the courage to frequent Donna Chiara, the beautiful nun who had fallen in love with him, and who transformed him into a serious and romantic jester who read the Song of Songs under the light of the moon. Whenever I was away from him, I would never neglect to forward a message. Once I sent a wolf to befriend him; another time a swarm of birds greeted him on my behalf.

When I heard that he was dying, I went to visit him on a mountain in Tuscany to which he had retired. Before he expired he thanked me for everything—for the sun, the strong and beautiful fire, the plants, the animals, the clear and chaste water. He even thanked me for his death; and before he subsided into it, we embraced, and I kissed the palms of his hands, whose skin had become so fragile that it cracked beneath the pressure of my lips, and a bit of blood mingled with my tears. None of Francesco's companions knew that I was present at his death, and not even Giotto, when he portrayed that moment years later, guessed my presence among them. Francesco helped me to cast off the dream in which I was immersed. From the moment I met him I stopped being mad, as though my jester had set me free, taking the madness unto himself as a joyful penance.

I descended from the mountain where he had left his remains, and on that same day I returned to the world. I found

myself among chestnut trees; I heard the rustle of brooks flow-
ing, and in the thick of the forest invisible birds made a veritable racket. Halfway down the slope I came upon a clearing
where shepherds grazed their meager flocks of sheep and
goats. Further down began the olive groves and the vineyards,
hardy, tormented plants from which came that land's riches of
oil and wine. The peasants toiled around the branches and
vines, hoeing, pruning, grafting, with an industry and skill that
put me in mind of jewelers modeling precious stones. While I
was lost in my madness, humanity had stubbornly insisted
upon furthering my creation, despite all the obstacles I myself
had not known how to remedy—the same humanity that had
driven me to insanity! Well, fancy that, I said to myself. I still
have things to learn.

Since I needed a spell of laborious and orderly life, I in turn
became a friar, and so the memory of Francesco still accompanied me.

I spent a part of my life in a great abbey built on the summit
of a hill, from where you could see, distant and glittering, a
vast valley flamed in the evening with dozens of bonfires. I realized how much life had changed since the days of Isidore and
how humanity's desire for death had become a slow awakening
toward life, accepted as it was, with all its faults and its unforeseen sweetnesses and delights.

I was assigned to the abbey's department of librarians. We
were a small group, three young men led by an older one, and
we spent our time copying manuscripts and arranging them
on the library's ample shelves. One of us was very skillful at
illustrating those texts, but we had to explain the contents to
him, since he did not understand Latin very well. He would
copy entire pages without knowing their meaning, then would
take fire with inspiration and draw miniatures around a capital
letter, and all of us would rush to admire his finished work on
the large page resplendent with colors. From the window before my writing desk I could see the convent's vegetable garden
where the field monks worked, bent over their seedlings. I
would catch myself thinking that we were doing something
quite similar, transmitting life in the fashion granted to us,

bearing witness to our love for it, as a sign of the presence of God. The texts that I copied traversed time as those plants crossed the seasons, blossoming again at the appointed time. I was thinking about this one spring morning as I transcribed an episode from a Latin poem, and my soul was filled with a restless yearning that forced me to leave the small hall, followed by the frowning glance of the old librarian. I went to my cell and flung myself upon my cot, and there I tried to pray.

I remembered the instructions of the spiritual director, who lived as a recluse in one of the monastery's wings and was writing a book called *On the Contempt of the World*. That year, on Good Friday, the recluse had appeared in the refectory and read to us several passages from his book, which no one had yet seen. "O brothers," the fasting man said, hovering over our meal of vegetables and dry bread, "remain as still as you can. *Sede in cella tua*. Do not allow yourself to be scized by the malady of unstable movement. But see to it that your cell does not become a prison; for the good monk the cell is a refuge of peace and quiet." Our director had also proscribed walking back and forth in one's habit as a flagrant sign of the *morbus vagationis*, and this was precisely what I was doing now as I tried to pray, without much effect.

I repeated to myself the glories of monastic life that I had been taught as a novice: "O my cell, tabernacle of the sacred militia, precinct of the triumphant army, *castra Dei*, field of the divine battle, arena of the spiritual clash, spectacle for the angels, trench of an advancing army, *munitio fortium!*" As I declaimed I realized that I was marching up and down within those four walls, and my head was filled with a warrior's ambitions. The military life certainly must have inspired the author of those prayers, since they were continually presenting the monk as a soldier of God. I felt my limbs tremble beneath my habit, as though I were wanting to plunge into a skirmish on the open fields, amid the trampling of horses and the clash of swords, as in the dreams that visited our silent nights on the peak of that hill. I remembered the time when I subjected myself to a monthlong penance for having dreamed that I was a soldier among others storming a small fortified citadel. I recalled the joy that had borne me through those walls, toward a cluster of frightened girls crouching on the ground. I shivered at the memory and stopped praying.

I found myself before a small window and through it I saw an oak tree struck by the evening light. I heard the bleating of flocks and the voices of peasants returning home after a day in the fields. Back to mind came the verses I had copied that day in the library, and I repeated them ecstatically with their beautiful Latin sounds: "And already in the distance smoke rises from the roofs of the huts and the shadows lengthen as they descend from the high mountains."

I don't know what seized me as I recalled those lines. As soon as night fell I was fleeing like a deserter from the holy militia of the monastery, racing through the fields toward an unknown freedom, happy to move, yearning for love, flying beneath the stars. And when the sun returned I saw with joyous amazement that the land was covered with hundreds of churches of the purest white, as far as my eye could see.

I stopped in one of these churches early in the morning after my flight from the monastery. I had taken off my habit and put on some rough homemade clothes I had bought at a nearby farm. Thus transformed, I entered the deserted, snow-white building. I was gripped by a powerful and profound emotion. I stood near the entrance, looking at a stained-glass window through which the sunlight filtered, taking on all its colors. There were angels, saints, and pilgrims to keep me company; beside me a statue of the Madonna cast a maternal gaze upon me. Again I felt a desire to pray, and fell to my knees. "But what shall I say?" I thought. I saw a woman's figure pass, her face hidden behind a veil, and the way she moved inspired in me such a feeling of tenderness that I was filled with trepidation and confusion. The woman disappeared but a scent hung in the air, and I caught myself giving thanks to God, to myself, for the existence of the world and for the act of hope that was creation, until I grew tired of speaking to myself and rose from the floor.

I came out of the church into the bright light of day. I breathed with joy as I stood before the portal adorned with sculptures of saints and beasts. Life was as novel as the first day of creation.

Suffering was present wherever I turned my gaze. But in my desire for recovery I tended to see it as an effort toward something positive, as if a series of defeats must precede the mysterious triumph that awaited me.

Tales of glorious times and deeds reached me—adventures, travels, loves, and conquests to the sound of clanging swords and the gallop of horses toward cities where women waited. My passions were rekindled. I wanted to travel, to write, to love, to do everything that gave life its majesty and joy.

I had settled in the region that runs from the southern coast of France to the Pyrenees, perfumed by the sweet names of its cities and towns. I reappeared as God of my world, still a strong full-grown man, without lines in my face. I was called Jauffré Rudel and owned a castle surrounded by vineyards to the north of Bordeaux. From the height of the castle's walls I would interrogate the horizon and the distant line of the sea. Below me climbed the village that clung around the castle. Off to one side gleamed the white tomb of Roland, the hero of Rouncesville, knight of Charlemagne, who had inflamed my youth with his wartime feats. From one of the castle's courtyards echoed the repeated and methodical clatter of the knights' weapons as they trained for tournaments and wars. For long hours I too practiced with sword and bow in the company of my squire, Fernando.

The hour of sunset would drive me in search of poetic solitude. I wrote verses, in love with the beauty that I was discovering in the universe. I delighted in the breeze that reached all the way to the castle's bastions, like a soft gust from paradise. I saw the lark flutter its wings in the last rays of daylight and then plunge, almost lifeless, its heart bursting with tenderness. I would inhale the wind until the sun disappeared beyond the horizon, then I would go down to the banquet hall.

I sat alone at the head of the table. I had not wanted to marry, seeing the fate of my noblemen friends, whose wives were smothered with children and destined to be grandmothers within a few years, while they vented their energy hunting in the woods and cavorting with peasant women in the haystacks. I preferred being alone. In the evening I would listen to the accounts of the visitors who stopped at my castle. Many of them were merchants, who recounted complicated intrigues of war and love. Others were pilgrims resting after their long journeys, and they reported on the various saintly exploits of their heroes. Both merchants and pilgrims ignited in me a bittersweet longing to hasten to the lands they described. I would listen to them spellbound, and my soul melted with desire. After everyone had retired I would stay up and walk through the silent castle, among those drowsing under the white moonlight. I was so deeply invaded by love for the mysterious, faraway regions of their tales that my body ached.

One evening I heard a group of pilgrims on their return from the Orient extol the beauty of a noblewoman who lived in a corner of the Mediterranean on the coast of Lebanon. That was all I had to hear; my soul was immediately afire. I would not let them leave. I forced them for days on end to tell me about her, distracting them from their holy thoughts. I asked to see her portrait, but they did not have one. They did their best to draw her face and her figure, but each one portrayed her in a different way, so that my love could only increase in impatience. They contradicted each other with words too. One described her as blond, another as brunette; one gave her eyes the color of the sky, another saw them as green as emeralds. But no one doubted her beauty. I thought of her as a goddess involved in some sort of continual metamorphosis, and in the fullness of my passion I decided to go and find her so as to admire her reality.

This was a time when the craze for the Crusades exploded throughout Europe. Had I not been in love, I would certainly not have left with the others, for what I heard on the subject of the First Crusade had left me with serious doubts. But such was my ardor that I did not hesitate to join the armies that gathered amid the plaudits of the clergy and the tears of the women left behind. Their husbands were in fact escaping from them, and the wives must certainly have been aware of this since they wept so bitterly. I on the other hand was hastening to meet my love, whom I had never seen before, and I was certain that I could find happiness only with her.

Together with Fernando and a group of knights, I caught up with the retinue of the king of France on its way to the Balkans.

I have unhappy memories of that voyage despite the gleam of light that awaited at its end. As in other wars in which I had chanced to fight, the high-mindedness inspired by our triumphal departure soon degenerated into a series of robberies and disembowelments, in the performance of which everyone tried to outdo the others in cruelty and treachery. The evil of the universe rose to meet me at each step of that journey. I fled from the Crusaders and from the religious unctuousness with which they anointed the slaughter. I set sail with Fernando in the direction of Lebanon, having cast off the insignia of warrior and Christian.

Toward the end of my sea-crossing, a mortal illness overtook me, and until landfall I repeated the name of the woman of my dreams. I lay on the beach and felt the Levantine sun beating down upon my head. News of my frantic search had reached my beloved, and she had fallen in love with me by hearing my story, as I had fallen in love with her by listening to the legends of her beauty. She hastened to my side after being informed of my arrival by messengers and held me close to her breast, and I felt the taste of her tears on my mouth. I could savor the perfume of her skin, but I could not see her face, my eyes obscured by the death that was overtaking me. I touched her hair to guess its color and implored her to describe her eyes for me. But even her words were unintelligible, and it was my fate to die without having contemplated her beauty. Just as I was about to expire, the imperious and fatal memory of my nature came back to me; the moan that came from my lips at that moment was a lament for a happiness I would never know, for the life that was escaping from me, for the burden of my divinity.

I WAS still getting over this disappointment when, a century later, I went to see Thomas Aquinas, pretending I was an Arab who admired Aristotle and bringing him some texts translated and commented upon by Averroës, the great Islamic scholar.

Thomas was just about to complete his major work. He was old by now and ready to die. Tranquil and corpulent as Thomas was, he spent the whole day at his desk, where he kept all the books he needed to consult and the paper on which to write, so that no unnecessary movements would distract his body and mind from the immense opus that had absorbed the last years of his life. That work, almost completed, was piled up before him like a vast castle, complete with towers, moats, draw-bridges, gangways, dungeons, and reception halls. Its architect was sailing toward the end of his life like a voyager certain of being on schedule, and was already thinking about his arrival in the immutable realm of eternity, where a still and silent God would preside over a world motionless in its perfection. I went to see him in his Dominican monk's cell, which was bare and unadorned.

The disputations about the proofs of my existence kept us up for nights on end. Thomas obstinately insisted on the num-ber of these proofs. They must be five, not one more or less. Discussing the number of proofs did not seem to me as impor-tant as examining the contents of each proof. I would have pre-ferred to work by day, but Thomas suffered from insomnia and would fall asleep only in the morning. He was absolutely frugal, despite his bulk, and occasionally I had to interrupt the work in order to restore myself with some fruit and biscuits, which I had brought with me because I knew he wouldn't have any-thing to offer. We worked with an enthusiasm that I had not experienced since that time atop Mount Sinai.

How could we prove my existence? "Ex ratione causae effi-cientis, ex parte motus, ex gradibus," we recited in unison, tri-umphantly. Who could doubt those three proofs? Obviously, what moves must be put into motion by an originally propel-ling cause. Encouraged, we continued our project. "A contin-gentia mundi." But this is where our disagreement began. The contingency of the world certainly proved my existence but not my superiority; indeed, it could have proved my precarious-ness. We quarreled at length, but then I resigned myself and let him have his way. He had more stamina than I, and when it was a matter of going the distance he always won. At the end of the argument, and almost in anger, I devoured an orange.

We then came to the final proof. "Ex ratione causae finalis!" Thomas chuckled joyfully as he recited it. "What final cause?" I retorted, pacing the cell and snatching away his manuscript to force him to listen. "What are you talking about? There is no final cause! I have no intention of taking all of you anywhere. I expect you to help me understand where I come from and where I am going." He would not listen to these words. Our breakup was inevitable, and it occurred after we had ceased our useless philosophical discussions. One morning, while he was saying Mass in a Neapolitan church, I was one of the young boys serving the Mass, and at one point I got so bored with the ceremony that I snorted with impatience. I can still see Thomas's mortified glance and the anguished face of Reginaldo, his dearest friend.

A crisis of silence followed my unfortunate outburst. Thomas stopped writing that same day and sank into a melancholy sloth. Reginaldo succeeded in coaxing a few words out of his pen, but Thomas told him to leave him alone, because now he was sure that all he had written was worthless. Consternation overwhelmed the monk's disciples. Within a short time, while returning to his monastery on the back of a mule, Thomas hit his head against the branch of a tree and fell to the ground in a faint. It was the beginning of the illness that soon carried him to his grave. The saintly man died commending his soul to the Church and entrusting his writings to the authority of the theologians. No one ever knew what had led him to such a state of anguish and distrust. But I know that at the Mass he had finally seen me as I was, bustling and impatient, and that at that moment his philosophical castle seemed to collapse before him. I left him there on his bed, praying for his soul to merge in peace with the nothingness that awaited it.

Not much later I would mention Thomas's name to a great admirer of his work, an exiled Florentine poet who was writing a book I had heard about. It was the story of a traveler who journeys through the realms of the divine in the hope of meeting me at the end. This subject fascinated me, and I decided to lend a hand to the project by going to meet the writer in person. I confess I would have liked his work to be written under my dictation, but this was not to be.

I hastened to seek out the proud and fugitive poet. I found him in a forested valley among the Tuscan mountains, in the freezing cold of an impossible winter, amid a howling snowstorm.

Dante had a sharp profile, a curved nose, and the rapid step of a shy but arrogant man. He was subject to incredible verbal rages and harbored a strenuous will for revenge against the makers of his misfortune. Perhaps there took shape in his soul the idea of a work that would restore order to the world: a book that would make him more spiritually powerful than the pope and the emperor, more Christian than any other Christian. It was a way of achieving immortality. I did not understand this right off, because immortality does not interest me. Perhaps I inherit it too naturally from myself, in the many and various forms of my being. But Dante was obsessed by the idea of death, and he thought of his book as a boat that would cross the seas of time.

When we met he had lost his way in the snow, cursing himself for having ventured into an unfamiliar forest in such weather. He trembled with fear at the sight of the animals that scurried across his path as he ran about in search of refuge; at the end he slipped and crashed down a slope, screaming with fright. I appeared to him as he was struggling to get to his feet, drenched in snow and mud, and this is what I said to him:

"I am God. I'm here to help you. Why don't you write about our encounter? Just start by telling how I saved you from this hopeless situation."

I led him out of the storm and accompanied him all the way to the door of a nearby castle. For days on end I hovered around the walls, peeking into his room. He was glued to his desk like a helmsman to his wheel. I kept encouraging him from a distance and promised to read his manuscript.

When I actually read it I was disconcerted. In his story everything that happened had been changed: the boars and hares that had fled through the snowstorm became wolves, leopards, and lions. He had written the first cantos of the *Inferno* in a

single outburst, and had completely redone what he had written before. The gate of the castle of his protectors had been
transformed into the gateway to hell; and the story of the death
of the lovelorn poet on the shores of Lebanon—which I had
told him during our long walk out of the storm—had been
turned upside down and had become the episode of Paolo and
Francesca, in which physical love between man and woman
was branded as sinful.

I did my best to explain to him that the very ideas of hell,
purgatory, and paradise did not hold. He must believe that
there is no life beyond life. This was an arduous truth to recognize, but indispensable for humanity if it wanted to emerge
from the childish state of its relationship to me. In order to
impress Dante, I rattled his windowpanes with stormy winds,
I glared at him with the power of a once-again resplendent sun,
I flashed between his feet in the shape of a tiny serpent, I
swooped down in large circles like an eagle dropping from the
mountain peak; yet he continued to compose verses about
landscapes in another world. I realized the dangers of the
beauty that he had at his command. Enamored of itself, his gift
was quite capable of producing lies, and with what tremendous
grace and conviction! The wind had become an infernal storm;
the eagle was the shade of Homer flying above other poets like
the king of birds; the souls of thieves were transformed into
snakes.

On the first day of spring, a cheerful party of the castle's
guests descended to the Tyrrhenian Sea. When the marine expanse appeared in the distance, Dante let out a cry that I again
encountered at the beginning of *Purgatorio,* on the beach at the
foot of the mountain where the pilgrims walked, leaving behind them the winter season. When a seagull darted toward
us, his gaze followed it, and in that instant the angel messenger
of God took shape in the poem. The poet was walking by himself, reciting snatches of verse. His vulture's nose turned in all
directions, as if the universe itself were his book's vocabulary;
and I, sand beneath his feet, became the image of shattered
and dissolved time.

My history with Dante did not end there. After he left to seek
a new protector, it took me quite some time to find him again.

More than ten years passed, during which I traveled all over Europe and the Orient, mingling with the crews of navigators who set out in search of new lands. I rubbed shoulders with those who were changing the created world: merchants who carried tools and textiles from continent to continent; bankers who exchanged goods and money; alchemists shut away in their cellars, tormenting themselves amid fumes and esoteric tools in the hope of converting base metal into gold. It was as though in everyone's soul it were written that things must be transformed and that man is in a hurry because he knows he is only a transient animal.

Scientists and inventors, scattered everywhere like an army of blind but industrious ants, groped in the world hoping to find the springs and gear-wheels of the great living organism, and I was made to see every part of myself in the vast mechanisms of creation they uncovered.

I landed next to a watchmaker in Nuremberg and rested as I watched him work. He must have felt my presence and, enraptured in prayer, he put together the first portable clock, which I immediately seized. The watchmaker, satisfied, fell asleep and dreamed of heavenly bells. With this device in my pouch, I crossed the Alps and became a traveler aboard a carriage headed for the republic of the Most Serene Venice. We descended from the German forests along tortuous Alpine paths. A single blanket protected me and a dignitary from the Visconti court in Milan, returning home after an ill-starred diplomatic mission in Germany. He was shivering with both fever and fear, so certain was he that his head would be chopped off. He got off in Milan, leaving the blanket all to me, and I continued the journey heartened by Dante's tercets, which I had now memorized.

We passed the pre-Alpine lakes, and at last the coach reached Verona, where I found that Dante had taken refuge in his later years, the guest of the city's rulers.

I managed to be introduced to him as a watchmaker, and he received me in the wing of the palace that was reserved for him. I was shocked when I saw him; he seemed so changed. It wasn't that he had grown older; rather, he seemed transfigured and close to becoming something else. The very game he played had imprisoned him. In the throes of his *Paradiso*, Dante was migrating toward the unearthly world he had invented, and his body was preparing itself. His skin seemed burned as by a constant flame, and his sunken eyes caressed the object I had set on the table. He remained in contemplation for a while and then left abruptly, without a word. The next day, as I was strolling through the rooms of the palace, he came to meet me and invited me into his study to read what he had composed the night before. He had set the description of the clock right before the canto dedicated to Saint Francis. I immediately recognized the talent that I knew so well, but I did not stop at those lines and took advantage of the opportunity to devour the entire poem.

Once again, my reaction was a mixture of admiration and shock. His choice of the damned and the blessed was surprising. A man who had inspired horrendous massacres, Saint Dominic, was placed in paradise in the company of my beloved Francesco! And this definitely was not our only point of disagreement. I was partly comforted by the thought that paradise does not exist; at least I could be sure that this sort of person would never be rewarded.

Later I told him the story of Odysseus, meaning to hold up the Greek hero for Dante's admiration. I told him that, after returning to his faithful Penelope, Odysseus had once again departed, this time to see the world that lay beyond the columns that Heracles raised in Gibraltar to prevent man from venturing beyond. I was trying to make him see that this was an example that should be emulated; people ought to consider carefully the true essence of their nature and follow their yearning for knowledge. Dante became excited over my story and rushed off to write his version, in which I punished Odysseus because of his excessive daring as a navigator. According to Dante, I caused Odysseus to sink into the sea at the very moment when the new land was sighted. Poor Odysseus was added to the phalanx of those damned in hell, and thus was extinguished my attempt to educate Dante in pagan values.

On another occasion, seeing Dante absorbed in sad meditation, I asked him what might be troubling him. He replied that he was very worried about the composition of *Paradiso*, because of the difficulty of conceiving the division of the heavens and the disposition of the angelic hierarchies. No one had ever seen them and so he did not really know how to describe them. In order to comfort him I told Dante how the Mohammedans had solved the very same problem and launched into a detailed geographical description of Allah's paradise. I was pleased that he didn't seem to miss a word and took a great many notes. I even illustrated my explanation with drawings, which Dante copied faithfully. Years later, in reading the finished poem, I noticed that Dante had used the arrangement of the Moslem paradise for his Christian heaven. "Trickster!" I thought. "But the day will come when you will be found out."

By now his paradise resembled a cathedral packed with people during the hour of High Mass, with the noble folk in their stalls and the hoi polloi pushed all the way to the back, all to attend Dante's coronation. It was the only way for the exiled poet to return at last to the house of God. Dante kept aloof and alert, so that nothing would distract him from the enchanted realm of infernal circles and purgatorial mountains and heavens that rotated around each other; and the blessed, clothed in ceremonial robes, applauded the pilgrim-poet as he laboriously climbed forth. I decided to wait for him at the manuscript's end, meanwhile contemplating Dante as he wrote by the light of his tallow candle, tormenting the syllables of each line. He reminded me of a geometer determined to square the circle and cudgeling his brain to come upon the formula he needs.

In order to help Dante with the last phase of his voyage to me, I gave him another gift. I had gone to Venice on a vacation and to escape the provincial and somewhat gloomy atmosphere of the court of Verona. In a corner of the piazza, between the antics of a mountebank dressed like Harlequin and a fire-eater dressed as a Turk, my attention was attracted by a peddler who was selling all sorts of merchandise: magic lamps, hangings filched from a church, a mismatched helmet and armor, the skirt of a Persian courtesan. I noticed a pair of minuscule pieces of glass mounted crudely in wood, glittering amid all that stuff. I held them up to my eyes, and everything around me became foggy and misty, a sign that I did not need spectacles. But I bought them anyhow, thinking that I could make a useful present of them to my friend the poet.

Judging by his eyes, reddened by his vigils in the wavering light of the torches, I had not been mistaken. This time too Dante welcomed me, puckering his eyelids in a squint, as he had been doing for some time. Without delay, I placed my Venetian purchase on the humped bridge of his nose. Joy lit his parched and wrinkled face, and he embraced me with a movement so quick that I could not avoid it. "It is not only for glory," I whispered into his ear. "It is not only the need to defeat fate. You do your best, as the caterpillar does with its spinning and the oak with its acorns and the jester with his somersaults. Now your eyes needn't hold you back."

I watched as Dante ascended toward me through the empyrean. I saw him approach, with veneration, Bernard of Clairvaux and the dignitaries closest to the emperor of heaven. I couldn't repress a feeling of antipathy for Bernard, who had promoted and inspired the Crusade of which I had been such an unhappy witness. I saw the mother of Christ, unrecognizable as the woman I remembered, wearing festive light like a celestial mantle. I saw faces bearing the legendary names that had perturbed the imagination of the Jews dispersed in Egypt: Rachel, Sarah, Rebecca, Judith, and Ruth. On the opposite side of the rows of the blessed I saw John the Baptist, and I recognized Francis and Augustine among God's courtiers; and very close to the throne, hidden in the splendor, I saw the most illustrious of them all, among them a fellow named Adam who had escaped my notice before, and Peter, and, next to Moses, John the Evangelist. Bernard spoke at length to the Virgin, and she turned her gaze to the place where I was hidden, asking me with her eyes to admit Dante to my presence; and the saints, all in unison, made prayerful gestures begging me to grant her request. I accepted the part entrusted to me by the poet and waited for him at the very end.

Dante had by now come close to me, and his eyes pierced my very being. I saw that he was wearing the glasses I had given him, and there was no doubt that at that moment he could see perfectly. I appeared to him as I was, without concealment. I saw him go pale and hesitate, like a man who has been dreaming and, returning to his waking senses, confusedly remembers his dream. The moment of recognition was dazzling and mysterious, as though the sea itself had become able to contemplate the ship plowing through it. He had seen me as I was, father and son of my very own self, the fire of intelligence that circulates through the cosmos and pours into humankind in order to attain the form of thought and words. Through his mind flashed the image of divine incarnation, the God who becomes man in order to be helped rather than to help. It was too much for the pilgrim-poet. Dante's mind renounced this final step. Like snow melted by the sun, like the ink of a manuscript erased by time, everything that he contemplated in me was swallowed into the account he gave of it.

I saw him give way to the sleep of oblivion, the pen laid down on the table. I left him at rest, with his head on his arm. I exited his book and then the castle and then Verona. Soon I was on the road again. I pawned the clock and with the money bought a woolen mantle for the rest of the winter.

Before long, I found myself a sailor in Columbus's crew on the way to the Indies.

The day before, a ship had set sail from Cadiz carrying several Jews expelled from Spain. My family and friends were on that ship, having refused to abjure the religion of our fathers. My fate was different. I had fled from the city of Cordova to the seacoast and had arrived in Palos de la Frontera, where, standing in the crowd, I listened to the inflamed words of an old sailor. Some time earlier he had had to cut short a voyage to the Sargasso Sea, and now he was urging the men present to participate in a new adventure. He loudly proclaimed the good fortune awaiting those who would depart on board the three caravels, for they would find earthly riches and eternal salvation, and their enterprise had the blessing of the most Christian king and the holy Queen Isabella. As I listened to the speech of Pedro Vasques (that's what they called him), something inside me responded.

In my bag there were a few possessions that I had been able

to save from the pogrom, among them Marco Polo's book, which had long fed my dreams. One chapter spoke of a distant land where gold covered the ground like pebbles along a path through the fields. No one had ever seen that land but there was no doubt about its existence. I also had a map that showed the white area beyond the sea to the south of the Indies, and on it you could read the inscription *terra non condita*, territory as yet unknown. When I read those pages and examined that map, confused emotions stirred in me. In the crowd at Palos de la Frontera I felt as though I were accepting a suggestion that had always been written in the pages of that book and the markings on that map. I went to the harbor and signed up under a Christian name.

I was more than thirty years old, but after they saw me at work they gave me the job of cabin boy. It didn't bother me; I had joined the ship to escape the fate of my people and remain a free man. I pretended I was mute, since my accent would have given me away as a fugitive Jew. I spoke with grunts and cries, like a bird of the air. They took me for an eccentric and treated me well. In fact, I was so well liked that I soon became Columbus's valet. I owed this position also to my being thought a mute: I would be unable to act as a spy for the sailors. I adapted to my new task. I was given a very small space, but I had it all to myself, and in the evening I could read the Bible and Marco Polo before falling asleep.

My cabin was adjacent to Columbus's, and if I put my ear against the wall I could hear him pray before going to bed. His prayers were a mixture of Spanish, Latin, and a Genovese dialect, and I didn't understand most of them. I remembered the story of the Tower of Babel that my father used to read to us when we were children and how God had mixed up the languages when man tried to reach heaven with the immense construction begun by Nimrod. What if the same thing were happening here? Why was this crew crossing an ocean that nobody had dared venture across before? The chief of the expedition spoke three languages, and perhaps he no longer knew what he was saying! His voice was drowned out by that of a boy charged with saying prayers on deck, who would begin the nightly invocation, *Amén y Dios nos de buenas noches.*

Wrapped in my blankets, in the small room lit by a smoky lamp, I would talk to myself in Ladino, reassuring myself that I had not ended up in another Tower of Babel, until I fell asleep. And then the dreams began. My wife, with a burst of laughter, welcomed my return. My mother watched the scene, looking out from the kitchen. My son stretched his arms out to me. And I cried in my sleep, without hope, because I knew that I would never see them again. When I was awake I envied the Christians because of their belief in another world, where fathers find their children again, and wives run to embrace their husbands.

However, there was the ocean, and memory of my divinity was appeased by its presence. After serving the meals at the commanders' tables and listening to the conversation, I could not get on deck soon enough to scrutinize the horizon, where the sky joined the ocean and where, at night, they melted together. Columbus was always in a hurry and paid no attention to his food. His desk was covered with geographical maps, which he would mark here and there, with a great shifting of compasses and rulers. Gutierrez, the second in command, would visit him, and together they would become absorbed in the study of the charts, discussing until late into the night what route they should take. It seemed clear to me that neither of them knew where we were going. I didn't care, but I knew that the sailors were restless. And then, with a shrug, I would say to myself, What difference can it make for me?

My recollection that I was God was imperfect at this point, since my soul harbored ill will, the most antidivine feeling of all. I thought that my life had come to an end, and I had only the slightest interest in the fate of others. To console me I had, besides my books, an instrument that I would take with me whenever I went on deck and walked toward the ship's prow. It was a magnetic needle that pointed north from any position, so that I always knew where we were going, and it seemed to me that I myself was guiding the ship toward its destination. "What Indies?" I asked myself, mocking the captain's plans. "Going in this direction we'll never reach them." I was sure that he was making a mistake, but this too did not interest me. I caught myself whispering absurd sentences before falling asleep. "What matters is not to live but to navigate," I remember thinking; it did not seem to make much sense.

Sorrow shook me periodically. I had not denied my faith, but by now I had become a deserter, separated from my own blood. I didn't care so much about the lost ceremonies and traditions, because I had always been a skeptic in that regard; but I felt the weight of my loneliness. I was rootless, a leaf at the mercy of wind and fate. I thought about my son in my wife's arms as they made their way toward Flanders, where the family had decided to take refuge. Whatever had led me to dissociate myself from their destiny? Why was I aboard the Santa Maria?

I asked myself these questions at night, when I was charged with turning over the small oddly shaped ampoule of sand, the device used to measure time aboard the admiral's flagship. As soon as all the sand had run through, I would turn the ampoule and mark a short dash on a sheet of paper, the sign that another half hour had passed. Had I fallen asleep and neglected to turn the hourglass, time would have escaped us and been lost in the nocturnal sky. "Time does not exist," I thought one night. "Time is nothing more than we ourselves crossing the ocean and counting the turns of the ampoule. On this ship it is I who decides whether time will be preserved or lost." From this to remembering that I was God was only a short step.

I spent another night measuring time, and then everything became comprehensible, like the pieces of a puzzle that are joined together after a long period of confusion. The separation from those dear to me, my loneliness, the fleet upon the ocean like a constellation traversing space toward an unknown destination, and I myself marking the sheet every half hour, close to the cabin where the admiral was snoring. If I listened intently I could hear, beyond the silence, the wash of the waves against the hull, and below us and around us the surreptitious trotting of mice on the stairs and in the hold. "Yes, I am God," I thought. "I no longer have a father and I no longer have a mother. I have lost my wife, I have lost my son. This is my solar system. I am inside a comet traveling across the water."

I went on deck to gaze at the stars. They were like an immense army traveling toward an undiscovered continent. I remained on the bridge until dawn, going below every so often to turn the ampoule; and when dawn cracked the sky behind us, I heard the morning hymn and wake-up call for the crew:

Bendita sea la luz
y la Santa Veracruz
y el Señor de la Verdad
y la Santa Trinidad

I gratefully welcomed the salute and then the cry that marked the beginning of the day's work. I heard the men summoned to assembly—"Al cuarto, al cuarto," the cabin boy shouted with enough force to raise the drowned. "Al cuarto que ya es hora! Leva, leva, leva!" I hopped about the bridge, smiling at everyone and waving greetings to the returning sun, whose rise at that point seemed miraculous to me and certainly worthy of a little demonstration. The sailors looked at me, astonished by so much enthusiasm, worn out as they were by the long voyage. I had to make an effort not to break my silence. I watched the birds that followed the ship day and night, the swarms of fish in the wake. The entire marine world was on the move.

Everything regained meaning, even the fact that I had lost faith in the Hebrew religion. "This is why you no longer believe," I told myself while I cleaned the admiral's room and his desk cluttered with compasses and charts. "This is why you cannot believe! You've known all along that there was something higher to reach for, something that would catch up with you and transform you into a wandering Jew." In my mind was born the idea of finding once again the Eden described in Genesis and about which the books dear to me fantasized. Perhaps that was where we were headed.

We sailed farther and farther to the west. Plants that we had never seen before appeared floating on the water, and in the sky unknown birds were flying. The entire firmament was changing position. The moon looked like a companion of other times. One night, leaning against the cabin wall, I listened to a conversation between Columbus and an officer who was devoured by anxiety that the voyage would never come to an end. Columbus's words reached me like a fragment from a philosophical discourse.

"You see," Columbus was saying to the officer, "we mustn't complain about our fate. It is true that we are on the high seas, far from home and uncertain about our destination. It is true that we dream, at the same time, about our arrival and our return. It is true that we interrogate the stars and entrust ourselves to the winds, and it is true that every night we must comfort ourselves with prayers. And all of this is often painful. But just think! What would we be doing if we were not at sea? Something cheerful and beautiful, or perhaps something even more painful and distressing? The second hypothesis is the more probable, if you think back on our past life. And even if we did escape pain and sorrow, do you know what might await us that is even more dreadful? Boredom, mankind's mortal enemy! Whereas here, on our journey, boredom, you'll have to admit, cannot take root. And how strong is the weight of one's memory during a voyage! What we had every day on land today seems all the more precious to us—flowers and young girls, rivers and fields of grain. Even the ground on which we walked. Who, if not sailors, ever thought of it as precious? As you see, we follow a dream and are fulfilled by the quest. And even as we seek new land, we are sustained by the memory of the land we have left. Ours is not an ugly fate!"

I no longer knew whether I was listening or dreaming. The ampoule was empty and I hurried to turn it over. The silence was now absolute beneath the cloud-covered sky. Where was the North Star? I walked up and down the bridge in the throes of thought. "Columbus is right," I said to myself. "He reasons well, this sailor from Genoa. Now I understand all these frantic explorations better. But his arguments don't apply to me. I was not bored! I was happy with my life and was not looking for this to happen. Mine is not a human destiny. Its only explanation is that it must be a divine one."

Walking to the entrance of the hold where the sailors slept, I stared into it without seeing anything. I was nailed to the spot by a strange fascination. I hesitated. Then I descended into that world which seemed to me, like the admiral's cabin, crowded with thoughts. But what thoughts were they? I stumbled among the mice that scurried below deck. I went ahead, groping and feeling my way until I was near the beds of the sleeping men and could hear the starts and moans of their sleep. I lingered to listen to them. Some were afraid of shipwreck, others fantasized about gold and diamonds, still others invoked their distant country and the names of those dear to them.

I stood there taking in the vast murmur of the exhausted and discontented crew. I rushed back to the deck just in time to turn the glass. In the next room the officer had left and gone to sleep, and Columbus paced about for a long time before lying down himself. I heard him pray, as was his habit before falling asleep. That night I told myself that God had chosen for his abode the body of a Jew aboard a ship owned by Christian persecutors, and all this so that I would become the explorer of a world of hope. I saw myself as a restless animal dispatched to investigate the world—a fox, an eel, a dolphin leaping through the seas. On the ship, only I and the cabin boy on duty, huddled in his blankets in a corner of the bridge, were awake.

It was precisely that cabin boy who, the following morning, let out the cry that all were waiting for: "Tierra, tierra! Señor, albricias!" And he claimed the reward promised to whoever first sighted land. Later on I remembered the extraordinary excitement of that moment and the crew wildly milling about on deck and the first tenders that were set ashore. We set foot on the island, which we baptized with a Christian name. The half-naked bodies of the natives and the friendly welcome convinced me that in this place it was possible to recommence the history of the world. But the last page that I read in Columbus's log declared his resolve to convert the natives to slavery.

It was then that I decided to go and live among the natives, and I moved from tribe to tribe, as the conquerors gradually advanced and subjugated the villages. I pushed inland, following rivers to their sources, traversing plains, scaling mountains, coming ever closer to myself and my original hopes, until every trace of my passage was lost and I was forgotten. It was as though God had been swallowed up by a swamp or a swift stream.

FRAGMENTS of this voyage came back to me in London, where, a very devout and sedentary little man, hunchbacked and lame, I was drawing geographical maps.

I lived alone, as was my habit. My mother had died the year before and joined my father in heaven, where I imagined him drawing maps for the angels. From him I had learned the art of cartography, and it suited me, given the body that fate had allotted me. I spent a large part of my time at home in a study lined with maps, books, compasses, globes, and a precious astrolabe made in Italy, which had reached my family after several peregrinations. It was rumored that it had belonged to Columbus during his first voyage to the Americas, but this was most certainly a legend. As far as my studies could determine, that great navigator was not equipped with one.

Some time before, my wife had fled from home, and I had no idea where she had gone. This had not shaken my conviction that in this world there existed a divine providence, a golden thread that runs through history and holds together the destinies scattered in the world. My son had disappeared with her. By now he was grown up, and perhaps he lived in London, in my very neighborhood. Glancing away from my work, I tried to figure out how old he would be. Was he eighteen or twenty? I could not reckon.

I had been working for years on a world atlas. By now I had prepared dozens of maps of continents, of regions and islands strewn across the surface of the globe. I devoted the most thorough attention to the shorelines, the marine depths, the heights of mountains, the courses of rivers, the jagged lines that separated nations and were altered after every war and every treaty. That is why I continued with my work, fearful of printing it until it was perfect and all the gaps had been filled. Because of the voyages and continuing discoveries, the form of the world was forever changing. I kept receiving reports from recent explorations, together with crude and approximate maps. I worked at deciphering those hasty hypotheses, convinced that I'd been given the task of reestablishing order in a universe long neglected and torn by violence.

I had become accustomed to the idea that my work would go on until my death and that I would then take it with me into the heavens to compare it with what my father, through the direct vision of the angels and the blessed, had drawn up there. At that time I would correct all my previous mistakes. I strode toward beatitude, oblivious of the bodily ailments and misfortunes that had stricken me. Although the memory of my divinity was dim and muddled by Christianity, I became certain that I had come down from heaven to map my possessions, like a surveyor who takes his measurements in the field and then goes home to proceed with calculations and inventories.

I was a suffering God, intent on re-creating the world in the only way that was granted to me. On the day of this revelation I began to work on a single map of the entire globe, within a network of longitudes that curved and dilated like the segments of a peeled orange. I was resolutely happy. My life brimmed with meaning, and the sheets of drawing paper filled up with vast and scattered tracts of color.

I almost never left my study, and I would lie down in a corner to sleep, in a bed that I myself made every day. One night I was awakened by a clamor at the door. I rose and went downstairs, stopping to listen. Outside, someone knocked and groaned in a stream of disconnected sentences. Overcoming my fear, I opened the door. I was struck by wind and rain, and then a body fell sprawling into the hallway, knocking me down in the process. The man cried out and lost consciousness. I managed to see his face in the uncertain light, and despite all the time that had passed and all the signs of the man's ruinous misfortune, I had no trouble in recognizing my son. I had not yet recovered when I felt my hand drenched by a hot jet gushing from his side. At that I plunged into the night and went stumbling through the streets in search of a surgeon. I found someone, and together we moved my son's body to my bed, where the doctor proceeded to treat him. He had lost a lot of blood, and the knife wound was deep. After some time I was left alone with him.

He was lost in sleep. I looked at him carefully. Cleaned up and wearing one of my dressing gowns, he was indeed my son, as beautiful as Adonis, without a trace of my ugliness. I thought he had returned to me as a gift of the providence that watched over my earthly passage. That night I promised myself that I would give myself to him, body and soul; it did not matter where he came from or what he had done. Observing him as he slept, I sharpened my pencils but drew not a single line.

When he woke up and was able to speak, he told me his story. He had eked out a living, dividing his time between the actors of a theater where he had occasional work and the taverns where the intrigues of London's underground life were concocted. He had been knifed during a brawl over a purse whose provenance he would not explain to me. I listened to him, saddened, but also with benevolence. So this had been his fate. But now heaven had delivered him into my hands, and I was going to take care of him.

I recall the excitement with which I went about looking for food and clothes, and how I would be visited by unexpected and daring ideas. I thought of him as Jesus, who had gone into the dark and violent world of men, been killed, and finally returned to his father's house, where I had always been waiting for him. His return seemed to me to be the certain proof of my achieved divinity. While he rested after a meal I had prepared for him, I returned to my work on the map of the globe and drew with an inspired hand the coast of an undiscovered land in the south, and I colored it a bright red that faded away toward the interior of the mysterious region. I too fell asleep, my mind filled with visions of unknown trees.

The next morning my son had gone, taking with him the garments I had bought him and all the money he had been able to find in the house. He could not have gone far, weak as he was. I assumed he would return, and for two days I listened intently for any sound at the door. Insomnia haunted me from the moment of his departure. I began to go out in the evening, bundled up in a heavy coat, and look for him in the taverns of the theater district.

There were many taverns and I wandered from one to the next. Some of them welcomed poor wretches and prostitutes; others were frequented by theater people, and there I looked for him more carefully. In vain I gazed into face after face, amid deafening racket. My search proved futile. Finally I sat down at a table in one of the taverns and ordered something to drink, I who never drank! I was so despondent that I was ready to give up and get drunk, when I noticed that someone had sat down at my table. He was a young man, but not as young as my son, shorter and less robust; and he was definitely more used to wine than I. He realized that I was looking at him and he began to talk to me. He told me a tangled story that did not make much sense; but in any case it became clear that he was an actor and dramatist. He complained a great deal about his success, which did not seem great enough to him and was imperiled by a conspiracy of his rivals. I let him talk, quite willing to listen to his grievances in the hope of forgetting my own troubles, and as he drank and spoke I kept looking at his unkempt head, his mustache damp with wine, his narrow shoulders and his gnarled hands.

I compared him to my son, who was more beautiful, albeit equally discontented and angry. And I cursed not having found him instead of this stranger who was telling me everything about himself. Suddenly he told me his name and I realized that I had heard of him. I had heard people mention some of his works, historical dramas, comedies, and mythological farces. He was a prolific and notably successful author. Why was he in such a bad mood? I sat there listening to him, a bit befuddled by the little I had drunk. The actor grew animated at the thought of his work and began to recite his lines with a stammering but nevertheless clear voice. The lines were very beautiful, but it seemed to me that they would have benefited from more description and less turgidity. Everywhere you could sense a declamatory intent that partially spoiled the effect, which was, otherwise, of the first order. I told him this quite frankly and as a result offended him. He stared at me with mocking dislike and scrutinized me thoroughly from head to foot. A gleam crossed his face and he pointed his finger at me, while with his other hand he gestured toward the room, demanding attention.

In an instant there was silence in the tavern, and as though by magic our table was transformed into a stage, with myself and him as actors, I still uncertain of my role. He launched into a monologue meant to describe me: lame, deformed, afraid of projecting my shadow on the walls—the sight of me so repulsive that dogs attacked me and women shrank from touching me. I listened, unable to move and with the curious feeling that his speech had been rehearsed, and that he was using it against me so as to gauge its theatrical effect. During the performance laughter began to move stealthily among our drunken audience until finally it swelled into a chorus of hilarity. Spurred on by his success, the actor rose to his feet and held his hand out toward me with a gesture of complete contempt. My face was aflame; I stood up with great caution, trying to control every move. A torch nearby projected the shadow of my hump onto the table. My first step was so tottering that laughter accompanied me all the way to the door. I vanished into the fog, humiliated.

Distressed as I was, I walked until I realized that I was lost. I continued through fetid, unfamiliar alleyways in absolute darkness. By some sort of evil magic, I had arrived in a world of blind dwarfs. The doors and windows of the huts were low and extremely narrow, and I was barely able to walk through the garbage in the streets. I tried to retrace my steps and got even more confused in the dense tangle of streets. All of a sudden, an unlikely procession began. It seemed as if I had entered hell. Beside me passed the blind, the maimed, the crippled, the mangy, the demented, the pustulous, the goitered, the hungry, the drunk, the scrofulous, the cancerous, the delirious, the fugitive, the dazed. I was in some court of obscene miracles. Old people and children fought over a piece of bread; even the air exuded dirt and stench. Nobody noticed me. All were caught up in some apocalyptic dream. Muffled in my coat, motionless in the mob, I saw myself as God descending incognito to visit the human sewers, and a sting of remorse entered my soul. I lingered to contemplate the debacle, leaning against the wall of one of the hovels. Then someone discovered me in the shadows; a hand reached out to me; the alleyway resounded with lamentation. I slipped out of my cape, which another hand had grasped, and fled blindly through the darkness.

This cannot be the world, I told myself. It cannot all be like this. There must be a part of it that is blossoming. I remember it, I've been told about it. Where is it?

Of course, if I had been an angel it would have been easy. I would have flown to the woods and lakes and shores that I had worked on for years, and there I would have fulfilled my dream of beauty. But I was lame and nearly faint with exhaustion. I scrambled through the night until I found myself in front of a theater. I entered it to regain my breath. The show had already begun; I bought a ticket for a seat that was still available in the first balcony, mounted the stairs, and let myself fall onto the bench.

That evening they were performing a mythological fable with dances and music and with a great coming and going of actors and lantern-bearers, all to the delight of a rowdy audience. The crowd was caught up in action taking place on several stages, encouraging and threatening the characters, shaking their fists and shouting. I did not enter into the enthusiasm, partly out of shyness and partly because I had arrived late and did not quite understand what was happening onstage; but I was captivated by what I saw after so many years of not having set foot in a theater. The movement, the lights, the beauty of the costumes worn by boys playing women's parts, the contagious sense of magic that animated the entire building, all of this came back to me like a memory of other days. At the end of the performance, I was surrounded by the crowd surging toward the exit.

Then I was in the streets of London again. I walked some distance, my eyes filled with a whirling turbulence of costumes and bodies. I went into a few more taverns, but in vain. Perhaps my son had lied to me and did not live around there. He certainly did not want me to find him. A great weariness drove me to my home, where I fell into a heavy, disquieting sleep.

I awoke in tears in the dead of the night. As I lay in bed clutching my blanket, the theater reappeared to me as though it were itself the world that I was drawing on a map—the stage a continent surrounded by seas, and hell beneath a trapdoor. I was playing a role, but whether a comic or a tragic one I wouldn't know until the end of the play, written by the Supreme Author. In the darkness of the room, I knelt on the floor and immersed myself in prayer. I asked to be forgiven the foolish thoughts that had distressed me, and I gave thanks for the gifts that had been bestowed on me as well as the infirmities that had saddled me since birth.

At that moment I realized that the poor old man did not want to be God anymore. I detached myself and watched him pray for a while. He was so absorbed that he did not hear me leave.

SOME time later I returned again to Italy, the country dreamed of among the northern mists. In Venice, after a wearying journey among the clouds, in the warm, damp air of the Veneto summer, I stood before the Bridge of Sighs. While the gondolas glided by, silent as butterflies, I brought back to memory the prisoners I had visited during the years of the Great Incarceration. One of them had been locked up in the Tower of London for thirteen years, busily writing the history of the world, of which I was the evident and hidden protagonist. I had spent a great deal of time with him in an effort to enlighten him, until they dragged him out to take him to the block. I was never able to discover what he thought of that final experience. Had that too been ordained by me?

I remembered the French gentleman who had chosen confinement in his study, where he withdrew to read ancient books and write down the thoughts inspired by his readings. The walls of the room were covered with scribblings in Greek and Latin; he never rose from his desk to look at the countryside from his windows. Nature did not interest him at all. He had once written, "We must do as the beasts who erase their tracks at the entrance to their dens," and his body, glued to the chair at the desk, had taken on the shape of an animal in its lair, a hare enclosed in darkness. Every day he would venture into the idea of Death until he breathed inside it, assuming the rigid immobility of someone buried alive. He would resume his normal state just in time to get dressed and hurry off to his duties as the town's mayor. I admired him for playing both roles so well.

I remembered, too, a visit with a faithful imprisoned Italian, a monk condemned because of his heretical views, who spent his time writing poems of condemnation for the world and praise for my justice. I don't know how he succeeded in seeing anything in the dark cell where he was shut away, surrounded by indescribable filth and the stench of his own excrement. He had feigned madness in order to escape death, so strong was his bond to the very life he despised in his poetry. I did my best to introduce some air into the fetid cell, and then he would awake from his torpor and jot down another chapter about the perfect society he meant to construct, a community dominated by priests—so little had he learned from his own fate. I would then seek solace in the studio of a painter in Amsterdam, where I posed without being asked, and many times he painted me on the pretext of painting himself. I still go to look at myself in those portraits to see how I appeared then.

Among so many memories of solitary persons stands out the love story of a Spanish nun. Teresa de Avila had adored me for some time in her fantastic and excessive way, and in a manner that was at once sweet and menacing she demanded the same sort of love from the friars and nuns around her. I had seen her during a procession, and I was struck by her face, devoured by a pale and inexhaustible flame. I went to visit her as she was praying in her cell, and I saw the configuration of the soul into which she had withdrawn like a bristling porcupine or like a turtle in its shell. Her soul was like a castle with seven concentric apartments, and at the center of the castle stood the room that awaited us as bride and groom. I was seduced by Teresa's beauty and ardor and accompanied her as she passed through the seven apartments. She traversed each room with a firm and light step, leaving earthly temptations behind. She had divested herself of all lust by the time she reached the nuptial chamber, where our encounter took place. We exchanged not a word; she asked nothing about life or about me. She only wanted to love me, and I was happy to have her do so, in the heart of her very soul. I recall her pleasure in the swift rhythms of prayer, her eyes rolled back, her breath jagged, her limbs gripped by ecstatic tremors. As I penetrated the folds of her soul, a scent of incense swathed the nuptial couch, and an ingenious carillon wrought in gold beat out a sound of bells: the third, the sixth, the ninth. My mistress dozed off in a vision of angels, who removed her mortal envelope and left her dressed only in her soul as if it were a nightgown.

Other moments were less joyful. Once I fell into a great depression and decided to put an end to my days. This is an idea that comes back to me every so often, and quite forcefully. I had become a dauber in Pisa, having persuaded myself that I could best express my divine nature to humanity through art. But my talent got me no further than drawing angels and madonnas on the walls of small churches lost in the countryside. I found that I had no hope of being called to paint in the big churches of the towns to which famous artists would come. I admired them from afar, without approaching them; then I returned to my brushes and the tins in which I mixed always the same colors. I was forced to acknowledge that I, God, was not in the same class as the masters, but I did not know how deeply disappointed I was by this.

One day a friend had the idea of showing me a work by Caravaggio, the criminal painter wanted by the police of half of Italy. It was a painting that my friend kept hidden in his house, waiting for the proper moment to sell it. He led me inside, and from a heap of other canvases in a dark corner of his attic he produced what he wanted to show me, bringing a torch closer to it so that I could see. It would have been better had I not seen that painting.

Before me loomed a scene so vivid that it filled me with religious stupefaction—precisely the feeling I had tried to inspire in the populace attending the churches whose walls I had frescoed. I was overwhelmed by the daring of the composition. At the center of the painting shone a light that erupted from some hidden source. It was so strong that it seemed to obscure the torch with which my friend illuminated the painting. All around this light writhed violent and ecstatic figures. Why do I say *writhed?* Because that was the sensation offered to my eyes, in a flaring up of colors, each of which seemed to be dreamed by the color next to it, so that the painting was like life but even more than life. As I became aware of my inadequacy, I could no longer breathe. My friend was whispering professional observations that I didn't bother to pay attention to, lost as I was in the whirlpool of my failure. I saw myself painting pictures that had to be set aside to make room for what I was now admiring. I was a sparrow or a thrush confronted by a soaring eagle! I fled from that house like a thief in the dark.

I spent a sleepless night. Beside me slept my lover, unaware of what tormented me. She was a naive admirer of my work and would forever believe that I was an artist, a Raphael and a Titian, and in her faith I saw a will to ignore my person, as though she did not wish to see me as I was.

I got out of bed and went to the studio. On the easel stood an Annunciation I had just begun. The Madonna was still only a study of lines and sketched draperies, for until then I had worked chiefly on the angel. I looked at the angel with hostility, still under the impression awakened in me by that other painting. It was a blond angel with a feminine face and a white and azure robe. One wing was finished and I was half done with the other. The hand that reached out to the Madonna still lacked fingers, which were barely sketched in with pencil, and the celestial messenger looked to me like a maimed and mutilated monster, stretched out toward a phantom wrapped in a thicket. What I saw seemed to me a summation of my aimless life and of my incomplete art, through which I passed like a blind wanderer pretending he can see. I thought that the fate awaiting that painting was to resemble the frescoes in my churches, unhappy to be finished and have their real nature exposed. And it was then that I wanted to die.

I had no idea how one goes about taking one's own life, and I left the house in order to think about it. Until dawn I roamed about outside the city, in the countryside swept by the sounds of the wind. I meditated on what was happening to me and reached a desolate conclusion: if I had failed, it was because I had not become the painter I should have been in keeping with my divinity. I had lost myself in the imitation of other artists. But perhaps in donning the artist's mask I had lost sight of my mission, which now I was no longer able to remember; I should rather have been a merchant, a baker, or simply a loving and faithful husband. Caged in this sort of fruitless speculation, I regretted having fallen so low in the divine trajectory.

I made a decision. I must free myself of all masks, including the bodily one, and emerge from myself in order to rise aloft again. But how? The dagger terrified me. I would never gather the nerve to cut myself. I didn't possess any poison and had no idea where to find some. At the first glimmer of dawn, I went to gaze at the Arno's waters; but the swirls of the current dissuaded me from the option of drowning. I reentered the city and stood below the leaning tower. Flooded by the rising sun the tower cast a shadow that fell in a long line across the piazza. I found the door open and climbed the steps all the way to the top.

Atop the railing on the side where the tower leaned toward the ground, I remembered the legend of the architect who had built it and had been awakened in the depths of the night by the howling of his workshop assistants, who feared the bell tower was collapsing. He had rushed to the spot, climbed all the way to the top, where I was at this moment, and measured the scope of the disaster. Such was his shame that he threw himself into the void, to be followed, in the course of time, by a long series of unhappy lovers and ruined merchants. Contrary to all predictions, the tower did not fall. For centuries it had been leaning ever closer to the ground as if it wanted to meet it as gently as possible.

There was a more recent story connected with that tower. I again saw Galileo's jovial body, his bearded and serene face—an image of satisfied divinity just the slightest bit perplexed by the confusion he saw all around, and in which he was trying to restore some order. One morning at the crack of dawn, as in that wretched moment of mine—and all along I continued to stare into the void with violent fascination—Galileo had also climbed the tower. He was not plagued, however, by thoughts of death. The story claimed, in fact, that Galileo had dropped from the top of the tower two objects of different weights, and that a student, who had remained below, had testified with shouts and gestures that both objects had reached the ground at the same instant, thus contradicting every previous hypothesis concerning falling weights. I could not understand why these two stories were combined into one and why, at that moment of mortal crisis, both seemed to signify something essential for me. Only one step away from the ultimate void, I clung to the railing with the strength of one who wants to retrieve the life that is escaping him. I looked at Pisa from above, and all the way to the sea, suffused by the sun, which was by now high in the sky. In the distance I saw the islands of Capraia and

Gorgona, and to the east the ring of the Apennine mountains. I went back down the circle of the stairs and came out into the piazza, already crowded with people.

As I turned to gaze at the tower, I could identify with the destiny of its builder, who had remained famous through time because of his unforgivable failure. And I thought that, if I had cast myself down, giving way to dismay, I would have reached the ground in the same amount of time as he had, a perfectly identical fate for a great artist and the most obscure dauber. I was not worthy of achieving equality with him in death.

I breathed with relief. The perfume of life was everywhere— I had never realized how strong it was. My lover was waiting for me, and I could hardly wait to embrace her and to go back to finish my mediocre painting, since even failure, I now understood, was part of my existence. The finished canvas that I took away as a souvenir of this adventure seemed not so bad after all.

My memory is woven out of small and great events in the fabric of time. Visiting great artists and artists manqué has always been one of my privileges. I happened to walk along with a young man by the name of Sebastian Bach when he could not afford to pay for a carriage home after listening to the great Buxtehude play the organ thirty miles away. I did so much for him during that long walk that he would benefit from it for the rest of his life. I was a good friend of Mozart, whose playfulness consistently amused me; and while he was composing his final *Requiem*, worn out and not knowing who was impelling him to write that work, I was at his side and kept talking to him. You can find some traces of our conversation inside that same music, and that is why I still love to listen to it.

I can see myself discoursing with the ill composer and repeating excitedly all the attributes of myself that I had recently read about in a theological treatise. "Listen to this, Wolfgang. You know what I am supposed to be? One and threefold, immense and individual, merged with everything, unified in my fragments. What alchemist could do better? I am visible and invisible, luminous without light, the beginning and end of ev-

erything, devoid of beginning and lacking an end, creator from
nothingness, the loftiest and the deepest. Ask a painter to paint
my portrait, if he can!"

Mozart remained impassive, immersed in his creation. He
was now composing one of the most majestic passages of his
work and was close to the end. He could hardly wait, since he
had arranged for an inviting lunch and the smells of the cooking reached us from the kitchen. I continued as if I were myself
inspired.

"Find me anyone else who can, like me, be situated in every
place and yet not be circumscribed in any place, and who can
move all things without moving! Would you like to compare
me to a monarch? Then let me tell you that I am forever ancient
and forever new, and have no need for descendants." I went
on and on this way, chirping about myself with borrowed
words like a second-rate poet.

Mozart stopped me when he had finished his scheduled
work for that morning. He put his pen down, closed the key-
board, and stood up to move to the other room. Before leaving
the studio, he looked at me for a moment (and I could see how
tired he was, notwithstanding all his creative energy). He
looked at me with no evident feeling, as if he were considering
my stature, or my temper, in a quite technical manner. It was
obvious that he believed in me, but he did not especially like
me. I think he considered God some sort of curiosity that one
cannot really ignore, but which should not be excessively admired. Having sized me up, he shrugged his shoulders and
rushed to his meal, regaining his playful mood.

I went to his scores and read what he had just finished composing. It was an aria in which my divine power was enthusias-
tically celebrated, with astounding musical effects. But I could
sense the composer giggling silently behind his music. So that
was my function: to inspire his music but not his reverence.

I often tried my own hand at music. Until meeting Mozart
I had treated it like a pleasant servant, but recently I had decided to make it my personal language. Learning from experience, I was careful not to compose anything myself. Instead, I
would descend into the body and soul of a musician and

emerge from it promptly when the creative work was done. The musicians sensed my arrival but did not know what name to give me or whence I came.

By frequenting their homes, I acquired proficiency with instruments: violins, bass fiddles, violas, clavichords and spinets, oboes and horns. It seemed to me that I had found the language I had long sought in the wind over the sea or the crash of cascading rivers or in lofty thunderclaps that pursued each other through the caverns of the sky. Humankind, this prodigious mimic, had captured my voices inside brasses, strings, and percussion. Enchanted, I devoted myself to liberating the songs that were imprisoned in humankind's magical instruments.

I had found refuge and release. As I roamed the world, I could hear rising from various points of the planet the chords and melodies that I had helped to make possible. O music, you have rendered my life infinitely luminous. Without you, there would be no consolation for my silent and solitary spirit.

4

Humankind and I grew old together. For a time I hid the fact of my age from myself, becoming the adolescent son of a French aristocrat and quite forgetting my divinity. And yet my family, at least, was ancient—so old that it had earned a viscountcy and an invitation to court every three weeks.

My father, the viscount, would spend entire evenings reading the philosophers he loved, the radical and innovative men of the Enlightenment, the libertines of thought, the demolishers of centuries-old certainties. How many times, during a conversation, did I hear him quote a sentence from his beloved Voltaire, accompanied by a smile and a shake of his head, as if to say, "What a great man!" I watched him read his masters, never removing his powdered wig and always perfectly garbed, in the reading room of the Paris mansion where generations of our family had lived.

Everything around me spoke of interminable durations. A proof of our old age was the way we dressed. I was oppressed by closets full of suffocating ceremonial garb. My father would have been shocked had he seen me come to table without my wig, and my mother would caress my face only when I appeared before her dressed elegantly enough for a carriage ride. To free myself from the clothes that tortured me, I took up riding and fencing. I would ride to the Bois de Boulogne and as soon as I arrived would throw off my riding costume. In trousers and shirt, I would spur on my mount with my heels, like the son of a peasant, and disappear among the trees before the eyes of the valet who escorted me. My furious ride would last an hour, and each time it was as though a new itinerary were opening within me.

I also loved to fence and was most skillful at épée. I longed for a war to prove my valor, but there weren't any wars for our kind of nobility, and we walked about with merely decorative dress-swords at our sides. I had struck up a friendship with André, my fencing teacher, a young bourgeois who had literary talent and paid the rent for his room in the Latin Quarter by offering himself as a master of arms. We used to shut ourselves in the room of the mansion set aside for exercise and fence in our shirtsleeves, animated by an almost ferocious will to outdo each other. In the end we were drenched in sweat and rushed to quench our thirst, still inflamed with rivalry.

PASSING one evening by my mother's boudoir, I noticed that her door was ajar, and on an impulse I stopped to peer inside. I saw my mother lying back on her sofa and reading a book, and from my hiding place I could just make out the book's title. It was a novel that had become extremely popular lately, a story of a tutor who falls in love with his pupil, who eventually marries another and dies at a still young age, overcome by the memory of her first love. I had heard many stories concerning the author of that novel, whose name was Jean-Jacques Rousseau. He was a rustic and solitary man, a lover of nature and enemy of social life, and my parents should have hated him because he detested everything they held true. And yet he was the favorite writer of the Parisian aristocracy. As I reflected on this curious fact, I was startled by a loud sob.

I looked at my mother. I had never seen her weep in that way and I wouldn't have thought her capable of it. They were bitter tears, violent, mixed with sighs and stifled cries. Over her face, as in a *tableau vivant*, swept every sentiment that had been packed into that book. I understood that the force of these emotions depended on her having no hope of experiencing them as her own. I slipped away from the door and realized that my eyes too were brimming because I had seen real tears. But my soul felt withered.

I was disturbed enough to go and tell my father what I had just seen. I found him sitting down, completely dressed in his nightly apparel, and he too was reading a book. Although surprised at my visit, he disposed himself to listen to me, keeping a finger between the pages, which made me nervous throughout our conversation. When I finished my story, he obliged me with a series of considerations, his gaze wandering over the

shelves filled with books, on which the flames from the fireplace cast a flickering light. He spoke about my mother as
though she were a person of another time, described to him by
someone who had known her, and he used her as an example to
prove a theory in which he seemed to set great store.

He explained to me that each individual follows an inevitable law, which is that of satisfying his or her pleasure. Those
who are selfish get pleasure from self-appeasement, while
those who are generous and altruistic get it from giving of
themselves to others; and in precisely the same way there are
those who kill and those who cure the sick. If my mother read
stories that made her cry, it meant that from this she obtained
her satisfaction. The equanimity of his speech made my soul
ache. I instinctively moved closer to the fireplace as if I had a
chill. "So there is no way that one can come out of oneself!" I
caught myself exclaiming in a voice too loud for that setting.

My father looked at me and said nothing. Perhaps he was
asking himself why indeed I should want to come out of myself
and, if so, to go where. Then he asked me what book my mother
was reading. When I told him, he thought for a moment and
then launched into a monologue.

"A novel about love," he reflected in a highly meditative tone.
"Indeed, falling in love is a natural temptation. It seems that I
too cannot avoid it from time to time. This means that love
must after all yield some sort of pleasure, despite the anxieties
it causes. Love is a bit like life. In fact it follows life's trajectory
exactly. In youth it is full of joy and hope and one feels capable
of conquering the world. But happiness does not last long, because we end by becoming accustomed to what we are and
what we have. At that moment desire leaves us and boredom
inundates us. At the age of maturity, love, like life, is almost
exclusively composed of habits. We live for the annoyances but
not for pleasure. Jealousy, distrust, the fear of being deserted,
these feelings attach themselves to the body's old age. Among
all the decrepitudes, that of love is the most disagreeable."

He was silent for a moment and then spoke again, almost
as if he were recounting a distant event to himself.

"A love that is ending resembles a becalmed sea, when you
are aboard a ship that is unable to reach shore. Everything is

calm and boring. You see land; you would like to disembark, but the ship doesn't move because the wind is no longer blowing. Passengers and crew plunge into a strange languorous state. Food and water no longer have the same taste. Those who fish don't know what to do with the fish they catch and are haunted by thoughts that never leave them. You live, but with great regrets. Even when you make an effort to feel desire, so as to throw off this pall, the desires that come to the fore are spent and without direction. In the end you lie down on the bunk in your cabin and close your eyes, waiting for the doldrums to end."

"But when do they end?" I cried. My father was startled. He stared at me, removed his fingers from the book, put the slim volume down at his side, and got up to go to sleep. As he passed near me, he stopped as if he were uncertain, and I sensed that he was about to caress me. He must have changed his mind, because he walked past me, and before leaving the room he turned to say, in a quiet tone, "Old age only ends in death." And he disappeared in the direction of his rooms.

Left alone, I was submerged in melancholy. So this is what I must expect from life, that my passion will become the faded flower of myself? I shuddered at the thought. Why did I feel so different from my parents? It did not occur to me that I was inhabited by a trace of divinity.

The nocturnal dialogue with my father remained with me like a kind of testament. A few months later his own doldrums came to an end and the winds of death flung him against a rock he had never encountered before. I went to look at him on his deathbed in the middle of the room, where he was laid out surrounded by tapers. His face had a curiously jovial expression, and his jaw had relaxed as though he no longer needed to control his gestures and feelings. I asked myself whether he hadn't found in some book a convincing definition of death and clear advice on how to face it and how to behave when it came. Or perhaps death demanded absolute spontaneity and it was impossible to playact once it came. I had a sudden burst of affection for him and his newly recovered sincerity. I left that room in the paternal house and lost myself in the city.

I walked all day, and in the evening I went to a public concert. I don't know what impelled me to go there. Perhaps it was the sight of the joyous and elegantly dressed people who entered the church, transformed into a concert hall. I sat in a corner, away from the orchestra, near the exit, for I did not know if I would stay.

The pianist entered to join the other musicians. My attention roamed, and I began to admire the ceiling of the church, so that the start of the music caught me by surprise, carrying me immediately to vertiginous heights, to the prodigious recesses beyond everyday reality. Perhaps that was what I searched for when I galloped my horse and fenced, and perhaps my mother's need for tears came from that source. My face dripped with tears—such were the extremes I had been carried to by the orchestra's violent opening chords.

When the piano broke in, I seemed to perceive the dialogue with my father on the night of our encounter. It contained everything, and it could not have been better said. The orchestra thundered in an inexorable crescendo while the piano pursued a subdued and determined work of persuasion. I recognized myself, split in my very own soul. Was this the human creature? Had God conceived a being that argues for its instincts in a tone of reason? Perhaps I too was always seeking the same thing on different and tragically contrasting levels. Would I ever find the harmony that I was searching for? I decided not to wait for the final moment, when the notes cease to roll and in the audience each soul suddenly separates from the movement that had united it miraculously with the souls of the rest. I rose and left the church, pursued by the voice of the piano, which gradually convinced the orchestra to dominate its impulses. Nighttime Paris welcomed me like a fugitive.

DURING the period that followed my father's death, I almost always lived away from home. I had become close friends with André, who introduced me to his circle in the Latin Quarter. His friends were very different from the people I used to meet at the receptions in my house. They held group readings, debated heatedly, wrote articles for the newspapers and short essays for the encyclopedia, got drunk, gambled with dice, ran after girls, and paid no attention to the clothes they wore. They associated with tradesmen, coopers, typographers, painters, opera singers, mountebanks, and poets. I was fascinated by that spectacle of human variety and moved from one world to the other without really knowing what I was looking for.

The years of the Revolution went by in a tumult beneath the windows of our house. André was a protagonist of the great events, and he fenced oratorically in the amphitheater of the National Assembly. I went to hear him, mingling with the crowd of bourgeois and working folk. My mother had found asylum in England, and from there she had written in vain for me to join her. I watched what was happening, though I took no active part in it. I asked myself why so many people were moving at the same time and in the same direction. It did not seem a good sign to me. But I felt sure that André would become a leader and restore the world to reason.

I deceived myself. André was arrested one day, together with his friends, and locked up in the dungeons that held political prisoners. One left that place only to be taken to the gallows. I set out to visit him, though I knew that I might be arrested for doing so. I was admitted into a large cellar bereft of light, and at first I had no hope of finding my friend. Then a hand gripped my arm and a shadow stood before me. It was he! We embraced and sought a quiet corner to talk. I had many things to ask him, and I found it difficult to formulate my questions, but in the end they all came down to a single one: "Why are you in this hell instead of being out there, honored by everyone?" André sensed my torment and gave me his answer without further prompting: "We must do all that we possibly can, always, but the result does not depend on us. You may lose every battle except the battle with yourself." We whispered in the dark, like two conspirators intent on re-creating man.

A few days later André was decapitated, and I myself was in danger. I fled Paris and sought refuge in the vicinity of Chantilly, in the company of two women friends who had joined me. I soon got accustomed to my new life, which certainly was not devoid of pleasures. I read and went hunting and horseback riding, and in the open air I practiced with the sword. Enchanting summer sunsets flared in the sky. I would sit in the garden to write my thoughts in a notebook, listening to the women laugh and chat as they prepared dinner. The three of us would sleep together, and mornings I would find them embracing in their sleep, breast against breast and their hair intermingled. It was like a sojourn in the Muslim paradise, amid a whirling of swords and the smacking sound of kisses!

Happy as I was, I might have continued in this fashion for an entire lifetime, immersed in the oblivion that enfolds mortals, collapsing only occasionally in anguished jolts. But deep inside I knew I was searching for an opportunity that would pull me away from the blessed idleness of Chantilly.

As I waited, I received a letter from my mother in London. She had married a marquis and had had a son with him. I had a little brother! But the second part of the letter contained an even more surprising revelation. In a long story, which seemed inspired by her favorite romances, my mother confessed to me that I was the fruit of a distant sin of love. The viscount had not been my father. My real sire was a footman for whom she had nourished a guilty passion and who had long since disappeared from her life.

Now I knew why I had always felt so different from my relatives. "A bastard!" I said to myself. "A bastard!" The word had an exhilarating rather than an offensive sound. It occurred to me that to be without ancestry or a family tradition is a divine situation. God himself is a bastard, excessively so. He comes from nowhere, he does not know his parents, he has all the qualities and defects of the self-made person. He must be rather like myself, I mused; trusting, sincere, never satisfied with himself, never keeping quiet, always running after love. Yes, that would be God all over.

It was evening, a beautiful autumn evening. I heard the voices of my women rise from the courtyard and reach me in the study, where I had just finished reading my mother's letter. A magpie alighted in the open window, looked inside, emitted a hoarse cry, and flew away. My eyes turned to the portrait of an ancestor who, I now knew, was no ancestor at all, and then fell upon a book on the desk, open to the poem that I had learned that day. Those lines spoke of life with an ineffable tenderness. A glorious melancholy so like the season of the year transfixed my soul. I was very close to remembering who I was, but right then my nymphs burst into the room and I was swept away by the games of love.

A few days later the echo of Napoleon's exploits in Italy reached us. I immediately left my friends and hurried away to enlist. I joined the army in Piedmont, experiencing the intoxication familiar to all those who participated in that adventure. The general seemed to everyone an archangel who had descended to bring justice back to earth, young, disinterested, audacious. Old age was left behind us, lost in the twilight between the centuries.

We fought without fear, almost as though death were a trivial incident of battle. We arrived in Milan and two months later we left and went on to besiege Mantua, where we were met by a jubilant citizenry who wanted nothing better than to be defeated by us. Then we crossed the Alps and set out for Vienna. I was once again filled with the chivalrous spirit that long ago had convinced me to join the Crusades. This time too, I did not stay to the end of my war.

On a winter morning, there was a skirmish between my squad and a reconnaissance platoon of mounted Austrian soldiers. I can still picture the mountains on the horizon and, close by, the gloomy forest of evergreens. I can see again my horse's mane and the frozen lake at the foot of the mountains. I was shouting an order when, for an interminable moment, during which I was unable to move, I saw the projectile flying toward me. It was swift and confused like a mortal thought. "No, not now," I caught myself thinking in furious irritation.

An instant later I was lying on the ground and had commenced the complicated journey from which I awoke in a hospital. I heard German muttered in the next room and someone answering in French. Through the window I saw a tree whose branches were covered with snow. Right then I remembered myself. I was God! I was close to death and there was no time to waste. I floated on the bed like a water lily on a pond, before rising to leave. I had lost all longing for military conquests.

"You are a bastard," I said to myself, with sudden cheerfulness. "That is why life loves you so much."

It was the first and last thought we really had together. He abandoned me almost immediately, or maybe I abandoned him; after such prodigious merging it was difficult to tell.

The years circled with the wind. Memories dispersed like leaves in the face of an approaching winter. I migrated to the North, into the depths of boreal melancholy. I could sense the fear of old age that had settled upon the world. Humanity was afraid that history had carried it too far from its origins. Sitting among the ancient pines I realized that I too had changed. Once upon a time I had run through woods and plains as if I were the very breath of the world. Everything had appeared suffused with celestial light. I was seized now by such nostalgia that I did not know whether I should mourn for those woods or for my own childhood.

It was during this period that I turned to the poets as to the heralds of new youth. One of my most memorable encounters was with Friedrich Hölderlin.

I had come to Germany, to the banks of the Neckar River, among vineyard-covered hills. On a day when I was changing the color of the swaying wheat fields, I appeared to a small, curly-headed boy. He attached himself to me at once, never again to leave me. He saw me as the ether that embraces the earth or the galloping horse or the deer that wades the stream. He heard me in the sound that a river makes in spring. When I returned to see him years later I entrusted him with the task of extolling the return of my divinity to the created world. I had no idea what effect my demand would have. The fact is, it deranged him.

I became aware of his madness one day in France, when I waded out of the Garonne after a swim. There he was in front of me, and he again recognized me. He had been in Bordeaux for a few months, working as a tutor for the Hamburg consul, and he seemed pale and ailing. He did not appear surprised to see me, almost as though he had been waiting for me.

"So, you see, I was right," he said in an ecstatic voice. "The gods walk among us and rise from the rivers' waters. And so it is day again! Now don't leave, for I am afraid that night might return."

His appearance worried me so much that, instead of answering him, I jumped back into my clothes and set off with him to town, where I tried to convince him to go and be examined by a physician. We got into a heated argument in front of the theater that was then under construction, among the women returning from the harbor with fish sticking out of their shopping bags. "I don't want to go to the doctor!" Friedrich shrieked in German, his cheeks inflamed by irritation. "How can it be possible that God should be concerned with this sort of thing? Lift me up in flight instead. Make a demigod of me! You're as frustrating to talk to as Goethe."

Thus was the image of the German poet conjured up—large, fleshy, vigorous. To Hölderlin all the will for health seemed concentrated in Goethe, and it left my protégé deprived and anxious. I myself could not help comparing Goethe's majestic attire with the miserable tunic that I saw before me, the trousers that dropped in untidy folds, the dirty clogs too big for his thin, bony feet. I withdrew into embarrassment, and he asked me in a hesitant tone, "Did you see him? Have you met him recently? So that's why I seem imperfect to you. You think I'm inferior to Goethe! Go ahead, tell me the truth."

I didn't quite know what to tell him about Goethe, who deftly avoided me whenever I set out to talk with him. In any event, I felt sure that Goethe too would have advised Hölderlin to see a doctor, and perhaps he would have succeeded, but I was unable to convince him. We wound up in a tavern eating a mediocre meal. Friedrich, lost in ecstatic resentment, did not touch the food. I devoured the sinewy steak and washed it down with harsh wine, hungry as I was after my afternoon swim. He watched me, a bit incredulous that the God he had dreamed about since adolescence should be showing such an appetite on the other side of that table, in a badly lit room in southwest France.

Hölderlin eventually returned to his native city, retired to a mill, and spent the rest of his life in solitude. I was moved to pity by his fate, but I did not go to visit him. I thought of him as a friend for whom running into God had been a decidedly unlucky turn. He was gripped by resentment that he too could not be a god, and so enclosed himself in silence like an eagle in its nest. He was more concerned with himself than with me, but I was fond of him all the same.

I set out into the world again and found that, not being able to change themselves for the better, humans had begun to build a great many machines. Perhaps they hoped that these machines might sooner or later transform them too. I frequented the inventors of instruments and the new infernos of the factories that replaced the ancient hell of farm life. As various animal species had done in the past, now the social classes took turns at dominating the world. The industrialists had no rivals. They acted nervously and aggressively, bringing to my mind the first mammals on Earth. Here were the new rodents, the new felines, the new wolves.

Human tides poured into the urban areas. In the suburb of one city, I happened to see again the bastard I had left behind in the Austrian hospital, still coming to grips with divine reminiscence. He had given up weapons and had devoted himself to philanthropy. Like his mother he had moved to England, where he had opened a model spinnery that employed a multitude of workers. He had married and led a virtuous life, and I was unable to find in him even a trace of the libertine impulses of his past. I told myself that I should have frequented him more often and rekindled his passions. I thought of paying him a visit, but at the moment I arrived something happened to prevent our encounter. The workers in the spinnery he had built rebelled and stormed the plant, destroying the looms, and he was pacing the site of the rebellion in dismay, a clutch of respectful police guards at his heels. I was busy and could not wait for him to calm down. Before leaving I read this sentence on his lips:

"And I did so much! I was like a father to them!"

Well, I thought, do you alone have the right to be a bastard? And where did all the gaiety that made you so attractive go?

Now he would have been able to explain to that wise viscount why men want to come out of themselves, whether it be to build machines or to destroy them. It is because they are unhappy, realizing dimly that they have not fulfilled their mission.

But the viscount had other things on his mind, under the ground as he was, giving life to an innumerable and filiform posterity.

People who did not give God a second thought were penetrating deep into the world of nature. Armed with their magnifying glasses and notebooks, they examined leaf after leaf, divided animals into species, brought fossils to light, and reconstructed the genealogical trees of semi-fantastic animals. They would meet on an island or on the banks of a river and would then continue on their own, individually, like strangers in a waiting room. I refused to pay any attention to them for quite a while, and certainly I did not think they were involved in the same mission I had entrusted to philosophers and poets. I considered them maintenance people who achieved an appearance of order by classifying and piling up plants in gardens, bones of reptiles in museums, manuscripts in libraries. All sorts of things came out of the ground: the skulls of humanoids, the bodies of Pompeii's inhabitants preserved in ash, funerary towns, carbonized trees. It was like overturning a family trunk.

In short, nature was not what it used to be. Quite a few poets were looking for me in the woods and in the rivers, but they could find me there only when I happened by. I busied myself more and more in the life of the cities, perhaps in order to forget my problems. Like other solitary malcontents, I sought refuge in crowds. I went to Boston, London, St. Petersburg, letting myself be jostled by the human tide.

I tried my hand at accumulating wealth. I delved into the life of a banker, staying awake with him to count profits. For a moment I exulted at the sight of all those coins that winked at me like clusters of light. But my excitement was short lived, and boredom took its place. Amassing possessions seemed to me a detestable occupation. Don't people who draw up accounts look at themselves in the mirror? And do they like what they see? I finally realized the answer had to be yes, they *do* like what they see! I should have better understood human nature by now.

Once, just for the sake of the experiment, I fused myself with a murderer of women, and I got out of there in a hurry, utterly disgusted. I waited for the moment of violence, thinking I might receive some big revelation. Not at all. It was the most vile and stupid experience you can think of. Hiding and pouncing and penetrating and killing—what a definite bore. I tried my best to have that man arrested, but I couldn't manage it.

For an evening I joined a drunkard who slept in the streets, but I couldn't bear the stench that rose from his clothes. All right, I thought to myself, I do not understand these people, be they rich or poor. I was being unfair. I should have known that the old mantle of suffering was upon them once again, suffocating them. Everybody was trying to escape from under it in one way or another. If I had problems dealing with pain, so did they.

The recurring desire to visit great spaces took me more and more frequently to the North American continent. I was in love with the United States, like a European youngster today who has seen all the western movies. But I was right in the heart of the action, moving along with the westward caravans, settling with the pioneers in the Ohio Valley, building boats on the Mississippi, growing corn and wheat and potatoes in Iowa, constructing railroads across the expanding nation.

There was something special about that country. One part of me was constantly dwelling there, hovering around the windows of the White House, looking inside the dossiers on the desk of the Oval Office when nobody was there, trying in many oblique ways to convince a succession of presidents to abolish slavery, until I finally managed to win one of them to that cause. I was thrilled at the idea that it was possible, after such a long human history, to build a country as if it were a new world. All this brought back to me distant memories and a nostalgia for origins. America was far from flawless, but it had the enchantment of a new beginning.

My favorite visits throughout that century were with the writers. They did not always recognize me or understand my words, but I kept trying, even more in the United States than among the great Russian authors. In part I favored America for the climate. The Russian cold was almost the end of me when I went to see Dostoyevsky in St. Petersburg. I had hoped to challenge his belief that one should commit a crime in order to have something worth repenting. I found the logic of it quite absurd, but I never got around to telling him so: a bout of pneumonia almost killed me first, and as soon as I had recovered, I left that frigid land and flew southward, while he continued to publish his stuff full of blood and repentances, blowing his breath over his fingers.

Of my encounters with American writers I retain some vivid memories. Emerson was very bright but also boring with his preaching attitude; he pretended to teach me what to think and what to do, until I decided to leave him talking to himself in his Massachusetts home. That was the same day I met Miss Dickinson, almost by chance, as she was taking a walk around her Amherst neighborhood. She was dressed in white, her hair tightly combed, her attitude a combination of audacity and shyness. I walked next to her on that short promenade until I watched her reenter the porch of her home. That was enough for me to fall in love with her. Past her silence I sensed a totally absorbing personality. On our walk I tried to communicate to her the idea and the necessity of writing, blowing a gust of wind through the foliage of a great elm. I noticed the way she glanced up at it in wonder. I had no more time to court her, however. I was due elsewhere for an appointment that seemed important at the time; now I cannot even remember what it was. See for yourself how memory works!

Not much later I ran into Melville. I was one of the sailors on a ship, and actually I didn't know what to think of that silent member of the crew who spent his evenings reading the Bible, and Shakespeare, and books about whales, and chronicles of marine journeys. One evening I talked to him, and he told me that he had been a clerk but had finally left his job because he could not stand saying yes to his boss anymore. So he had become a sailor, but he really wanted to be a writer. Then he returned to his usual silence, without an inkling whom he had been talking to. But when I finished my service as a sailor, I found a way to take the measure of the strange, insomniac

writer Melville had become. I was intrigued by his obvious failure to recognize me, and so, as if taking up a challenge, I entered one of his books as I might enter a world, and I lived in
it as if it were my home.

It was quite an experience, and I don't recommend making
a habit of it. Being God, I can do such a thing without going
mad or being destroyed; a person might slip into a volume but
would run a serious risk of getting permanently lost in it. Only
God and silverfish can safely get inside books.

Even for me it was complicated enough. I entered *Moby Dick*
as the man who narrates the story and calls himself Ishmael,
and from the beginning I was led into a series of entrapments.
I realized soon that I would not easily exit those pages, and for
a while they became my real world. I roamed through them as
a fish swims in the water and a fox meanders in the woods. I
dealt with all sorts of surprising characters, from Queequeg to
Starbuck to Pip. I listened to myself recounting the worldly
history of whaling. I took part in the harpooning of the great
animals. I squeezed the sperm from the body of a killed ceta-
cean. I wondered about the philosophical implications of sailing through the ocean waters. I compared the land to the sea
and the Pacific to the Atlantic. I interrogated existence on the
seas as if I were creating a watery universe of which I was the
mysterious ruler, like a born-again Neptune.

I had one obsession that was shared by everybody else on
that ship, namely the presence of Captain Ahab. I did not like
that man; he seemed to me to embody all the evil that could
be found in the world. I saw in his dark ambition the result
of some metamorphosis that had contorted humankind into a
villainous animal intent on subjugating nature and even myself. Once I heard him crying to me, perhaps sensing that I was
nearby, looking at him among the other sailors: "Oh, thou big
white God aloft somewhere in your darkness!" His voice had
a harsh, obscure, deadly pitch. I don't think I've ever heard a
less attractive tonality of speech. He was speaking from down-
town hell, or so it seemed.

From that point on, I could not bear Ahab's gaze. I forced
myself to leave the body and soul of Ishmael, who had fallen
prey to an unwilling admiration for this megalomaniac. I had

to find a way of getting out of a book that looked more and more like a prison to me. I could only do so by punishing the dictator of that sinister, loveless society. I left Ishmael while he was sleeping, and actually he was never to recall my visit. I jumped into the ocean and swam for a long time, until I found the Great White Whale. It could not avoid me, for all its efforts to do so; I possessed its body and conquered its will. I became Moby Dick, navigating the seas, waiting to confront the hunter who was spending his life in my pursuit. I was the book's title, its subject, its motivation.

I don't have a happy memory of that adventure. Being a whale was quite a burden, and it reminded me of that ancient time I spent in the sea, trying to escape my destiny. I was swimming like a whale, eating like a whale, feeling like a whale. All in me was whalishly ponderous. Only my candid color reminded me of my real purpose: to find Ahab and to finish with him, so that I could go back to the whole of life from which I had been severed. "That's it with books for me," I would mumble in the water, releasing great bubbles of air.

The memory of Miss Dickinson kept coming to me throughout that marine odyssey. I thought of her in my sleepless nights (I didn't know that whales suffered from insomnia) and during my interminable meals. I had been transformed into an eating machine, swallowing anything that appeared before me. I swam and ate and dreamed for the entire duration of the novel, while Ishmael was elaborating his narration. I often got impatient with the unusual length of the story. "Couldn't we cut a few pages here and there?" I thought to myself beneath the waves, like an editor at large. If anyone heard me, they pretended not to; it is easy to disregard a whale's complaint. As for Melville, I didn't even know where he was. Perhaps he had gone away and left his novel unattended. Or perhaps he was watching us, as God watches the world.

Ahab and I finally met at the climax of the tale. We fought for three chapters, from top to bottom. Salty water flowed over us, and I bounced from wave to wave. Boatloads of men launched their harpoons at me. I saw Ahab and I heard him cry, "Toward thee I roll, thou all-destroying but unconquering whale; to the last I grapple with thee; from hell's heart I stab

at thee; for hate's sake I spit my last breath at thee. . . . *Thus,
I give up the spear!*" What a way to settle a dispute! There
seemed no chance of common ground and no way to reconcile
ourselves: it was either him or me. He lunged at me and
attached himself to me with harpoon and cord, and we
bounded into the ocean like newlyweds. I abandoned him as
soon as possible and I left the whale as well. What a relief to
be out of that book! I never could read it again without it giving
me the chills.

I rushed to Miss Dickinson and found her walking in the
small garden of her house, her eyes turned toward the branches
of that big elm. She did not want to look at me, but I knew
that she had felt my presence. We walked again together as we
had the first time. We never spoke to each other, and I understood that that was the way it should be, that I should respect
her virginity forever, and that her way of recognizing me would
always be a keen one, an oblique one, a mysterious one—like
the embroidering of a thousand small flowers on a bride's robe.
I savored all the mute intensity of that brief encounter on the
grass outside her home. When I left her, I turned back to wave
farewell. She was standing on the porch, looking away from
me and yet looking at me, smiling and yet not. Her dress was
whiter than the whale's skin.

Toward the end of that crowded and busy century, I was seized
by a desire to go to Vienna to enjoy the sight of that old city
and the courtesy of its inhabitants. I felt a great need for good
manners after several experiences in metropolises populated
by thieves and bums and would-be poets. I spent days visiting
museums and savoring sweets in a coffeehouse with large arm-
chairs and deep carpets. This was the only time in my life when
I fell prey to gluttony. I did so for the sake of Sacher tortes,
and the experience resulted in a nausea that still sometimes
overtakes me when I look into the window of a pastry shop.

That orgy of sweet and pleasant idleness ended, in fact, in
an illness severe enough that I took to my hotel room. The next
day I was still so sick that I had to call for a doctor. A young
man with a black beard and pince-nez arrived, and his exami-

nation was elaborate and formal. I remained clothed from head to foot, and he groped beneath my vest to palpate my abdomen and stomach, while I contemplated the landscape in a painting, making an effort to keep my food down. Despite my firmest intentions, however, vomit gushed from my throat and fell into the towel that the doctor was holding, which was immediately rolled up and placed in a basin in a corner of the room. At that point I started blubbering like a child, my face streaming with tears. "Well," I spluttered through a mist of bitter chocolate, "the nausea is gone. What I need now is chamomile." I watched the doctor wash his hands and felt as though I had been to confession.

At night I went to sleep, and while I slept my indigestion took its revenge. I was visited by a shapeless thing that twisted and contracted before me, like a beast lurking in the dark, ready to pounce and swallow. I awoke trembling and drenched in sweat, certain that I had encountered God's unconscious. For a long time I felt afraid, as if my true enemy were hiding in that memory, an indestructible opponent against whom I would forever struggle.

It was then that, without realizing it, all by myself and without any help whatsoever, I invented psychoanalysis. I shut myself up in the house with a provision of tea and probed into my soul as an explorer ventures into a cave. I penetrated as far as I could but couldn't tell where I was because the place was so dark. It was as though I were following a cavern toward the far side of the globe, the antipode of Vienna. The cavern was crammed with the buried skeletons of animals and plants, as if it had been the playroom of my divine infancy. I came upon two flowers encased in amber, and looking at them I remembered the time when I had created the sexual organs before I created the animals themselves, designing models that lived on, independently, as orchids, tulips, and their multiform kin. One of these preserved specimens was so like a vagina that I looked at it with stupefaction.

I went farther down and reached the point to which I had descended in my dream, the bowels of the earth. There the cave ended. I felt an impulse to turn around and go back up, where a cup of hot tea was waiting for me, but I summoned up all my courage—until the form of my dream appeared to me and sniffed me like a dog.

Of course I couldn't see it, but I perceived it with my whole being. I had the impression I could touch it, but at the same time I knew that it was an illusion, because it could not be reached or seen. It was the enemy that had appeared to me when I was an infant and that I had always wanted to forget! It was *It*, it was nothingness.

During all that time, I had done my best to believe, as humans do, that the opposite of life is death, while death is but the dark side of life. One without the other could not endure, and both take turns and support each other to escape It, which now stood before me in silent mockery, the beast waiting on the threshold, the hole into which sooner or later everything falls. This hole was nothingness, and against it I had erected the immense ramshackle structure of the cosmos. I was paralyzed by fear, but I managed to regain control of myself and turn back. I passed skeletons of never-before-seen whales and trees that had grown upside down. I trampled on crustaceans set in ice and on deposits of gold and diamonds. I splashed through blackish, pitchy liquid that fifty years later would become as precious as gold, but at the time I scarcely gave it notice.

I clambered to the surface and returned to the room where my tea was waiting, lukewarm by now; and precisely in that instant the little doctor of the day before called on me again. I was so distressed by my journey that I had to tell him everything, as if he were the closest of my friends. I did not tell him who I was, but I revealed to him that *I had an unconscious*, and that perhaps everybody did, and that all this was very exciting. Inside the soul was a cellar, and perhaps an attic as well; a hidden truth was deposited there and I thought I had just glimpsed it. I realized now that I had always been tormented by the fear of non-being, and this fear probably explained many of my eccentricities.

I spoke quite deliriously, but the doctor did not seem discomposed. He administered a sedative and ordered me back to bed. This is how my first meeting with Dr. Freud came to an end. I left Vienna the very next day.

During that period I ran into somebody else who was to become very important to me. Our first encounter took place by
chance, a few years before the end of the century, when I began
a journey through the regions of Europe. I went to Nancy and
then to Strasbourg and then moved down through Alsatia and
into Germany, through the Black Forest, and down toward Ba-
varia. I was traveling by train. It was the first time I spent an
entire day watching cities and countryside roll by.

When I arrived in Munich, my soul, perhaps because of the
excitement of the journey, brimmed with lofty thoughts. I sat
down at a table in a beer hall on a June afternoon, and the
foamy brew filled me with a gaiety at once ribald and solemn.
On that journey I had regained total consciousness of myself,
as if opening a photograph album or rereading one's old letters.

All around teemed a Sunday-like crowd of contented people,
and for a short while I fantasized that they perceived my discreet presence. A band scattered musical notes through the air.
A platoon of mounted soldiers in their parade uniforms passed
in front of the beer hall, and the band struck up a military
march to wild applause. A spontaneous chorus flowed from the
tables toward the riders, who were moving away, seated above
the horses' waving manes. The people were singing. Why were
they singing? Perhaps because the riders were handsome, or
perhaps because the smell of the dust raised by the horses'
hooves filled the throat with something that resembled the
taste of blood?

I did not know the answer. Among the excited and laughing
people I had the look of a God perplexed by the spectacle he
himself had set in motion. As I nursed my glass of beer with
a pensive air, Albert Einstein saw me and immediately recognized me.

He was a little boy, sitting at the table next to mine, with
his parents in their Sunday best. He too seemed surprised by
the scene he was witnessing and could not understand it. I noticed that he stuttered when answering a question from his parents, almost as though he had a speech impediment. We looked
at each other, and I felt that he was penetrating into my territory. He contemplated me with religious astonishment. I asked
myself if I had arrived here only to leave again for distant re-

gions. Why did I place the money on the table with such haste and get up as if it were urgent for me to leave? And why did I turn to stare at him from the street? He was watching me, absorbed in his vision, and I knew that we would encounter each other again.

When I saw him the second time I had just bought my first automobile. I was traveling in the direction of where he lived, thinking back over recent events. A few years before I had gone into voluntary exile, delving deep into the forests of Canada and not speaking to a living soul. That long period of isolation had helped me to clarify for myself my own intentions: *I wanted to leave!* I felt that I should emigrate from the world, and with that perception everything became clearer. Humanity's persistent rummaging in every corner of the earth and dragging into the light every forgotten thing finally made better sense. Anyone who wants to leave someplace needs an inventory in order to find out what he should take along; I saw science as the sum total of all the preparations for a journey. Humans had understood what I needed before I could grasp it myself. They were showing me the way! They were kicking me out.

I asked myself why I wanted to leave, and I found the answer. I already knew that my world was an imperfect work, a sort of sketch that needed a good deal more work. I had finally come to accept that this revision could not be made on this planet, and with these inhabitants. What I had created could deteriorate but could not be erased or adjusted; the mess we had arrived at was by now overwhelming. I had reached the end of my attempts to use humankind to improve my creation. They could only help me to leave.

One Sunday morning I left the Canadian woods for the nearest town and bought all the magazines and newspapers that I could find, looking for a sign of my presence anywhere in the world. By then I had learned to read newspapers. I knew that the important news was never on the first page. It would be hidden in a corner, on the inside, brief and without elaboration, as though the reporter had been taken by surprise and did not know what more to say. Or perhaps a newspaper dreams, and its dreams surface only in the occasional small article on the local-news page. But it is there that humanity recognizes itself, even as the poor editor wonders why in the world he is publishing that piece of information. After ransacking thousands of pages filled with almost useless information, I pieced together something that suggested an important development. It seemed that, in various parts of the world, men who knew nothing of each other were all building flying machines, bizarre in shape and fragile in appearance. One of the articles showed drawings that struck my imagination more forcefully than any description. I was seized by the desire to fly a contraption through the sky.

I discovered that I did not have to travel far. In North Carolina the construction of an airplane was under way. The two brothers who had initiated the undertaking needed a mechanic and a handyman, and they hired me. I did a bit of everything. For months on end I worked for them in the hope of seeing that strange wooden bumblebee, shut away in a hut at night, rise into the air with me on board. Although we worked together, no friendship sprang up between us. The two brothers lived in a secretiveness that kept me at a distance. We spoke only in connection with the work, and they had not the slightest idea what was going through my mind.

In the evening, while the two brothers studied their drawings inside the house, I would enjoy the cool air in the garden, and I would light my pipe. I haven't smoked a pipe since then, and I recall this habit as proof of the patience that sustained me in those days. I kept thinking about the plane locked, like a sleeping insect, in that box without windows. I was certain that this craft's maiden voyage would be only the sign of greater events approaching. But first this threshold had to be crossed.

One morning, in the dewy twilight of winter, I started walking toward the wind tunnel in which the brothers simulated the conditions with which the airplane would have to contend. Then suddenly I saw the wings of the wooden bumblebee oscillate above me in the misty sky. In my excitement I dropped the cleaning tools I was holding, and I joined my soul to the soul of the brother who had remained on the ground, anxiously following the flight from a corner of the large meadow. The plane's flight was very short, and soon after the brothers rushed

to meet each other, forgetting all about me. I stood there waving my arms as though I had engineered the miracle myself.

I would have liked to climb into the flying machine, but it
was not granted me. There was space for only one pilot, and I
had to content myself with watching their trials as each time
they lengthened the flight a few more yards. I would clean the
motor at the end of the day, before locking the plane away. In
the end, I understood that humankind sensed I wanted to leave,
and in some obscure way their flying machines were the first
of their efforts to keep up with me.

These were the memories that preoccupied me as I drove
my car through the valleys and lakes on the way to Zurich,
where Einstein lived. I reached the town on a placid Sunday.
When I finally got hold of his address and found his apartment,
I let myself in and gently pushed Albert's door open. The room
was dark, the windows shut, in fact, to afford Albert a bit of
rest after a night spent writing in his notebook. A flood of light
accompanied my entrance. I stood still so as not to wake him,
but it was too late. He moved on the bed, shook the sleep from
his head, and glanced in my direction.

I don't know whether he saw me clearly or how I must have
appeared to him, standing in the doorway at the center of that
cascade of light, but certainly the doubts that had been tormenting him were dispelled as if by magic. On entering I had
raised some dust from the rug that covered the floor; his eyes
met the luminous breach crisscrossed by minuscule granules
like a swarm of microscopic insects. He rose on his elbows to
survey the unexpected apparition. I felt that he knew who I
was. Simultaneously, we were overcome by the discovery that
light is composed of particles, just as a wave is made up of
infinitesimal drops of water. We both recalled another occasion when, tumbling through the air like a dolphin in water, I
had convinced another scientist that magnetic waves run
through the ether like rivers of light pouring into a sea.

I sat down next to him to savor the joy of discovery. It was
a poetic moment, cut short by a hubbub from the street that
reminded me that I had parked my car illegally. I rushed downstairs, but I was unable to avoid a fine, the first of a long series.

This was the beginning of an intense friendship. Albert remembered me from that distant day in the Munich beer hall, and since that time he had been waiting for me. He was a man of extraordinary gentleness, and coming into contact with God did not inspire any pride in him. Quite soon, however, I found out how much he had idealized me.

Einstein was convinced of my honesty and of my inability to cheat at any game, which was true, but not in the sense in which he understood it. Cheating is contemptible, and my numerous losses should be evidence enough of my aversion to it. But what he wanted to believe was that I don't play games at all, and here he was mistaken. In one sense my universe is an interminable game of cards, each player concealing his hand. A bluff is not the same as a fraud. It is part of the game to agree upon certain acceptable tricks, because life, like a game of poker, cannot do without simulation and dissimulation.

Einstein, however, saw me as an angel occupying heaven and Earth, passionately bent on a marvelous construction, an enchanted palace where celestial music is played. I let him believe all this, lest he quit my employ; I needed him too badly. Finding a right-hand man equal to my requirements was never an easy business, as I had long since discovered. But now I needed something different. My youthful excursions among the stars were a distant memory, when I remembered them at all; I had no notion how I had managed them. I needed Albert to help me leave. So I resigned myself to a masquerade that would preserve Albert's respect and devotion: assuming (not for the first time) the role of the all-seeing master of the cosmos who waits for man to discover the truth that already shines before him. Impersonating this sort of divinity, I would wake up each morning with unimaginable power, my eyes piercing the daylight.

Light was the great subject of my conversations with Albert, perfectly in keeping with my sudden apparition to him.

Once, in an indirect way, I told him about my plan to leave. We had spent a day in the study and I had protected his tranquillity in every possible way. In the evening we went out for a stroll and sat on a bench in the Prater public park amid a multitude of people. I surreptitiously observed his seraphic profile out of the corner of my eye and racked my brain trying to find a way to begin what I had to say.

I was aided by an unexpected scene. A pretty mother walked past us, holding by the hands identical twin children dressed identically. Albert observed them with an amused expression, and there and then I invented a story that proved quite successful. I told him that I too was a twin and that my twin brother had ended up in a very, very distant region, from which he wanted to return. I portrayed this brother of mine in all the colors of goodness and benevolence, almost convincing myself that he was in fact a part of me that I had forgotten, and I insisted on the necessity of my going forth to retrieve him. But how could I get to him across such a vast space? I watched Albert as he absorbed this problem as a sponge absorbs water. We were on the brink of another sleepless night.

On returning home he locked himself in his study in the dark, as he would often do. Stretched out on a small sofa in another room, I gazed through the window at a magnolia tree stirring against the sky. Beyond the tree I saw the stars congregate again in the sky for the nightly dance of the constellations. I remembered the times when I had relied on painters and poets to communicate with the world. It was now fated that for my departure I should use this meditative thinker, who instead of images or words employed numbers and alphabetic symbols and squared the universe with all the courage of his timid soul.

With this thought I fell asleep and had a dream. My twin was waiting for me at the far side of the sky with a watch in his hand. I was rushing to him on a plane and was also checking the time, afraid that I would arrive late and find him grown so old that I would not recognize him. I tossed and turned, unnerved by the idea.

The next morning Albert awoke me with an air of triumph. During the night, while I was asleep or busy revising sea currents or reactivating some extinct volcano, he had approached the solution to the problem I had presented to him. He had identified the vehicle of my travels. It could only be light. Not only because it was the fastest element he had been able to think of, but also because its speed was always constant, so that we could count on its punctuality.

We almost embraced in our excitement. The sun was pouring into the house through the window, and once again I remembered that I had appeared to him in a shaft of light; this was further proof that I had always been right in mistrusting darkness.

We ate breakfast together and then I hurried off. I was anxious to test Albert's suggestion. I had the impression that he wanted to add something, but I was already far away, aboard my train of light. I didn't even know how to buy a ticket; I just jumped inside the first beam that I found passing on the corner.

The journey seemed instantaneous. In a moment I was launched into the firmament, contemplating the astral expanses that surrounded me. I reached the rim of the majestic wheel rotating in space, and I noticed that all the stars moved away from the wheel's center, and the further away they moved from the nucleus, the faster they entered the abyss. From that height I was an explorer of the extreme boundaries. I observed all about me the stellar conglomerates, some round and flat, some oval, some spherical, some gibbous, and others shapeless like clumps thrown into space, all of them blossoming in the air like unending fireworks. There was not a star that remained still; the entire universe was exploding toward its outer limits. I had the impression of being in an enormous railway station with convoys leaving in all directions, without any assurance of returning. I cast a glance toward Earth, and my eyes came to rest on a small train station lost in the midst of the Russian forest, where an old man had gone to catch a train in order to join me. I recognized him, since I had many times seen his photograph in the newspapers and had read and admired his books. It was he, Tolstoy! But how old and anguished he had become. I saw him collapse on a wooden bench and die before he was able to climb into the coach that would bring him all the way to me after his long and useless search. I called to him from that distance, but he could no longer hear me, and his soul was dispersed in the pollen of the ethereal wind. I cast another glance about me before returning to Earth, and in what had seemed the blink of an eye ten years had passed on the green, white, and blue planet.

My return was dramatic. I rolled headfirst into a muddy ditch, beneath a leaden sky, alongside bodies that appeared motionless in sleep, until I realized that I was in a trench after some military assault. But who was fighting whom, and how had this come about? I climbed up until I was on level ground and roved over the vast plain that opened before me. In the distance, almost undistinguishable, loomed the trees of a forest like a mirage. I headed for them, scrabbling in the mud and tripping over roots.

I felt that I had plunged into a black nightmare. "And yet I have known war," I repeated to myself, panting on my muddy path. "This is certainly not the first one I've seen. I would have done well to read the newspapers instead of distracting myself in the cosmos. Then I'd know what is going on here."

I continued walking over terrain strewn with bodies. I smelled the odor of blood and excrement and feared I might faint in that putrid inferno. After a while I leaned against a shattered tree. In the distance I saw human shadows moving about, and I understood that they were looking for the wounded.

Then I heard a moan nearby. I saw a human form moving with great effort and anguish. I went to help, and as I got near him, the soldier saw me and I read the fear in his gaunt, bearded face. I didn't have time to say anything to reassure him nor even to make a gesture of help. A word, a sound, issued from his throat and faded away into the air like a stunted curse or an aborted prayer, and he went to join his comrades in muddy oblivion, his nose planted in a clump of earth. The rescuers were now close by, but they would not pick him up.

A vertical plunge had snatched me from dizzy astral heights, and I was buried now in the shadows of an unknown countryside, beneath a black sky in which explosions ripped chasms open. "Where are the wings I had a short while ago?" I caught myself thinking. I was troubled by the suspicion that the soldier beside me had recognized me and with his dying breath had insulted me. If that was the case, he had become aware of my past and of the past of the species. They say it happens to people who, at the point of death, rise beyond themselves and see everything about the elapsed world and the future one, only to plunge again straight into the void. The soldier had barely begun his quick journey, and I could feel him escaping me, irreparably.

Something moved in the mud and slithered over my leg. I was overcome by revulsion and thought of running. But something inside me prevented me. I looked again at the soldier's face, half sunk into the mud. I lifted him and turned him on his back. I closed his eyes and restored a bit of order to his countenance. The rain had begun to pour down on us and had partly cleaned the dead soldier's face. His mouth had closed tightly in a grimace. I removed a glob of mud from one of his ears and decided to do something for him, the unknown soldier of all the wars that had swept over my world.

I went through his pockets and found a damp, dirty wallet, together with a tobacco pouch and a box of matches that miraculously could still be lit. By striking them one after the other and protecting the tenuous flame in the palm of my hand, I deciphered the poor fellow's name and address, written by hand on a pass. Otto Müller, I repeated to myself several times, Otto Müller, Gottfried Strasse, Vienna. I put everything back in its place and returned the wallet to where I had found it. "Goodbye, Otto," I murmured. The name had a strangely solemn ring in the darkness in which we had become brothers.

So Austria was at war. At least this much I knew. I made my way to a village and bought some newspapers, all of them in French. I had alighted in Gallic territory, where the soldier Otto had been killed, and after some inductions and deductions I succeeded in understanding who was at war. The reasons for the conflict remained obscure to me, but so they were even to the combatants, in spite of their illusions to the contrary.

I went down from Lorraine toward Vienna, flying over battlefields and peaceful hamlets buried among the mountains. The gaiety that I remembered had deserted the city, replaced by a monotonous and unadorned severity that was interrupted only by the patriotic demonstrations that occasionally filled the boulevards. I went to the address I had found in Otto's pocket and arrived in a quiet, modest quarter on the outskirts of town. I paced back and forth in front of the house of the dead soldier. I had decided to bring his wife the news of his death and to offer her words of comfort that I imagined she would need. But before knocking at the door I peered inside through a window that faced out on the garden.

I saw a room in which a white canopy loomed large over a bed. I had difficulty discerning anything in the room's dim light, but when colors and shadows began to separate, I could make out two shapes moving as one on the bed, almost like a cloud changing shape as it travels, and I was seized by dismay. Who was this unknown man who had taken Otto's place while he was decomposing in a corner of nature's slaughterhouse? I compared the mud of the front lines with all that brilliant whiteness, and I gave up the mission I had assigned myself. I returned to the center of the city, where I sat down at a café, repressing a great craving for chocolate.

It was inevitable that I should recall the little doctor who had examined me at the time of my Sacher-torte indigestion. After a short inquiry, I found that the name of Sigmund Freud was on everyone's lips, since he had become famous in the world of science. I went to the library to read up on him, and I could not help but notice that he had taken the idea of the unconscious from me. But I didn't resent it. It seemed impossible for any idea to pass into history under my name, so it was just as well that this one should carry Dr. Freud's. What I read interested me very much, and I made up my mind to meet him again. I set about tracking him down, because somehow I knew that I would never meet him at any of those patriotic manifestations that filled Vienna's squares. Freud spent his days among patients and disciples, and then would read and write till late at night. I trailed after him during the walks he took with his wife, to whom he rarely addressed a word, and he did his best not to see me, though I beckoned to him at every street corner.

Finally I appeared at his house, and at first he quite curtly refused to receive me. Twice he forbade me access to his study, leaving me to pace in his hallway under the eyes of his wife and servants, who were mildly curious about my presence. I had decided not to disguise my identity any further, and perhaps this was the reason for his refusal to see me. I persisted; after a few days the door opened, and Freud appeared in its frame. I looked at him, holding my breath. He stared at me in turn for a few moments, then went back into his study, leaving the door open behind him. I interpreted this as an invitation and followed him inside. He sat down behind his desk, and I sank into an armchair beside bookshelves incredibly crammed.

The sound of a piano reached us from some recess of the house. For a whole minute I abandoned myself to my favorite game: who had composed that music? I placed it in time without difficulty: it was from a period of brief human rejuvenation that I remembered with great nostalgia. I would have ventured the name of Beethoven, but there was something else, the trace of a secret and perhaps definitive truth, a message left by a visitor brimming with grace, the thrill of a dance that took me back to a different world. I was tapping the motif on the armrest of my chair when Freud's attentive eye caught mine. I stopped tapping.

"It's Haydn," he announced in a tone of defiance. I could not help but reply in the same tone.

"Indeed, it is Haydn. I was just about to get it. But certain passages go beyond his own music. In fact, it is Haydn surpassing Haydn, as anyone does who truly creates, as Beethoven does, and as you do. As I did, some time ago. I'm in a position to know, I believe."

"But you *didn't* guess it," Freud retorted, putting an end to the exchange while he was ahead, with a satisfaction that seemed to me a bit childish. "You never change! I should have kept you waiting in the hallway. You do not control your world. An infinite number of things escape you. Your omnipotence and your omniscience are purely imaginary."

"I'm the first to admit it," I explained. "I never claimed that I possessed either. But you ought to have understood me by now."

Freud suffered from a tic that caused him to pucker his lids behind his spectacles. At these words of mine he stared at me inquisitively, and I detected not the slightest benevolence in his eyes.

"What is it that I should have understood?" he finally asked me, with a touch of bitterness.

I felt the need for friendship. I wanted us to get along.

"You don't know me yet," I answered, "nor do you know my nature. For instance, you don't know the first thing about my origins. Until you do, you'll never recognize me properly."

Freud avoided my gaze.

"So let's hear it. How were you made?"

"I don't even know whether there was any choice on my part," I began. "I was simply there, and the universe could not have turned out differently, unless it started all over again without me. I cannot be still. If I stop moving I can feel the end coming. Do you have any idea of how many things I am initiating and bringing to term at this very moment, and with how many I will be occupied when I next remember this encounter of ours? Just thinking about it makes my head spin. I continually do and undo, because destruction and creation seem to need each other."

This is not what I wanted to say to him, I thought, as the words flowed unchecked from my lips. Why am I here boasting about how busy I am? Am I just trying to make an impression? I stopped and let a brief pause intervene. Freud had removed the spectacles from his nose and was cleaning them with his handkerchief. His eyes without glasses looked like those of a fish that has just been caught. He took advantage of the silence to ask me, without looking at me, "Well?"

"Well, I want you to understand me," I continued emphatically. "Both God and men are compelled to invent, just as a river is driven to flow—not even ice can enchain it. But it has taken me time to understand that to create can be a violent act! I've just returned from battlefields strewn with corpses, and I now understand that people go to war because war seems to them more creative than peace. After seeing these things, I've almost lost all hope. I've also just made an inspection tour of the sky, and I can tell you that the universe has already taken off and is leaving all of us behind."

This part of my argument did not interest Freud, for he suffered from agoraphobia and could not tolerate the thought of such open spaces. He wouldn't think of flying in a plane. He tended to lock himself away within four walls, surrounded by books, rummaging in drawers and tidying up his desk and his notes. But my reflections on life and death had finally gotten his attention, and he told me what he had been thinking about human nature since the beginning of the conflict.

It was far from happy. Freud conjured up a hypocritical and ferocious humanity, a primitive horde thirsting for blood behind a screen of false pretexts. And while I was up there measuring incredible distances, this horde had seized the opportunity to inundate the plains of Europe. "Where were you when you were needed?" Freud asked in a barely controlled voice, forgetting that I never started a war (never mind that I was incapable of preventing one). He had me thoroughly intimidated, and at that moment his superiority seemed overwhelming. I cowered in my comfortable leather chair and listened to him, thinking of disappearing into the night that was enclosing Vienna. I again felt a yearning for chocolate, which I immediately repressed.

Freud turned from me to his desk and bent over the notes for his most recent essay, beneath the light of the gas lamp. Watching him at work, I was reminded of another scene. I concentrated in order to retrieve it from my memory, and finally it appeared to me as crystal clear as when I saw it happen: the face of Moses as he sat behind that big rock on the top of Mount Sinai, illuminated by the torch's flame. As I recalled Moses, I squirmed in my seat. My eyes met Freud's. I was about to tell him what I had remembered, when something unexpected happened. He became ill.

His face was ashen and his eyes as if hidden behind a veil. His hand rose to his chest, then to his head, and finally came to rest on the desk, while his body waited for the attack to leave him. After a while he slowly stood up, walked around the desk, and went to lie down on a couch, where he remained with his eyes closed, no longer paying any attention to me. I went over to him and sat down at his side and took his hand; his pulse was very weak and somehow inert. He lay on that couch, dressed from head to toe, and I thought it would do him good to be liberated from his heavy clothes.

It was hard to undress him, but he did not resist and lay there in timorous passivity. I began with the spats, which Freud wore even in his study as he read in the evening; then the jacket of heavy and rather coarse cloth; the immaculate, tightly buttoned vest; his bow tie under the starched collar, the latter requiring a separate operation; the starched and pleatless shirt; the thin-striped trousers, which I slipped off with great difficulty because, as he shifted on his temporary bed, trying to be helpful, he proved far from agile. He remained in his cotton undershirt, woolen underpants that reached down to his knees, and woolen socks that covered his calves.

I had the impression of performing an act to which he submitted himself with the spirit of a patient. Only his most intimate garments separated me from his nudity. I had removed his eyeglasses, and his myopic gaze appealed to me for help. I noticed a dressing gown hanging from a hook and went to get it. Freud put it on with great effort; his face was returning to normal and his pulse was stronger. I withdrew to my armchair, waiting for him to fall asleep. I watched him as he sprawled limply on the cushions of the couch. I was struck by the fragility of one of my most daring inventions. How precarious that body appeared to me! It looked crushed by something too strong for it; the soul perhaps? A vast soul for such a limited receptacle; a soul overflowing its limits, to the point of becoming a torment to its own corporeal domain.

But where was this soul? "Seele," I said aloud in German, as if to gain his attention; but by now he was asleep and had begun to snore lightly. His head rested on his shoulder, and his dressing gown had fallen open. To my embarrassment I realized that the great man had wet himself.

I was not prepared for this and wondered if it would be best for me to leave. But I told myself that when he awoke Freud would be mortified at the thought of having peed on himself in the presence of God. I wanted to spare him that painful realization. For the first and last time I set about changing a sleeping adult's underwear.

I could not help looking at him, though fleetingly. His penis and testicles lay limply between his thighs, as if they too were asleep. I thought of the complex articulation hidden in every part of that tired and inert body. I considered the penis, which I was now covering with a pair of long underwear I found in a chest. In my mind I reexamined this accomplishment of life's mysterious engineers: the blood vessels and the spermatic sac; the tunicae albuginea testis and vasculosa testis; the digital fossa, the vas deferens, the glans penis, the bulbocavernosus, and the corpus cavernosum urethrae. And all the rest of his body was just as variegated, including the brain, whence the sleep that now enswathed him had come, issuing from some region of the fasciculus solitarius or the gracilis nucleus, down over the cascade of nerves all the way to the tarsi and phalanges of the feet, on which I replaced the slippers. And the soul—now lost in some dream or rooting about in the back rooms of the body—where was the soul in a structure so perfected that it could not change except by deterioration and illness?

"Another of my mistakes," I said to myself. "I should have created a more resilient body, capable of sheltering the most restless soul."

When I was certain that he was sound asleep, I turned off the light and set forth again into the world's web.

I WENT to see Einstein in order to bring him up to date on my heavenly explorations. Once again I was forced to traverse the war-torn territories to reach him in Berlin, where he had moved.

He listened intently to my account of my lightning-like journey. I was once more the universal master that he wanted to find in me, always occupied with mysterious and noble enterprises. The only part of my report that he did not believe was my news that the universe is expanding infinitely. Albert's orderly mind could not accept this idea. He was convinced that once one set out, one must arrive somewhere; and if the cosmos exploded endlessly, there was no question of arrival. I did not argue the point, because I would not have convinced him, and I asked him to describe for me the conclusions he had reached on his own.

Albert had not wasted his time. He informed me, quite happily, that the problem of leaving would be much more simple than expected, inasmuch as the force of gravity does not op-

erate in the way generally thought. He had discovered a law
that he assumed I already knew—and in fact I did my best to
nod frequently while I listened, as if he were repeating well-
established things. This law declared that if you abandon a
body in space it is impossible to determine whether that body
falls toward the earth or the earth runs to meet the body, and
that this truth held for the entire universe. The question thus
became, would I be setting forth or would the firmament be
coming to meet me? In short, was I proposing to leave or to
be caught up with?

Furthermore, I learned that if I were to be shot toward the
stars, I would never travel in a straight line, since space actually
curves. Albert lost himself in a lyrical description of celestial
hills and valleys, and through his words I could picture a train
of light climbing high and then descending again from station
to astral station. He said that those ascents and descents were
the effect time had on space, and that this great undulation
would prevent me from traveling like an arrow. The idea of
curved space delighted Albert. We spent hours trying to figure
out what would happen if I and a fiancée of mine were forced
to leave from different points of the earth for distant galaxies.
If space were straight, we would never again see each other;
but if it were curved, our trajectories would eventually meet.
He demonstrated this for me with pencil and paper, still with
the air of repeating things that I must already know. I too was
smitten by the idea that it was impossible to lose sight of a
beloved in the space-time of my universe.

That encounter truly was a picture of philosophical and serene times. And yet each of us was convinced that the other
was his guide. Perhaps we would meet again in a corner of the
cosmos to scrutinize the same point, conjecturing about the
curvature of space and the lines that cut through it.

Albert asked me when I intended to leave. I realized that I
was not quite ready—there were yet a few lives I wished to live
before saying goodbye.

I left Albert and took up the life of a Portuguese trader, Fernando. I was very much in love with my woman, Tareja, and

we would walk down the streets of Oporto together, holding hands in spite of our advancing age. People were pleasantly puzzled by us; we were thought of as two eternally betrothed who had decided to postpone their marriage indefinitely. It was as if we belonged to some exotic but harmless sect—those happily and forever in love. I was inhabited by God, but I did not know it until the end.

I would often have to leave on business for days at a stretch, wandering from place to place, always anxious to get back home. Tareja was an artist who painted canvases that nobody ever bought, and she would rarely show them. She thought of her work in the reserved, private way in which many of us think of our bodies. She created only for herself, with abandoned rapture, and after working she would sleep for hours, exhausted. Her paintings, drenched in light, had a mysterious beauty: they depicted plants of ivory and ebony, stretches of sky like endless corridors in astonishing colors, bizarre creatures with perfectly human gazes. When she was alone, she always worked at night.

I too would spend many late hours alone, repeating to myself this or that poem. I had been blessed with an extraordinary memory and had learned by heart the entire *Odyssey* and all of Dante's *Inferno* in Portuguese translation after reading them only a few times. It was the same for music: note after note, with the precision of a well-rehearsed orchestra, I could repeat the part of any instrument. My memory had become a local legend, and I was very proud of my talent. I exercised and cultivated it, learning all that I could learn. I would take a book and print it in my mind. It was as if I carried a library with me at all times. I would softly recite to myself for hours and hours during my travels, while everyone else was asleep. I had worked out a timetable for it. The whole *Odyssey* could be recited in the span of a few nights, giving each scene its proper emphasis—a few nights of euphoria for the lover far from home. *The Thousand and One Nights* was for longer trips. Dickens's novels would take weeks and weeks, while the average span for a single poem, all pauses and rhetorical effects considered, was a good half hour. This is how I measured my time.

Whenever I returned home, Tareja and I were completely

happy and would throw a party at which we were the only guests. We were the very ideal of a perfect love epic—the absolute version, at once solemn and playful, of what in common experience ends as conditional love, betrayed love, compromising love. None of that could happen to us, and we had reached a point beyond which lovers could not go. It seemed as if we had been granted some exemption from all catastrophes. But we were to be hit by the most unsuspected and irrevocable misfortune.

This is what happened, and I recall it with fear: my memory began to swell to unprecedented dimensions. I noticed it when, one morning, after barely glancing at my newspaper, I was able to recite it to Tareja from the first word to the last. At first we both laughed about it, but soon we were alarmed. My memory became unarrestable, and I could not forget anything that attracted my attention. From that moment on, I appreciated the positive value of Forgetfulness, and I began to invoke her as a new muse, almost as often as I had called upon Mnemosyne, the goddess of remembrance. Now I called them both, imploring the first, "Do not leave me!" and the second, "Please, Memory, take it all away!"

Imagine to yourself that everything that ever happened to you came back, surfacing like seaweed from the sandy bottom, floating together to make the sea an unnavigable marsh. To me, all the past became suddenly present: every awakening of every morning, every cup of coffee, the daily papers, the meals, the cities I had visited, the smells of all the fish I had eaten, all the love stories I had heard mixed in an interminable melodrama. I myself, Fernando, a mere fragment of the universe, had become as big as a galaxy.

Tareja would look at me, helpless, unwilling to ask anything for fear of setting off an avalanche of memories. "I am sick," I told her. And sick I was indeed. Only two days had passed since the onset of this crisis, and the burden of my memories had grown incessantly. Lying in bed, I found it hard to move, as if under an immense weight. I stretched my hand toward her with considerable effort. She came to me and held my hand. "Dear," she murmured softly.

Then and there I realized that there would be no cure for

my illness. That one simple word, "dear," overwhelmed me, as if all the debris of time had fallen upon me. The memory of each occasion when I had heard that word filled my mind to the brim. My very soul swelled, sweaty, crowded. I heard inside my head my mother calling me "dear" on my return from school, one windy day in April. "Dear Fernando," said a young girl, my first sweetheart. A boatman I had known began every other sentence with a "my dear." "This suit is rather dear," I heard someone complain in a store. "Freedom is too dear to me," an old friend of mine had written to me, before doing himself in. "Dear Fernando" began all the letters I had received up to that very day. "My dear" was the way my father's friendly lectures invariably began. "Dear love," Tareja had said after our first kiss. A web of hundreds of such utterances spun tightly around me. I gripped Tareja's hand to beg her silence.

That evening, my gentle painter of skies and whimsical creatures prepared a special dinner, uncorked a bottle of wine, and moved lightly around her paralyzed Fernando, who was inhabited by a God sick of memories. She began to find innocent words for her love. They were poisonless words, incapable of awakening any memories in me, ingenious, unexpected words, shining with freshness. They were German words that she had studied in school and that had stayed buried in her like dragonflies almost detached from their meaning. "Dunkel," she shouted, laughing, from the other room; and I felt that word, unattached to anything, reach me like a balsam. "Heimlich," I heard her call from the kitchen as she mixed the salad; "unerklärbar" as she opened the bottle; "rätselhaft" as she took the cake out of the oven; "unverständlich" as she kissed me; "doppelsinnig" as we sipped an after-dinner grappa. The sweetness of that farewell night surpassed all our expectations. I could understand every word by her intonation, and each was one of fondness and mystery.

I know, however, that as we lay on our bed holding hands, as I felt eternal sleep descend like the most beautiful of gifts, Tareja sensed me drifting away. She turned toward me and looked at me as if I were part of one of her paintings, and deliberately whispered the ultimate, eternal word of lovers for all seasons. She called me "love." She knew what she was doing.

My frail resistance was immediately overcome. I descended among the algae of my memories like a sleeping sailor, and I was finished by them. I took with me the voice of the woman I had loved, like a promise or a theft. And I hoped that the afterlife would be free of memories, like icy plains, like the mind of a newborn infant.

I traveled inconclusively from one end of the blood-drenched globe to the other. I whiled away some of the time aboard a boat owned by Norwegian sailors, fishing for salmon near the mouths of Scandinavian rivers. One day I heard a story about dramatic events that were changing the world's configuration. A Russian soldier who had joined our ship told us about the revolution that had flared up in his country. A shiver of fearful admiration ran through the crew as they listened to his story. I was seized by the desire to go and witness those events that had already found their place in history. The hunt for salmon had begun to bore me, and I did not hesitate to leave. I chose a night in December for the great bound beyond the Baltic all the way to the steppes rigidified by freezing cold.

Sometimes we know how we leave, but not how we arrive, or where. At the end of my nocturnal journey I found myself inside the skin of an old woman. I was aware of the change in my being, since my body now moved with wooden slowness. I looked in the mirror and saw my face covered with wrinkles. My eyes were sunk deep in their sockets, and they looked at me with astonishment. The rest of my body was covered by a heavy dressing gown. On my head I wore a kerchief that perhaps I had always possessed. I gazed at myself fixedly. Who was I and what was I doing in those clothes?

I sat down on the bed, closed my eyes, and drew a deep breath. I felt it rise again from my lungs, all the way through my throat and across my palate, and then it was released into the air. I breathed again, in a docile tranquillity. At that moment I heard an infant's cry from the other room. I rushed to Dunya's side, picked her up, and held her against my bosom. She stopped crying and her little body strained toward the obscure donor of sustenance. I carried her into the kitchen, warmed the milk, and in the silence of the house fed her. Standing in the century-old kitchen, I nourished my half-asleep great-granddaughter with the sense of performing an act of lasting significance.

I went back to my room and made an effort to read, but I soon stopped. I began contemplating the garden and the frozen branches of the peach and almond trees beyond the window-panes, and the past returned to me with the force of a gust of wind.

I saw myself as a young woman, many years before, in front of that same window. I was in love with myself, married to a man in whose eyes I saw the same admiration for my beauty. Making love bestowed on me an immediate joy, as if I had come to know myself truly and without pretenses. So did dancing. I danced with such love for myself that my partners seemed faceless, one indistinguishable from the next.

One night I awoke beside my sleeping husband, both of us still naked after our amorous embrace. Suddenly I did not recognize him. I was lying there as in a foreign land, covering my nudity. A ray of moonlight entered the darkness of the bedroom. I saw it touch the room's furniture, the mirror, the rugs, the white counterpane, the sheets. It scattered a silvery powder over everything. I kept watching it, until it disappeared and the room became dark again.

I rose and dressed quietly and slipped out into the wintry night. The wind piled up the clouds and blew them apart in bizarre shapes. Swathed in my fur coat, with my kerchief and my huge snow boots, I seemed to be as lost down here on Earth as the friendly moon aloft in the heavens, and I asked myself what purpose my life had. I could not answer. It was as though I had known it once, if only for a moment, and then I had forgotten. This idea struck me forcefully. For hours I roamed the night, following the friend who had awakened me, until it disappeared behind a bank of clouds and sank below the horizon. I sat down on the snow and almost fell asleep in the cold dawn.

They found me there when the sled caught up with me. They had looked for me everywhere and now they were taking me home. My husband sat beside the driver; my nurse sat next to me and made sure that I was well covered. I understood then that I would have died had they not found me. The sun was rising on my right, flashing behind a forest of oak and fir, almost like a bird jumping from branch to branch so as not to lose sight of me. On the other side the fields lay beneath a rosy veil. Against the snow the hills and houses stood out like blossoming flowers. I watched the dogs running over the snow, I felt my nurse's hand warming mine. I gazed at the fields bathed in light. At that moment I reattached myself to life with a tacit oath.

When I became a mother, it was as if the sun was born from the corner within me where tranquil clarity is hidden. Thanks to my children I grew through an extended youth. For years my husband watched me run about the house and the garden, resigned to receiving only the reverberations of my flight. My sons Nikolai and Anton took possession of me for more than twenty years.

But my hopes for those boys were disappointed. They grew up as if one son were a violation of the other, and they were both incomplete and unhappy. Nikolai became a physician, married early, and withdrew into a provincial and mediocre life, from which I sometimes tried to extricate him. I would go to visit him in his big house on the outskirts of a small town in Georgia. I would converse with his wife, who certainly did not love me, and play games with their children. Whenever I managed to speak to Nikolai himself, I would see before me a tired and frustrated man. He drank vodka as he spoke, and he was thinking already about a quiet retirement, in yearning expectation of his death. An avalanche had passed over his soul and left it sorrowful and deserted. I always left with a feeling of sadness, until I stopped those visits altogether.

Anton hated his older brother, who embodied everything that he strove to destroy. From its very beginning I saw his life evolve in a constant reversal of everything Nikolai personified. He refused to get married and have a career, he didn't touch liquor, he longed for a swift death, without ever achieving it. He abandoned his studies in order to join an anarchist sect and later a group of revolutionaries who lived in hiding and planned radical upheavals. I never knew where he lived, and so it was he who came to visit me, always unexpectedly and in a hurry. I saw him go through two failed revolutions, escaping capture both times.

Once he hid with me, and this was the only opportunity we had to talk at length in many years. I came out of it defeated, in a way different from the results of my rare conversations with Nikolai. Anton's arrogance was boundless. For him, I too was part of a world that must be torn down as soon as possible. It did not help that in his eyes I was more Nikolai's mother than his.

Following that conversation with Anton, I left my home and my husband and moved to a village on the Volga, where I taught the local children. I had been married three times, once to my husband and twice to my male children, and to the latter I had given a love that my husband never knew. I would watch the falling snow and feel that it was the longing for the sun's return that made this a joyful event. I had to discover where I had lost myself.

Not far from my house there was a sawmill, and one day I met Boris, its owner. I visited his forests and we went together to watch the workers as they cut timber and heaved the logs into the river. Three miles farther down, where his property ended, the logs would be gathered in front of his house. He took me there, and he himself cooked the evening meal that one of his assistants served to us.

He told me about his project. He wanted to go to Siberia and set up a large tree nursery with an irrigation system that he had invented; he was waiting to receive a patent for his invention and then sell his properties and the sawmill and leave for the north. As I listened I must have looked like one of my own schoolchildren, staring without interrupting, and the trees that were to be transplanted appeared to me like animals that must be pursued to the ends of the world. I went to embrace him and rested my head on his chest. There began my one and only love story.

When Boris left he told me that he would write and arrange for me to join him. The last month of lessons came, and I began to teach in the open air, on the meadow behind the building, close to the path that led to the river. From there I could see the abandoned sawmill. Since Boris had sold it, the logs no longer came down the river. One day, while the boys and girls sat on the grass and sang, a barge passed by and disappeared behind a river bend where the trees were thick. As I watched it I sensed that the unthinkable had occurred. After the lesson, I walked to the water's edge, and by the time I got there I was certain I would never hear from Boris again.

ONE day Nikolai wrote me that he was very ill and that he needed my presence. I went to see him where he lived, at the other end of Russia. I found him withered, frail, close to his end, abandoned by all but a sullen sixteen-year-old daughter and a few servants. When he saw me he burst into tears, and he seemed to me much older than myself. He was dying of cirrhosis of the liver due to his excessive drinking. He no longer drank; he no longer needed to. The thought of death is enough to fully occupy a person, and he thought of nothing else. He insisted on talking to me about it at all costs. I listened unwillingly and watched him expire.

My granddaughter informed me that she would soon leave to join her uncle Anton, whom she had met and to whom she had become close in connection with his clandestine activities. Nikolai had never mentioned this to me, absorbed as he was with the thought of his death, but she made a point of letting me know. As she spoke, I understood the apparent bitterness with which she had nursed her father. I also understood Anton's spell over her: they both loved one thing out of hatred for another. I did not attempt to dissuade her.

At the time of the revolution, all of Russia was turned upside down. Back home, convoys of troops began passing down my road, and I would go to the window and try to identify them. One day my servant Tanya told me that the legendary train that traversed the territories of the revolution with its leaders aboard would stop for several hours in our village. I decided to go and see it and I had Tanya drive me in a carriage to the station, bouncing along the frozen road. We were able to venture as close as two hundred feet from the train before we were barred from going farther. I watched the train through the bare, skeletal trees and the armed men that guarded it. I had a flash of perception that inside the train, behind its barred windows, a murky family history was being played out.

When Tanya and I returned home, I found Anton waiting for me with Nikolai's daughter, who by this time followed Anton wherever he went. The train had brought them. It was years since I had last seen my second son, and at first I did not recognize him. He was now thin, willowy, and animated by a cold energy entirely unlike Nikolai's soft languor. My granddaughter kept silent throughout our conversation. In her arms she held a newborn, who slept quietly: it was Dunya, her little daughter. They had come to see me because of her, and Anton now asked me to take care of the child while they resumed their journey. I took the little girl from the arms of my granddaughter, who then turned away and gazed at some uncertain point in the distance. I did not answer Anton's question about what money I would need. He fell silent, then turned abruptly and vanished through the door. The young woman ran after him.

I thought of Dunya as a part of myself that once had left and now had returned at the end of a tortuous path. I was by then certain that God takes refuge in people, and I was feeling him operate inside me. I was nearing the end of a difficult experiment. I prayed in my own fashion. Surrounded by ice, I breathed warm air. I left tracks in the snow. I perceived my existence to lie in a certain music that I was trying to overtake.

One morning I went out for a long walk through the fields. The sun burst out from behind the clouds and pierced through the trees, reaching all the way to me as it once had in my youth, on my return home after a moonlit night asleep in the snow. The message of existence was there, before me and inside me, intact in its significance, and the two dawns were one and the same dawn. The light that enfolded me glittered with dazzling hieroglyphs, and I walked beneath the ageless trees.

I felt that I was coming close to separation. In the clear light of the full day I saw the God whose name I had never uttered, the God to whom I had never directly prayed, leap through space and come to me, and I was moved that he would let me distract him from the events that ravaged the earth. I kept him beside me until I slowly dozed off. Before dying, I had the curi-

ous vision that he hailed from a place of lush greenery and
trickling streams.

I wondered if I would be able to do without love in the new
world I was beginning to project. I looked around me, and love
was scattered everywhere, a myriad of drops in the sea of being.
I threw myself into an amorous exploration, and I soon realized
that love could not be transplanted elsewhere. There was no
way that such an essence could be exported. Every love carried
baggage along with it: individual dawns and sunsets, the taste
of a meal, the color of a room, the books and music of the
moment, the name of the beloved, the sound of a voice. Every
love story was formed out of the entire world, and I could not
uproot it. Love was a boundless territory, and there was no
space for it in the bag I was packing.

I imagined my long voyage through the cosmos to the outer
borders of the constellations, with the books, the photograph
albums, the recordings of music, the human and animal genes
with which I would start over on some new planet. But I was
doubtful that the plants would be able to make the transition,
and there was no question but that I would have to leave love
behind. When I realized this I decided to satiate myself with
these things as with a fruit soon to be out of season. I ran
through the woods, meadows, and hothouses of the world to
breathe in the fragrance of plants, and I immersed myself in
whirlpools of love.

My awakening was swift and painful. A new and more
dreadful war spread through the world. It caught me by surprise, in the midst of my overflowing expressions of tenderness.
I tried in vain to come up with a remedy by redoubling my
efforts at love, like adding bricks to a dike to hold back the tide
of violence. People passed and pushed me aside. "Force must
be met with force," I heard them hiss at me.

Before me paraded the new-age works of art that were sup-
planting paintings, music, and books: they were resplendent
battleships, fighter planes, tanks that crisscrossed the battlefields. It was hard not to fall prey to their fascination. After an

intoxicating race at the bottom of the sea aboard a submarine, I asked myself how man could possibly resist the lure of violence when even I was stirred by it.

I knew that I could not appeal to people's yearning for happiness. Happiness was not a good criterion for establishing what was right. I had never seen men more enthusiastic than during wartime, as long as they were hopeful of victory. As soon as this hope abandoned them, their nature seemed to change. They became negative philosophers, shipwreck victims looking for rescue. I witnessed all manner of devastation: routed armies pursued by victors, piled-up dead, razed farmlands, cities transformed into cathedrals of rubble, the smoke of human flesh rising from ovens. It was more than I could endure.

I went to Italy, north of Milan, and isolated myself from everything. One evening I took a walk along a path in the countryside. I carried a small pad of paper with me, and every so often I would stop to make a note of what I wanted to preserve of the world. Before it turned dark I discovered a tiny rose in the grass and almost trampled on it. I stopped to look at it. What was it doing there, so perfect and so far from all eyes, and how many things like that rose were hidden within the folds of life? I wondered whether it wasn't hidden beauty that sustained the world, but I told myself not to harbor any illusions. If it concealed itself, it was only so as not to be destroyed.

I thought better of picking the rose and headed for home. Along the way I met an old couple who, like me, were taking an evening stroll. The man smiled at me and pointed to my shoes. "Your shoelace is undone, sir." I bent down to tie it and was swept by emotional dizziness. He had said that to me as if there were nothing else for which to reproach me! I imagined many honest, courteous men living a retiring life and coming out at sunset to meet God and bring to his attention some small thing that was not right.

The next day I walked through the village and noticed a change of atmosphere. A gloomy silence had descended upon the houses, broken by shouts and commands, among which German accents seemed to predominate. Along the streets you could see only soldiers; something serious was afoot. Finally I learned that American troops had arrived south of Milan and that the Germans and the Italian Fascists were evacuating the lake area. I continued on into the silent landscape. Soon the calm was broken by the croaking of a motor. At a bend in the road before me there appeared four German soldiers in a small vehicle. As I wondered what to do, from an invisible spot among the bushes came sharp and prolonged bursts of rifle fire. The vehicle swerved and jolted to a halt off the road, under the hail of bullets. None of the soldiers on board had had time to respond to the fire, and all of them seemed mortally wounded except for one soldier, who crawled out of the vehicle and flung himself on the ground, where he was hit by a rifle shot and lay motionless. I saw some men come out from behind the bushes and walk off in the direction of the hills, and once more I was alone, a hundred feet away from the bullet-riddled vehicle. The attack had lasted not more than half a minute.

I headed toward the car and saw that the three men who had remained inside were dead. I watched them impotently, and all of a sudden I was surrounded by a group of Italian Fascist soldiers. They hustled me into the German vehicle at gunpoint, and we headed north, the opposite direction to where I wanted to go. I sat crushed on all sides by a group of men who neither spoke nor looked at me, except for a little soldier who seemed very young and stared at me with open friendliness. At a certain point he offered me his canteen of water. I drank a long draft and gave it back to him, receiving in return a broad smile that split his face.

We reached a temporary field hospital packed with wounded Italians and Germans. Some of them were in critical condition and were waiting to be operated on. There was only one doctor and a couple of nurses; I offered to help and became absorbed in the work without thinking any more of my problems. I had been trained as a nurse in the past and I knew what to do. I struggled until late at night, without a pause and without eating anything. Finally I collapsed beside a wounded man they were operating on. I fell into a faint, and the world around me dissolved like mist in the dark.

I woke up on a cot in a tent, beside some of the wounded. My throat was parched and my face covered with sweat. I found it hard to breathe. I got up and left the tent to look for some water. The encampment was immersed in silence, and there did not seem to be any sentinels. I approached a large tent, from which I heard voices. I was certain it was the headquarters of this hospital in limbo, between an army in flight and another about to arrive. I kept walking and quite soon I was far from the encampment, surprised at the ease of my flight. I turned to look at the lights behind me, and as I did so I stumbled into somebody moving on the ground. The unknown shadow and I struggled briefly without knowing why, and then we separated to look into each other's face. It was the little soldier who had given me the canteen when I was taken prisoner. We were both dumbfounded.

"What do you think you're doing?" he finally said.

"I'm escaping," I replied, deciding not to lie. Then, almost imploring him, I added, "I'm thirsty." I really was terribly thirsty. He smiled and I recognized him completely.

"Here," and he handed me the canteen with the same gesture of the day before.

"I too am escaping," he confided cheerfully as he watched me drink. "We can go on together."

"Where are you going?"

He mentioned a small town near Milan, and it seemed to me as good a destination as any. We walked on together in silence. I could hear our footsteps on the grass. Up there on high hung Ursa Major, sinking toward the horizon.

Then came the moment of dawn. The stars suddenly disappeared and the sky paled behind us until it was tinted pink, then vivid red, and finally blue. We greeted the day with a joyful shout. We walked through a village that was still asleep, reached the fields again, picked apples from the trees, ate our breakfast without stopping. We came to a clearing surrounded by barbed wire. It wasn't easy, but we made our way through the wire and continued on. Now I could feel the sun on the nape of my neck and on my shoulders.

Suddenly the shadow next to mine detached itself and moved forward. I looked up and saw my friend run, his arm pointing toward a distant spot where two white horses stood. They were grazing beyond the barbed wire, where the clearing met the woods. The little soldier shouted excitedly as he ran, and the horses, disturbed by the noisy apparition, moved away at a gallop.

He let out another shout and stopped in the middle of the clearing, a hundred feet beyond me. He turned toward me, and I saw him panting, out of breath from running. Again he gave me that splendid grin that cut his face in two, as though it were a watermelon. I made a jocular threatening gesture and continued to walk toward him. He pretended to be afraid and moved around the meadow in a circle with a comical dance step. I watched him and laughed, and suddenly I saw him leap in a blue-gray cloud. An instant later his body lay motionless on the ground, while I ran gasping toward him.

He had stepped on a mine. He was unrecognizable, his face a bloody pulp with no trace of the clownish smile that had graced it a moment before. I looked at it incredulously, then I raised my eyes, astonished by the silence. I saw a flock of birds that had risen in flight at the roar of the explosion disappear behind the woods. I was alone at his side, and I did not even know his name.

I remained for a long time on my knees beside his body, deprived of all energy by my sorrow. When I got up I noticed that the horses had returned to graze on the same spot as before. The sun had reached a higher point and my shadow had shortened.

My divine soul shook with rage. I covered many miles, seized by the wish to confront those responsible for all the slaughter that I had witnessed. At least one of them could not be far off.

I found Mussolini more quickly than I expected. He was climbing into a military truck, disguised as a German corporal. I sat down next to him. I wore the uniform of a soldier in his army, and he immediately understood that I had recognized him. He refused to meet my gaze and obstinately looked at the landscape outside. I was nervous and impatient to confront him, but there were too many people with us and I could not speak to him. Perhaps my thoughts reached him, but he gave no sign at all. At one point he pulled the rim of his helmet over his eyes and seemed to fall asleep.

The journey ended when a group of Italian partisans

stopped the truck to search it. Mussolini was recognized and taken away. I followed the group, and later on I slipped into the room in which Il Duce had been locked up. He was sitting at a table beneath the acid light of a bulb that hung from the ceiling. I sat down in front of him, and now he could not possibly avoid me. He stared straight into my eyes. I found him enormously changed since the last time I had seen him, at the beginning of his ascension to power, when I had walked across a piazza crowded with people listening to one of his speeches. He had become old, and his face was scored with lines and folds. We each waited for the other to break the silence.

As I looked at him I realized that his death was near. It had the shape of an insect that crawled over the collar of his shirt, and I followed it with my eyes until it disappeared behind the nape of his neck. In the end he was the one to speak.

"So you've decided to come."

I did not hide my surprise.

"Were you expecting me? So you did recognize me in the truck."

He nodded, as though to cut things short.

"I was waiting for you to come much earlier. It certainly took you a long time to find me again."

"What are you talking about?" I asked. He had piqued my curiosity.

And so he told his story. When he was a young socialist in exile in Switzerland he was invited to give a lecture. Halfway through his speech he stopped and placed his watch on the table. "If within two minutes God does not show himself," he proclaimed, "it means that he does not exist." After the two minutes passed, he put his watch back in his pocket and was acclaimed by his audience.

"Now here you are, at last," he concluded. "Are you here to get your revenge? You certainly know how to wait."

"I knew nothing about that stunt," I said. "I'm here now because of the mess that you and your associates produced later on. I've just concluded a trip around the continent, and I've come to demand an explanation."

While I was speaking, an irritating cough had risen in my throat, and it prevented me from continuing. The effect of my words was diminished because of this, but Mussolini did not notice my discomfort. When he spoke again it was as if he had prepared his answer long ago.

"You know whose fault all this has been. We only executed the will of those who wanted us to lead them. The dog with a thousand heads! Whenever I stood on a balcony above the crowd, I could feel that dog suck the words from my mouth, and they came out with the force of a torrent. Perhaps those were the very words hidden in all those heads and unable to come out by themselves. But why do you demand explanations from me of all people? I'm no more responsible than anyone else for what has happened. My only failing is that I have lost. The ideals of the victors are no better than mine, but they will now receive all the applause. Never mind, I've already had my share. Why didn't you come before? You would have found me better fit to confront you."

I had managed to recover enough to be able to speak.

"I don't call on those who win at the power game," I said. "They usually aren't capable of seeing me. I don't frequent army generals, I've never called on the pope or the cardinals, I don't show myself to the wealthy. Why should I ever have come to see you? Once you entered this labyrinth, there was no hope of your approaching me. During his rallies your friend Hitler communed with the gods of Wagner: Siegfried, Brunhild, Lohengrin, the Valkyries. But what would I have to say to such a fanatic? If I come to you now, it's because you have already lost everything, and I thought there was a tenuous chance that you might be able to recognize me, that perhaps fate had made you wise in spite of yourself."

Halfway through my speech, Mussolini's attention seemed to wander. His face had become pale and tense; I again saw death, which had returned to ripple across his skull, reach all the way down to his brow.

"Hitler was not my friend," he muttered, and then he launched into elaborate recriminations about alliances and failed strategies. When I next spoke my voice trembled with indignation.

"The moment is almost at hand, you cretin! Look back and admit that your entire story is the tale of an imbecile—noise and rage adding up to nothing! An entire life without improving life. You will get what you deserve."

Mussolini was speechless. The dread of judgment seemed to overwhelm him. I would have continued my tirade had I not been seized by another coughing fit so violent that it propelled me out of the room. I left half stifled, my face wet with tears, and I could not say why they came.

So ended my encounter with the defeated dictator. I felt in my soul that I should have said more and said it better. I lingered nearby, long enough to witness Mussolini's execution in front of a low wall on a path across the fields. This time death positioned itself arrogantly inside the barrel of a tommy gun and struck him between his half-open lids.

I called on the other protagonists of the war, beginning with the losers. I flew to Germany and whirled around the bunker where the German dictator was holed up, but he was so pigheadedly determined not to recognize me that even defeat could not convince him to open his door to me. I could not tell what I thought of him. I hastened to the victors, hovering over their tables during meetings in secluded locations, where they were discussing the fate of the planet. They did not even deign to look at me, intent on the chessboard of territories to be divided up and powers to be consolidated. As I listened to them, I became sure that this war would repeat itself again and again. It was like an eternally recurring dream that would cease only when the victors assembled to acknowledge a vast defeat.

I recalled my comment to Mussolini that I had refused to visit the pope, and desirous as I was for any sort of company, I wondered if I had been too puritanical on this point. I entered the Vatican and was surprised at the ease of my admission. I visited halls overflowing with paintings and rugs and tapestries, interminable corridors and monumental stairways. As I advanced I could feel my confidence diminish and almost evaporate in the space surrounding me. All that exaltation of power made me feel like a stranger, as though it were addressed to a brother of mine who vaguely resembled me. When I entered the papal study, I caught the pontiff at prayer. He was dressed in white, his face bent over clasped hands in the dimness of the simply furnished room.

I approached until I could almost touch him with my hand. He was startled, and when he turned to look at me his eyes brightened with white-hot passion. "You have come at last," he whispered. "I've been waiting for you so long. Why did you not come earlier? Where did you spend this infamous time? Why were you not here to advise me? All the weight of the world has rested on my sinful shoulders!"

Our meeting place seemed to fill with the light of wonder and astonishment. I felt as if caught up in a vision. I was appearing to a pope, and I was overwhelmed by insecurity. I even asked myself whether I was dressed appropriately, like a pilgrim who comes from afar and is on the point of being admitted to the presence of my vicar-on-earth. I was afraid that my long journey across the blood-soaked continent had left mud on my shoes. The pope's appearance was so incredibly noble. I was about to fall to my knees and ask him to give me a sign of paternal welcome, but I caught myself just in time. "It is I who am his God," I repeated to myself several times.

A great opportunity was being offered to us. I had never spoken to a pope before, and who knows what essential things we could tell each other for the fate of the world. There was an interval of intense expectation, like the trepidation of birth. The entire world seemed centered on that small unadorned room, where the white figure and the mud-covered pilgrim faced each other. What a moment! But it was destined to pass. No sooner had the pope absorbed the reality of my presence than he closed his eyes and erased me from his gaze. I did not correspond to his image of me. In his imagination he stooped to clean my shoes, and as he did so I abandoned him and resumed my travels.

I descended along the small peninsula as it celebrated the victory of one army over the other, and reached the Tyrrhenian coast, at the mouth of the Arno, on a warm summer afternoon. As I wandered through that landscape that was so dear to me, memories swarmed through my mind. More than a hundred years earlier, on that same beach, I had recognized the body of Shelley cast ashore after a storm. I remembered my sorrow at that now distant event. I spoke with him across time, and my words mingled with the wind, confused among the cries of the gulls, beneath clouds shaped like roses. Not many miles away, another poet was now imprisoned for treason. I watched him from a distance, while he wrote his poems among the prisoners of that camp by the ocean. Perhaps it would be better if poets did not try to change the world, I said to myself.

Pursued by my memories and regrets, I had gone all the way to the pine groves that lay beyond Marina di Pisa. I was tired of my peregrinations and needed some rest. From the distance I heard the waves shatter against the rocks. The nearby village was plunged in meridian silence, and the sun reached me in fragments through the century-old pine trees. I would have liked at that moment to become a pine tree or a grain of sand or a thorny bush or a bird asleep on a branch. I was overcome by an invincible weakness and stretched out on the pine-grove sand. That is when I made the mistake for which I was to pay dearly. Right beside me I saw a lizard dozing on the sand. It seemed so trusting that in the end I fell asleep in it. I sank into my lizard-sleep as into a childhood bath. It was a dreamless sleep, fraught with oblivion, the true slumber of an animal.

When I awoke I was in the hand of a boy who stared at me closely with eyes that were immense and cruel. He was the leader of a gang roaming the grove in search of pine nuts and of animals to torture. Now I was aloft, suspended, kicking furiously. The eyes of the boy who gripped me vibrated, brown and greenish, beneath thick lashes.

I squirmed in the air and still hoped that the gang would let me go. I sensed their uncertainty. The executioner vacillated! That instant might have been the turning point for the world, but the boys did not release their prey. Everything was ready for the game in which I was to be the victim.

Suddenly the gang leader laid me out on the ground and began to cut me into strips with a sharply honed knife. What a curious sensation. Violent pain, then only a soft prickling as the blade entered my body and severed it into many fragments, like railroad cars detaching themselves from a train. The head was noticing everything. You see that I say "the head" instead of "I"; and indeed what was an "I" divided into so many pieces? In that interregnum I was separate and yet whole, held together only by the fingers that pinned me down. I still saw everything, in a strange and hallucinatory way. One of the boys had moved away from the group and had gone to vomit behind a bush.

Now that I was all cut up, the second part of the game began. After a pause, the fingers let go of the prey, and my body exploded like a firework. The pieces flew off across the sand, blindly bouncing about; only I (I mean, my head) did not move, but lingered to watch. So that was the amusement I had not been able to avoid at the end. I looked at my persecutors. I, a dwarfed and toothless crocodile who fed on grass, caterpillars, and insects, observed the giants above me with their keen and pensive eyes. I watched them as the fly watches the spider, already captured in the aerial and multiform net. I was a point in the trajectory of evil, something between a fly and a child in the interminable scale of violence, there under the pine trees and under the sky, between sea and countryside, in the ardent noon, in the twentieth century, millions of miles from the sun.

In the last shiver of my life as a lizard, I summoned the sinews of my body, like a defeated and dispersed army, and leaped into the pale animals with the cruel eyes. A piece of me ended up inside each one of them, and I walked through the labyrinth of their souls. The torturers of lizards were invaded by God. One shook me off. One carried me with him on a journey of which I have lost all traces, but which I will recall again when my story is written by a hundred hands. Still another deposited me in a drawer of his soul and forgot me for so long that when he reopened it he was faced with a memory that seemed to belong to someone else.

Through the pine wood wafted a breath of hope that someone would find a bit of me in a corner of the world, so that I would be able to recognize myself again after my innumerable oblivions.

EPILOGUE

One part of me remained hidden in that pine grove, close to the site of the sacrifice, within the soul of a poor man meditating in a secluded hermitage.

I go and see this man from time to time, and pray with him. God while praying is something to see. I pray to become better than I am, while my solitary believer prays for me to have mercy on him. Mercy on him! I should be grateful to him, to the deep probity showing through his face. "Have mercy on me, if you ever know me," I whisper to him; "and do not ask me too many questions! I wouldn't know the answers." At that moment he feels that God is near, closes his eyes, lowers his head in humility. "He is so unassuming," I think to myself. "Goodness is so bashful. That's why he seldom ventures out."

Another part of me wanders across the earth with an army of refugees and returning veterans. Some of them are escaping hunger, some are fleeing from the cruelty of their leaders, some others are simply running away from the enigmas of existence.

I leave the usual signs behind me: winter and summer, springtime and autumn, assorted missives that every so often reach their destination. Many of those letters remain unopened and pile up in life's basements. One day they will be burned, together with all the unanswered mail; and so the sheets of paper, the envelopes, the stamps, the postmarks, the fingerprints of the clerk, the dust of the cellars, the match that has lit the fire—all will return to ashes.

Occasionally I take a cab and wander for hours in some city. I do it in Lyons, in San Francisco, in Moscow, in Hong Kong. I look at people as attentively as I can. I go to the factories and look at workers, I go to the offices and look at business people. I notice the ways people think of me, usually without realizing that they are thinking of me. They glance at their watches, and they do not know that they are thinking of me. They caress their lovers, and they do not know that they are thinking of me. They wake up after a dream they have already forgotten about, and that is the moment when they are closest to me. People should not run to those places where divinity is celebrated! I am less likely to be found there than between trains and appointments.

Often I concentrate in order to become aware of myself. I do it in various ways. The simplest trick is to become an object: a mountain, an armchair in some hotel room, a house on the seashore, a drop of water from a faucet. But whenever I am at rest, something strange happens to me. I become agitated and feel an impelling force inside me like a buried fire, or like ice on the verge of melting.

I think of when I exploded over Japan, liberating the energy of my every particle, a bomb not much larger than a cake. As I rose again in the form of a mushroom cloud, I rushed away from Earth so as not to hear my laments and sorrows down there, in the suffering inferno that was also myself. I caught up with the pilot who dropped me, like the unknown father who in the time of times abandoned me in space to create my universe. I wanted to speak to him but did not succeed. I returned to Earth with the crew, listening to their banter from a corner of the military plane, looking at the clouds through which we passed like hurrying archangels.

I know the reason why the memory of myself came back to me while I was in front of the television set. It is because I also nest there, in the space between the programs, like a spider in a hole in the wall or an astral signal at the crossroads of galaxies. Television and the atomic bomb are different signs of my existence, and both show how difficult it is to grasp my entireness; as that bomb, I was to explode above another part of myself. Every time I see the mushroom cloud on the small screen, I see myself arising on the stage of life, like the dawn of a day when everything begins all over again. When I mirror myself in that way, I would rather be a flower on a pond—so calm and green and suffused with azure light—or the flavor of ice cream in the mouth of a child heading home after school.

I hide in the laboratories where the devices of nature are being manipulated, and I entertain the idea of an animal that can reproduce beauty and knowledge as organs of its own body. Then I remember that beauty and knowledge were supposed to be remedies against the pain of existence. What would they do in a world that does not suffer? I am now and forever the artificer of the world's imperfections.

I go to the hospitals to watch people die. Some take a long time, some do it in a second. Death walks busily through the corridors, in and out of the rooms. She wears blue jeans and a cotton sweater. She wears dark glasses and I cannot look into her eyes. I move to the maternity wing and watch the birth of children. What a fight to come into the world! Life is always here, and she is as busy as her sister down the hall, but her eyes are not hidden and I gaze into them. From time to time Death comes and takes a child or a mother away, or both of them. When that happens, the two sisters do not even look at each other. They do what has to be done.

If I am more curious than ever about what happens in the world, it is because I have decided that the time for my departure is almost at hand. By now everything is almost squared away. I feel nostalgic already. But I have no doubts about my resolution. Light will be my means of transportation, and I am entitled to an open ticket good all the way to the borders of the universe. It is a one-way ticket to the unborn world where I want to rest in the late ripeness of my years. I am not afraid of the cold anymore.

Nostalgia for love affects me especially. Lovers sitting on park benches, lying together in bed, missing one another when apart, have always had me at their side, and they've guessed as much. I look at children, lost in the dream of play, walking on the verge of creation, knocking at my door. I sit on the grass, and I am unseen, but I am felt by all of them.

Of all my intentions, at least my departure should not fail. In order to make reliable plans I use a computer, the most recent gift from the active and disorderly human race. It takes up no more space than an attaché case, so the baggage problem is solved. Still, I find myself ogling more recent models, the notebooks that contain more and more memory, entire centuries in a small disk. What would one human have to do to amass even a small part of such memory? If I put this question to the computer, it flashes and blinks, then stops, because my question has no answer. I have never seen anything less vain. It could become my best friend if not for its deep inability to make decisions. What if I found myself in need of counseling?

I go back and forth, make the rounds, close the doors, turn off the lights. My anxiety about watering the plants before I leave has made me overflow more than one region. My moving the furniture and my emptying the drawers has caused some recent earthquakes that could have been avoided with more caution on my part. I feel sorry about that.

I put away books, I switch off the music, I turn the pictures to the wall. Obedient to the signal, humanity has almost stopped creating, and feeds on the past. Scraps of discarded music and leftover pictures decorate the departure lounge that the world has become. The malls and the supermarkets stock preserved images of creation—endless warehouses of the useless and forgotten.

The New York skyscrapers rise ever higher, like the control towers of an airport. I often find myself on their peaks, taking my bearings, charting my course. I lose myself in fantastic conjectures. What would have happened if I had created two thinking animals? Perhaps things would have turned out better. I imagine, for instance, man and dog walking together and talking about the existence of God or some equally compelling matter, trying to overcome their deeply hostile feelings toward one another. The world would become accustomed to every manner of doggy development, including canine architecture and a running debate on whether or not foxes and jackals belong to the same race. Maybe the dogs would think of me as a great Saint Bernard type or as a mountain wolf.

The news of my departure is spreading around, although I have not talked much about it. Some react to it by pushing and shoving, as if they imagine they also could leave and are afraid of not finding room on board. Some think that poverty will make it difficult for them to find a place at my side and do their best to accumulate wealth. Some travel frenetically during their summers, possibly training for the greatest journey of them all.

I have decided on the date of my departure. The idea came

to me as I was watching an athletic competition. Halfway between a hurricane in China and a migration of Canadian ducks toward the Gulf of Mexico, I took a rest, stopping in the stadium at Barcelona to watch my favorite athletic events: pole vaulting and the hundred meter run. They were both exceedingly beautiful, and in the pole vault a world record was achieved. As the pole vaulter ran around the track amid the applause, I resolved to depart on the day when the last record in that event is set—and that day will come for all competitions. I open the newspaper to the sports pages and check my travelers' advisory. The record is at five meters ninety, six meters twelve, six meters twenty! I vibrate with expectation, like the transverse pole grazed by the vaulter.

A majestic feeling pervades me. It is summer. I am flying from Colorado to Alaska over water, forests, and glaciers. The sun penetrates the clefts in the clouds. I peer through the white cotton, and all around me the interminable blue opens up. It won't be easy to abandon such beauty.

Confused prayers reach me, intersected by electrical signals. I can barely make out the words.

A NOTE ON THE TRANSLATION

This English edition of *Il Mondo Creato* often departs freely from the Italian original and at points is better characterized as an adaptation than as a translation. Some passages have been dropped, and the author has added two new episodes. The author and the publisher thank Rosemarie LaValva, Anthony Oldcorn, and John Grossman for their assistance with the translation.

We note with sadness the death of Raymond Rosenthal on 24 July 1995, before the editing of this translation was complete.